The
Literary
Traveler

Also Edited by Larry Dark

THE LITERARY LOVER

THE LITERARY GHOST

LITERARY OUTTAKES

The
Literary
Traveler

AN ANTHOLOGY
OF CONTEMPORARY
SHORT FICTION

Edited and with an Introduction by

Larry Dark

VIKING

VIKING
Published by the Penguin Group
Penguin Books USA Inc., 375 Hudson Street,
New York, New York 10014, U.S.A.
Penguin Books Ltd, 27 Wrights Lane,
London W8 5TZ, England
Penguin Books Australia Ltd, Ringwood,
Victoria, Australia
Penguin Books Canada Ltd, 10 Alcorn Avenue,
Toronto, Ontario, Canada M4V 3B2
Penguin Books (N.Z.) Ltd, 182-190 Wairau Road,
Auckland 10, New Zealand

Penguin Books Ltd, Registered Offices:
Harmondsworth, Middlesex, England

First published in 1994 by Viking Penguin,
a division of Penguin Books USA Inc.

1 3 5 7 9 10 8 6 4 2

LIBRARY OF CONGRESS CATALOGING IN PUBLICATION DATA
The literary traveler: an anthology of contemporary short
fiction/edited and with an introduction by Larry Dark.
p. cm.
ISBN 0-670-84578-7
1. Voyages and travels—Fiction.   2. American fiction—20th
century.   3. Travelers' writings, American.   4. Short stories,
American.   5. Travel—Fiction.   I. Dark, Larry.
PS648.T73L58   1994
813'.0108355—dc20   94–8796

This book is printed on acid-free paper.

Printed in the United States of America
Set in Granjon
Designed by Ann Gold

For Asher—

and all the places he will go

CONTENTS

Contents

INTRODUCTION

Traveling with too many expectations is like traveling with too much baggage. Just as some travelers pack clothing for every social situation and every type of weather, only to find that most of it is never even taken out of the suitcase, so too do some carry inside themselves hopes and fears and rationalizations for every eventuality they feel they might meet, only to find that this emotional baggage does nothing more than stand in the way of their immediate experience. The stories in *The Literary Traveler* are about more than the places people go and what happens to them; they are also about the expectations people bring to their travels, whether these expectations are met or not, and how they change along the way.

One likely result, when hopes are too high and expectations too narrow, is disappointment. The protagonist of William Maxwell's "The Gardens of Mont-Saint-Michel" is incapable of enjoying a family trip through France because of changes there since he and his wife visited eighteen years before. On returning to Normandy with his family, he finds that the quaint hotel where they stayed on their last trip has been modernized and expanded and that Mont-Saint-Michel is now overrun with tourist buses and souvenir stands:

> Reynolds was quite aware that to complain because things were not as agreeable as they used to be was one of the recognizable signs of growing old. And whether you accepted change or not, there was really no preventing it. But why, without exception, did something bad drive out something good? Why was the change always for the worse? . . . Once in a while, some small detail represented an improvement on the past, and you could not be happy in the intellectual climate of any time but your own. But in general, so far as the way people lived, it was one loss after another, something hideous replacing something beautiful, the decay of manners, the lapse of pleasant customs, as by a blind increase in numbers the human race went about making the earth more and more unfit to live on.

It's easy to understand this view of the world and, sadly, there is some truth to these sentiments. Yet to experience the world through the mediation of our expectations is to blind ourselves to what is present in the moment. The children, though seemingly blasé, have never been to France before. For them, this is the experience against which they will measure any return trip, just as Reynolds's first visit set the standard for his expectations.

While change is certainly not always for the worse, it is true that even positive progress can bring about undesirable results. The fall of Communist regimes in Eastern Europe, for instance, has left an ideological vacuum that has been filled on the one hand by nationalism and bloodshed and on the other by capitalism in its most base form: voracious consumerism. Fay Weldon's "Wasted Lives," set in a post-Communist Central European city, most likely Prague, opens with a comparison of the city to

Introduction

Disneyland and sightings of the Body Shop, Benetton, and McDonald's among the charming old façades. The icons of Communism, Lenin and Marx, have been torn down, only to be replaced by the leading icons of consumerism, Mickey Mouse and Ronald McDonald.

For better or worse, Anglo-American culture has become a dominant influence worldwide, and traces of it turn up everywhere in these stories, from the ubiquitous American overseas newspaper the *International Herald Tribune* to a Dixie Fried Chicken joint in Lagos, Nigeria, to Buddhist monks sipping Pepsi-Colas at a restaurant near a holy city in Thailand. In James Lasdun's "Delirium Eclipse," the owner of a small hotel in the Indian city of Varanasi turns out to be an Anglophile working his way through an alphabetical trove of English delicacies. The *M*'s, for instance, include muffins, macaroons, marmalade, and Marmite. While the spread (no pun intended) of familiar culture offers comfort to less adventurous travelers, it also represents an erosion of uniqueness.

Other dashed expectations to be found in these stories include Inca ruins that seem at first sight parched and ugly; the river Ganges, which Lasdun's protagonist sees as "a massive brown tract of water, calm beneath an oily haze"; the Black Sea, which turns out to be pale blue in color; and a mossy Blarney Stone covered with lipstick prints. In Paul Theroux's "Portrait of a Lady," Harper, a young American courier, even manages to have a bad time in Paris:

> He thought: All travelers are like aging women, now homely beauties; the strange land flirts, then jilts and makes a fool of the stranger. There is less risk, at home, in making a jackass of yourself: you know the rules there. The answer is to be ladylike about it and maintain your dignity. But he knew as he thought this that he was denying himself the calculated risks that might bring him romance and a memory to carry away.

Harper's rigid perception of the world blinds him to all that is wonderful about Paris, and even though he understands this about himself, he is, to his own detriment, unable and unwilling to change.

For those who are looking for flaws, it is possible to not see the tropical island for the souvenir stand, but there are rewards for the traveler who can look past the obvious shortcomings of a place. The Inca ruins in Sue Miller's "Travel" turn out, upon closer examination, to be full of beautiful and moving details. And after the protagonist of Lorrie Moore's "Which Is More Than I Can Say About Some People" kisses the Blarney Stone, she does become more eloquent, just as the legend promises. In "Great Barrier Reef," by Diane Johnson, a cruise that is at first disappointing turns out to yield a far deeper experience than the narrator could have anticipated, and the reef itself proves to be a living wonder.

Despite the preconceived notions we bring to travel, there is usually something to surprise us and almost always much to be gained from the experience of leaving home to explore different parts of the world and encounter other cultures. In "Summer Opportunity," by Maria Thomas, a bookish, overweight African-American college student travels to Nigeria on a summer fellowship. Not only does Gwendolyn find a new sense of freedom in a place where every police officer, doctor, nurse, judge, teacher, and telephone operator is black, but she finds that for the first time in her life she is attractive to men—her figure even resembles those of the female fertility statues carved by local artisans. In "Verona: A Young Woman Speaks," by Harold Brodkey, we experience the wonder of travel through the eyes of a woman remembering an enchanted childhood trip across Italy with her parents.

Expectations aren't always detrimental to an experience of travel; sometimes it can enhance a trip to know what you want out of it. In "Succor," by Allen Barnett, a young man diagnosed as HIV-positive revisits Rome, his vision of the city informed by memories of his student days and the stark parallels he observes between the plagues of the Middle Ages and the new plague of AIDS. Although Kerch knows he can't turn back the clock on his life or his illness, he makes the trip as a tonic to his soul and because he wants to see Rome once more before he becomes too sick to do so. "Cruise," by John Updike, presents truly literary travelers who embark on a tour of the Mediterranean, Ionian, and Aegean seas to re-create the wanderings of Ulysses. As the voyage progresses, the cruise transcends its stuffy academic origins and assumes mythic proportions. In "Hold Me Fast, Don't Let Me Pass," by Alice Munro, a widow travels to the Scottish village her husband talked of in his war stories, hoping to find some connection to a past in which she played no part. Although Hazel meets the people her late husband mentioned, they say they don't remember him. Still, her journey affords her insight into his past and takes her to the cusp of greater knowledge of herself.

This is not unusual. Travel, like literature, has among its highest aims a deeper understanding of the self and our place in the world. In *The Literary Traveler* we encounter characters who travel as an antidote to boredom, as a means of self-fulfillment, to satisfy their curiosity about other places, for work or study, in an attempt to renew themselves, or in an effort to revive a floundering relationship. What they get out of the experience varies widely depending on the company they keep, the destinations they choose, the people they meet along the way, the weather, the terrain, and other contingencies. But one thing is certain: Those travelers who take their own small worlds with them wherever they go might just as well stay home. For only when we put aside our narrow expectations and rigid preconceptions can we discover the wonders of the world outside ourselves, and within.

LARRY DARK

WILLIAM MAXWELL

The Gardens of Mont-Saint-Michel

The elephantine Volkswagen bus didn't belong to the French landscape. Compared to the Peugeots and Renaults and Citroëns that overtook it so casually, it seemed an oddity. So was the family riding in it. When they went through towns people turned and stared, but nothing smaller would have held the five of them and their luggage, and the middle-aged American who was driving was not happy at the wheel of any automobile. This particular automobile he loathed. There was no room beyond the clutch pedal. To push it down to the floor he had to turn his foot sidewise, and his knee ached all day long from this unnatural position. "Have I got enough room on my right?" he asked continually, though he had been driving the Volkswagen for two weeks now. "Oh God!" he would exclaim. "There's a man on a bicycle." For he was suffering from a recurring premonition: *In the narrow street of some village, though he was taking every human*

1

precaution, suddenly he heard a hideous crunch under the right rear wheel. He stopped the car and with a sinking heart got out and made himself look at the twisted bicycle frame and the body lying on the cobblestones. . . . A dozen times a day John Reynolds could feel his face responding to the emotions of this disaster, which he was convinced was actually going to happen. It was only a matter of when. And where. Sometimes the gendarmes came and took him away, and at other times he managed to extricate himself by thinking of something else. At odds with all this, making his life bearable, was another scene—the moment in the airport at Dinard when he would turn the keys over to the man from the car-rental agency and be free of this particular nightmare forever.

Dorothy Reynolds, sitting on the front seat beside her husband, loved the car because she could see out of it in all directions. Right this minute she asked for nothing more than to be driving through the French countryside. Her worries, which were real and not, like his, imaginary, had been left behind, on the other side of the Atlantic Ocean. She could only vaguely remember what they were.

"In France," she said, "nothing is really ugly, because everything is so bare."

"In some ways I like England better," he said.

"It's more picturesque, but it isn't as beautiful. Look at that grey hill town with those dark clouds towering above it," she said, turning around to the two older girls in the seat directly behind her. And then silently scolded herself, because she was resolved not to say "Look!" all the time but to let the children use their own eyes to find what pleased them. The trouble was, their eyes did not see what hers did, or, it often seemed, anything at all.

This was not, strictly speaking, true. Reynolds' niece, Linda Porter, had 20/20 vision, but instead of scattering her attention on the landscape she saved it for what she had heard about—the Eiffel Tower, for example—and for the mirror when she was dressing. She was not vain, and neither was she interested in arousing the interest of any actual boy, though boys and men looked at her wherever she went. Her ash-blond hair had been washed and set the night before, her cuticles were flawless, her rose-pink nail polish was without a scratch, her skirt was arranged under her delightful young bottom in such a way that it would not wrinkle, her hand satchel was crammed with indispensable cosmetics, her charm bracelet was the equal of that of any of her contemporaries, but she was feeling forlorn. She had not wanted to leave the hotel in Concarneau, which was right on the water, and she could swim and then lie in the sun, when there was any, and she had considered the possibility of getting a job as a waitress so she could spend the rest of her life there, only her father would never let her do it. She had also considered whether or not she was in love with the waiter in charge of their table in the dining room, who was young and good-looking and from Marseille; when a leaf of lettuce leaped out of the salad bowl, he said *"Zut!"* and kicked it under the table. He asked her to play tennis with him, but unfortunately she hadn't brought her own racquet and he didn't have an extra one. Also, it turned out he was married.

How strange that she should be sitting side by side with someone for whom mirrors did not reflect anything whatever. Alison Reynolds, who was eleven and a half, considered the hours when she was not reading largely wasted. "If Dantès has had lunch," she once confided to her father, "then I have had lunch. Otherwise I don't know whether I've eaten or not." With a note of sadness in her voice, because no matter how vivid and all-consuming the book was, or how long, sooner or later she finished it, and was stranded once more in ordinariness until she had started another. She couldn't read in the car because it made her feel queer. She was very nearsighted, and by the time she had found her glasses and put them on, the blur her mother and father wanted her to look at had been left behind. All châteaux interested her, and anything that had anything to do with Jeanne d'Arc, or with Marie Antoinette. Or Marguerite de Valois. Or Louise de La Vallière.

Because her mind and her cousin's were so differently occupied, they were able to let one another alone, except for some mild offensive and defensive belittling now and then, but Alison and her younger sister had to ride in separate seats or they quarrelled. Trip was lying stretched out, unable to see anything but the car roof and hating every minute of the drive from Fougères, where they had spent the night. It didn't take much to make her happy—a stray dog or a cat, or a monkey chained to a post in a farmyard, or an old white horse in a pasture—but while they were driving she existed in a vacuum and exerted a monumental patience. At any moment she might have to sit up and put her head out of the car window and be sick.

They passed through Antrain without running over anybody on a bicycle, and shortly afterward something happened that made them all more cheerful. Another salmon-and-cream-colored Volkswagen bus, the first they had seen, drew up behind them and started to pass. In it were a man and a woman and two children and a great deal of luggage. The children waved to them from the rear window as the other Volkswagen sped on.

"Americans," Dorothy Reynolds said.

"And probably on their way to Mont-Saint-Michel," Reynolds said. "Wouldn't you know." They were no longer unique.

He saw a sign on their side of the road. She also noticed it, and they smiled at each other with their eyes, in the rearview mirror.

Eighteen years ago, they had arrived in Pontorson from Cherbourg, by train, by a series of trains, at five o'clock in the afternoon. They had a reservation at a hotel in Mont-Saint-Michel, but they had got up at daybreak and were too tired to go on, so they spent the night here in what the "Michelin" described as an *"hôtel simple, mais confortable,"* with *"une bonne table dans la localité."* It was simple and bare and rather dark inside, and it smelled of roasting coffee beans. It was also very old; their guidebook said it had been the manor of the counts of Montgomery, though there was nothing about it now to indicate this. Their room was on the second floor and it was enormous. So was the bathroom. There was hot water. They had a bath, and then they came downstairs and had an apéritif sitting under a striped umbrella in front of the hotel. He remembered that there was a freshly painted wooden fence with flower boxes on it that separated the table from the street. What was in the flower boxes? Striped petunias? Geraniums? He did not remember, but there were heavenly blue morning-glories climbing on strings beside the front door. Their dinner was too good to be true, and they drank a bottle of wine with it, and stumbled up the stairs to their room, and in the profound quiet got into the big double bed and slept like children. So long ago. And so uncritical they were. All open to delight.

In the morning they both woke at the same instant and sat up and looked out of the window. It was market day and the street in front of the hotel was full of people. The women wore long shapeless black cotton dresses and no makeup on their plain country faces. The men wore blue smocks, like the illustrations of Boutet de Monvel. And everybody was carrying long thin loaves of fresh bread. A man with a vegetable stand was yelling at the top of his lungs about his green beans. They saw an old woman leading a cow. And chickens and geese, and little black-and-white goats, and lots of bicycles, but no cars. It was right after the war, and gasoline was rationed, but it seemed more as if the automobile hadn't yet been heard of in this part of France.

They were the only guests at the hotel, the only tourists as far as the eye could see. It was the earthly paradise, and they had it all to themselves. When they came in from cashing a traveller's check or reading the inscriptions on the tombstones in the cemetery, a sliding panel opened in the wall at the foot of the stairs and the cook asked how they enjoyed their walk. The waitress helped them make up their minds what they wanted to eat, and if they had any other problems they went to the concierge with them. The happier they became the happier he was for them, so how could they not love him, or he them? The same with the waitress and the chambermaid and the cook. They went right on drinking too much wine and eating seven-course meals for two more days, and if it hadn't been that they had not seen anything whatever of the rest of France, they might have stayed there, deep in the nineteenth century, forever.

Reynolds thought he remembered Pontorson perfectly, but some-thing peculiar goes on in the memory. This experience is lovingly remembered and that one is, to one's everlasting shame, forgot-ten. Of the remembered experience a very great deal drops out, drops away, leaving only what is convenient, or what is emotion-ally useful, and this simplified version takes up much more room than it has any right to. The village of Pontorson in 1948 was larger than John Reynolds remembered it as being, but after eigh-teen years it was not even a village any longer; it was now a small town, thriving and prosperous, and one street looked so much like another that he had to stop in the middle of a busy intersec-tion and ask a traffic policeman the way to the hotel they had been so happy in.

It was still there, but he wouldn't have recognized it without the sign. The fence was gone, and so were the morning-glories twisting around their white strings, and the striped umbrellas. The sidewalk came right up to the door of the hotel, and it would not have been safe to drive a cow down the street it was situated on.

"It's all so changed," he said. "But flourishing, wouldn't you say? Would you like to go in and have a look around?"

"No," Dorothy said.

"They might remember us."

"It isn't likely the staff would be the same after all this time."

Somewhere deep inside he was surprised. He had expected everybody in France to stand right where they were (one, two, three, four, five, six, seven, eight, nine, *stillpost*) until he got back.

"I never thought about it before," he said, "but except for the cook there was nobody who was much older than we were. . . . So kind they all were. But there was also something sad about them. The war, I guess. Also, there's no place to park. Too bad." He drove on slowly, still looking.

"What's too bad?" Alison asked.

"Nothing," Dorothy said. "Your father doesn't like change."

"Do you?"

"Not particularly. But if you are going to live in the modern world—"

Alison stopped listening. Her mother could live in the modern world if she wanted to, but she had no intention of joining her there.

They circled around, and found the sign that said "Mont-Saint-Michel," and headed due north. In 1948 their friend the concierge, having found an aged taxi for them, stood in the doorway waving goodbye. Nine kilometres and not another car on the road the whole ride. Ancient farmhouses such as they had seen from the train window they could observe from close up: the weathered tile roofs, the pink rose cascading from its trellis, the stone watering trough for the animals; the beautiful man-made, almost mathematical orderliness of the woodpile, the vegetable garden, and the orchard. Suddenly they saw, glimmering in the distance, the abbey on its rock, with the pointed spire indicating the precise direction of a heaven nobody believed in anymore. The taxi-driver said, "Le Mont-Saint-Michel," and they looked at each other and shook their heads. For reading about it was one thing and seeing it with their own eyes was another. The airiness, the visionary quality, the way it kept changing right in front of their eyes, as if it were some kind of heavenly vaudeville act.

After the fifth brand-new house, Reynolds said, massaging his knee, "Where are all the old farmhouses?"

"We must have come by a different road," Dorothy said.

"It has to be the same road," he said, and seeing how intently he peered ahead through the windshield she didn't argue. But surely if there were new houses there could be new roads.

Once more the abbey took them by surprise. This time the surprise was due to the fact they were already close upon it. There had been no distant view. New buildings, taller trees, something, had prevented their seeing it until now. The light was of the seacoast, dazzling and severe. Clouds funnelled the radiance upward. It seemed that flocks of angels might be released into the sky at any moment.

"There it is!" Dorothy cried. "Look, children!"

Linda added the name Mont-Saint-Michel to the list of places she could tell people she had seen when she got home. Alison put her glasses on and dutifully looked. Mont-Saint-Michel was enough like a castle to strike her as interesting, but what she re-membered afterward was not the thing itself but the excitement in her father's and mother's voices. Trip sat up, looked, and sank back again without a word and without the slightest change in her expression.

The abbey was immediately obscured by a big new hotel. Boys in white jackets stood in a line on the left-hand side of the road, and indicated with a gesture of the thumb that the Volkswagen was to swing in here.

"What an insane idea," Reynolds murmured. He had made a reservation at the hotel where they had stayed before, right in the shadow of the abbey.

At the beginning of the causeway, three or four cars were stopped and their occupants had got out with their cameras. He got out too, with the children's Hawkeye, and had to wait several minutes for an unobstructed view. Then he got back in the car and drove the rest of the way.

At the last turn in the road, he exclaimed, "Oh, *no!*" In a huge parking lot to the right of the causeway there were roughly a thousand cars shining in the sunlight. "It's just like the World's Fair," he said. "We'll probably have to stand in line an hour and forty minutes to see the tide come in."

A traffic policeman indicated with a movement of his arm that they were to swing off to the right and down into the park-ing lot. Reynolds stopped and explained that they were spending the night here and had been told they were to leave the car next to the outer gate. The policeman's arm made exactly the same gesture it had made before.

"He's a big help," Reynolds said as he drove on, and Trip said, "There's a car just like ours."

"Why, so it is," Dorothy said. "It must be the people who passed us."

"And there's another," Trip said.

The Gardens of Mont-Saint-Michel

"Where?" Alison said, and put on her glasses.

They left the luggage in the locked Volkswagen and joined the stream of pilgrims. Reynolds stopped and paid for the parking ticket. Looking back over his shoulder, he saw the sand flats extending out into the bay as far as the eye could see, wet, shining, and with long, thin, bright ribbons of water running through them, just as he remembered. The time before, there were nine sightseeing buses lined up on the causeway, from which he knew before he ever set foot in it, that Mont-Saint-Michel was not going to be the earthly paradise. This time he didn't even bother to count them. Thirty, forty, fifty, what difference did it make. But the little stream that flowed right past the outer gate? *Gone....* Was it perhaps not a stream at all but a ditch with tidal water in it? Anyway, it had been just too wide to jump over, and a big man in a porter's uniform had picked Dorothy up in his arms and, wading through the water, set her down on the other side. Then he came back for Reynolds. There was no indication now that there had ever been a stream here that you had to be carried across as if you were living in the time of Chaucer.

The hotels, restaurants, cafés, Quimper shops, and souvenir shops (the abbey on glass ashtrays, on cheap china, on armbands, on felt pennants; the abbey in the form of lead paperweights three or four inches high) had survived. The winding street of stairs was noisier, perhaps, and more crowded, but not really any different. The hotel was expecting them. Reynolds left Dorothy and the children in the lobby and went back to the car with a porter, who was five foot three or four at the most and probably not old enough to vote. Sitting on the front seat of the Volkswagen, he indicated the road they were to take out of the big parking lot, up over the causeway and down into the smaller parking lot by the outer gate, where Reynolds had tried to go in the first place. The same policeman waved them on, consistency being not one of the things the French are nervous about. With the help of leather straps the porter draped the big suitcases and then the smaller ones here and there around his person, and would have added the hand luggage if Reynolds had let him. To-

9

gether they staggered up the cobblestone street, and Reynolds saw to his surprise that Dorothy and the children were sitting at a café table across from the entrance to the hotel.

"It was too hot in there," she said, "and there was no place to sit down. I ordered an apéritif. Do you want one?"

And the luggage? What do I do with that? his eyebrows asked, for she was descended from the girl in the fairy tale who said, "Just bring me a rose, dear Father," and he was born in the dead center of the middle class, and they did not always immediately agree about what came before what. He followed the porter inside and up a flight of stairs. The second floor was just as he remembered it, and their room was right down there—where he started to go, until he saw that the porter was continuing up the stairs. On the floor above he went out through a door, with Reynolds following, to a wing of the hotel that didn't exist eighteen years before. It was three stories high and built in the style of an American motel, and the rooms that had been reserved for them were on the third floor—making four stories in all that they climbed. The porter never paused for breath, possibly because any loss of momentum would have stopped him in his tracks. Reynolds went to a window and opened it. The view from this much higher position was of rooftops and the main parking lot and, like a line drawn with a ruler, the canal that divides Brittany and Normandy. He felt one of the twin beds (no sag in the middle) and then inspected the children's room and the bathroom. It was all very modern and comfortable. It was, in fact, a good deal more comfortable than their old room had been, though he had remembered that room with pleasure all these years. The flowered wallpaper and the flowered curtains had been simply god-awful together, and leaning out of the window they had looked straight down on the heads of the tourists coming and going in the Grande Rue—tourists from all over Europe, by their appearance, their clothes, and by the variety of languages they were speaking. There were even tourists from Brittany, in their *pardon* costumes. And they all seemed to have the same expression on their faces, as if it were an effect of the afternoon light. They looked as if they were soberly aware that they had come to a dividing place in their lives and nothing would be quite the same for them after this. And all afternoon and all evening there was the sound of the omelette whisk. In a room between the foyer of the hotel and the dining room, directly underneath them, a very tall man in a chef's cap and white apron stood beating eggs with a whisk and then cooking them in a long-handled skillet over a wood fire in an enormous open fireplace.

Reynolds listened. There was no *whisk, whisk, whisk* now. Too far away. A car came down the causeway and turned in to the parking lot. When night came, the buses would all be gone and the parking lot would be empty.

In this he was arguing from what had happened before. The tourists got back on the sightseeing buses, and the buses drove away. By the end of the afternoon he and Dorothy were the only ones left. After dinner they walked up to the abbey again, drawn there by some invisible force. It was closed for the night, but they noticed a gate and pushed it open a few inches and looked in. It was a walled garden from a fifteenth-century Book of Hours. There was nobody around, so they went in and closed the gate carefully behind them and started down the gravel path. The garden beds were outlined with bilateral dwarf fruit trees, their branches tied to a low wire and heavy with picture-book apples and pears. There was no snobbish distinction between flowers and vegetables. The weed was unknown. At the far end of this Eden there was a gate that led to another, and after that there were still others—a whole series of exquisite walled gardens hidden away behind the street of restaurants and hotels and souvenir shops. They visited them all. Lingering in the deep twilight, they stood looking up at the cliffs of masonry and were awed by the actual living presence of Time; for it must have been just like this for the last five or six hundred years and maybe longer. The swallows were slicing the air into convex curves, the tide had receded far out into the bay, leaving everywhere behind it the channels by which it would return at three in the morning, and the air was so pure it made them light-headed.

Before Reynolds turned away from the window, three more

cars came down the causeway. Here and there in the parking lot a car was starting up and leaving. Though he did not know it, it was what they should have been doing; he should have rounded up Dorothy and the children and driven on to Dinan, where there was a nice well-run hotel with a good restaurant and no memories and a castle right down the street. But his clairvoyance was limited. He foresaw the accident that would never take place but not the disorderly reception that lay in wait for them downstairs.

□   □

On the way into the dining room, half an hour later, they stopped to show the children how the omelettes were made. The very tall man in the white apron had been replaced by two young women in uniforms, but there was still a fire in the fireplace, Reynolds was glad to see; they weren't making the omelettes on a gas stove. The fire was quite a small one, though, and not the huge yellow flames he remembered.

"*Cinq,*" he said to the maître d'hôtel, who replied in English, "Will you come this way?" and led them to a table in the center of the dining room. When he had passed out enormous printed menus, he said, "I think the little lady had better put her knitting away. One of the waiters might get jabbed by a needle." This request was accompanied by the smile of a man who knows what children are like, and whom children always find irresistible. Trip ignored the smile and looked at her mother inquiringly.

"I don't see how you could jab anybody, but put it away. I want an omelette *fines herbes,*" Dorothy said.

The maître d'hôtel indicated the top of the menu with his gold pencil and said, "We have the famous omelette of Mont-Saint-Michel."

"But with herbs," Dorothy said.

"There is no omelette with herbs," the maître d'hôtel said.

"Why not?" Reynolds asked. "We had it here before."

The question went unanswered.

The two younger children did not care for omelette, famous or otherwise, and took an unconscionably long time making up their minds what they did want to eat for lunch. The maître d'hôtel came back twice before Reynolds was ready to give him their order. After he had left the table, Dorothy said, "I don't see why you can't have it *fines herbes.*"

"Perhaps they don't have any herbs," Reynolds said.

"In *France?*"

"Here, I mean. It's an island, practically."

"All you need is parsley and chives. Surely they have that."

"Well maybe it's too much bother, then."

"It's no more trouble than a plain omelette. I don't like him."

"Yes? What's the matter with him?"

"He looks like a Yale man."

This was not intended as a funny remark, but Reynolds laughed anyway.

"And he's not a good headwaiter," she said.

The maître d'hôtel did not, in fact, get their order straight. Things came that they hadn't ordered, and Trip's sole didn't come with the omelettes, or at all. Since she had already filled up on bread, it was not serious. The service was elaborate but very slow.

"No dessert, thank you," Reynolds said when the waiter brought the enormous menus back.

"Just coffee," Dorothy said.

Reynolds looked at his watch. "It says in the green 'Michelin' there's a tour of the abbey with an English-speaking guide at two o'clock. We just barely have time to make it. If we have coffee we'll be too late."

"Oh, let's have coffee," Dorothy said. "They won't start on time."

As they raced up the Grande Rue at five minutes after two, he noticed that it was different in one respect: The shops had been enlarged; they went back much deeper than they had before. The objects offered for sale were the same, and since he had examined them carefully eighteen years before, there was no need to do anything but avert his eyes from them now.

The English-speaking tour had already left the vaulted room it started from, and they ran up a long flight of stone steps and caught up with their party on the battlements. A young French-man with heavy black-rimmed glasses and a greenish complexion was lecturing to them about the part Mont-Saint-Michel played in the Hundred Years' War. There was a group just ahead of them, and another just behind. The guides manipulated their parties in and out of the same rooms and up and down the same stairs with military precision.

"There were dungeons," Alison Reynolds afterward wrote in her diary, "where you could not sit, lie, or stand and were not al-lowed to move. Some prisoners were eaten by rats! There were beautiful cloisters where the monks walked and watered their gardens. There was the knights' hall, where guests stayed. The monks ate and worked in the refectory. . . ."

"It's better managed than it used to be," Dorothy said. "I mean, when you think how many people have to be taken through."

The tour was also much shorter than Reynolds remembered it as being, but that could have been because this time they had an English-speaking guide. Or it could just be that what he sus-pected was true and they were being hurried through. He could not feel the same passionate interest in either the history or the architectural details of the abbey that he had the first time, but that was not the guide's fault. It was obvious that he cared very much about the evolution of the Gothic style and the various uses to which this immensely beautiful but now lifeless monument had been put, through the centuries. His accent made the chil-dren smile, but it was no farther from the mark than Reynolds' French, which the French did not smile at only because it didn't amuse them to hear their language badly spoken.

When the tour was over, the guide gathered the party around him and, standing in a doorway through which they would have to pass, informed them that he was a student in a university and that this was his only means of paying for his education. The in-tellectual tradition of France sat gracefully on his frail shoulders, Reynolds thought, and short or not his tour had been a model of clarity. And was ten francs enough for the five of them?

Travelling in France right after the war, when everybody was so poor, he had been struck by the way the French always tipped the guide generously and thanked him in a way that was never perfunctory. It seemed partly good manners and partly a universal respect for the details of French history. A considerable number of tourists slipped through the doorway now without putting anything in the waiting hand. Before, the guide stood out in the open, quite confident that no one would try to escape without giving him something.

At the sight of the ten-franc note, the young man's features underwent a slight change, by which Reynolds knew that it was sufficient, but money was not all the occasion called for, and there was a word he had been waiting for a chance to use. "*Votre tour est très sensible,*" he said, and the guide's face lit up with pleasure.

Only connect, Mr. E. M. Forster said, but he was not talking about John Reynolds, whose life's blood went into making incessant and vivid connections with all sorts of people he would never see again, and never forgot.

The wine at lunch had made him sleepy. He waited impatiently while Dorothy and the children bought slides and postcards in the room where the tour ended. Outside, at the foot of the staircase, his plans for taking a nap were threatened when Dorothy was attracted to a museum of horrors having to do with the period when Mont-Saint-Michel was a state prison. But by applying delicate pressures at the right moment he got her to give up the museum, and they walked on down to their hotel. When he had undressed and pulled the covers back, he went to the window in his dressing gown. Some cars were just arriving. American cars. He looked at his watch. It was after four, and the parking lot was still more than half full. On the top floor of the hotel just below, and right next to an open window, he could see a girl of nineteen or twenty with long straight straw-blond hair, sitting on the side of a bed in an attitude of despondency. During the whole time he stood at the window, she didn't raise her head or move. He got into his own bed and was just falling asleep when somebody came into the courtyard with a transistor radio playing rock and roll. He got up and rummaged through his suitcase until he found the wax earplugs. When he woke an hour later, the courtyard was quiet. The girl was still there. He went to the window several times while he was running a bath and afterward while he was dressing. Though the girl left the bed and came back to it, there was no change in her dejection.

"That girl," he said finally.

"I've been watching her too," Dorothy said.

"She's in love. And something's gone wrong."

"They aren't married and she's having a baby," Dorothy said.

"And the man has left her."

"No, he's in the room," Dorothy said. "I saw him a minute ago, drinking out of a wine bottle."

The next time Reynolds looked he couldn't see anyone. The room looked empty, though you couldn't see all the way into it. Had the man and the girl left? Or were they down below somewhere? He looked one last time before they started down to the dining room. The shutters in the room across the court were closed. That was that.

□　　□

At dinner Reynolds got into a row with their waiter. For ten days in Paris and ten more days at a little seaside resort on the south coast of Brittany they had met with nothing but politeness and the desire to please. All the familiar complaints about France and the French were refuted, until this evening, when one thing after another went wrong. They were seated at a table that had been wedged into a far corner of the room, between a grotto for trout and goldfish and the foot of a stairway leading to the upper floors of the hotel. Reynolds started to protest and Dorothy stopped him.

"Trip wants to stay here so she can watch the fish," she explained.

"I know," he said as he unfolded his napkin, "but if anybody comes down those stairs they'll have to climb over my lap to get into the dining room."

"They won't," she said. "I'm sure it isn't used." Then to the children, "You pick out the one you want to eat and they take it out with a net and carry it to the kitchen."

"I have a feeling those trout are just for decoration," Reynolds said.

"No," Dorothy said. "I've seen it done. I forget where."

Nobody came down the stairs, and the trout, also undisturbed, circled round and round among the rocks and ferns. Though the room was only half full, the service was dreadfully slow. When they had finished the first course, the waiter, rather than go all the way around the table to where he could pick up Reynolds' plate, said curtly, "Hand me your plate," and Reynolds did. It would never have occurred to him to throw the plate at the waiter's head. His first reaction was always to be obliging. Anger came more slowly, usually with prodding.

The service got worse and worse.

"I think we ought to complain to the headwaiter," Dorothy said. Reynolds looked around. The maître d'hôtel was nowhere in sight. They went on eating their dinner.

"The food is just plain bad," Dorothy announced. "And he forgot to give us any cheese. I don't see how they can give this place a star in the 'Michelin.' "

When reminded of the fact that he had forgotten to give them any cheese, the waiter, instead of putting the cheese board on the table, cut off thin slices himself at a serving table and passed them. His manner was openly contemptuous. He also created a disturbance in the vicinity of their table by scolding his assistant, who had been courteous and friendly. In mounting anger Reynolds composed a speech to be delivered when the waiter brought the check. Of this withering eloquence all he actually got out was one sentence, ending with the words "*n'est plus un restaurant sérieux.*" The waiter pretended not to understand Reynolds' French. Like a fool Reynolds fell into the trap and repeated what he had said. It sounded much more feeble the second time. Smirking, the waiter asked if there was something wrong with their dinner, and Reynolds said that he was referring to the way it was served, whereupon the waiter went over to the assistant

and said, in English, "They don't like the way you served them."
It was his round, definitely.

□   □

Reynolds glanced at his wristwatch and then pushed his chair
back and hurried Dorothy and the three children out of the dining room and through the lobby and down the street to the outer
gate, and then along a path to higher ground. They were in
plenty of time. The sunset colors lingered in the sky and in the
ribbons of water. The children, happy to have escaped from the
atmosphere of eating, climbed over the rocks, risking their lives.
Dorothy sat with the sea wind blowing her hair back from her
face. He saw that she had entirely forgotten the unpleasantness in
the dining room. She responded to Nature the way he responded
to human beings. Presently he let go of his anger, too, and responded to the evening instead.

"What if they fall?" she said. "It could be quicksand."

"If it's quicksand, I'll jump in after them. Isn't it lovely and
quiet here?"

For in spite of all those cars in the parking lot they had the
evening to themselves. Nobody had come down here to see the
tide sweep in. At first it was silent. They saw that the channels
through the sandbars were growing wider, but there was no visible movement of water. Then suddenly it began to move, everywhere, with a rushing sound that no river ever makes on its
way to the sea. It was less like a force of Nature than like an
emotion—like the disastrous happiness of a man who has fallen
in love at the wrong season of life.

When it was over, they walked up to the abbey in the dusk,
by a back way that was all stairs, and down again along the outer
ramparts, looking into the rear windows of houses and restaurants, and were just in time to be startled by a bloodcurdling
scream. It came from a brightly lighted room in a house that was
across a courtyard and one story down from where they were. It
could have been a woman's scream, or a child's. There was an
outbreak of angry voices.

"What *is* it, Daddy?" the children asked. "What are they saying?"

"It's just a family argument," Reynolds said, making his voice sound casual. His knees were shaking. Listening to the excited voices, he made out only one word—*"idiot."* Either the scream had come from a mental defective or somebody was being insulted. The voices subsided. The Americans walked on until they came to a flight of steps leading down to the street in front of their hotel.

When the children were in bed, Reynolds and Dorothy sat at the window of their room, looking out at the night. "The air is so soft," she said, and he said "Ummm," not wanting to spoil her pleasure by saying what was really on his mind, which was that they should never have come here and that nothing on earth would make him come here again. In a place where things could easily have been kept as they were—where, one would have thought, it was to everybody's advantage to keep them that way—something had gone fatally wrong. Something had been allowed to happen that shouldn't have happened.

And it was not only here. The evening they arrived in Paris, the taxi-driver who took them from the boat train to their hotel on the Left Bank said, *"Paris n'est plus Paris."* And in the morning Madame said when she gave them their mail, "Paris is changed. It's so noisy now." "New York too," he said, to comfort her. But the truth was that nowhere in New York was the traffic like the Boulevard Saint-Germain. The cars drove at twice the speed of the cars at home, and when the lights changed there was always some side street from which cars kept on coming, and pedestrians ran for their lives. Like insects. The patrons who sat at the tables on the sidewalk in front of Lipp could no longer see their counterparts at the Deux Magots because of the river of cars that flowed between them. The soft summer air reeked of gasoline. And there was something he saw that he could not get out of his mind afterward: an old woman who had tried to cross against the light and was stranded in the middle of the street, her eyes wide with terror, like a living monument.

Reynolds was quite aware that to complain because things were not as agreeable as they used to be was one of the recognizable signs of growing old. And whether you accepted change or not, there was really no preventing it. But why, without exception, did something bad drive out something good? Why was the change always for the worse?

He had once asked his father-in-law, a man in his seventies, if there was a time—he didn't say whether he meant in history or a time that his father-in-law remembered, and, actually, he meant both—when the world seemed to be becoming a better place, little by little. And life everywhere more agreeable, more the way it ought to be. And then suddenly, after that, was there a noticeable shift in the pattern of events? Some sort of dividing line that people were aware of, when everything started to go downhill? His father-in-law didn't answer, making Reynolds feel he had said something foolish or tactless. But his father-in-law didn't like to talk about his feelings, and it was just possible that he felt the same way Reynolds did.

Once in a while, some small detail represented an improvement on the past, and you could not be happy in the intellectual climate of any time but your own. But in general, so far as the way people lived, it was one loss after another, something hideous replacing something beautiful, the decay of manners, the lapse of pleasant customs, as by a blind increase in numbers the human race went about making the earth more and more unfit to live on.

□   □

In the morning, Reynolds woke ready to pay the bill and leave as soon as possible, but it was only a short drive to Dinard, and their plane didn't leave until five o'clock in the afternoon, so after breakfast they climbed the steps of the Grande Rue once more, for a last look at the outside of the abbey, and found something they had overlooked before—an exhibition marking the thousandth year of the Abbey of Mont-Saint-Michel. There were illuminated manuscripts: St. Michael appearing to Aubert, Bishop of Avranches, in a dream and telling him to build a chapel on the

The Gardens of Mont-Saint-Michel

Mount; St. Michael weighing souls, slaying dragons, vanquishing demons, separating the blessed from the damned; St. Michael between St. Benoît and the archbishop St. William; St. Michael presenting his arms to the Virgin; St. Michael the guardian of Paradise. There was a list of the Benedictine monks living and dead at the time of the abbot Mainard II, and an inventory of the relics of the monastery at the end of the fifteenth century. There was the royal seal of William the Conqueror, of Philip the Fair, of Philip the Bold, of Louis VIII, of Philip Augustus. There was an octagonal reliquary containing a fragment of the cranium of St. Suzanne the Virgin Martyr. There was a drawing, cut by some vandal from an illuminated manuscript, of Jeanne d'Arc, Alison's friend, with her banner and sword, corresponding exactly to a description given at her trial, and a letter from Charles VII reaffirming that Mont-Saint-Michel was part of the royal domain. There were maquettes of the abbey in the year 1000, in 1100, in 1701, and as it was now. There was an aquarelle by Viollet-le-Duc of the flying buttresses. There were suits of armor, harquebuses, a pistolet, and some cannonballs. There was far more than they could take in or do justice to. When they emerged from the exhibition rooms, dazed by all they had looked at, Reynolds remembered the little gardens. It would never do to go away without seeing them. He couldn't find the gate that opened into the first one, and he wasn't sure, after eighteen years, on which side of the Mount they were, but Dorothy had noticed a sign, down a flight of steps from the abbey, that said "The Bishop's Garden." They bought tickets from an old woman sitting at a table under a vaulted archway and passed into what was hardly more than a strip of grass with a few flowers and flowering shrubs, and could have been the terrace of a public park in some small provincial French town. Reynolds began to look for the medieval gardens in earnest, and in the end they found themselves in what must once have been the place they were looking for. It was overrun with weeds, and hardly recognizable as a garden, and there was only that one.

Later, after he had closed and locked his suitcase, he went to the window for the last time. The shutters of the room that had contained so much drama were still closed. Looking down on the courtyard between the new wing of their hotel and the hotel in front of it, he knew suddenly what had happened. The medieval gardens didn't exist any more. To accommodate an ever-increasing number of tourists, the hotels had been added on to. So that they could hold thousands of souvenirs instead of hundreds, the souvenir shops had been deepened, taking the only available land, which happened to be those enchanting walled gardens. The very building he was in at that moment, with its comfortable if anonymous rooms with adjoining bath, had obliterated some garden that had been here for perhaps five hundred years. One of the miracles of the modern world, and they did just what people everywhere else would have done—they cashed in on a good thing. And never mind about the past. The past is what filled the gigantic parking lot with cars all summer, but so long as you have the appearance you can sell that; you don't need the real thing. What's a garden that has come down intact through five hundred years compared to money in the bank? *This is something I will never get over,* he thought, feeling the anger go deeper and deeper. *I will never stop hating the people who did this. And I will never forgive them—or France for letting them do it. What's here now is no longer worth seeing or saving. If this could happen here, then there is no limit to what can happen everywhere else. It's all going down, and down. There's no stopping it. . . .*

In order to pay the bill, he had to go to the cashier's desk, which was at the far end of the dining room. As he started there, walking between the empty tables, he saw that the only maître d'hôtel in the whole of France who looked like a Yale man was avoiding his eyes—not because he felt any remorse for putting them next to the fish tank with a clown for a waiter, or because he was afraid of anything Reynolds might say or do. He didn't care if Reynolds dropped dead on the spot, so long as he didn't have to dispose of the body. He was a man without any feeling for his métier, *tout simplement,* and so the food and the service had gone to hell in a basket.

□   □

While Reynolds was at the concierge's desk in the foyer, confirming their reservations at the airport by telephone, a gentle feminine voice said behind him, in English, "Monsieur, you left your traveller's checks," and he turned and thanked the cashier profusely.

He started up the stairs to see about the luggage and the concierge called after him, "Monsieur, your airplane tickets!"

They had banded together and were looking after him.

The same boy who carried the luggage up four flights of stairs now carried it down again and out through the medieval gate to the Volkswagen. "We were here eighteen years ago," Reynolds said to him as he took out his wallet. "You have no idea how different it was."

This was quite true. Eighteen years ago, the porter was not anywhere. Or if he was, he was only a babe in arms. But he was a Frenchman, and knew that a polite man doesn't sneer at emotions he doesn't feel or memories he cannot share. He insisted on packing the luggage for Reynolds, and tucked Dorothy and the children in, and closed the car doors, and then gave them a beautiful smile.

It's true that I overtipped him, Reynolds thought. But then, looking into the porter's alert, intelligent, doglike eyes, he knew that he was being unjust. The tip had nothing to do with it. It was because he was a harmless maniac and they all felt obliged to take care of him and see him on his way.

DIANE JOHNSON

Great Barrier Reef

The hotel had smelled of cinder block and cement floor, and was full of Australian senior citizens off a motor coach, but when we waked up in the morning a little less jet-lagged, and from the balcony could see the bed of a tidal river, with ibises and herons poking along the shallows, and giant ravens and parrots in the trees—trees strangling with monstera vines, all luridly beautiful—then we felt it would be all right.

But then when we went along to the quay, I felt it wouldn't. The ship, the *Dolphin,* was smaller than one could have imagined. Where could sixteen people possibly sleep? Brown stains from rusted drain spouts spoiled the hull. Gray deck paint splattered the ropes and ladders, orange primer showed through the chips. Wooden crates of lettuce and cabbages were stacked on the deck, and a case of peas in giant tin cans. This cruise had been J.'s idea, so I tried not to seem reproachful or shocked at the tiny, shabby vessel. But I am

25

not fond of travel in the best of circumstances—inconvenient displacements punctuated by painful longings to be home. For J., travel is natural opium.

J. was on his way to a meeting in Singapore of the International Infectious Disease Council, a body of eminent medical specialists from different lands who are charged with making decisions about diseases: Should the last remaining smallpox virus be destroyed? What was the significance of a pocket of polio in Sri Lanka? Could leprosy be finished off with a full-bore campaign in the spring? Was tuberculosis on the way back now via AIDS victims? What about measles in the third world? I had not realized until I took up with J. that these remote afflictions were still around, let alone that they killed people in the millions. A professor of medicine, J. did research on the things that infected their lungs.

He had always longed to visit the Great Barrier Reef. Afterward he would give some lectures in Sydney and Wellington, and we planned en route to indulge another whim: skiing in New Zealand in the middle of summer, just to say we'd skied in August and to bribe me to come along, for I will go anywhere to ski, it is the one thing. For me, too, the voyage was one of escape from California after some difficult times, and was to be—what was unspoken by either of us—a sort of trial honeymoon (though we were not married) on which we would discover whether we were suited to live together by subjecting ourselves to that most serious of tests: traveling together.

A crewman named Murray, a short, hardy man with a narrow Scots face and thick Aussie accent, showed us our stateroom. It had been called a stateroom in the brochure. Unimaginably small, two foam mattresses on pallets suspended from the wall, and a smell. Tall J. couldn't stand all the way up in it. The porthole was seamed with salt and rust. Across the passage, the door of another stateroom was open, but that one was a large, pretty room, with mahogany and nautical brass fittings, and a desk, and the portholes shone. It was the one, certainly, that had been pictured in the brochure.

"This one here, the Royal, was fitted for Prince Charles,

Prince of Wales, when he come on this voyage in nineteen seventy-four," Murray said.

"How do you book the Royal?" I asked.

"First come, first service," Murray told us. Australian, egalitarian, opposed to privilege.

Up on deck, thinking of spending five days on the *Dolphin,* I began to be seized by emotions of panic and pain I couldn't explain. They racketed about in my chest, my heart beat fast, I felt as if a balloon was blowing up inside me, squeezing up tears and pressing them out of my eyes, and thrusting painful words up into my throat, where they lodged. What was the matter with me? Usually I am a calm person (I think); five days is not a lifetime; the aesthetics of a mattress, or its comfort either, is not a matter for serious protests. A smell of rotten water sloshing somewhere inside the hull could be gotten used to. Anyone could eat tinned peas five days and survive, plenty of people in the world were glad to get tinned peas; I knew all that. I knew I wasn't reacting appropriately, and was sorry for this querulous fit of passion. Maybe it was only jet lag.

All the same, I said to J., "I just can't," and stared tragically at the moorings. He knew, of course, that I could and probably would, but he maintained an attitude of calm sympathy.

"You've been through a rough time," he said. "It's the court thing you're really upset about." Maybe so. The court thing, a draining and frightening lawsuit, had only been a week ago, and now here we were a hemisphere away.

The other passengers came on board, one by one or two by two. Cases clattered on the metal gangs. To me only one person looked possible—a tall, handsome, youngish man with scholarly spectacles and a weathered yachting cap. The rest were aged and fat, plain, wore shapeless brown or navy blue coat-sweaters buttoned over paunches, had gray perms and bald spots, and they all spoke in this accent I disliked, as if their vowels had been slammed in doors. They spoke like cats, I thought: *eeoooow.* Fat Australians, not looking fond of nature, why were they all here?

"Why are these people here?" I complained to J. "What do they care about the Great Barrier Reef?"

27

"It's a wonder of the world, anyone would want to see it," J. said, assuming the same dreamy expression he always wore when talking about or thinking about the Great Barrier Reef, so long the object of his heart.

I hated all the other passengers. On a second inspection, besides the youngish man, only a youngish couple, Dave and Rita, looked promising, but then I was infuriated to learn that Dave and Rita were Americans—we hadn't come all this way to be cooped up for five days in a prison of an old Coast Guard cutter with other Americans, and, what was worse, Rita and Dave had drawn the Prince Charles cabin, and occupied it as if by natural right, Americans expecting and getting luxury.

Of course I kept these overwrought feelings to myself. No Australian complained. None appeared unhappy with the ship, no satirical remark, no questioning comment marred their apparent delight with the whole ship-shape of things, the cabins, even the appalling lunch, which was under way as soon as the little craft was under way, pointing itself east toward the open sea out of McKay Harbor.

After we lost sight of land, this mood of desperate resentment did not disappear, as J. had predicted, but deepened. It was more than the irritability of a shallow, difficult person demanding comfort, it was a failure of spirit, inexplicable and unwarranted on this bright afternoon. How did these obese Australian women, these stiff old men, clamber so uncomplainingly below deck to their tiny cells, career along the railings laughing crazily as they tripped on ropes? Doubtless one would fall and the voyage would be turned back. When I thought of the ugliness of the things I had just escaped from—the unpleasant divorce, the custody battle, the hounding of lawyers and strangers—only to find myself here, really unmanageable emotions made me turn my face away from the others.

Dinner was tinned peas, and minted lamb overdone to a gray rag, and potatoes. J. bought a bottle of wine from the little bar, which the deckhand Murray nimbly leapt behind, transforming himself into waiter or bartender as required. We sat with the promising young man, Mark, and offered him some wine, but he said he didn't drink wine. He was no use, he was very, very prim, a bachelor civil servant from Canberra, with a slight stammer, only handsome and young by some accident, and would someday be old without changing, would still be taking lonely cruises, eating minted lamb, would still be unmarried and reticent. He had no conversation, had never been anywhere, did not even know what we wanted from him. Imagining his life, I thought about how sad it was to be him, hoping for whatever he hoped for, but not hoping for the right things, content to eat these awful peas, doomed by being Australian, and even while I pitied him I found him hopeless. Even J., who could talk to anyone, gave up trying to talk to him, and, feeling embarrassed to talk only to each other as if he weren't there, we fell silent and stared out the windows at the rising moon along the black horizon of the sea.

There didn't seem a way, in the tiny cabin, for two normal-sized people to exist, let alone to make love; there was no space that could accommodate two bodies in any position. Our suitcases filled half the room. With summer clothing, our proper suits to wear in Wellington and Sydney, and bulky ski clothes of quilted down, we were ridiculously encumbered with baggage. It seemed stupid now. We were obliged to stow our bags and coats precariously on racks overhead, our duffel bags sleeping at the feet of our bunks like lumpy interloper dogs. J. took my hand comfortingly in the dark across the space between the two bunks before he dropped off to sleep; I lay awake, seized with a terrible fit of traveler's panic, suffocating with fearful visions of fire, of people in prison cells or confined in army tanks, their blazing bodies emerging screaming from the holds of ships to writhe doomed on the ground, their stick limbs ringed in flame, people burned in oil splashed on them from the holds of rusted ships, and smells of sewers, smells of underground, the slosh of engine fuel from the hell beneath.

□   □

As is so often the traveler's fate, nothing on the cruise was as promised or as we had expected. The seedy crew of six had tourist-baked smiles and warmed-over jokes. There was a little faded captain who climbed out of his tower to greet us now and then, and a sort of Irish barmaid, Maureen, who helped Murray serve the drinks. The main business of the passage seemed to be not the life of the sea nor the paradise of tropical birds on Pacific shores nor the balmy water but putting in at innumerable islands to look at souvenir shops. J., his mind on the Great Barrier Reef, which we were expected to reach on the fourth day, sweetly bore it all, the boredom and the endless stops at each little island, but I somehow couldn't conquer my petulant dislike.

It fastened, especially, on our shipmates. Reluctantly I learned their names, in order to detest them with more precision: Don and Donna from New Zealand, Priscilla from Adelaide—portly, harmless old creatures, as J. pointed out. Knowing that the derisive remarks that sprang to my lips only revealed me as petty and querulous to good-natured J., I didn't speak them aloud.

But it seemed to me that these Australians only wanted to travel to rummage in the souvenir shops, though these were all alike from island to island: Dream Island, Hook Island—was this a cultural or a generation gap? I brooded on the subject of souvenirs—why they should exist, why people should want them, by what law they were made to be ugly—shells shaped like toilets, a row of swizzle sticks in the shapes of women's silhouetted bodies, thin, fatter, fat, with bellies and breasts increasingly sagging as they graduated from SWEET SIXTEEN to SIXTY. I was unsettled to notice that the one depicting a woman of my age had a noticeably thickened middle. These trinkets were everywhere. I watched a man buy one, a fat one, and hand it to his wife. "Here, Mother, this one's you," he said. Laughter a form of hate. It was not a man from our ship, luckily, or I would have pushed him overboard. I brooded on my own complicity in the industry of souvenirs, for didn't I buy them myself? The things I bought— the (I liked to think) tasteful baskets and elegant textiles I was always carting home—were these not just a refined form of souvenir for a more citified sort of traveler?

Statuettes of drunken sailors, velvet pictures of island maidens, plastic seashell lamps made in Taiwan. What contempt the people who think up souvenirs have for other people. Yet our fellow passengers plunked down money with no feeling of shame. They never walked on the sand or looked at the colors of the bright patchwork birds rioting in the palm trees. Besides us, only the other Americans, Rita and Dave, did this. It was Dave who found the perfect helmet shell—a regular treasure, the crew assured them, increasingly rare—protected, even, you weren't supposed to carry them away, but who was looking? I wanted it to have been J. who got it.

□   □

Each morning, each afternoon, we stopped at another island. This one was Dream Island. "It's lovely, isn't it, dear?" Priscilla said to me. "People like to see a bit of a new place, the shopping, they have different things to make it interesting." But it wasn't different, it was the same each day: The crew hands the heavy, sacklike people grunting down into rowboats, and hauls them out onto a sandy slope of beach. Up they trudge toward a souvenir shop. This one had large shells perched on legs, and small shells pasted in designs on picture frames, and earrings made of shells, and plastic buckets, and plastic straw hats surrounded with fringe, and pictures of hula dancers.

"I don't care, I do hate them," I ranted passionately to J. "I'm right to hate them. They're what's the matter with the world, they're ugly consumers, they can't look at a shell unless it's coated in plastic, they never look at the sea—why are they here? Why don't they stay in Perth and Adelaide—you can buy shells there, and swizzle sticks in the shape of hula girls." Of course J. hadn't any answer for this, of course I was right.

I wandered onto the strand of beach and took off my shoes, planning to wade. Whenever I was left alone I found myself harking back to the court hearing, my recollections just as sharp and painful as a week ago. I couldn't keep from going over and over my ordeal, and thinking of my hated former husband, not really him so much as his lawyer, Waxman, a man in high-heeled boots and aviator glasses. I imagined him here on Dream Island. He has fallen overboard at the back of the ship. I am the only one to notice, and I have the power to cry out for rescue but I don't. Our eyes meet; he is down in the water, still wearing the glasses. I imagine his expression of surprise when he realizes that I'm not going to call for help. What for him had been a mere legal game, a job, would cost him his life. He had misjudged me. The ship speeds along. We are too far away to hear his cries.

□   □

It was the third day and we had set down at Happy Island. Here we had to wade across a sandbar. This island had goats grazing. "This is the first we've gotten wet," I bitterly complained. We stood in ankle-deep water amid queer gelatinous seaweed. I had wanted to swim, to dive, to sluice away the court and the memories but hadn't been permitted to because these waters, so innocently beautiful, so seductively warm, were riddled with poisonous creatures, deadly toxins, and sharks.

"Be careful not to pick up anything that looks like this," the first mate, Murray, warned us, showing us a harmless-looking little shell. "The deadly cone shell. And the coral, be careful a' that, it scratches like hell. One scratch can take over a year to heal. We have some ointment on board, be sure to tell one of the crew if you scratch yourself."

From here, I looked back at the ship, and, seeing the crew watching us, I suddenly saw ourselves, the passengers, with the crew's eyes—we were a collection of thick bodies, mere cargo to be freighted around, slightly volatile, likely to ferment, like damp grain, and give trouble—difficult cargo that sent you scurrying unreasonably on tasks, boozed, got itself cut on coral, made you laugh at its jokes. I could see that the crew must hate us.

Yet, a little later, I came upon Murray tying up a fishhook for old George, whose fingers were arthritic. Murray was chatting to him with a natural smile. I studied them. Perhaps Murray by himself was a man of simple good nature, but the rest, surely, hated us. The captain, staring coolly out from his absurd quarterdeck, made no pretense of liking us, seemed always to be thinking of something else, not of this strange Pacific civilization of Quonset huts and rotting landing barges and odd South Sea denizens strangely toothless, beyond dentistry, beyond fashion, playing old records over and over on PR systems strung through the palms. You felt the forlornness of these tacky little islands that should have been beautiful and serene. I even wondered if we would ever get back to America again. Not that I wanted to. America was smeared with horrible memories, scenes of litigation. Why shouldn't J. and I simply stay here? Why—more important—was I not someone who was able, like the lovely goat that grazed on the slope near here, to gaze at the turquoise sea and enjoy the sight of little rose-colored parrots wheeling in the air? Why was I not, like a nice person, simply content to be, to enjoy beauty and inner peace? Instead I must suffer, review, quiver with fears and rages—the fault, I saw, was in myself, I was a restless, peevish, flawed person. How would I be able to struggle out of this frame of mind? Slipping on the sandy bank, I frightened the little goat.

□   □

By the third day I began to notice a sea change in our shipmates, who had begun in sensible gabardines and print dresses, but now wore violently floral shirts and dresses, and were studded with shells—wreaths of shells about their necks and at their ears, hats with crabs and gulls embroidered on. By now I knew a bit more about them. They were all travelers—George and Nettie, Fred and Polly, had been friends for forty years, and spent a part of each year, now that they were all retired, traveling in Europe in their caravans. Dave and Rita were both schoolteachers, and Rita raised Great Danes. Priscilla was going along on this cruise with her brother Albert because Albert had just lost his wife. Mark was taking his annual vacation. Don and Donna were thinking of selling their Auckland real estate business and buying a sailboat to live on and sail around the world. J. told me that George was a sensitive and sweet man who had lived his whole life in Australia and only now in his retirement had begun to see something of the world. "And he says that the most beautiful place in the world is someplace near Split, in Yugoslavia, and if I take you there, my darling, will you for God's sake cheer up now?" But I couldn't.

Tonight we were dining ashore, in a big shed on Frenchie's Island, in a shabby tin building. Music was already playing on loudspeakers. Groups of people from other ships or hotels strolled around carrying drinks. A smell of roasted sausages, someone singing "Waltzing Matilda" in the kitchen at the back. The *Dolphin* passengers were lined up at the bar and in the souvenir shop. In the big hangar of a room little tables encircled a dance floor, and at one end a microphone stood against a photo mural of the South Seas, as if the real scene outdoors were not evocative. The sun lowered across the pink water, setting in the east, and the water in the gentle lagoon was as warm as our blood. "I wish a hurricane would come and blow it all away," I said to J.

When the diners had tipped their paper plates into a bin, they began to sing old American songs. Sitting outside, I could hear Maureen singing "And Let Her Sleep Under the Bar." Then came canned music from a phonograph, and people began to dance—the ones who were not too decrepit. I tried to hear only the chatter of the monkeys or parrots in the palm trees, innocent creatures disturbed by the raucous humans. J. was strangely cheerful and shot some pool with a New Zealander, causing me all of a sudden to think, with a chill of disapproval, that J., possibly, was an Australian at heart and that I ought not to marry him or I would end up in a caravan in Split. His good looks and professional standing were only a mask that concealed ... simplicity.

It didn't surprise me that people liked the handsome and amiable J.; it didn't even surprise me that they seemed to like me. I had concealed my tumult of feelings, and I was used to being treated by other people with protective affection, if only because I am small. This in part explained why the courtroom, and its formal process of accusation, its focus on myself as a stipulated bad person, had been such a shock. It was as if a furious mob had come to smash with sticks my porcelain figure of my self. I had a brief intimation that the Australians with their simple friendliness could put me back together if I would let them, but I would rather lie in pieces for a while.

The moon was full and golden. "What a beautiful, beautiful

night," said Nettie from Adelaide, the sister of George, coming out onto the beach. Who could disagree? Not even I. The ship on the moonlit water lapped at anchor, resting, awaiting them, looking luxurious and serene. J. came out and showed us the Southern Cross. At first I couldn't see it, all constellations look alike to me, I have never been able to see the bears or belts or any of it. But now, when J. turned my chin, I did see it, and it did look like a cross.

□   □

In the night I had another dream, in which the lawyer had said, "Isn't it true that you have often left your children while you travel?" He had been looking not at me but at a laughing audience. He was speaking over a microphone. The audience wore plastic, fringed hats.

"Not willingly, no," I had said. "Not often."

"How many times did you go on trips last year and leave them at home?"

"Oh, six, I don't know."

"That's not often?"

"Just a day or two each time. A man takes a business trip, you don't call it leaving, or 'often.'" But I was not allowed to speak or explain.

"We're looking at how often you are in fact away from your children."

Here I had awakened, realizing that it was all true, it wasn't just just a dream, it was what had happened, not of course the audience in plastic hats. Even though in the end I had been vindicated, I felt sticky with the encumbrance of their father's hate. All I had wanted was to be free and now I was so soiled with words spoken at me, about me, by strangers, by lawyers I had never seen before, who had never seen me. It didn't seem fair that you could not prevent being the object of other people's emotions, you were not safe anywhere from their hate—or from their love, for that matter. You were never safe from being invaded by their feelings when you wanted only to be rid of them, free, off, away.

35

□ □

In the morning I had wanted to swim, to wash in the sea, to wash all this stuff off, splash; my longing must have been clear, because Cawley, the other deckhand, laughed at me. "Not here you don't, love," he said. "There's sharks here as long as a boat."

The captain, Captain Clarke, made one of his few visits. He had kept aloof in the little pilot cabin above, though he must have slipped down to the galley to eat, or maybe the crew took him his food up there. Now he invited his passengers two by two to his bridge. When people were tapped, they hauled themselves up the metal ladder, helped by Cawley or Murray, then would come down looking gratified. Alfred, who went up alone, suggested that he had helped avoid a navigational accident.

J. and I were invited on the morning of the fourth day, the day we were to arrive at the reef itself in the late afternoon. I went up despite myself. Captain Clarke was a thin, red-haired man sitting amid pipes and charts. He let us take the wheel, and showed us the red line that marked our route through the labyrinth of islands shown on a chart. His manner was grave, polite, resigned. No doubt these visits were dictated by the cruise company.

"But there are thousands of islands between here and the Great Barrier Reef!" said J., studying the charts.

"Souvenir shops on every one," I couldn't help saying. J. fastened me with a steady look in which I read terminal exasperation.

"These islands are not all charted," said the captain. "The ones that are were almost all charted by Captain Cook himself, after he ran aground on one in seventeen seventy. He was a remarkable navigator. He even gave names to them all. But new ones are always being found. I've always hoped to find one myself."

"What would you name it?" J. asked.

"I would give it my name, or, actually, since there is already a Clarke Island, I would name it for my wife, Laura, Laura Clarke Island, or else for Alison, my daughter."

"Do you keep your eyes open for one?"

"I mean to get one," he said.

□　　□

When we went down to the deck again, Maureen was gazing at the waves. "It's getting choppy," she observed, unnecessarily, for the boat had begun to rear up like a prancing horse.

"Right, we probably won't make it," Murray agreed.

"What do you mean?" I asked, alarmed by the tinge of satisfaction that underlay their sorry looks.

"To the reef. No point in going if the sea's up, like it's coming up, washed right up, no use going out there. If it's like this, we put in at Hook Island instead."

Astonished, I looked around to see if J., or anyone else, was listening. No, or not worried, would just as soon have Hook Island. They continued to knit and read along the deck, which now began to heave more forcefully, as if responding to the desire of the crew to return to port without seeing the great sight.

"How often does it happen that you don't go to the reef?" I asked, heart thundering. The point of all this, and J.'s dream, was to go to the reef, and now they were casually dismissing the possibility.

"Oh, it happens more often than not. This time of year, you know. Chancy, the nautical business is."

"Come out all this way and not see it?" I insisted, voice rising.

"Well, you can't see it if the waves are covering it up, can you? You can bump your craft into it, but you can't see it. Can you?"

"I don't know," cried I. "I don't even know what it is." But the shape of things was awfully clear; given the slightest excuse, the merest breeze or ripple, the *Dolphin* would not take us to the Great Barrier Reef, and perhaps had never meant to. I thought in panic of not alerting J., but then I rushed to tell him. He put down his book, his expression aghast, and studied the waves.

The midday sky began to take on a blush of deeper blue, and, now that our attention was called to it, the sea seemed to grow dark and rough before our eyes. Where moments before it had been smooth enough to row, we now began to pitch. The report of the prow smacking the waves made me think of cannons, of Trafalgar. In defiance of the rocking motion, the Australian passengers began to move around the cabin and along the deck, gripping the railings, looking trustfully at the sky and smiling. Their dentures were white as teacups.

"Christ," said Murray, "one of these bloody old fools will break a hip. Folks, why don't you sit down?" Obediently, like children, the Australians went inside the main cabin and sat in facing rows of chairs. Despite the abrupt change in the weather, the ship continued its course out to sea. J. and I anchored ourselves in the prow, leaning against the tool chest, resolutely watching the horizon, not the bounding deck beneath our feet, a recommended way to avoid seasickness. In twenty minutes the sea had changed altogether, from calm to a thing that threw the little ship in the air. We felt as if we were slithering along the back of a sea monster who toiled beneath us.

The dread specter of seasickness was promptly among us. The captain, rusty haired, pale eyed, as if his eyes had bleached with sea wind, climbed off the bridge and glanced inside the cabin at his passengers.

"Oh, please, they want to go, they'll be all right," I called to him, but the words were swept off by the wind.

The others were so occupied with the likelihood of nausea that they hadn't grasped that the ship might turn back, and they seemed rather to be enjoying the drama of getting seasick. Every few minutes someone would get up, totter out to the rail, retch over it, and return to the laughter and commiseration of the others. The friendly thing was to be sick, so I was contrarily determined not to be, and J. was strong by nature. One of the Australians, Albert, gave us a matey grin as he lurched over our feet toward a bucket. I looked disgustedly away, but J. wondered aloud if he should be helping these old folks.

"Of course they'll use this as an excuse for not going," I was saying bitterly. These barfing Australian senior citizens would keep us from getting to the Great Barrier Reef. My unruly emotions, which had been milder today, now plumped around in my bosom like the smacking of the boat on the waves. J. watched the Australians screaming with laughter, and telling each other, "That's right, barf in the bin."

"This is a rough one," Albert said, and pitched sharply against the cabin, so that J. leapt up to catch him. Murray, tightening ropes, called for him to go back in the cabin.

"Tossed a cookie meself." He grinned at J. and me.

"We don't think it's so rough," I said.

"I've seen plenty rougher," Murray agreed. "Bloody hangover is my problem."

When the captain leaned out to look down at the deck below him, I cried, "Oh, we just have to go to the reef, we have to! Oh, please!"

"What's the likelihood this sea will die down?" J. shouted to the captain. The captain shrugged. I felt angry for the first time at J., as if he were a magnet. It was unfair, I knew, to say it was J.'s fault—the storm, the tossing sea, the *Dolphin,* and of course the rest. J. who had signed us up for this terrible voyage, during which we would be lost at sea, before reaching the Great Barrier Reef, whatever it was, and who had caused the sea to come up like this.

All J.'s fault. If I ever saw the children again, it would be a miracle, or else them saying in after years, Our mother perished on the high seas somewhere off Australia. What would they re-member of me? The sight of the boiling waves, now spilling over the bow, now below us, made me think of throwing myself in— just an unbidden impulse trailing into my mind, the way I half-thought, always, of throwing my keys or my sunglasses off bridges. Of course I wouldn't do it.

The ship pitched, thrust, dove through the waters. Yet we had not turned back. "Whoooeee," the Aussies were screaming inside the lounge. Life was like this, getting tossed around, and then, right before the real goal is reached, something, someone, makes you turn back.

"J., don't let them turn back," I said again, for the tenth time, putting all the imperative passion I knew into my voice. Without hearing me, J. was already climbing the ladder to the bridge. I looked at my fingers whitely gripping the rope handle on the end of the tool chest. A locker slid across the deck, back, across, back, and once, upon the impact of a giant wave, a dead fish stowed in it sloshed out onto the deck. Then, in the wind, I heard Murray's thin voice call out, "It's all right, love, we're going to the reef! The captain says we're going to the reef!"

□　　□

As abruptly as the storm had started, it subsided meekly, the sky once more changed color, now to metallic gray, lighter at the horizon, as if it were dawn. Ahead of us an indistinguishable shape lay in the water like the back of a submerged crocodile, a vast bulk under the surface. The captain had stopped the engines, and we drifted in the water. "The reef, the reef!" cried the Australians, coming out on deck. I shouted too. The crew began to busy themselves with readying the small boats, and the other passengers came boisterously out of the cabin, as if nothing had been wrong. "Ow," they said, "that was a bit of a toss."

"You'll have two hours on the reef, not more," the captain told us before we climbed again into the rowboats. "Because of the tide. If you get left there at high tide, if we can't find you, well, we don't come back. Because you wouldn't be there." The Australians laughed at this merry joke.

J. handed me out of the boat and onto the reef. My first step on it shocked me. For I had had the idea of coral, hard and red, a great lump of coral sticking out of the ocean, a jagged thing that would scratch you if you fell on it, that you could chisel into formations dictated by your own mind. We had heard it was endangered, and I had imagined its destruction by divers with chisels, carrying off lumps at a time.

Instead it was like a sponge. It sank underfoot, it sighed and sucked. Shocked, looking down, I could see that it was entirely alive, made of eyeless formations of cabbagey creatures sucking and opening and closing, yearning toward tiny ponds of water lying on the pitted surface, pink, green, gray, viscous, silent. I moved, I put my foot here, then hurriedly there, stumbled, and gashed my palm against something rough.

"Where should you step? I don't want to step on the things," I gasped.

"You have to. Just step as lightly as you can," J. said.

"It's alive, it's all alive!"

"Of course. It's coral, it's alive, of course," J. said. He had told me there were 350 species of coral here, along with the calcareous remains of tiny polyzoan and hydrozoan creatures that helped to form a home for others.

"Go on, J., leave me," I said, seeing that he wanted to be alone to have his own thoughts about all this marine life, whatever it meant to him. It meant something. His expression was of rapture. He smiled at me and wandered off.

I had my Minox, but I found the things beneath my feet too fascinating to photograph. Through the viewer of my camera they seemed pale and far away. At my feet in astonishing abundance they continued their strange life. I hated to tread on them, so at length stood like a stork, and aimed the camera at the other passengers.

These were proceeding cautiously, according to their fashion, over the strange surface—Mark in his yachting cap, with his camera, alone; the Kiwis in red tropical shirts more brilliant than the most bright-hued creatures; even the crew, with insouciant expressions, protectively there to save their passengers from falls or from strange sea poisons that darted into the inky ponds from the wounded life beneath the feet. For the first time, I felt, seeing each behaving characteristically, that I knew them all, and even that I liked them, or at least that I liked it that I understood what they would wear and do. Travelers like myself.

I watched J. kneeling in the water to peer into the centers of the mysterious forms. Almost as wonderful as this various life was J.'s delight. He was as dazzled as if we had walked on stars, and indeed the sun shining on the tentacles, wet petals, filling the spongy holes, made things sparkle like a strange underfoot galaxy. He appeared as a long, sandy-haired, handsome stranger, separate, unknowable. I, losing myself once more in the patterns and colors, thought of nothing, was myself as formless and uncaring as the coral, all my unruly, bad-natured passions leaching harmlessly into the sea, leaving a warm sensation of blankness and ease. I thought of the Hindu doctrine of *ahimsa,* of not harming living things, and I was not harming them, I saw—neither by stepping on them nor by leaving my anger and fears and the encumbrances of real life with them. Almost as wonderful as J.'s happiness was this sense of being healed of a poisoned spirit.

□   □

At sunset we headed landward into the sun, a strange direction to a Californian, for whom all sunsets are out at sea. We would arrive at McKay at midnight—it also seemed strange that a voyage that had taken four days out would take only six hours back, something to do with the curve of the continental shelf. A spirit of triumph imbued our little party—we had lived through storms and reached a destination. People sat in the lounge labeling their rolls of film.

Maureen came along and reminded us that, as this was our last night on board, there would be a fancy dress party. When we had read this in the brochure, I had laughed. It had seemed absurd that such a little ship would give itself great liner airs. J. and I had not brought costumes. In our cabin, I asked him what he meant to wear. Since my attitude had been so resolutely one of noncompliance, he seemed surprised that I was going to participate in the dressing up. Now it seemed too churlish to object. "I know it's stupid, but how can we not?" I said. "It would be so pointed, with only sixteen of us aboard."

J. wore his ski pants, which were blue and tight, with a towel cape, and called himself Batman. I wore his ski parka, a huge, orange, down-filled garment. The others were elaborately got up, must have brought their masks and spangles with them. Rita wore a black leotard and had painted cat whiskers on her face, and Dave had a Neptune beard. Nettie wore a golden crown, and Don a harlequin suit, half purple, half green. I drew to one side and sat on the table with my feet drawn up inside J.'s parka, chin on my knees, watching the capers which now began. "I? I am a pumpkin," I explained, when they noticed the green ribbon in my hair, my stem. It wasn't much of a costume, but it was all I could think of, and they laughed forgivingly and said that it looked cute.

J. won a prize, a bottle of beer, for the best paper cutout of a cow. I was surprised, watching him with the scissors making meticulous little snips, to see how a cow shape emerged under his hands, with a beautiful delicate udder and teats, and knobs of horn. I had not thought that J. would notice a cow.

"I have an announcement," Mark said, in a strangely loud and shaky voice, one hand held up, his other hand nervously twisting his knotted cravat. The theme of his costume was not obvious.

"Excuse me, an announcement." The others smiled and shushed. "I've had word from my friend—a few months ago I had the honor to assist a friend with his astronomical observations, and I've just had word that he—we—that the comet we discovered has been accepted by the international commission. It will bear his name, and, as I had the honor to assist, I'll be mentioned too. Only a little comet, of course, barely a flash in the sky. There are millions of them, of course. There are millions of them. But ..."

A cheer, toasts, Mark bought drinks for everybody. The crew bought drinks for the guests, dishing up from behind the little bar with the slick expertise of landside bartenders. They seemed respectful at Mark's news. I raised my glass with the rest and felt ashamed at the way I had despised Mark's life—indeed a nice life, spent exploring the heavens with a friend—how had I thought him friendless, this nice-looking young man?

"Split, Yugoslavia, is the most beautiful place on earth," George was telling me. "Like a travel poster. I've been almost everywhere by now, except China, but there, at Split, my heart stopped." My attention was reclaimed from my own repentant thoughts; for a second I had been thinking that he was describing a medical calamity, and I had been about to say, "How terrible!"

But no, he was describing a moment, an experience, the experience of beauty. He had the long, bald head of a statesman, but he was a farmer, now retired, from Perth. I was ashamed that it had taken me so long to see that the difference between Americans and Australians was that Americans were tired and bored, while for Australians, stuck off at the edge of the world, all was new, and they had the energy and spirit to go off looking for abstractions like beauty, and comets.

"Let me get you another one of those," George said, taking my wineglass, for a pumpkin cannot move.

"How long have you been married?" asked Nettie, smiling at me. I considered, not knowing whether I wanted to shock them by admitting that we were not married at all. "Two years," I said.

"Really?" Nettie laughed. "We all thought you was newlyweds." Her smile was sly.

I felt myself flush inside the hot parka. The others had thought all my withdrawn unfriendliness was newlywed shyness and the preoccupations of love. They were giving me another chance.

"It seems like it." I laughed. I would never marry J., I thought. He was too good-natured to be saddled with a cross person like me. And yet now I wasn't cross, was at ease and warm with affection for the whole company. Don and Donna were buying champagne all around, and the crew, now that they were about to be rid of this lot of passengers, seemed sentimental and sorry, as if we had been the nicest, most amusing passengers ever.

The prize for the best costume was to be awarded by vote. People wrote on bits of paper and passed them to Maureen, who sat on the bar and sorted them. There was even a little mood of tension, people wanting to win.

"And the prize for the best costume," she paused portentously, "goes to the pumpkin!" My shipmates beamed and applauded. In the hot parka I felt myself grow even warmer with shame and affection. People of goodwill and good sense, and I had allowed a snobbish mood of accidie to blind me to it. Their white untroubled smiles.

In a wrapped paper parcel was a key ring with a plastic-covered picture of the *Dolphin,* and the words GREAT BARRIER REEF around the edge of it. I was seized by a love for it, would always carry it, I decided, if only as a reminder of various moral lessons I thought myself to have learned, and as a reminder of certain bad things about my own character.

"Thank you very much," I said. "I'll always keep it. And I'll always remember the *Dolphin* and all of you"—for at the moment I thought, of course, that I would. J. was looking at me with a considering air, as if to inspect my sincerity. But I was sincere.

"I know I've been a pig," I apologized to him later, as we gathered our things in the stateroom. "These people are really very sweet."

"I wonder if you'd feel like that if you hadn't gotten the prize," he said, peevishly. I was surprised at his tone. Of course it wasn't the prize, only a little key chain, after all, that had cured me, but the process of the voyage, and the mysterious power of distant places to dissolve the problems the traveler has brought along. Looking at J., I could see that, for his part, he was happy but let down, as if the excitement and happiness of seeing the reef at last, and no doubt the nuisance of my complaining, had worn him out for the moment, and serious thoughts of his coming confrontations with malaria and leprosy and pain and sadness were returning, and what he needed was a good night's sleep.

WARD JUST

I'm Worried About You

At Verdun it began to leak rain, staining the concrete of the monument, the Ossuaire. She insisted on taking a photograph of Marshall and Harry, who stood uncomfortably on the steps in front of the building. They were as gray as the day, dressed in floppy hats and trench coats. French tourists moved around them, apparently oblivious; one old man stood staring at the graves, wiping his eyes. Janine fiddled with the camera and finally snapped the picture of the men, who looked off to one side, casually, as if they did not know they were being photographed.

Later, the three of them went to the Tranchée des Baïonnettes, hustling because they were late; Harry had to catch a train. He kept looking at his watch while Marshall and Janine circled the trench. He knew the battlefield well. Look, he said finally. Look carefully in there. You can still see their bayonets pointed up. Killed where they stood, buried. See the bayonets?

It was true, the points of the bayonets poked through the soft earth, a grim iron garden. There was also a bent and rusted rifle barrel. It was a memorial to one of the great legends of the first war, members of the 137th Infantry Regiment holding the line, though bombarded and eventually interred by German artillery.

She said, You can't mean that the bodies are still there?

No, Harry said, looking at his watch. They have buried the men in the Ossuaire but left their weapons in place. It's to give you an idea of how it was in the spring of 1916. *La gloire, Mort pour la France*. The goddamned French, he said savagely. This place is a monument to death.

Janine stood looking at the trench, shaking her head.

We have to go now, Harry said. My train.

I've been waiting for twenty years to see Verdun, Marshall said. I want to see Douaumont, and Fort de Vaux. Then we can go. You won't miss your train.

Inside Fort de Vaux, they stood next to one of the French 75s. On a sunny day there would have been a fine, clear field of fire. They stood silent a moment, oppressed by the closeness and thickness of the walls and the low ceiling, the dampness and the mass of the gun, silent for sixty-eight years. Fort de Vaux had been taken when the defenders had run out of water and ammunition; later, it was retaken. There were no graffiti on the walls and everything seemed to be as it was then. The rain had turned to a sporadic drizzle, almost a fog. Marshall looked at the fields below and imagined line upon line of German troops. He turned to his wife and said, Can you imagine the racket in here when the gun was firing? My God.

She said, I can't forget the old man at the Ossuaire.

At last they were en route to Bar-le-Duc, where Harry would catch his train. He had the schedule in his hand and was calculating whether it would be better to go to Metz or to Nancy. They were very late. The pavement was slippery and Marshall drove slowly, taking no chances; he did not know the road. Harry kept looking at his wristwatch and sighing. He was returning to Paris to have a farewell dinner with a girl. He intended to say good-bye to her at the dinner and break off their affair.

You can pass that truck, he said.

No, I can't, Marshall said.

Harry said, This is very stressful.

We'll get there in time, Marshall said.

I never should've come, Harry said. I should have stayed in Paris. Then he began to talk about the girl in short sentences, non sequiturs. Marshall only nodded, keeping his eyes on the road. He did not know the girl well; really, he did not understand what had gone wrong except that it was another busted love affair. There was a snapshot in Harry's Paris apartment, the girl in dishabille, sitting on a cocktail table. She was wearing one of Harry's oxford shirts, the shirt unbuttoned all the way down. She was sitting Indian-fashion, leaning forward, her head a little to one side. It was a low glass cocktail table and the photographer had been above her, shooting down; the result looked professionally made, grainy and slightly off focus. It looked like Harry's work. A cigarette hung from her lower lip, the smoke just visible around her head, a goofy smile curling around the cigarette. She held a champagne flute at an angle, so anyone looking at the picture wanted to cry out, Watch it! You're going to spill your wine! The whorish effect was comical because the girl was very well groomed, short hair, fine bones, and a cleft chin; a model's composed face. She was lovely to look at. It was just a snapshot stuck in a bookcase, but it caught everyone's eye. It made people, men mostly, smile when they looked at it.

The girl's name was Antoinette, and she came from a very old French family. Her great-grandfather, the viscount, was mentioned by Proust as a habitué of the many soirées chez les Verdurin. Harry said she reminded him of an earlier, happier, more organized time. She made him laugh. He called her Off-With-My-Head Antoinette.

He said, I'm worried about her.

Marshall said, We're almost there.

Harry said, As a matter of fact, I think that was the first thing I said to her in seriousness, the night we met: I'm worried about you. I was too. She didn't look well. She was mixed up with a bad crowd. And she still is. But the hell with it, it's all in the past. At my age you're happy for whatever you get, for whatever duration. And we had a great six months. These women today, they're too modern for me. But I came in at the end of everything—colonialism, the novel, decent movies, worthy women. And she's so goddamned young, only thirty-five. I kept telling her that. And that I couldn't ever be French. I'm an American and I don't want to be French. The goddamned French. So I'm going to end it tonight, and put myself out of my misery. Her too. She has a right to her own life, don't you think? Can't you hurry it up, Marsh?

Here we are, Janine said from the rear seat. Bar-le-Duc.

You two have been great, Harry said.

Marshall said, Good luck.

His hand on the door handle, Harry turned all the way around to smile nervously at Janine. His mind was still on Antoinette. He said, Were you surprised by Verdun?

She smiled back. She said, Surprised is not the word.

He nodded. Well, then, did you like it? A lot of people can't take it. And why should they? It's an ugly place that only a Frenchman could've designed. All that concrete, those crosses and the bayonets. But it's something that you have to see, once. It's where Europe died.

She said, I didn't *like* it, Harry.

He patted her knee with his free hand. You know what I mean, he said, sighing again, looking at his watch and then out the window. They were stopped at a traffic light. He said, This is ridiculous, we'll never make it. I'll have to go to Strasbourg with you. I don't know what'll happen to her, that's the thing. I just want to get it over with.

The train was in the station when they pulled up. Harry opened the door and flew out of the car. Marshall parked, and he and Janine strolled back to the platform. The train was already moving, Harry waving at them from the vestibule of the first-class coach. They watched the train disappear and then they turned and looked at each other. Janine closed her eyes. A great weariness came upon her, and she slumped against Marshall's shoulder. He sensed her mood at once, steering her firmly off the platform and into the waiting room and around the corner to the buffet. They drank one glass of wine and then another, and when at last they were on the road again, Janine realized she was tipsy. Her vision was blurred and she felt exhausted. She put her head back but was unable to nap. The snap of the windshield wipers and the whine of the little car's engine irritated her. It was gray and raining all over the place. Dusk was coming on. When Marshall lit a cigarette, she turned to him and said sharply, You're smoking too much. Why did we have to go to Verdun?

□   □

They did not make Strasbourg that night, choosing instead an auberge in a tiny hillside town near Nancy. It was almost eight-thirty when they arrived. Without a booking, Marshall wanted to secure a room immediately. The auberge was highly recommended, and popular on weekends. But Jan wanted to talk, to clear her head, to breathe deeply, to get the kinks out; really, she was tired of rushing. This was supposed to be a vacation, a *holiday,* their first in three years; it wasn't supposed to be a forced march, or a memorial service for the death of Europe. And Europe wasn't dead; it was only temporarily out of service, for the moment elusive in the darkness.

Your friend Harry, she began.

Our friend, he corrected.

Harry, she said, then didn't finish the sentence. Harry was Harry was Harry was Harry, and if he wanted to believe that Europe was dead, he had the right. She wondered why he hadn't added Europe to the list of things he had come in at the end of. She would listen to it, but she didn't have to believe it. She didn't have to *like* it.

They walked the few feet to the graveyard of the old church and stood looking over the stones into the valley. It was very dark now and no one was about; light rain obscured the view, and she wondered if there was a town and farmhouses below, or whether there was only forest. There was no light anywhere, but she heard the sound of rushing water. Something made her turn, and she saw a priest glide soundlessly from the side door of the church. Inside were the dim yellow lights of candles; a vigil. She might not have noticed him at all, except that the white of his collar glittered in the candlelight. The priest locked the door and moved down the path, picking his way. He was a portly priest, no stranger to the cuisine of Lorraine. He looked over at them, seemed to hesitate, and then went on.

Spooky, she thought. She turned to Marshall to say something, but he was distant. His mood reminded her of Harry on the way to the railway station—sighing, consulting his wristwatch, distracted, worried that he wouldn't catch the train, worried about Antoinette mixed up with a bad crowd. Marshall stood with his hands plunged into the pockets of his trench coat, looking like a sentry doing disagreeable duty.

It's chilly, Marshall said.

Yes, she said. It's good autumn weather, football weather, but nice, so quiet and dark. Let's walk just a minute more. She took his hand and pulled him along, past the graveyard to the road leading into the valley. There were silent, shuttered houses on either side of them, and she wondered if the town was a summer resort, like Edgartown or Wellfleet, unoccupied until the summer season. Then she saw a sliver of light behind one of the shutters, a dancing blue fluorescence; television. She turned quickly away.

It's time to get back, he said.

Just a minute more, she pleaded, one minute. She took a step forward. The road sloped down to the right and was lost to view. She wanted to follow it into the valley. She said, Isn't it great to be here? She heard him fumbling in his pocket and then he lit a cigarette, the match flaring and the smoke hanging in the heavy air. She was looking again into the darkness, listening to the rushing water and wondering where the road went. His hand was on her arm. She tried not to notice his impatience. She felt somehow that the place was enchanted and that her own life was entering a new chapter. No one in the world knew where they were.

Jan?

Shhh, she said.

He moved close to her and explained that they had to get

things settled. He had to speak to the patron to see to the booking here, and get the luggage up to the room—assuming that there was a room—and find out about dinner. It was already close to nine, and the chef was no doubt temperamental. If the chef closed his kitchen down, well then, they'd had it. Also, he had to cancel the booking in Strasbourg. And Harry had made a reservation for them at that restaurant, whatsitsname, and it was important that they cancel that. Two telephone calls.

Gosh, she said. All in one night?

And I want a drink, he said.

All right, she said. OK.

He said, I hate these details.

She said, Me too.

But we don't want to be stranded, he said.

She said, Do you love me?

Yes, he said.

I love you, too.

He laughed and took her hand, and when they turned around, they saw the auberge, its lights rosy and welcoming through the rain. It was like a mirage in the desert, or an advertisement for gastronomic France—a pretty sign, and flowers in pots outside. Wonderful smells came from the kitchen. She suddenly felt very hungry.

They stood for a moment without moving. Marshall smelled escargots, and smiled to himself because escargots meant traditional cooking—heavy, rich sauces and large portions. He hated the delicate nouvelle cuisine.

This town, she said.

What about it? He pitched his cigarette into the street.

She said, It's insecure. It looks dead, doesn't it? Feels dead. An Ossuaire, and I've had enough of Ossuaires. No one's home in this town. Did you notice the priest, so furtive? Listen to the water, there must be a river in the valley. What a strange place this is. What's its name?

But Marshall had forgotten the name of the town.

She said, I'll call it Forlorn.

He said, It's late, that's all.

How did we happen to come here? she asked.

He took her hand and they began to walk. You found it in the Michelin, he said.

That's right, she said.

And a good thing we did. Good for you, finding Forlorn. We'd still be on the road, otherwise.

She opened her mouth to say something, then didn't. The odd thing was, this village in Lorraine reminded her of the town they lived in, an anonymous suburb north of Boston. In the suburb no one moved after dark, and the streets were always silent, blue fluorescence everywhere. They had lived in the same house for three years, and knew no one on their block; it was too much to call it a neighborhood. Of course, the shape of their suburban town was familiar; it held no surprises.

□   □

The next day they moved on to Strasbourg, and the day after that to an inn at Hirschegg in the Kleinwalsertal. It was a punishing drive, and they stayed at the inn two days, taking a long hike on the second day. The following afternoon they found themselves in Freiburg, where they dropped off the car. After lunch, they visited the cathedral, taking a seat quietly because a *son et lumière* was in progress. The narration was in German and they understood very little, so after fifteen minutes they left their seats and padded around the inside perimeter of the church. Then they left the way they had come, by the west porch, the one with the frieze depicting a princely Satan leading a procession of virgins; the *son et lumière* continued, in hostile, incomprehensible German.

Outside, in the shadow of the great cathedral, a crowd had gathered around a brightly colored Gypsy caravan. Two mute white-faced clowns, one grim and the other merry, were shilling for a circus due in Freiburg the next day. Marshall and Jan pressed close, watching the pantomime. The caravan was filled with animals, and these the clowns introduced one by one: a boar, a goat, a monkey, two hobbled doves, three roosters, a terrier, a black cat, a wee Shetland pony, and, finally, rats. One gray rat after another appeared on the steeple of a misshapen cuckoo clock in an alcove in the front of the caravan. The dour clown gathered them up and let them crawl on his shoulders and around his neck. He seemed not to notice his necklace of rats. He put the largest in his shirt pocket, its long snout moving this way and that, like a cobra's head. Meanwhile, the goat and the boar nuzzled each other, and the pony sat down with the dog. From its perch on a three-legged stool, the black cat eyed the doves. The monkey moved to the feet of the dour clown and he picked it up roughly, cradling it in his arms; the monkey's odor was pungent, and the rats ceased to move, except the shirt-pocket rat, whose snout swayed from side to side, sniffing the monkey. The cheerful clown reached inside the alcove and brought out a cassette, which he punched into the tape deck on the pavement. It was a Mozart concerto, scratchy, badly modulated. The cheerful clown began to hop in time with the music, while his confederate stood to one side, blank-faced, rats motionless on his shoulders.

When the dwarf burst through the little door below the alcove, the crowd laughed and cheered. Marshall gaped. The dwarf was the smallest man he had ever seen. He seemed scarcely larger than the monkey, yet he had a beard and heavy, powerful arms. The dwarf pirouetted once and crashed to the pavement, all this without a sound. The crowd cheered again, and the dwarf doffed his derby. The dour clown gave the dwarf a rat, which he placed in the crease of the derby. With a look of disapproval, the other clown shooed the black cat off the stool.

The doves waddled away.

The boar nudged the dog.

The crowd began to chant.

The cavorting dwarf embraced the boar, caressing it, muttering something into its ear, laughing soundlessly, then deftly plucked the gray rat from the crease of his derby and stuffed it violently down the animal's throat—though that may have been an illusionist's sleight of hand, it was so sudden and unexpected. The crowd gasped, delighted, then roared its approval. With a malicious grin, the dwarf released the boar and advanced on the Shetland, creeping really, moving on all fours like an ape, his

55

hands scraping the ground. The roosters and the goat backed away and settled under the caravan, alert and wary. The two clowns stood off to one side, bored and weary, as the music ran down, now off-key, sounding more like Kurt Weill than Mozart. A strange nervousness swept the crowd; no one knew what might come next. The dwarf, sensing this, paused and turned his heavy head left and right, leering, the muscles in his forearms bulging—and in a moment had flung himself into a front flip, landing on the pony's tiny back. He crouched, his cheek touching the shaggy withers, looking for all the world like a professional jockey approaching the starting gate; the dwarf and the pony were in perfect proportion to each other. They looked like toys. The pony moved hesitantly, a step at a time, as if walking through a minefield, its eyes wide and terrified. When the dwarf opened his mouth and howled—the sound seemed scarcely human—the pony flared and stepped crabwise, moving in a circle around the other animals, which remained rigid. The dour clown had moved surreptitiously to the front of the caravan, and now began feeding the rats back into the mouth of the cuckoo clock; show almost over. The dwarf was balancing himself on the pony's back, and now laboriously lifted himself in a handstand, to thunderous applause. The pony cautiously picked up speed and the other animals retreated, scuttling under the caravan or into the arms of the clowns. A single rat remained on the clock's steeple. Still upside down, his eyes wide open, the dwarf fixed on a point in the middle distance. He clenched his hands, digging into the pony's flesh. The pony shuddered. Then the dwarf began to do something else, one-handed, and Marshall turned away.

He said, Jesus Christ.

Jan said, I think we are very far into Europe.

And with that, the great bells of the cathedral began to toll.

□   □

Marshall was sleeping badly. He would wake up at two or three o'clock in the morning, the room cool but his body slick with sweat. It always took him a moment to remember where he was, whether this was Hirschegg or Nuremberg. The first few nights

he thought he was coming down with something, the flu perhaps, but after a week he put it down to nerves, a kind of unease
that he could neither define nor suppress. He would lie awake for
three hours, then fall asleep and snap to punctually at nine. He
had two books in his bag, one a book of history and the other a
novel. The history book was dense, and he began with that after
an hour's sleeplessness one night. The preface to it was a lovely
thing, the historian's memories of conversations with friends. He
mentioned one particular friend, and the many talks they'd had
sitting beneath cedar trees at Souget, his friend's house in the
Jura. Marshall was beguiled by the preface, so rigorous and civilized, and whenever he thought about the horrors of war, he
thought not about young children with their lives ahead of them
but about the two old men, two of the most learned men in Europe, sitting beneath cedars on the lawn of a house in the Jura,
trading memories.

The book of history was so demanding that after thirty minutes Marshall would put it aside, twenty pages read, and turn to
the novel. This was the novel about old Sartoris. On this particular early morning Marshall tried to enter the life of the page, the
lines of type that always reminded him of the formation of infantry regiments of the nineteenth century. He allowed the lines of
type to advance, and to overwhelm him. It was necessary for him
to open himself to any possibility, to enter fully into the spirit of
the transaction. He allowed himself to feel the heat and fragrance
of the Deep South in order to come to know the novel's characters, and the great burden of the past. These were characters who
seemed to have no future. They were in chains to the past,
moored as securely as any vessel in a swift-running river. At the
end of the hour, Marshall realized that he was not understanding
what he was reading. He parsed the page a word at a time, the
words not windows but mirrors, and the story not the novelist's
but his own. Old Sartoris receded, and finally disappeared. Only
the lines of type remained, motionless.

When he put the book aside and turned to look out the window, it was dawn, gray and uninviting; cloud cover shrouded
Western Europe. His body was dry and he pulled the covers up,

fearful of a chill; his nose was cold and his feet numb, and his mind thick with sleeplessness, though he knew he had been dozing while he read. Perhaps he had only dreamed the business about the two old men sitting under cedar trees, reminiscing. Outside, traffic began to move. He heard the clang of a trolley's bell and, far off, the hoot of an ambulance, *eine kleine Nachtmusik*. Except it was not night; it was dawn, six o'clock by his watch. He heard Jan turn and sigh in the next bed, then mumble something in German. Amused, he raised his head to look at her, concealed under the covers; her face was hidden, but her familiar hair was sprayed carelessly on the pillow. She knew no German, and in his muddled state he wondered if somehow he had wandered into the wrong room. Wrong room, wrong Fräulein. He looked out the window again and decided to take a long morning's walk while she slept. His clothes were slung over the chair across the room. He could stroll to the square and have a cup of coffee and watch the city wake up, read the *Herald Tribune* and catch up on the ball scores and the campaign, connect again to American time. But it was very gray outside; the streets were desolate. Turning over, Marshall fell asleep.

□   □

In Berlin they found a gallery that specialized in German Expressionists. They bought four posters: two of Beckmann, two of Grosz. The posters were exceptionally cheap, so on a spree they bought an Otto Dix lithograph as well. They spent two exhilarating hours in the gallery, wishing they had ten thousand dollars to spend instead of two hundred. How thin and flimsy and self-indulgent the American moderns seemed beside the prewar Germans. A little bit perverse, she thought, bringing these Germans to their quaint Boston suburb. Beckmann's thick black lines, Grosz's pig-faced capitalists, Dix's oppressed masses. But it was a way of retaining something of Europe, and especially of Germany, which had come to mean so much to both of them: a way to measure themselves, and their own time, and their own country.

On the street again, the posters and the Dix secure in a cardboard tube, they walked up the Kurfürstendamm to their hotel. The street was thick with youngsters, teenagers of every nationality. A city of children, he thought. A curt cabdriver had told them they were mostly young men avoiding the draft in Holland, Scandinavia, France, and the United States. Divided Berlin was the gathering place of the youth of all nations, so eager to evade their responsibilities. Drugs were cheap and plentiful. There was no discipline in Berlin.

Marshall said, There is no draft in the United States. The United States is not at war.

Ach, the driver said, is that so? No military service at all? Then why are there so many American young in Berlin?

Marshall had no answer to that.

Jan tugged at his arm as they walked up the great glitzy boulevard, brilliant with light. For their last night in Germany, she thought they should ignore the tyrannical Guide Michelin. They should trust to instinct, find a place that looked cheerful and not too expensive, and tuck into it for a feast. She tapped him on the shoulder with the tube, grinning. Their luck had turned; how else to explain finding the gallery with its trove of German Expressionists?

She led the way, past the sidewalk troubadours, off the Kurfürstendamm, to a small, noisy restaurant. They ordered a bottle of wine, sausage, and sauerkraut—specialties of the house. She was animated, talking about the first afternoon at Verdun, the drive to Bar-le-Duc, and, later that night, the town she had named Forlorn. Some of the details had gotten out of hand, but all in all they had done well. Perhaps in the future they would plan a real itinerary, not leave quite so much to chance. But it was difficult, traveling in a strange country, not knowing the language or the customs.

She said, The other night you were muttering in German.

He laughed. I was? So were you.

In your sleep, she said. You talked.

I wonder what I was saying, he said.

The sausages and sauerkraut arrived, and they began to eat. He was trying to remember the clowns in the square at Freiburg, and the exact sequence in which the animals had appeared. She was silent, her head bent over her plate. He said, What a menagerie! Narrative by the Brothers Grimm. Grosz could have done something with the clowns and the dwarf on the pony's back. He said, You were right when you said we were very far into Europe. Marshall signaled for another bottle of wine, then noticed that Jan wasn't eating.

He said, Is something wrong?

She said, The sauerkraut reminds me of my mother. She made such good sauerkraut, it was just the best sauerkraut, my mom's. Sorry.

She was crying. He leaned across the table to touch her hand and she looked at him, biting her lip, trying and failing to smile. Her hand was hot and damp. The noise rose around them, and they drew closer; it was as if they were in a cocoon, wrapped in hostile foreign voices. He murmured something to her, but she didn't hear. He said, You are my one and only. She made a little ambiguous gesture with her hand, pushing at her food with a fork. He filled her glass with wine and she raised it, toasting him, and drained it, every drop. Presently she began to eat and then, impulsively, leaned across the table, closed her eyes, and kissed him.

At the Café Einstein, where they went for a drink after dinner, she was pensive again, inspecting the room, scrutinizing the intellectuals. Conversation around them was low and intense. They were served cognac by a sullen Asian in black tie. Marshall wondered if he was Vietnamese; his English was flawless, idiomatic American.

She said, I'm sorry I was so mean to Harry. I didn't understand his life, the way he lives, what he has to cope with. He said he was an American and couldn't ever be anything else, but I'm not so sure. I think I understand him better now. This has been such an experience for me. I'll never forget it, ever. I feel as if we've been in Germany for a hundred years. I feel pushed back in time. I find myself remembering the strangest things, old emotions, memories. What was it that Harry said about Germany that I didn't believe?

Marshall looked up and shook his head. He didn't remember. She said, This is the place where all modern history begins.

□   □

They were to meet Harry at his apartment, then go on to dinner. But driving in from the airport, Marshall had a sudden inspiration. It was afternoon in Paris, the trees turning and the weather warm. The French strolled hand in hand, animated, dressed in summer colors. He leaned forward and tapped the cabdriver on the shoulder and told him to take them to the Brasserie Flo. He wanted a plate of oysters and a bottle of Sancerre. They jumped from the cab with four pieces of luggage and settled around a table. Flo was crowded and cheerful. The oysters arrived, along with the Sancerre. They ate a dozen oysters apiece and ordered a second bottle. They were trying to remember the precise moment they had fallen in love; it had been eleven years before, and they had both been married to other people. He insisted it had to be the same moment, and she said that was just like a man, an *American* man, searching for symmetry when there was none. She offered a preposterous version of events that had him roaring with laughter. She insisted that he had entrapped her, a kind of con. They were leaning across the table, head to head, talking now in their private language, on familiar ground. They remained that way for some time in the amiable, boozy atmosphere of Flo. They had finished the second bottle and knew now that it was time to go. But neither wanted to speak first, to break the spell and reintroduce the old world of promises and obligations. Knowing that, they looked up simultaneously and winked at each other. Time for the check. Time to go meet Harry.

They were very late, but in any event, Harry was not at home. He had left them a note in his difficult, spidery handwriting. Make free with the apartment. He had gone to Cyprus on assignment; it was either assignment or assignation, hard to tell which. There was altogether too much commotion and turbulence in Paris. Too much anxiety, and the weather had been lousy, pissing down rain. However, he and Antoinette had reached an accommodation; in fact, she was with him in Cyprus, surprise, surprise. It turned out that the quarrel had been the result of a simple misunderstanding, and he had taken her to Kyrenia to sort it out once and for all. She was a good egg, really, though a little off the wall. Wish me luck. There was a bottle of champagne in the fridge. How was your trip? Do you like the Jerries?

Marshall and Jan tumbled into bed, and it was after nine when they rose and bathed. While Jan was still in the bath Marshall wandered into the kitchen and popped the bottle. It was warm in the apartment, and he opened one of the kitchen windows. He poured two glasses and walked into the living room, pausing at the bookcase to look for Antoinette in dishabille.

He heard Jan laughing in the tub.

She called to him, Remember the German on the mountain in the Kleinwalsertal?

He did, vaguely. They had taken a picnic into the mountains, leaving the hotel at noon, winding higher and higher along the macadam path. The view was gorgeous. There were many hikers in lederhosen, carrying backpacks and walking sticks, who looked at them with disapproval. They were dressed for a stroll on Boston Common. Marshall carried a plastic bag from the supermarket, with sausage and cheese and a bottle of wine. At midafternoon they left the path and began to strike for the summit, ascending through pastureland in lazy S curves. They stopped to eat, wondering whether to resume the climb or start back. It was then that Jan saw the German and called to him.

She was still laughing, recalling the conversation, a clutter of German, French, and English. No, the German had said, they must not go higher. The north slope was already in shadows and the snow six inches deep. He pointed at their shoes and laughed. They were not properly equipped for the journey. Heavy sweaters were required; darkness came quickly on the mountain, and with it the cold, and it was so very easy to lose your way. He produced a map that explained the difficulty. He said, Take the funicular, it takes five minutes. And you only have to hike one way and it's easier walking down than walking up. Or take the funicular both ways and save your energy. They shared their wine with him. He was an engineer from Darmstadt, on a hiking holiday in the Kleinwalsertal. Leaving them, he wagged a finger and pointed at their feet. Next time, bring boots! He strode away very confidently, descending, and in a few minutes he was an inch high, merging with the other hikers on the lower slopes, heading for the village in the valley.

She laughed again. He could hear her splashing in the tub.

He had forgotten all about the hiker, a large, good-looking German of the blond, Nordic type. He had given them sound advice. Marshall stood in front of the bookcase, two glasses of champagne in his hand. Jan called to him, but he did not answer. He felt the beginnings of a headache and looked at his watch. In fourteen hours they would board their plane for Boston. Seven hours across the Atlantic, then customs at Logan, and another forty-five minutes by train to the anonymous suburb—a tedious day. He looked around the apartment, depressed by its sudden familiarity. It was only a bachelor's pad, with the bachelor's fussy confusion of transience and stability, but its atmosphere nagged at him. His eye swept the bookcase—a pretty edition of Proust, Baedekers, histories of European wars, biographies of statesmen—but Antoinette's photograph was not to be seen. He searched and searched, then found it tucked between volumes four and five of Proust. He looked at her, a captivating off-focus European, a woman about to spill her wine. She had a carnival aura, a dangerous woman worth worrying about. That seemed to be what careless Harry desired. It was what made him laugh. No doubt he was attracted to her ironic glare and her bad crowd. Marshall stood motionless, staring at the photograph, stunned, knowing the most profound ambivalence.

Jan was in the doorway then, naked, dripping water.

He turned to face her, the headache beginning to tighten behind his eyes.

She said, Are you all right?

I'm all right, he said.

You look so sad.

No, he said, forcing a smile. I was just remembering us, a

63

couple of middle-aged Bostonians, touring Europe. Thinking about Harry, and what made him laugh. Thinking about this apartment, thinking about us. Thinking about tomorrow.

Tomorrow, she said. Well, then, where's the champagne?

He said, You're drinking too much, and extended to her the hand that held the two glasses. She took one, sipped it thoughtfully, then drained the glass—and with a triumphant look that went back to the first day they met, she flung it with all her force into Harry's tiny fake fireplace. The glass exploded into bits, fragments everywhere, and he recoiled, surprised. *There,* she said, laughing. Isn't that what you're supposed to do at a celebration?

He said, What's the celebration?

Oh, Marsh. This is our last night! She laughed. And here I am, naked in Paris.

La gloire, he thought. He realized he was still holding Antoinette's photograph, and gently pushed it back between volumes four and five. He said, I found Antoinette.

I didn't know she was lost, Jan said, looking at him, grinning, giving a little toss of her head; droplets flew from her hair, catching the light, stardust. The glow from the single floor lamp accentuated the lines of her breasts and belly. She spread her arms wide and popped open the palms of her hands, an actress accepting the applause of a grateful audience.

But he was in another realm, forced there against his will; in the end, no two people could know one another, even if they loved each other and traveled well together. He thought of Harry and modern history, and remembered suddenly the trench of bayonets. He said, I hate the thought of going home. Maybe this is where we belong.

Not me, she said.

Yes, he said. That's right. Not you.

She said, There's always a limit to things, a time to say Enough. I'm ready to leave. We've had a fine time. We had a fine time this afternoon, and we're having a fine time now. Aren't we? But I want to go home. We're only visitors here.

He listened carefully but did not commit himself.

It's been a strange time, she continued. At Verdun I didn't

think it was going to be so great. We didn't seem to know who we were and what we were seeing. It was all so alien, and grim. It didn't seem safe. Freiburg was so weird, and the mountain, the pictures that we bought, and the last night in Berlin ... She turned, presenting her profile. His headache, forgotten these last few moments, returned. He stepped to her side and they stood together at Harry's picture window, looking out over the rooftops, sharing the last glass.

Really, she murmured. Do you want to stay?

Yes, he said. But his voice did not carry conviction and of course she perceived that, having lived with him so long, knowing him so well. Marsh always had trouble letting go. She put her bare arm around his waist. She said, I understand.

I know you do, he said.

Europe would always be here, she thought. But the idea did not console her, so she said nothing; in any case, it was true whether she said it or not.

SUE MILLER

Travel

The room at the tourist hotel was small, with casement windows that opened out over the kitchen annex. Starting at about seven in the morning, the happy incomprehensible banter of the kitchen staff, the crash and clatter of garbage cans and dishes, would rise into Oley and Rob's room. Oley lay in bed and listened. From the bathroom floated in the smell of fermenting strawberries. Oley and Rob had bought them at the market on their first day in Trujillo. An impassive Indian woman had sat next to an enormous basket of the fruit, a deep basket at least four feet in diameter. It seemed romantic, the luxuriance of so many strawberries gleaming uniformly fat and red, so unlike the parsimony of pint boxes in the supermarket at home, boxes in which only the top layer of fruit was red; the buyer knew that distributed underneath were the ones with hard white patches or soft sides. Oley and Rob bought a large bag of the fruit from the

Indian woman, and a bottle of wine. On their first night in the hotel they'd played gin rummy in their room, eating and drinking. Then, drunk, full, they'd made love, smelling the strawberries in each other's mouths, and then on each other's skin, everywhere.

Rob was gone from the bed already. Probably out taking pictures. He was doing a travel article. It had been gray and overcast since they'd arrived in Trujillo, so he didn't want to do the ruins yet, or the plaza. He got up early to do interiors—churches, museums—before they were crowded with people, whose appeal or lack of it to potential tourists he couldn't control. Once she would have gone with him, held the cameras and lenses he wasn't using. But there was some silent agreement they'd reached about this now and he let her sleep on alone.

She got up and went into the bathroom. The smell of fermenting strawberries was much stronger, almost sickening, in here. The plastic bag rested on the windowsill, and she could see that the strawberries had exuded a little pool of pinkish liquid, in which they sat. She picked up the bag and dropped it into the wastebasket. A little of it had oozed out onto the sill.

As she hunched over on the toilet, the complicated, funky smell of their lovemaking the night before rose to her nostrils too. She reached over to the sink and filled the water glass. She lowered it between her legs and splashed herself with little handfuls of the warm water four or five times. She stood up and dabbed at herself with a towel. Bright laughter floated up from the kitchen. She pushed the heavy nickel handle and the toilet flushed violently.

Rob came back full of energy, with presents for Oley. He dumped them on her naked thighs as she lay stretched out on the bed, and then sat in the room's only chair, the desk chair, to watch her open them. There was a little white box that held silver earrings and a necklace nested in slightly soiled cotton; a tiny, brightly colored basket in a brown paper bag; and a greenish fruit he couldn't remember the name of. She thanked him over and over. She put on the jewelry and looked at herself in the hand mirror he gave her. The dangling earrings brushed against the sides of her neck.

"And pictures?" she asked. She was trying to be generous too. "Did you get any good pictures?"

He raised the camera, as though to fiddle with it. Then it was in front of his face. It clicked. "One, anyway," he said, and smiled at her.

□   □

Olympia had flown to Lima with money that Rob had mailed to her. He'd called her long-distance three times from Peru before she'd agreed to join him. She had at first been determined not to. Rob had decided only two months earlier that he couldn't marry her. They'd been living together for more than a year. She had asked him to move out.

He wanted her to join him, he said on the phone, because he was lonely, because they'd always traveled so well together. Why couldn't they still be loving friends, especially in a faraway place? She ought to see Peru at least this once. He'd be more than happy to pay all her expenses.

Oley had missed Rob, the excitement he brought into her life. She'd grown up in a safe, small town and was a little afraid of anything new or random. In New Haven she was a teacher; her work was regular and held no surprises for her. When Rob had lived with her, was her lover, she liked the feeling of involvement with passing events he introduced her to, the way life seemed to reach in and touch him. His voice on the telephone seemed like that exciting, random touch. She decided to go.

After she'd made the decision, when she began to think about seeing Rob again, Oley felt, in spite of herself, a return of the hope that had fueled her during their year together: the hope that given enough time, she could will Rob into the kind of love that would make him want to stay. She had to consciously remind herself that she was going only to have a good time, only to travel.

And at first it had seemed as though it might work on that

basis. In the airport, watching him walk toward her, tanned, his hair longer than when she'd last seen him, she felt a rush of intense passion that made her throat hurt. They'd had the night with the strawberries and for a few days after that they'd been happy. Rob made little ceremonies of every meal, every gift he gave her. She spoke no Spanish and so he had to act as her interpreter to the world. She felt sheltered and protected, cared for in a way that hadn't been possible for a long time at home. There her toughness, her competence, had been things she felt she needed to stress as it became clearer and clearer to her that he was choosing not to marry her.

But as the slow days passed in Trujillo, Oley came to resent the very gifts, the courtliness that had at first charmed her. She was sometimes unpleasant to Rob, petulant. She didn't like herself then, but she wasn't able to stop. Everything he gave her, everything he did for her, reminded her only of what he wouldn't give, wouldn't do.

□ □

As they crossed the plaza on their way to the bakery, three little boys with shoeshine kits followed them, their clothes ragged, their faces dirty. They were always on the plaza, noisy and cheerful. The first day, Rob and Oley had decided to have a shoeshine, and had hired the two thinnest, smallest boys. A group of ten or so, all with their wooden kits, assembled to watch the process, chatting and commenting while the chosen boys stylishly and elaborately polished and buffed. On the final buffing, their cloths took on a life of their own, cracking and whipping through the air.

The second day, in their eagerness for business, the boys had followed Rob and Oley without noticing that they were both wearing sandals. Rob had stopped finally and pointed this out. He'd asked them what color they would polish his bare feet, and they'd laughed at this joke, at themselves. Now they always trailed behind Rob and Oley, laughing, calling out. They seemed to like Rob. He told Oley that they'd become very familiar, were sometimes quite insulting in their comments on the condition of his Frye boots, of Oley's shoes.

Today Rob delivered a long dramatic monologue to the boys as they crossed the plaza, his face and voice mournful. The boys laughed and danced around him, egging him on. Oley felt edged out, ignored.

They crossed to a side street, leaving the ragged group behind, and Oley asked him what he'd been saying.

"Long sad story," said Rob. He lifted an imaginary violin and began to play. "I'm so poor I can't afford even a shoeshine. And if I had the money I ought to take it home to my even poorer mother, who sits alone with fourteen babies, trying to make supper from a cup of meal and one starving guinea pig. In fact, if I had the money, I ought to take it home to the guinea pig of my mother, who hasn't had anything to eat since . . ." He stopped abruptly, looking at Oley.

"Not funny, O?" He bent to look at her face. "You no like?"

She shook her head. They walked a block in silence. The dark men turned to stare at Oley, who was tall and fair, with straight blond hair hanging down her back and over her shoulders.

"Well, I'd hate to ask you *why*," Rob said finally, with hostility in his voice. "I'd be so fucking scared you'd tell me."

She pressed her lips together, and then spoke. She'd never felt more like a schoolteacher. "It seems unkind," she said, "when by their standards we're so rich, for you to make fun of their poverty."

He shrugged. "Therein, of course, lies the joke," he said. They turned into the bakery, pushing aside the beaded curtain. Everyone looked up at them for a moment, at the tall, long-haired man dressed a little like a cowboy in his jeans and work shirt, and his blond companion. "Clearly they thought it was funny," he said, behind her. "If they can laugh at it, then there must be some level on which it *is* funny."

There were empty tables in the back, and they walked toward them through the groups of Peruvians nearer the front. There were mostly men in the bakery, except for the women who worked behind the counter.

"The trouble with you, Oley, is that you always imagine everyone else has exactly your sensibility." As he said this, Rob was pulling the chair out for Oley. She sat down. "And they don't. They don't. By and large, the human race is tougher and has a better sense of humor than you do, O."

He sat down opposite her and Oley looked at him. She would never, she felt, not find him attractive.

"That's just how *you* imagine them," she said. "And that's just because you think everyone is like *you*. So you see, we're not really so different after all."

□   □

Oley had met Rob when he came to take photographs of the preschool kids she taught. Oley, who was often somber and shy when she met new people, whose high school yearbook photo had "Still Waters Run Deep" under it, was animated and energetic around the children. Rob took as many pictures of her as he did of the kids.

She was aware of using her playfulness with the children to charm him, and felt, a few times during the day, guilty enough about this element of duplicity to draw back suddenly into a shy stiffness. But the children insisted on the Oley they knew. "Not *that* way, Oley," they'd say. "Do it the *other* way, the *silly* way."

He took her out for dinner that night. The combination of his own almost childish energy and his having seen her earlier so full of life made it easier for her to continue what she couldn't help thinking of as a charade during the meal. Even as they made love back in her apartment, she wanted to tell him he'd made a mistake, that she wasn't who he thought she was.

□   □

As the week in Trujillo went by, Oley and Rob spent more and more time after dinner in the hotel bar. They played gin rummy, keeping a running score, and drank foaming, lemony Pisco sours. The bar was as old as the rest of the hotel, paneled in mahogany and mirrored on one side. Louvered doors opened into the dining room and the lobby. A large fan with wooden blades twirled slowly overhead. The bartender, a short, plump Indian man with liquid black eyes, stared at Oley almost constantly; at her size, they speculated, at her blondness, her freckles.

"And my boobs," Oley said. She was drunk. "Boobs'll do it every time, the world over. It's amazing how predictable it all is."

"I'll drink to that. I'll drink to predictability," he said, spreading his cards on the table, "and I'll go down with three."

"Bastard," she said.

They still made love every night, always with the same skillful familiarity with each other's bodies, but they postponed until later and later the time when they'd leave the warm light of the bar and climb the wide wooden staircase together. Each night, undressing, getting ready for sure pleasure, Oley felt increasingly that it was a capitulation that shamed her somehow. More than once they were the last people to leave the bar, but the solemn, handsome bartender never complained, never rushed them, never stopped staring and blushing.

"He loves you, O," Rob said. He lay naked on the bed, watching Oley undress.

"I know," Oley said sadly. She carefully folded her jeans and shirt, then came to sit on the edge of the bed.

"You know how I know?" Rob asked.

"No."

" 'Cause he doesn't charge us for about half of what we drink. Your half, I figure." He had moved over to accommodate her. Now he began to stroke her back and arms.

Oley looked at him. "Is that true?"

"As sure as I'm about to screw you madly."

"No, wait. Tell me the truth." She put her hands on his, to still them. "He's been giving us free drinks?"

"Yes. *You,* anyway. I asked that Chilean guy, you know, the one with the fat wife and all the kids?" Oley nodded. "I asked him if he was getting free drinks and he said not. Said it must be because the guy's so smitten with you. *Everybody* knows it, Oley. My big, blond Oley."

She turned from him. "Oh, that's so sad."

"Why? What's so sad about it?"

"I don't know. Everything. That he's a grown man; and his world is so small that he sees me as some kind of *princess*. And all he has to offer me is Pisco sours. And I'm up here fucking you, who couldn't care less at some level. And he ends up, really, giving *you* the drinks. It just all seems so ... misplaced and pathetic."

Rob was silent a moment. Then he began stroking her arm again. His hand touched lightly the side of Oley's breast and she felt the dropping sensation inside that was, for her, the beginning of desire. "Well, he can't give you the drinks without treating me too. That's just how it is."

"I know. That's what I mean."

They sat in silence. Then Rob said, "I *do* care, O. I can't do it your way, but I do care."

"I know," she said. And then, because she was very drunk, she said again, "That's what I mean."

□   □

Oley had thought she wouldn't hear from Rob again after their first night together. She had gotten used to this in New Haven, though it was something she'd been unprepared for when she first arrived—that men could sleep with you and then simply never call you, never try to see you again. She had had one lover all through college, actually someone she'd known a little in high school too, so her experience was limited. And such a thing would have been in some sense impossible in the town where she'd grown up, if only because she would have known the man, or at least who he was, before she slept with him, and would have continued to see him at least occasionally afterward. In New Haven, men could just disappear, and did; although she would occasionally glimpse someone she'd slept with going into a bookstore or crossing a street. A few times she'd waved or said hello, but she realized by their lack of response that she wasn't supposed to do that. She wasn't supposed to exist anymore; she was just a place they'd been, a town they'd passed through and chosen not to visit again.

After the painful shock of the first few times, that was all right with Oley. It gave her a kind of freedom she hadn't imagined possible, and she discovered a side to herself sexually that was different and wilder than any of the parts of herself that lived responsibly day by day in New Haven.

Besides, she had come to understand that the men who would call her back were people she thought of as thick, dull; people who saw only the good, steady side of herself. The men she liked, the men who let her imagine herself as other than the way she was, were not men who wanted to spend much time with quiet young Head Start teachers.

And so, when Rob called back, she was surprised and even a little disturbed. There was a part of her that didn't want to have to cope with him as a real possibility, as a real disappointment. But she told him she'd meet him for a drink Friday evening to look at the proofs of the pictures he'd taken; and when she saw them, she saw suddenly who she could be, how she could be, with him. Off and on during the difficult year he'd lived with her, Oley would look at the pictures he'd taken of her before he knew who she was, in order to remind herself of what she could be to someone else.

□   □

Rob left Oley alone in the hotel for two days. A reporter they'd met who was covering the revolutionary movement for a British paper had told him that the rebels were planning to take over the train from Cuzco to Machu Picchu. Rob thought he should fly in right away and get his pictures. He didn't think it was a good idea for Oley to come along. It was as he stood peeling bills from a roll of money he carried with him that Oley understood how completely dependent on him she'd let herself become in this world. She was actually frightened to be alone.

The first day she didn't deviate from the routines they had set up together. Wherever she went, she smiled and nodded at the people who spoke to her. Laboriously she counted out money when she made a purchase, and occasionally she murmured the Spanish Rob had taught her for "I don't understand" when someone seemed to expect her to respond. Otherwise she was silent and alone all day. In the evening she ate in the hotel dining room and went to bed early, without stopping in the bar.

But the next morning the sun was shining for the first time since Oley had arrived in Peru, and after breakfast she went to the desk in the hotel lobby and asked the clerk about transportation to the ruins.

"Ah, the Professor!" the clerk said, and made a quick phone call. Then she explained to Oley that there was a local expert on the ruins who would take her on a guided tour for free, a kind of promotional deal he offered. He would come for her in his car later in the afternoon.

He showed up at about three-thirty. Oley was surprised at his appearance. He looked like a Latin crooner, a slicked-back Andy Williams. He wore pale clothes and a golfer's sweater, buttoned casually at the waist. His mustache was thin, his hair a preposterously brilliant black, and he spoke careful, formal English. He smiled at Oley and revealed elaborate structures of gold where most of his teeth should have been.

When Oley went outside with him, she discovered that his car was an ornately finned American model from the fifties, badly repainted a bilious green. There were several other passengers in it, other distinguished visitors to Peru, the Professor told Oley. The car had been fitted with a broken plastic cap on its roof, which now read TAX. Oley hesitated a moment, then inquired whether she could not pay the Professor something for the privilege of taking the tour with him. The Professor assured her that it was his privilege, he was pleased to do it *gratis,* in order to let people know about his shop, a shop specializing in reproductions of the ruins' artifacts.

As Oley got in, the Professor introduced the other tourists. The Indian man behind the wheel revved the car noisily, and they sped away from the tourist hotel, leaving a trail of rubber and exhaust to delight the shoeshine boys gathered on the plaza.

Travel

The car had no shocks at all, and on every bump and curve, Oley and the other passengers were thrown and swung from side to side in the back seat. The Professor sat in front with a massive Dutch woman, who had, like him, a small mustache. He rested his arm along the back of the seat, and with his face turned to his group, he made conversation in his stilted English about the ruins, about their countries of origin, about Peru.

Oley, glad to have an opportunity to speak English at last, grew expansive. She chatted with the massive Dutch woman and her shy female companion, and with the skinny and uncommunicative German student who completed their group.

It took about fifteen minutes to get to the ruins. They loomed ugly and unpromising in the flat terrain, so many dirt piles. Up close, more of what they might once have been was visible, and there were groups of archaeology students working to restore them; but Oley was disappointed. She was in the process of deciding that she preferred the living, slightly decrepit town to the parched desolation of the ruins, when they came to the sections where intact samples of the relief work remained in the sand. Abruptly her disappointment vanished. The artwork here was both stylized and sexual, and Oley found herself moved by it. But the Professor's explanations of the meaning of the figures irritated her. He kept talking about things like the symbolic fusion of the spirit and the will as he stood in front of the intertwined tongues and bodies. The Dutch woman, her friend and the German student stood, listened, nodded. But Oley began to lag behind the group. The Professor frowned at her, calling out from time to time that she was missing the discussion of the detail. Momentarily she would rejoin them; but then she would again find his monologue maddening, and drop back. She felt as though she were a naughty American child among adults.

On their way back to town, the driver pulled off the highway into what looked like an abandoned gas station. It was the Professor's gallery. The group of gringos clambered obediently out of the car, which rose several inches with each one's departure. The shop was sweltering. It was full of black-and-white prints, scrolls and little clay sculptures. The Professor swung into a sales pitch.

He had a way of unrolling the prints that reminded Oley of the shoeshine boys, their elaborate display with their cloths.

The Dutch woman seemed interested. After looking at what seemed to Oley an endless number of samples, she bought two prints. Oley had moved nearer to the door, waiting for the transactions to be over. The reproductions in the shop were stark, precise, Egyptian. They had none of the sensuality of the actual reliefs, and they seemed expensive to Oley. And even though there were a few less expensive, less unattractive pieces of sculpture, Oley didn't want anything. The moment the Professor had gone into his pitch, she felt angry at him for trapping her here, for his false generosity. She was determined to buy nothing.

The German student liked one of the prints, but said that the price was too high. Oley moved into the doorway to try to catch a breeze as she watched the Professor at work. He came down a bit; the student, more animated than he'd been all day, pushed for an even lower price. Slowly they narrowed in on the range they could agree on, and the purchase was made. Then the little group was left standing in the shop, waiting for a signal from the Professor that they could leave, that his driver would take them back. But it became clear that he, in turn, was waiting for Oley to buy something. Everyone else had paid the price for the tour. It was her turn. The group looked expectantly at her.

The Professor walked over closer to her and picked up one of the clay figures. "You have, perhaps, found something you would like, Miss Erickson?" he asked.

"No. Nothing," Oley answered. She could hear the defiance in her own voice.

The Professor paused for only a moment. "Ah, well, then," he said. "Perhaps I can point out to you some things which you may not have noticed." He gestured to where the scrolls lay rolled up like tubes of wallpaper on the shelf.

There was another moment of silence. Then Oley, still standing in the doorway, said, "I'm not going to buy anything, Professor. I'm sorry, I misunderstood your meaning, and really thought the tour was free." Oley thought she could feel the group recoil from her slightly in the shop. "Besides," she said, "I really can't afford it."

She turned and walked outside, let herself into the car. The driver, leaning against the auto in the hot sun, looked confused. Slowly the little group of tourists meandered out too. Last came the Professor, looking seedy and defeated. Oley felt sorry for him, actually. The driver took his silent lurching load back to town.

When Oley got back to the tourist hotel, she went up to her room. She ran herself a deep tub and lay in it for a long while, occasionally twisting the old-fashioned nickel-plated knob with her toes to let more hot water in. Her breasts floated above the water. The nipples tightened in the cool air. Oley dipped a washcloth into the steaming tub and laid it across her chest.

She lay in the tub until the sky outside turned purple; then black. When she got out, her fingers and toes were wrinkled into what she and her mother had called "raisin skin" when she was small. She noticed, on the windowsill, a little red stain the maid had missed when she cleaned, the hardened juice of the strawberries.

She dressed and went to the bar. She sat at one of the wooden tables by herself and ordered a Pisco sour. The table was next to the louvered windows which opened out onto the plaza. Through the slats she could see, in the glare of the fluorescent streetlamps, the shoeshine boys, their workday over, huddled in a tiny group around one bench. She watched them.

From time to time during the evening, one of the other guests with whom she was familiar—the fat wife of the Chilean, the British reporter—came and talked to Oley for a while. But for the most part she sat alone. The bartender brought over a fresh drink or bowl of peanuts as soon as she'd finished the one before. Slowly the boys on the plaza drifted away. When the last two lay down on one of the benches, Oley got up. She bumped into a chair on her way to the bar, and its legs scraped noisily on the bare floor.

She asked the bartender how much everything was. He looked at her, his eyes blazing with devotion, and shook his head.

"Please," she said in Spanish, "how much?" Again he shook his head. Oley felt her eyes fill with tears. "You are very generous," she said in English. "Too generous." He smiled shyly, partly, Oley saw, because he was missing several teeth. "Thank you," he said in slow English. She reached over and touched the immaculate sleeve of his white coat. "No," she said. "Thank *you*. Gracias. Thank you." She patted his arm gently; then turned and carefully walked out of the bar.

□   □

Rob came back early the next morning. Oley was still in bed, a little hung over. Rob was excited. He had met a man on the plane from Cuzco who wanted to buy American dollars and would meet him on the plaza in half an hour. Oley got out of bed and dressed slowly. Rob paced the room impatiently, leaned out the casement window into the kitchen noise. Oley knew it wasn't just the illegal exchange rate that excited him, but the idea of the black market, of doing something illicit. She was familiar with this impulse of his. He'd once, for the same reason, bought a gun from a black guy they'd met at a bar in New Haven. He didn't want it for anything. He had kept it for months in the bureau drawer in her apartment.

He and Oley had made a special trip to Block Island by ferry in order to get rid of it, finally. They hadn't even stayed over-night. They just took the ferry over, dropping the gun in the water on the way, and returned that evening.

As they stepped out of the hotel lobby, Oley looked over to-ward the plaza. The sky was white again today with high clouds. The flat gray stones in the plaza still gleamed darkly from their daily early-morning washing. The shoeshine boys, six or seven of them today, stood near the fountain at the plaza's center, talking and gesturing. Two of the cement benches that studded the radi-ating pathways of the plaza were occupied, one by an itinerant secretary, the typewriter on his knees clattering faintly in the morning air as the old man next to him dictated, the other by a man in a sports jacket and sunglasses, holding a briefcase on his lap.

"Is that the guy?" Olympia asked.

"The very one," Rob said. He patted his shirt pocket. Before they'd left their room, he'd put eight hundred-dollar bills into it, folded in half. Oley had protested that it seemed too much, but he'd said they would need it in Arequipa, the next city on their itinerary.

The shoeshine boys spotted Rob and approached, waving and calling out. Even though Rob barely nodded to them, they followed him and Oley over to the man. But when Rob and Oley sat down and began talking, they fell back slightly. A few of them set their kits down and sat on them at a little distance, watching the trio on the bench.

The man chatted politely with Oley and Rob for a while, at first about how they liked traveling in Peru. Their enthusiasm seemed to amuse him. He was slim and good-looking. His face was slightly pockmarked. He began to talk about himself. He seemed anxious to explain himself to Oley in particular. He spoke fluent English, with only a slight accent. He'd gone to school in America, UCLA, he told Oley, and majored in engineering. He wanted to leave Peru, where his opportunities were so limited, to move to the United States; but the government wouldn't let him take Peruvian money out of the country. "They would strip me of my birthright, as it were," he said. "My parents are not wealthy, but they have worked hard all of their lives for me, for their only son. But the government would have me leave the country a pauper. You, a rich North American, must understand that I cannot go to the United States a pauper."

"I'm not rich," said Oley.

"Of course you are," said the man politely.

"No." Oley shook her head. "Really. I'm a schoolteacher. Schoolteachers aren't rich."

"Schoolteachers in America are rich," the man announced in his gentle, apologetic voice. "They own houses, cars, land."

Oley thought of her tiny apartment on the fringe of the ghetto in New Haven. She felt, suddenly, a pang of homesickness for its bare familiarity. She wanted to describe it to the man, but she knew there was no point.

"And here I find you traveling in my country," he persisted gently. "Such travel is expensive, is it not?"

Rob was watching Oley with interest. Oley saw that he expected her to say that the money was his, to separate herself from him, repudiate him, as she'd done in one way or another, she realized, all week. She felt suddenly as though she should apologize to him.

"Yes, you're right," she said to the man. Her voice was soft and regretful, as though she were acknowledging something shameful about herself. "It is terribly expensive."

She felt Rob's eyes on her.

"Well, then," the man said. "You understand my circumstance entirely, then. Americans don't like poor foreigners, so that I must be certain, before I leave, to amass enough money to fit easily and smoothly into your world."

He turned to Rob and they proceeded to the details of their exchange. Oley watched them. Rob's face was animated, lively, full of the energy that had always attracted her, that she had always wanted to have herself, but didn't. He and the man laughed about something. Oley looked over at the shoeshine boys. She felt like them, shut out, an onlooker.

The man opened the briefcase on his knees. He left the lid up to shield the interior from view, but the shoeshine boys had caught a glimpse of its contents. They seemed in unison, audibly, to draw their breath in. They approached slightly nearer and made a silent semicircle around the three adults on the bench. In the briefcase, neatly banded, were stacks of Peruvian currency, perhaps more than most of the shoeshine boys would earn in a lifetime. They watched with rapt attention, whispering a little among themselves, as Rob and the man exchanged dollars for soles. Oley noted that when she and Rob got up and walked away, the shoeshine boys for the first time didn't follow or call to them. Unmolested, she and Rob walked back into the cool, dim lobby of the tourist hotel.

When they got up to their room, Rob began pulling the money from his pockets and throwing it on the bed. "We're rich,

Oley! Rich! Rich!" he cried. Oley sat in the chair and watched him. When he'd emptied his pockets and turned to her, grinning, she said softly, "I've got to go home, Rob." He looked at her for a moment, the smile fading, and then he sat down on the bed without pushing the money out of the way.

"Oley," he said. He shook his head. "Olympia. How come I knew you were going to say that?"

□   □

In late August, Oley found a manila envelope leaning against the door to her apartment. It was postmarked New York and stamped PHOTOGRAPH. DO NOT BEND. Because it was very hot outside and she'd been at a faculty meeting all day, she went around the apartment throwing open the windows and then she fixed herself a glass of iced tea before she opened it. Inside was a blowup of the picture Rob had taken of her in the tourist hotel in Trujillo. Oley felt in the corners of the envelope for a written message, but there was none. Just the picture. She looked at it carefully.

Wearing the delicate necklace and earrings that she still had in the dresser in her bedroom, the Oley in the picture stretched out naked on the bed and looked directly into the camera. Rob had lightened her body and darkened the background, so she seemed almost to float toward the camera, her gaze blankened and bold.

Oley looked at the picture a long time, trying to recognize herself in it. Then she picked up her iced tea and carried it into the bedroom. The cubes clinked gently together as she walked. She set the glass down on top of the bureau, opened the top drawer, and took out the necklace and earrings. Standing in front of her full-length mirror, she took off all her clothes and put on the jewelry. She looked at her familiar reflection—the solid wide hips, the large breasts, the pubic hair dark in spite of her blondness. She stood in her bedroom and looked at herself. On the breeze that stirred through the apartment and lightly touched her body floated the sound of someone's transistor radio, the rhythm of teenaged voices in conversation. She closed her eyes and tried to imagine herself making love with Rob, the familiar sequence of sensations she had thought of as shapes they made together. She couldn't. That possibility seemed remote, as far away as the small town she'd grown up in, as far away as the Olympia Rob had created in the photograph.

JAMES LASDUN

Delirium Eclipse

L ewis Jackson had about ten million dollars of multinational aid at his disposal. It was a large sum for a man as young as himself to be tending, but he was properly aware of his responsibilities, and confident in his ability to shoulder them.

His ascent through the hierarchies of his career had been rapid and smooth. His still-boyish face was glazed with the patina acquired by people who work in the medium of success. He now found himself representing quite a substantial node in the planet's economic grid, and he could feel the hum of power in his veins.

His assignment—the first serious one he had been given—was in the south of India, where he was to budget the finances for a series of projects ranging from the sinking of village wells to the planting and irrigation of thousands of hectares of new orchards.

There were six weeks to go before he was due

to begin, and he decided to fill the interval by visiting the great Mogul sites in the north of the country.

Shortly before he left, he met a girl called Clare at a party in a Kilburn squat. They could see the bronze glitter of the canal from the window where they stood. The brick houses facing it were sepia in the lamplight, and the sky was violet.

"Imagine if that canal was the river Ganges, and those houses were temples," was Jackson's opening line, after which he was able to steer the conversation quite naturally around to his ten million dollars and his projects. He spoke of peaches, plums, mangoes, and limes, of fungicides and fertilizers, of crop yields waiting to be multiplied tenfold or more. . . . His eloquence was lit up with the immediacy of personal involvement, so that even if Clare wasn't interested in the subject matter, she couldn't help noticing the energy with which it was communicated, and this energy drew her toward him.

She was carefree, relaxed, and quite without guile. She lived on the dole, and spent her time at the dance, language, and craft classes her local council provided for its unemployed, at a nominal fee.

Her hair was a very shiny gold on the top, but increasingly dark toward its roots—burnt stubble colors. It was thick and unkempt, and hung in a tea-towel girdle like a sheaf of wheat. Her eyes were a pale slate color when looked at; a perfect blue when remembered. Her face was broad and strong, but also faintly childish in a Nordic way. It looked well accustomed to expressing pleasure, and little else. A Kirlian photograph of her would have revealed a brilliant aura burning about her body like Saint Elmo's fire, indicative of unusual spiritual and physical vigor.

Within minutes of meeting her, Jackson had set his heart on taking her with him to India. There was some urgency, for he intended leaving in a few days, but as he unfurled before her his visions of plenty, he felt certain that whatever it would take of charm, cunning, and willpower to persuade her to come, he possessed it in abundance. He felt invincible. In the event, the only serious obstacle he had to overcome was her reluctance to let him pay her way, she having no money of her own. She allowed herself to be swayed when he told her how much he was being paid, and hinted at the latitude of his expense allowance. It was as much the spontaneity of the idea that appealed to her as its promise of adventure, and having agreed to it, she couldn't wait to go. Jackson congratulated himself on his good fortune in finding a traveling companion as pleasant and equable as Clare, though he didn't doubt he deserved it.

□   □

Pearl mosques, incense, cane juice, desert forts, the deft hands of itinerant foot masseurs, the unearthly sound of vultures at carrion . . . They traveled in a leisurely way, stopping for everything.

They enjoyed each other's company. Clare, a natural hedonist and libertine, was content to focus the entire range of her sensuality on Jackson alone, which made him feel like a prince. His health was so good that he soon gave up dissolving chlorine tablets in his water, and joined Clare, who disdained such precautions, in drinking from the tap. He was in fine, magnanimous humor. He scattered coins before beggars, gave liberal tips to rickshaw drivers, and patronized street vendors avidly, accumulating garlands of colorful bead necklaces, shiny silk scarves, and innumerable little trinkets, decking Clare out in increasingly sumptuous combinations of his purchases.

The closest they came to a quarrel was outside the Red Fort at Agra, where Jackson wrote a warm, witty postcard to someone whom he had only that morning described to Clare in terms of the most crushing contempt. Clare colored as she read it.

"You shouldn't send that," she said.

"Why on earth not?"

"It's hypocritical."

Jackson told her not to be so silly, but she persisted in a slow, painfully obstinate way. "I wish you'd tear it up," she said, and, "I would never send a postcard like that to someone I despised."

Finally, Jackson snapped at her: "If you attach your integrity to something as trivial as a postcard, then it can't be worth much. I reserve mine for more important things."

She recoiled into a puzzled, hurt silence, while Jackson went off to buy a stamp.

He was pleased with his retort; at first because it seemed so clever, and then because it began to seem true. It crystallized the Jesuitical sense he had that the gravity of his work licensed him to trade with impunity in the sort of deceptions Clare objected to. A mission to irrigate orchards guaranteed your soul against damage from these minor acts of dissembling. If anything, the more you exposed yourself to them, the stronger your conviction was proved to be. Reaching that conclusion, Jackson felt a twinge of pity for Clare, who had nothing weightier in her life than the sincerity of her postcards against which to measure herself. He bought a sapphire from a gem hawker outside the post office, and gave it to Clare when he got back to the tea stall where she was waiting for him.

"There you are," he said, "that's what I call an important thing."

She looked at him warily, uncertain whether to believe him. He faced her with his most unflinchingly honest gaze. As he watched her gradually giving him the benefit of the doubt, he felt a curious, complex sensation of joy: he had made her believe the sapphire was a token of love, which it wasn't, by sheer force of will, and it gratified him to see that he possessed this power. But simultaneously, the sight of Clare *accepting* it as a token of love gave him a rush of the kind of elated yearning he had only previously felt for complete strangers—beautiful women at airports or concerts, whom he would never talk to and never see again. . . . To feel like that about a girl who was looking at him as lovingly as Clare was now, whom if he wanted he could take back to their room this minute and ravish, was blissful.

□   □

Mr. Birla, the manager of their hotel in the holy city of Varanasi, was a friendly young man dressed in jeans and a tight floral shirt. He spoke English well, and informed them he was an Anglophile. He said he had a stock list of English delicacies which he was working through alphabetically. Last month his kitchen had been filled with boxes of lime cordial, lemon curd, and luncheon meat. This month it was marmalade, muffins, macaroons, malt loaf, and Marmite. He sincerely hoped they would not feel homesick.

He showed them to a room with a small balcony from which they could just see the far shore of a massive brown tract of water, calm beneath an oily haze: the river Ganges.

He said they had arrived on a very important day. There was to be a partial eclipse of the sun that afternoon, an event of great significance in the Hindu calendar. There would be processions along the river, chanting, "all these kind of things." He offered to accompany them.

The streets were already beginning to swarm as they set off. Sadhus were striding about singing and praying. A Mercedes van with smoked-glass windows pulled up on one street and disgorged a dozen pink-skinned devotees of Krishna, who danced off like fully wound-up clockwork toys, banging cymbals and drums, and singing their song. Here and there they or the sadhus sent a charge of fervor rippling through the crowds gathering around them, though it was still a tentative, experimental fervor, and a man seized by it one minute might easily break off to buy a popadum or a cup of hot spiced milk the next.

Everyone was making for the great stone steps that led down to the Ganges. These were carpeted with people, milling, jostling, weaving about in processions. . . .

Jackson could see that Clare was already entering into the spirit of the occasion. A look of delight was fixed on her broad, healthy face She beamed at everyone who passed. An old crone, muttering an incantation, was reeling from person to person, anointing foreheads with greasepaint. Mr. Birla saw her off with a little gesture of disdain. Jackson followed suit. But Clare solemnly parted her hair and lowered her head toward the woman, rising again with a smudge of red above her eyebrows. "Who was she?" she whispered to Mr. Birla. "Holy woman," he answered, in a matter-of-fact voice. Clare looked exultant. A moment later she was caught in a crush of human traffic. She rose a few inches into the air, and glided along, borne by the pressure of the crowd. She turned round to look at Jackson, shaking the dark golden mass of her hair out of her eyes. She was smiling rapturously at him. As he smiled back, Jackson's heart swelled with pride, as if he himself had conjured this radiant creature into being.

They were down at the river now. Rowboats tethered to jetties jostled each other in the brown water. People were swimming and washing themselves. Jackson could see trickles of effluvia, glistening like snail tracks, dribbling into the water. Right beside him, a boy was washing a herd of water buffalo in the shallows, scraping the matted dung off their rears, scrubbing their dusty black hides until they looked Brylcreem-slick, and the sunlight made a blue gleam on the cusp of each muscle corrugation in their necks.

A surge of noise, cymbals crashing, drums ... Something happened to the daylight. It didn't darken so much as distort. The whole dome of sky was like an eye being squeezed askew. Jackson could hear a roaring, but far away; he was fixed in the space immediately about him, as if in bending it had become vitreous—a great glass orb. He squinted up at the sun: quartz-cold brilliance. "Do not look at the sun," he heard Mr. Birla say. It cut a glittering trail of light across his vision as he turned away; coruscating, like diamond dust. For an instant he was snow-blind, his insides curling from some obscure discomfort. The sun had been misshapen. He had the impression of having seen a scimitar edge of absolute blackness probing into it—a tiny penetration of darkness into the source of light itself.

On the way back to their hotel, they passed the general post office, which Jackson had given as a *poste restante* to his employers and family, should they wish to contact him. Leaving Clare with Mr. Birla, he went in to see if there was anything waiting for him. A telegram was eventually handed over the counter. He tore it open. "Agency closing down. Funds transferred. All projects cancelled. All staff kaput. Please no more expenses. Will explain on your return."

He sat down on a bench at the back of the stuffy, paper-strewn room, breathing deeply, to regain his composure. He was acutely conscious of the fatigue of his body, which flushed all over like a fanned ember when he looked at the telegram again. When he could, he stood up and walked slowly toward the exit. On his way out, he crumpled up the telegram and threw it into a bin.

"Anything?" Clare asked.

"No. Nothing at all."

□   □

The following morning Jackson's eyes were ablaze with conjunctivitis. Scarlet threads of vein straggled out from each canthus toward the pupil. His eyeballs felt as if they'd been doused in acid. He smeared them with Chloromycetin ointment from a tube in his washbag. As he looked at himself in the mirror, he flinched, as if he had seen not himself but some unsavory acquaintance from long ago in the past, who was swimming up to him, grinning like a blackmailer

"Don't even think about it," Clare whispered, kissing his eyelids. "It'll soon disappear." He said as little as possible to her; he was still trying to calculate how much of his news he could conceal from her, and how she would react to what he chose to reveal.

They walked down to the river, Jackson's eyes streaming behind a pair of sunglasses. There was a bitterness at the back of his throat, where some of the ointment, diluted by tears, had trickled down his sinuses.

They had planned to swim, but when they actually reached the river, Jackson began to have doubts. He could see one of the snail trails of sewage he had observed the day before, trickling into the water. There was a smell of barbecued meat on the air from the Burning Ghats, where corpses were cremated on wooden pyres, their ashes sent floating out onto the river on little rafts. He had read the passage in the guidebook describing the miraculous medicinal properties attributed to the Ganges; tests—"scientific tests"—had shown that water from cholera-ridden tributaries was purified within seconds of its penetrating the holy river. The time when these myths would have sufficed, and he would have plunged in without hesitation, already seemed remote from him.

"You go in. I'll wait here with the things."

Dressed in a blue swimsuit, Clare stepped down through the sandy mud to the river. Her skin looked very dusky in the gloom afforded by Jackson's sunglasses. She waded into the water, splashing it on her waist and shoulders before kicking herself free of the ground and plunging in. She swam out from the shore, covering yards with each thrust of her strong arms and legs. Her body churned the water into bronze scoops and billows that fanned out behind her, tiger-striping the surface with big ripples. Jackson watched her, his mind a jumble of desire and misgivings: the free abandon with which she plunged and twisted in the water had in it something distantly threatening as well as graceful. A dangerous self-sufficiency. Perhaps after all he ought to join her in the water; it might make her less likely to suspect there was anything seriously the matter with him.

He stripped to his trunks and stepped gingerly down to the river. He felt peculiarly naked and vulnerable, as if he had taken off not only his clothes but also a layer of skin, and there was now nothing between his internal organs and the water. Clare waved, and called to him. She was a good thirty yards out. He could hardly retreat now. Goosebumps swarmed over his back and shoulders. The water was warm and thick with detritus. His toes sank deep into the soft riverbed. He kicked free and started to swim toward Clare. Something solid bobbed against his thigh. A fish, he tried to think, but could only imagine human excrement, or charred human remains; a burnt hand touching his thigh, a blackened tongue ... An involuntary spasm quivered through him, and he panicked, jackknifing around, thrashing wildly at the water in his haste to get out. Quite soon he was shivering.

□   □

He lay alone on the sagging double bed. That morning he had taken his temperature, and sent the silver thread straight up to a hundred and two.

Clare was with Mr. Birla, who had invited them to visit his family's carpet factory that day. She had offered to stay behind with Jackson, but he could see she wanted to go, and although he would have preferred not to lose sight of her, he decided there was less to be lost by a show of carefree acquiescence than one of possessiveness.

He was in quite a bad way. There was a fever ache in his bones, and dysentery in his bowels. His eyes were still so inflamed that direct sunlight caused him unbearable pain. The curtains were shut, the dark room stifling. Now and then he had to drag himself upstairs to squat at the cracked and stinking porcelain throat that connected the hotel with the river. He voided himself there with a ferocity that left him shattered. He was in a groggy, twilit stupor of aspirin, streptomycin, and Chloromycetin. Thoughts drifted through him, but he hadn't the energy to seize hold of one for more than a few seconds. They slipped by, inconclusively. The telegram had blown him wide open. He didn't know what to do. He wondered what the matter with him was; he seemed to have lost all his power of resistance. Clare wasn't getting ill. Had her life provided her with some crucial immunity that his own had not? He remembered himself as a schoolboy; shy, insecure, unaccustomed to attention, deeply affected by it when it came his way. A washroom surrounded with mirrors ... Someone teasing him for his baby face ... He'd blushed with pleasure as the insults flew at him. Nothing like this had happened to him before; he was being celebrated, never mind why. He started laughing wildly, braying. He could see himself in the mirrors. His face was incapable of expressing so much ecstasy, and it began to twist and curl in all the wrong ways, absolutely out of control. Finally tears started pouring down his cheeks—"It's all right," he sobbed, "I'm still laughing, I'm still laughing," and the place had frozen up in an embarrassed silence.... It was that schoolboy's face he had seen in the mirror yesterday morning. What is wrong with me? The question hung in abeyance. He was sleepy by the time Clare returned.

She was in a jubilant mood: "What a place!"

She whisked open the curtains, letting in a bright sunbeam that hit Jackson's eyes like a punch.

"Don't."

Instead of closing the curtains, she picked up Jackson's sunglasses and stuck them on his face. "There we are. No need for Clare to sit in darkness all afternoon, is there?" She kissed him on the forehead. She had never babied him before, and the unprecedented tone had a faintly depressing effect on him.

"There were huge copper vats full of dye, and bales of thread the most gorgeous colors stacked all over the place. And then these little children, tiny little things, just everywhere, little mice ..." She giggled. "They get four rupees a day, which Shiva says is a fortune for them—"

"Shiva?"

"Mr. Birla. He's a lovely man ... I told him all about your projects. He'd love to talk to you.... I said you'd like that too and he could come up anytime. He took me into a room completely covered with the carpets they make. I wish I could describe them to you...." She attempted, and even though she stumbled clumsily from one superlative to another, her words worked on Jackson's drowsy imagination to produce an impression of bright patterns, stylized animals, birds, flowers, all glimmering through a medium of peacock plumage alloyed with silver and mother-of-pearl. She was more than usually voluble; the place had evidently had an effect on her.

"The best thing was how they were made—you'd've adored it, Lewis. Half a dozen of these toddlers sit in a pile of thread weavering away like mad, with an old man beside them just singing, and the thing was that what he sang was the pattern of the carpet, which was how the children knew what to do. What they wove depended on what he sang. Do you see? Isn't that good? The carpet is a song turned into a silk tapestry. Lewis? Lewis?" She lowered her voice to a whisper. "Are you awake?"

"Hm."

How tired he felt. He yawned. He could hardly hear what Clare was saying. Was she saying anything now? A hand touched his forehead. His various discomforts floated away just far enough to let his mind relax its vigil over his body. . . .

He woke up at dusk, his head reverberating with an absurd dream phrase spoken in Clare's voice: "Shivaring away like mad." She wasn't in the room. His sunglasses had been placed on the bedside table, on top of a note. "Back soon."

He wondered what she could be doing. An idea came to him: she was downstairs having sex with Mr. Birla. He sent it packing. He wished he could read a book, or get up and go for a walk. He turned over the bolster and straightened the sheet on top of him. He could feel the idea hovering in the wings. Shivaring away like mad. Resist it, he told himself. He tried to think of something else. Nothing. A pulse of alarm struck up beneath his ribs. An image of Clare and Mr. Birla locked together in a naked embrace blossomed in his mind like a big pink and brown flower. He winced, shook his head. But there was nothing between him and the idea. He seemed to have as little immunity to it as he had against the microbes swarming in his body. Here was Clare again. It was like a film, a conscientiously scrupulous porno-graphic film. He sat up and tried to block it out by reciting the only thing he knew by heart, which was the Lord's Prayer. Our Father which art in heaven, Hallowed be Thy name . . . but there was Clare sighing while Mr. Birla's fingers slid under her loose silk shirt to fondle her breasts. . . . Thy kingdom come. Thy will be done, on earth as it is in heaven. Give us this day . . . and Mr. Birla was underneath her while she slid the cushioned chassis of her hips to and fro astride him, a flush of pink washing her body. . . . Jackson sat up appalled. A cold veil of sweat surfaced on his brow. Give us this day our daily bread and forgive us our trespasses; as we . . . and there were two Mr. Birlas now, one of them calmly fucking Clare from behind, the other stroking the golden hair buried in his groin. Why is this happening to me, Jackson thought. He did not want to see these things.

He looked around the shadowy room for something to dis-tract himself with. The room service buzzer . . . If he pressed it and Mr. Birla came up within . . . within a minute, that would bring an end to these anxieties. He pressed it.

Mr. Birla arrived with such alacrity that Jackson hadn't even begun to think what he would actually say to him. But he was spared the trouble by Mr. Birla himself.

"Hello," the summoned manager said. "I was just thinking of popping up and looking in. How are your spirits?"

He hardly looked like a cuckold-maker—tight polka-dot shirt shadowed at the hollows of his bony shoulders and collarbone, a crumbling battlement of dentistry silhouetted in his grin.

"I'm all rights, thanks," Jackson said, feeling a little relieved.

"Oh, good." Mr. Birla stepped right inside the room. "I understand you are engaged on important business. Distributing welfare, is it?" He half *v*'d the *w* of welfare, and concluded with a charming smile, eager for conversation.

"Oh, yes. That's right," Jackson said. Now of course it was necessary to get rid of the man. "I wondered, actually, could I . . ." Inspiration struck him: "Could you bring me some muffins, please, with marmalade, and Marmite?"

Mr. Birla looked momentarily startled. His smile went glassy as he reverted from would-be conversationalist to hotel manager.

"Of course," he said. "Thank you."

Clare had been swimming. She came back with wet hair, and hung her costume up to dry.

□   □

Like his dysentery, Jackson's feelings of jealousy were tidal. They could ebb so far away that they would seem no more than a vague, dispersed nightmare. But when they rose, they engulfed him, and this they tended to do whenever Clare went out. Within minutes of her departure, her blithe, relaxed manner began to curdle in Jackson's memory. He realized her poise was a sham, performed in order to quell precisely the suspicions he was harboring. The realization coexisted with a full awareness that it was groundless, but this didn't in the least diminish its effects. His imagination began to seethe, his fever to rise; he would start trembling and sweating. Finally he would hit the room service buzzer, summoning Mr. Birla, whom he would scrutinize with increasingly blatant hostility before ordering a plate of macaroons, or a muffin, or a slice of malt loaf. An incidental benefit of this procedure was that it supplied Jackson with nourishment bland enough for him to consume: he had come to regard eating Indian food as a form of Russian roulette, where every mouthful might be loaded. He had lost his taste for it.

The frequency with which he summoned Mr. Birla increased rapidly. Soon he had him running up and down stairs five or six times a morning. By then he hardly knew why he did it, but it satisfied him in an obscure way to exercise the power. "Thank you," Mr. Birla always said when Jackson finally snapped his order at him. He didn't try to engage Jackson in conversation again.

Meanwhile Jackson was growing steadily more ill. His eyes were swollen and rheumy. He developed a streaming cold. A small colony of itchy red spots between his toes ran riot, covering both feet with a livid, burning rash. He lay all day in shadow. Sometimes he would be aware of Clare lying beside him, talking about her day, cooling his forehead with a flannel. Then somehow she would have vanished, and in no time Jackson would have to hit the room service buzzer again. . . .

One day she produced from her bag a bottle of Dr. Collis Brown—an opium-based panacea which she had discovered in the bathroom cupboard of her squat. It was the only medicine she had brought.

"Why don't we try this for a change?" She poured out a spoonful for Jackson. It was sweet and fiery.

"Maybe I'll have some too." She took a swig straight from the bottle, and passed the bottle back to Jackson, smiling mischievously. "Go on. . . ." By the time they had finished it, Jackson was feeling a pleasant, slightly drunken sensation. Clare snuggled up next to him on the bed. Her bushy hair brushed against his skin, and set him tingling. He was floating, immensely happy. A lot of time went by very quickly, or else a little, slowly. His body wasn't hurting at all. He plied his fingers through Clare's hair. A rustle like a breeze through copper-colored leaves ... Tiny golden sparks began to tumble out of it with each stroke. The more he brushed the brighter they grew, and when he stopped they faded.

"Are you seeing things too?" Clare asked in a faraway voice.

"Oh, yes ... so I am ..."

They lay still. He was in a room like this but different. Clare was kneeling by the bed.

"Look," she said, placing a hand on each side of her head. "Look ..." She lifted away the top of her head. Jackson peered over: a crystalline, miniature landscape ... mountains with snow and dark green pines. Still blue lakes, and on a far shore an icy blue sea with motionless white crests ...

"Now you ..." she said. But he was looking at the wall. There was a hole in it he hadn't seen before, with a bird's nest inside. A spider the size of a hand was sitting on the twigs, its black head probing down into the broken shell of a pale blue egg. A bead of golden yolk was sliding down the side of the shell. "Make me come," he heard Clare whisper. She was naked, aroused. Her breasts had turned a rosy color at their tips. She pressed them to his face and wrapped her legs around him. "Come on ..."

"Look at the spider," Jackson said. It took him hours to form the syllables. She knelt up slowly on the bed and leaned toward it. As she did so, the bird's nest disappeared, and the hole shrank to a shallow cavity of flaked-away plaster. There was no trace of the egg or its liquid treasure. "Sweet little spider." She reached her hand toward it and picked it up very gently by one leg. It wriggled, grappling with the air close to Clare's naked skin. Jackson had to close his eyes for a moment. When he opened them again she was at the window talking to the spider, wishing it a pleasant journey to the ground. It was much smaller than he had imagined. "Bye, bye, little spider," Clare said. She drifted back to bed and covered Jackson's face with kisses. He rolled away. "Don't feel like it," he said. "Sleep."

□   □

It was evening. Beyond the window the dark pink sunset was drawn, like a conjuror's silk handkerchief, through a band of clouds, from which it emerged a watery blue. Jackson stretched and sat up. He could feel the imprint of the sweaty, crumpled linen on his cheeks. Clare wasn't there. He had no idea when he had last seen her.

There was something on the floor by the bed. Jackson peered down, touched it.

It was a rolled-up carpet about six feet in width. He stared at it a moment, wondering where it had come from. Clare couldn't possibly have afforded to buy a carpet from the pocket money he gave her, and he was certain she had no secret stash of her own. He checked his own wallet; nothing was missing. How had she got hold of it? It must have been a gift. Jackson felt the familiar signals of alarm go off in his body. He pressed the buzzer. A minute went by, two minutes. He pressed it again. An old woman he hadn't seen before finally appeared, wheezing and dragging her feet. She tilted her chin at Jackson, questioningly.

"Mr. Birla?" he asked. She shook her finger and gestured with it toward the window: gone out. Jackson thanked her, and she shuffled off.

He lay back on the bed with a feeling of acute consternation. He told himself over and over that there was absolutely no basis for his anxieties; and meanwhile he grew quite frantic. Images of Clare and Mr. Birla played in his mind with the intensity of an hallucination. He had nothing to fight them with, and they took on a life of their own, commandeering his imagination, like the amoebas in his bowels. He started shaking. Fever flushes rushed through his body. The intensity and luridness of his imaginings proliferated until he began to feel he was losing his grip. He had to move.

He climbed out of bed and put on a pair of light cotton pajamas. His legs were wobbly from lack of use, though this had the effect of making him feel oddly light rather than heavy. He took his wallet and documents so that he could leave the door unlocked in case Clare came back before him. The evening light being just tolerable, he left his sunglasses behind. The old woman was sitting at Mr. Birla's desk in the lobby. She looked at him impassively as he stumbled by her, out onto the street.

After a few yards he was panting; he was in no condition to

be out. He waved down a bicycle rickshaw and climbed into the chariot-like seat. They rumbled over the cobbles, into the maze of alleys that led down the steps.

The city was coming to life as the day cooled. People were out strolling. The street markets, some of them already lit with kerosene lamps, were trading busily. There was food everywhere. There seemed to be a surplus of it. Unwanted mangoes and limes lay in broken crates outside shops, fermenting into chutney; Jackson could smell the sweet syrup odor of fruit rot as he went by. Apple scab, he remembered from his training, potato canker, honey fungus, white rot, black rust . . . Pomegranates and papayas tumbled from overladen stalls onto the cobbles, where their heedless owners watched them disappear into the mitts of furtive monkeys. A skew-horned cow patrolling one of the alleys dragged, like a prisoner's ball, a giant watermelon she had stamped on, and which no one had troubled to prize from her hoof. There was meat in abundance too—garroted guinea fowl, skinned lambs dressed in living fleeces of big black flies, goats' heads, foamy swathes of what looked like, but surely could not have been, tripe still green with cud. . . . Jackson watched a begger tip ruefully from his brass bowl a mound of sticky rice that even his elastic appetite had been unable to accommodate. There were smells of cooking in the air—garlic and coriander, spice smells of cardamom and cinnamon, acrid odors from the dung-burning stoves over which soot-blackened vats simmered and steamed, and floating over these, the soapy smells of incense, frangipani, sandalwood. . . .

Too much was going on. Radios and klaxons were blaring out, flutes, drums, voices. . . . There were too many people and the rickshaw driver kept stopping to let them pass in front of him. Dogs and monkeys were rooting in the gutters. Cows choked up the alleys until they felt like ambling on. Jackson had an urgent desire to get down to the river. It made him feel uncomfortable to dawdle among all this plenty. He felt lost and insignificant. "I'm in rather a hurry," he said to the rickshaw driver, who smiled and said nothing. They were hardly moving. Come on, come on, Jackson thought. "Come on," he shouted. He could see knotted veins bulging like worm casts on the driver's skinny calves. Looking at them he had a brief intimation that if he'd had a whip, he would have used it. His fever was running high.

It was almost dark by the time they reached the steps that led down to the river. Fires were burning here and there, and the level sun made the sullage in the water look like gold dust. The steps were staggered, uneven, muddied by a mulch of crushed marigolds and rose petals. The whole higgledy-piggledy embankment with its crooked paths and terraced buildings stacked precariously on top of each other, saris flapping on the vast web of lines stretched between them, was more like vegetation than carefully assembled stone. The budding tip of a new shrine pushing its way through a crack in the ground would not have been an altogether surprising sight. Jackson climbed down, scanning the water for Clare. He was in a particular state of mind that internalizes everything perceived, giving it the viscosity of a dream landscape—temples flowed past him, people in prayer or meditation dissolved into the glare of torchlight, shadowy figures swam into focus and then ceased to exist. His head was throbbing. The steps seemed endless and unreal.

He was still some way from the water when a head of fair hair rose up from it, followed by a body in a dark blue swimsuit. Before the body had reached full height, the head of hair had already bushed out from its water-sleeked anonymity and taken on a burnish of firelight. Water streamed from the body, draping it for a second like a glassy dress; leaving behind a few beads in which the last of the light took refuge. . . . She walked slowly out of the water, smiling faintly to herself. Jackson stayed very still. He felt invisible. He watched her stoop for her towel and hold it round herself with one hand, while with the other she slid the swimsuit from her body. She knelt down to dry herself. There was nothing but twilight between her nakedness and the eyes of people wandering by the river. She was oblivious. She dried herself slowly and carefully, luxuriating, it seemed, in the sensations of her body. She put on a dress and strolled toward the steps, several yards along from where Jackson stood.

He hung back, following her from a short distance, half-thinking Mr. Birla was suddenly going to appear at her side, half-knowing he would not.

A figure approached her from the shadows ... not Mr. Birla, but a leper hobbling on a pair of makeshift crutches tied under his shoulders. His feet were bandaged in rags and his skin was mottled like a wall with bad damp. There was a box hanging from his neck. Clare fumbled in her purse for coins, which she held out to him at arm's length. The leper stood still with his head bowed as she dropped the coins in his box. From where Jackson stood, along the steps, he could see it dawning on Clare that the man had interpreted her outstretched arm as a sign that he was to come no closer. A look of anxiety at her unintended coldness crossed her face as the leper thanked her and turned to go. "Oh ... wait." She put her hand on his shoulder to detain him, and as he heaved himself back round on his crutches, she ran her fingers lightly down his arm, resting her hand a moment on his scabbed stump. The leper stood obediently still while Clare stared at him, her mouth open as if she were on the point of uttering some phrase that would magic away his disease. Then, remembering herself, she dug into her purse again, taking out not coins, but something that sparkled as she dropped it into the box: the sapphire Jackson had given her.

Jackson watched it all with a feeling of vertiginous wonder. What was he to make of this? There was too much new, bewildering information crammed into Clare's gestures and actions for him to comprehend it all at once. It was like being dazzled by a glare. As he watched her disappear into the dark city, he realized he had seriously underestimated her. There was a side to her he had failed to appreciate. Her uncomplicatedness wasn't the same as simplicity: he had glimpsed behind it, into a world where his own labyrinthine relations with people and possessions had no place, where you gave and took as you felt like or needed, and that was that. He walked back slowly, feeling faintly ashamed of his furtive behavior, and trying to assess how much damage it had done. He resolved never to indulge his suspicions again, and as he did so, it occurred to him that the only probable explanation for the presence of the carpet in their room was that Clare had borrowed it, just so that she could show him one. How extraordinarily thoughtful she was. He felt like someone coming out of a delirium: feeling his way back along a frail vein of reality. And it was the way back to health too; all he had to do was concentrate on holding on.

There was no one at the desk when he reentered the hotel. He climbed up the stairs, feeling rather stronger on his legs than he had when he'd set out. I'm recovering, he told himself, and felt an anticipatory buzz of well-being. The dimly lit staircase smelled of stale incense and drains: not a place he would be sorry to leave. There was enough money left for another week or so. They could go somewhere they hadn't planned to visit: Assam perhaps, or Kashmir, hire a wooden houseboat on Lake Srinagar—mountains and snow, lush valleys ... There was time to make a fresh start. He would tell her about the agency closing down; she wouldn't give a damn. He'd pretend he'd just been down to the post office, and found the telegram.

The light was on, peeping under the door, but the door was locked. He rattled the handle. "It's me." Scuffling sounds, a delay. "Open up, it's me." Clare opened the door: "Oh, there you are. Where on earth have you been? We thought you'd been kidnapped." Mr. Birla was in the room. Jackson stepped inside, screwing up his eyes against the electric light. He looked at Clare, and at Mr. Birla. Clare was talking breathlessly. "Did you see this carpet Shiva gave us?" he heard her say. "Isn't it beautiful? Look—" She knelt down and began to unroll it. Flowers and grasses appeared, tree trunks, boughs, foliage.... Jackson stared at it intently while Clare went on talking: "Have you ever seen anything so lovely ..." A dizzy feeling went through him as he tried to resist wondering why the door had been locked, why Mr. Birla was there, and why Clare was talking so wildly. Bright lemons and limes hung between the leaves on the carpet, and on one tree there were big lustrous peaches, shaded at the cleft and toned miraculously through from yellow to scarlet. "A small gift," Mr. Birla said. Jackson peered even closer as Mr. Birla edged behind him toward the door. He noticed how the leaves were individually veined, how some were curled to show a paler reverse, how there was even a silvery down of furze visible on the peaches if you looked carefully. "I have received my new shipment," Mr. Birla was saying as he backed into the corridor. "Nesquik, Nutella, a box of nougat—I'll bring you some nougat." Then Clare stepped forward with his sunglasses. "There's too much light in here," she said, "it's too bright for you. You'll damage yourself." She stuck them on his face and went out, saying she'd be back in a while, that she wouldn't be long.

FAY WELDON

Wasted Lives

They're turning the City into Disneyland. They're restoring the ancient façades and painting them apple-green, firming up the medieval gables and picking out the gargoyles in yellow. They're gold-leafing the church spires. They've boarded up the more stinking alleys until they get round to them, and as State property becomes private, the shops that were always there are suddenly gone, as if simply painted out. In the eaves above Benetton and the Body Shop, cherubs wreathe pale, cleaned-stone limbs, and even the great red McDonald's sign has been especially muted to rosy pink for this, its Central European edition. Don't think crass commerce rules the day as the former Communist world opens its arms wide to the seduction of market forces: the good taste of the new capitalist world leaps yowling into the embrace as well—a fresh-faced baby monster, with its yearning to prettify and make

105

the serious quaint, to turn the rat into Mickey Mouse and the wolf into Goofy.

Milena and I walked through knots of tourists, toward the famous Processional Bridge, circa 1357. I had always admired its sooty stamina, its dismal persistence through the turbulence of rising and falling empire. It was my habit to stay with Milena when I came to the City. I'd let Head Office book me into a hotel, to save official embarrassment, then spend my nights with her, and some part of my days, if courtesy so required. I was fond of her but did not love her, or loved only in the throes of the sexual excitement she was so good at summoning out of me. She made excellent coffee. If I sound disagreeable and calculating, it is because I am attempting to speak the truth about the events on the Processional Bridge that day, and the truth of motive seldom warms the listener's heart. I am generally accepted as a pleasant and kindly enough person. My family loves me, even my wife Joanna, though she and I live apart and are no longer sexually connected. She doesn't have to love me.

Milena is an archivist at the City Film Arts Institute. I work for a U.S. film company, from their London office. I suppose, if you add it up, I have spent some three months in the City over the last five years—before and after the fall of the Berlin Wall and the Great Retreat of Communism, a tide sweeping back over shallow sand into an obscure distance. Some three months in all spent with Milena.

Her English was not as good as she thought. Conversation could be difficult. Today she was not dressed warmly enough. It was June, but the wind was cold. Perhaps she thought her coat was too shabby to stand the inspection of the bright early-summer sun. I was accustomed to seeing her either naked or dressed in black—a color, or lack of it, that suited the gaunt drama of her face—but today, like her city, she wore pastel colors. I wished it were not so.

Beat your head not into the Berlin Wall but into cotton wool, machine-pleated in interesting baby shades, plastic-wrapped. Suffocation takes many forms.

"You should have brought your coat," I said.

"It's so old," she said. "I am ashamed of it."

"I like it," I said.

"It's old," she repeated, dismissively. "I would rather freeze."

For Milena the past was all dreary, the future all dread and expectation. A brave face must be put on everything. She smiled up at me. I am six foot three inches and bulky: she was all of five and a half foot, and skinny with it. The sweater was too tight: I could see her ribs through the stretched fabric, and the nipples, too. In the old days she would never have allowed that to happen. She would have let her availability be known in other, more subtle ways. Her teeth were bad: one in the front broken, a couple gray. When she wore black, their eccentricity seemed a matter of course; a delight, even. Now she wore green, they were yellowy, and seemed a perverse tribute to years of neglect, poverty, and bad diet. Eastern teeth, not Western. I wished she would not smile, or trust me so.

The Castle still looks down over the City, as does the extension to that turreted tourist delight—the long, low stone building with its rows of identical windows, tier upon tier of them, blank and anonymous, to demonstrate the way brute force gives way to the subtler yet more stifling energies of bureaucracy. You can't do this, you can't live like that, not because I have a sword to run you through but because Our Masters frown on it. And your papers have not risen to the top of the pile.

Up there in the Castle that day, a newly elected government was trying to piece together from the flesh of this nation and the bones of that a new, living, changing organism, a new constitution. New, new, new. I wished them every luck with it, but they could not make Milena's bad teeth good, or stop her smiling at me as if she wanted something. I wondered what it was. She'd not used to smile like this: it was a new trick: it sat badly on her doleful face.

We reached the Processional Bridge, which crosses the river between the Palace and the Cathedral. "The oldest bridge in Europe," said Milena. We had walked across it many times before. She had made this remark many times before. Look left down the river, and you could see where it carved its way through the

107

mountains that form the natural boundaries of this small nation; look right, and you looked into mist. On either bank the ancient city crowded in, in its crumbly, pre-Disney form, all eaves, spires, and casements, spared from the blasts of war for one reason or another, or perhaps by just plain miracle. But Emperors and Popes must have somewhere decent to be crowned, and Dictators, too, need a background for pomp and circumstance, crave some acknowledgment from history: a name engraved in gold in a Cathedral, a majestic tomb in a gracious square still standing. It can't be all rubble, or what's the point?

I offered Milena my coat. It seemed to me that she and I were at some crucial point in not just our story but everyone's—that the decisions we made here today had some general relevance to the way the world was going. I could at least share some warmth with her. My monthly Western salary would keep her in comfort for a year, but what could I do about that? If she wanted a new coat from me, it would have nothing to do with her desire to be warm; she would want it as a token of my love. She didn't mind shivering. Her discomfort was both a demonstration of martyrdom and a symbol of pride.

"I am not cold," she said.

□   □

The City is a favorite location for film companies. The place is cheap, its money valueless in the real world, and its appetite for hard currency voracious, which means good deals can be had. The quaint, colorful locations are inexpensively historicized—though the satellite dishes are these days becoming too numerous to dodge easily. And there are few parking problems, and highly trained postproduction technicians, efficient labs, excellent cameramen, sensitive sound men, and so on—and cheap, so cheap. Those who lived in the City had escaped the fate of so many of the hitherto Russian-dominated lands—the sullen refusal of the oppressed and exploited to do anything right, to be anything other than inefficient, to be sloppy and lazy, in the hope that the colonizing power would simply give up and go away, shaking the dust of the conquered land from its feet. And the power it had amassed lay not of course in the strength of the ideology it professed, as the West in its muddled way assumed, but in the strength of arms and organization of that single, colonizing, ambitious nation Russia. Ask anyone between Budapest and Samarkand, Tbilisi and the Siberian flatlands, and they would tell you whom they feared and hated. Russia, the motherland, announcing itself to a gullible world as the Soviet Union. Harsh mother, pretending kindness, using Marxism-Leninism as the religious tool of government and exploitation, as once in the South Americas Spain had used Christianity.

In the City they kept their wits about them: too sophisticated for the numbing rituals of mind control ever quite to work, for the concrete of the workers' blocks quite to take over from the tubercular gables and back alleys, to stifle the whispers of dissent, to quieten the gossip and mirth of café society. McDonald's has achieved that now, with its bright, forbidding jollity, and who in the brave new world of freedom can afford a cup of coffee anyway, has anything interesting or persuasive to say, now that everyone has what they wanted? Better, better by far, to travel hopefully than to arrive, to have to face the fact that the journey is not out of blackness into light but from one murky confusion into another. Happiness and fulfillment lie in our affections for one another, not in the forms that our societies take. If only I were in love with Milena, this walk across the bridge would be a delight. I would feel the air bright with the happiness of the hopeful young.

Be that as it may, the City was always better than anywhere else for filming. Go to Romania and you'd find the castles still full of manacled prisoners clanking their chains; try Poland and you'd have to fly in special food for your stars; in Hungary the cameraman would have artistic tantrums. But here in the City there would be gaiety, fun, sometimes even sparkle—the clatter of high heels on cobblestones, sultry looks from sultry eyes, and of course nights with Milena in the fringy, shabby apartment with the high, white-mantled brass bed, and good strong coffee in porcelain cups for breakfast. Milena, forever languidly busy, about my body or about her work, off to the Institute or back from it. Women worked hard in this country, as women were accustomed to all over the Soviet Union. Equality for women meant an equal obligation to work, the official direction of your labor, sleeping with your boss if he so required, the placement of your child in a crèche, as well as the cultural expectation that you get married, run a home, and empty the brimming ashtrays while your husband put his feet up. Joanna would have none of that kind of thing; for the male visitor from the West the Eastern European woman is paradise, if you can hack it, if your conscience can stand it—if you can bear being able to buy affection and constancy.

I hadn't been with Milena for three months or so. Now I found her changed, like her city. I wondered about her constancy. It occurred to me that it was foolish of me to expect it. As did the rest of the nation, she now paid at least lip service to market forces: perhaps these worked sexually as well. Rumor had it that there were now twenty-five thousand prostitutes in the City and an equal number of pimps, as men and women decided to make the best financial use of available resources. I discovered I was not so much jealous as rather hoping for evidence of Milena's infidelity, which would let me off whatever vague hook it was I found myself upon. Not so difficult a hook. She and I had always been discreet: I had not mentioned our relationship to a soul back home. Milena was in another country; she did not really count: her high, bouncing bosom, her narrow rib cage and fleshless hips vanished from my erotic imagination as the plane reached the far side of the mountaintops—the turbulence serving as some rite of passage—to reimprint the attraction only as I passed over them once again, on my return.

The cleaning processes had not yet reached the bridge, I was glad to see. The stone saints who lined it were still black with the accumulated grime of the past.

"Who are these saints?" I asked, but Milena didn't know. Some hold books, others candles; noses are weather-flattened. Milena apologized for her ignorance. She had not, she said, had the opportunity of a religious education: she hoped her son Milo would. Her son lived with Milena's mother, who was a good

Catholic, in the Southern Province—a place about to secede, to become independent, to ethnic-cleanse in its own time, in its own way.

"I didn't know you had a son," I said. I was surprised, and ashamed at myself for being so uncurious about her. "Why didn't you tell me?"

"It's my problem," Milena said. "I don't want to burden you. He's ten now. When he was born I was not well, and times were hard. It seemed better that he go to my mother. But she's getting old now, and there's trouble in the Southern Province. They are not nice people down there."

Once the City's dislike and suspicion had been reserved for the Russians. Now it had been unleashed and spread everywhere. The day the Berlin Wall fell, Milena and I had been sitting next to each other in the small Institute cinema, watching the demonstration reels of politically sound directors available for work, in the strange, flickering half-dark of such places. Her small white hand had strayed unexpectedly onto my thigh, unashamedly direct in its approach. But then exhilaration and expectation, mixed with fear, were in the air. Sex seemed the natural expression of such emotions, such events. And perhaps that was why I never quite trusted her, never quite loved her, found it so easy to forget her when she wasn't under my nose—I despised her because it was she who had approached me, not I her. If Joanna and I are apart it's because I'm so conditioned in the old, prefeminist ways of thinking that I'm impossible for a civilized woman to live with, or so she says. I am honest, that is to say, and scrupulous in the investigation of my feelings and opinions.

"Why didn't you put the child into a crèche?" I asked. It shocked me that Milena, that any woman, could give a child away so easily.

"I was in a crèche," she said bleakly. "It's the same for nearly everyone in this city under forty. The crèche was our real home, our parents were strangers. I didn't want it to happen to Milo. He was better with my mother, though there are too many Muslims down there. More and more of them. It's like a disease."

I caught the stony eye of baby Jesus on St. Joseph's

111

shoulder—that one, at least, I knew—and one or the other sent me a vision, not that I believed in such things, as I looked down at the greeny, sickly waters of the river. I saw, ranked and rippling, row upon row of infants, small, pale children, institutionalized, deprived, pasty-faced from the atrocious city food—meat, starch, fat, no fruit, no vegetables—and understood that I was looking at the destruction of a people. They turned their little faces to me in despair, and I looked quickly up and away and back at Milena to shake off the vision; but there behind her, where the river met the sky, I saw that nation grown up, marching toward me into the mists of its future, a sad mockery of those sunny early Social Realist posters that decked my local, once Marxist, now leftish bookshop back home: the proletariat marching square-jawed and determined into the new dawn, scythes and spanners at the ready. Here there were no square jaws, only wretchedness: the quivering lip of the English ex-public-school boy, wrenched from his home at a tender age, now made general; the same profound, puzzled sorrow spread through an entire young population, male and female. See it in the easy, surface emotion, the facile sexuality, the rush of tears to the eyes, uncontrolled and uncontrollable, pleading for a recognition that never comes, a comfort that is unavailable. "Pity me"—the unspoken words upon a nation's lips—"because I am indeed pitiable. I have been deprived of freedom—yes, of course, all that. And of proper food and of fancy things, consumer durables and material wealth of every kind, all that. But mostly I have been robbed of my birthright, my mother, my father, my home. And how can I ever recover from that?" Then there is a murmur, as a last, despairing cry, the latest prayer—"Market forces, market forces." Say it over and over, as once the Hail Mary was said, to ward off all ills and rescue the soul, but we know in our hearts it won't work. There is no magic here contained. Wasted lives, lost souls, unfixable. Pity me, pity me, pity me.

□   □

"I think the fog's coming down," said Milena, and so it was. The new dawn faded into it. A young man on the bridge was selling black rubber spiders: you hurled them against a board and they crept down, leg over leg; stillness alternating with sudden movement. No one was buying.

"Well," I said, "I expect you made the right decision about Milo. What happened to his father?" I turned to button her jacket. I wanted her warmed. This much, at least, I could do. Perhaps if she was warm she would not feel so much hate for the Southern Province and its people.

"We are divorced," she said. "I am free to marry again. Look, there's Jesus crucified. Hanging from nails in his hands. At least the Communists took down the crosses. Why should we have to think about torture all the time? It was the Russians taught our secret police their tricks: we would never have come to it on our own."

I commented on the contradiction between her wanting her son to have a Catholic upbringing and her dislike of the Christian symbol, the tortured man upon the cross, but she shrugged it off: she did not want the point pursued. She was not interested in it. She saw no virtue in consistency. First you had this feeling; then that: that was all there was to it. No parent had ever intervened between the tantrum and its cause; no doubt Milena, along with the rest of her generation, had been slapped into silence when protesting frustration and outrage. She was wounded; she was damaged: not her fault, but there it was. What I'd seen as childlike, as charming, in the early stages of a relationship was in the end merely irritating. I could not stir myself to become interested in her son or in a marriage that had ended in divorce. I could not take her initial commitment seriously.

"I'm pregnant," Milena now says. "Last time you were here we made a baby. Isn't that wonderful? Now you will marry me, and take me to London, and we will live happily ever after."

Fiends come surging up the river through the mist, past me—gaunt, soundlessly shrieking. These are the ghosts of the insulted, the injured, the wronged and tortured, whose efforts have been in vain. Those whose language has been taken away, whose bodies have been starved; they are the wrongfully dead. All the great rivers of the world carry these images with them; over time

113

they have infected me by their existence. They breathe all around me. I take in their exhalations. I am their persecutor, their ruler, the origin of their woes: the one who despises. They shake their ghoulish locks at me; they mock me with their sightless eyes, snapping to attention as they pass. Eyes right! Blind eyes, forever staring. They honor me, the living.

"Is something the matter?" asks Milena. "Aren't you happy? You told me you loved me."

Did I? Probably. I remind her that I've also told her that I'm married.

"But you will divorce her," she says. "Why not? Your children are grown. She doesn't need you anymore. I do."

Her eyes are large in their hollows: she fears disaster. Of course she does. It so often happens. I can hardly tell whether she is alive or dead. To have a child with a ghost!

Milena is perfectly right. Joanna doesn't need me. Milena does. The first night I went with Milena she was wearing a purple velvet bra. It fired me sexually, it was so extraordinary, but it put too great an element of pity into what otherwise could have been love. There seemed something more valuable in my wife's white Marks & Spencer bra with its valiant label, 40A. Broad-backed, that is, and flat-chested. I supposed Milena's to be a 36C. English women lean toward the pear-shaped; the City women toward the top-heavy. It's unfashionable, dangerous even, to make comparisons between the characteristics of the peoples of the world—this tribe, that tribe, this religion or that. The ghouls that people the river, who send their dying breath back, day after day, in the form of the fog that blights the place, mists up the new Disney façades with mystery droplets, met their end because people like me whispered, nudged, and made odious comparisons, and the odium grew and grew and ended in torture, murder, slaughter, genocide. Nevertheless, I must insist: it is true. Pear-shaped that lot, top-heavy this. And if I suspected Milena's purple velvet bra of being some kind of secret-police state issue, or part of the Film Arts Institute's plan to attract hard currency and Western business, an end toward which their young female staff were encouraged, even paid, it is not surprising. Had I been of

114

her nationality, I knew well enough, her hand would not have strayed across my thigh in the film-flickering dark. I was offended that the Gods of Freedom, Good Health, Good Teeth, Good Nourishment, Prosperity, and Market Forces, whom I myself did not worship, endowed me with this wondrous capacity to attract. I could snap my fingers and all the girls in Eastern Europe would come trotting and fall on their knees.

"Milena," I said, and I was only temporizing, "I have no way of knowing this baby is mine, if baby there be."

Milena threw her hands into the air, and cried aloud—a thin, horrid squeal, chin to the heavens, lips drawn back in a harsh grimace. There were few people left on the bridge. The fog had driven them away. The seller of rubber spiders had given up and gone home. Milena ran toward the parapet and wriggled and crawled until she lay along its top on the cold stone, and then she simply rolled off and fell into the water below; this in the most casual way possible. Between my straightforward question and this dramatic answer only fifteen seconds can have intervened. I was too stunned to feel alarm. I found myself leaning over the parapet to look downward; the fog was patchy. I saw a police launch veer off course and make for the spot where Milena fell. No doubt she had seen it coming or she would not have done what she did—launched herself into thick air, thin, swirling water. I had confidence in her ability to survive. Authorities of one kind or another, as merciful in succor as they were cruel in the detection of sedition, would pull her out of the wet murk, dry her, wrap her in blankets, warm her, return her to her apartment. She would be all right.

I walked to the end of the bridge, unsure as to whether I would then turn left to the police pier and Milena or to the right and the taxi rank. Why had the woman done it? Hysteria, despair, or was it some convenient local way of terminating unwanted pregnancies? I could take a flight back home, if I chose, forty-eight hours earlier than I had intended. The flights were full, but I would get a priority booking, as befitted my status, however whimsical, as a provider of hard currency. The powerful are indeed whimsical: they leave their elegant droppings where they choose—be they Milena's baby, Benetton, the Marlboro ads that now dominate the City: no end even now to the wheezing, the coughing, the death rattling along the river.

I turned to the right, where the taxis stood waiting for stray foreigners anxious to get out of the fog, back to their hotels.

"To the airport," I said. The driver understood. "To the airport" are golden words to taxi drivers all over the world. This way, at least, I created a smile. To have turned left would have meant endless trouble. I was thoroughly out of love with Milena. I wanted to help, of course I did, but the child in the Southern Province would have had to be fetched by the Catholic mother, taken in. There would be no end to it. My children would not accept a new family: Joanna would be made thoroughly miserable. To do good to one is to do bad to another. But you don't need to hear my excuses. They are the same that everyone makes to themselves when faced with the misery of others; though they would like to do the right thing, they simply fail to do so and look after themselves instead.

WILLIAM TREVOR

In Isfahan

They met in the most casual way, in the up-stairs office of Chaharbagh Tours Inc. In the downstairs office a boy asked Norman-ton to go upstairs and wait: the tour would start a little later because they were having trouble with the engine of the minibus.

The upstairs office was more like a tiny waiting-room than an office, with chairs lined against two walls. The chairs were rudimentary: metal frames, and red plastic over foam rubber. There was a counter stacked with free guides to Isfahan in French and German, and guides to Shi-raz and Persepolis in English as well. The walls had posters on them, issued by the Iranian Tourist Board: Mount Damavand, the Chalus road, native dancers from the Southern tribes, club-swinging, the Apadana Palace at Persepolis, the Theological School in Isfahan. The fees and conditions of Chaharbagh Tours were clearly stated: *Tours by De Lux microbus. Each Person Rls. 375 ($5). Tours* *in French and English language. Microbus comes to Hotel otherwise you'll come to Office. All Entrance Fees. No Shopping. Chaharbagh Tours Inc. wishes you the best.*

She was writing an air-mail letter with a ballpoint pen, leaning on a brochure which she'd spread out on her handbag. It was an awkward arrangement, but she didn't seem to mind. She wrote steadily, not looking up when he entered, not pausing to think about what each sentence might contain. There was no one else in the upstairs office.

He took some leaflets from the racks on the counter. *Isfahan était capitale de l'Iran sous les Seldjoukides et les Safavides. Sous le règne de ces deux dynasties l'art islamique de l'Iran avait atteint son apogée.*

"Are you going on the tour?"

He turned to look at her, surprised that she was English. She was thin and would probably not be very tall when she stood up, a woman in her thirties, without a wedding ring. In a pale face her eyes were hidden behind huge round sunglasses. Her mouth was sensuous, the lips rather thick, her hair soft and black. She was wearing a pink dress and white high-heeled sandals. Nothing about her was smart.

In turn she saw a man who seemed to her to be typically English. He was middle-aged and greying, dressed in a linen suit and carrying a linen hat that matched it. There were lines and wrinkles in his face, about the eyes especially, and the mouth. When he smiled more lines and wrinkles gathered. His skin was tanned, but with the look of skin that usually wasn't: he'd been in Persia only a few weeks, she reckoned.

"Yes, I'm going on the tour," he said. "They're having trouble with the minibus."

"Are we the only two?"

He said he thought not. The minibus would go round the hotels collecting the people who'd bought tickets for the tour. He pointed at the notice on the wall.

She took her dark glasses off. Her eyes were her startling feature: brown, beautiful orbs, with endless depth, mysterious in her more ordinary face. Without the dark glasses she had an Indian look: lips, hair and eyes combined to give her that. But her voice was purely English, made uglier than it might have been by attempts to disguise a Cockney twang.

"I've been writing to my mother," she said.

He smiled at her and nodded. She put her dark glasses on again and licked the edges of the air-mail letter-form.

"Microbus ready," the boy from downstairs said. He was a smiling youth of about fifteen with black-rimmed spectacles and very white teeth. He wore a white shirt with tidily rolled-up sleeves, and brown cotton trousers. "Tour commence please," he said. "I am Guide Hafiz."

He led them to the minibus. "You German two?" he enquired, and when they replied that they were English he said that not many English came to Persia. "American," he said. "French. German people often."

They got into the minibus. The driver turned his head to nod and smile at them. He spoke in Persian to Hafiz, and laughed.

"He commence a joke," Hafiz said. "He wish me the best. This is the first tour I make. Excuse me, please." He perused leaflets and guide-books, uneasily licking his lips.

"My name's Iris Smith," she said.

His, he revealed, was Normanton.

□   □

They drove through blue Isfahan, past domes and minarets, and tourist shops in the Avenue Chaharbagh, and blue mosaic on surfaces everywhere, and blue taxi-cabs. Trees and glass had a precious look because of the arid earth. The sky was pale with the promise of heat.

The minibus called at the Park Hotel and at the Intercontinental and the Shah Abbas, where Normanton was staying. It didn't call at the Old Atlantic, which Iris Smith had been told at Teheran Airport was cheap and clean. It collected a French party and a German couple who were having trouble with sunburn, and two wholesome-faced American girls. Hafiz continued to speak, in English, explaining that it was the only foreign language he knew. "Ladies-gentlemen, I am a student from Teheran," he announced with pride, and then confessed: "I do not know Isfahan well."

The leader of the French party, a testy-looking man whom Normanton put down as a university professor, had already protested at their guide's inability to speak French. He protested again when Hafiz said he didn't know Isfahan well, complaining that he had been considerably deceived.

"No, no," Hafiz replied. "That is not my fault, sir, I am poor Persian student, sir. Last night I arrive in Isfahan the first time only. It is impossible my father send me to Isfahan before." He smiled at the testy Frenchman. "So listen please, ladies-gentlemen. This morning we commence happy tour, we see many curious scenes." Again his smile flashed. He read in English from an Iran Air leaflet: *Isfahan is the showpiece of Islamic Persia, but founded at least two thousand years ago!* Here we are, ladies-gentlemen, at the Chehel Sotun. This is pavilion of lyric beauty, palace of forty columns where Shah Abbas II entertain all royal guests. All please leave microbus."

Normanton wandered alone among the forty columns of the palace. The American girls took photographs and the German couple did the same. A member of the French party operated a moving camera, although only tourists and their guides were moving. The girl called Iris Smith seemed out of place, Normanton thought, teetering on her high-heeled sandals.

"So now Masjed-e-Shah," Hafiz cried, clapping his hands to collect his party together. The testy Frenchman continued to expostulate, complaining that time had been wasted in the Chehel Sotun. Hafiz smiled at him.

"*Masjed-e Shah,*" he read from a leaflet as the minibus began again, "*is most outstanding and impressive mosque built by Shah Abbas the Great in early seventeenth century.*"

But when the minibus drew up outside the Masjed-e-Shah it was discovered that the Masjed-e-Shah was closed to tourists because of renovations. So, unfortunately, was the Sheikh Lotfollah.

"So commence to carpet-weaving," Hafiz said, smiling and shaking his head at the protestations of the French professor.

The cameras moved among the carpet-weavers, women of all

ages, producing at speed Isfahan carpets for export. "Look now at once," Hafiz commanded, pointing at a carpet that incorporated the features of the late President Kennedy. "Look please on this skill, ladies-gentlemen."

In the minibus he announced that the tour was now on its way to the Masjed-e-Jamé, the Friday Mosque. This, he reported after a consultation of his leaflets, displayed Persian architecture of the ninth to the eighteenth century. *"Oldest and largest in Isfahan,"* he read. *"Don't miss it! Many minarets in narrow lanes!* All leave microbus, ladies-gentlemen. All return to microbus in one hour."

At this there was chatter from the French party. The tour was scheduled to be conducted, points of interest were scheduled to be indicated. The tour was costing three hundred and seventy-five rials.

"O.K., ladies-gentlemen," Hafiz said. "Ladies-gentlemen come by me to commerce informations. Other ladies-gentlemen come to microbus in one hour."

An hour was a long time in the Friday Mosque. Normanton wandered away from it, through dusty crowded lanes, into market-places where letter-writers slept on their stools, waiting for illiterates with troubles. In hot, bright sunshine peasants with produce to sell bargained with deft-witted shopkeepers. Crouched on the dust, cobblers made shoes: on a wooden chair a man was shaved beneath a tree. Other men drank sherbet, arguing as vigorously as the heat allowed. Veiled women hurried, pausing to prod entrails at butchers' stalls or to finger rice.

"You're off the tourist track, Mr. Normanton."

Her white high-heeled sandals were covered with dust. She looked tired.

"So are you," he said.

"I'm glad I ran into you. I wanted to ask how much that dress was."

She pointed at a limp blue dress hanging on a stall. It was difficult when a woman on her own asked the price of something in this part of the world, she explained. She knew about that from living in Bombay.

He asked the stall-holder how much the dress was, but it turned out to be too expensive, although to Normanton it seemed cheap. The stall-holder followed them along the street offering to reduce the price, saying he had other goods, bags, lengths of cotton, pictures on ivory, all beautiful workmanship, all cheap bargains. Normanton told him to go away.

"Do you live in Bombay?" He wondered if she perhaps was Indian, brought up in London, or half-caste.

"Yes, I live in Bombay. And sometimes in England."

It was the statement of a woman not at all like Iris Smith: it suggested a grandeur, a certain style, beauty, and some riches.

"I've never been in Bombay," he said.

"Life can be good enough there. The social life's not bad."

They had arrived back at the Friday Mosque.

"You've seen all this?" He gestured towards it.

She said she had, but he had the feeling that she hadn't bothered much with the mosque. He couldn't think what had drawn her to Isfahan.

"I love traveling," she said.

The French party were already established again in the minibus, all except the man with the moving camera. They were talking loudly among themselves, complaining about Hafiz and Chaharbagh Tours. The German couple arrived, their sunburn pinker after their excursions. Hafiz arrived with the two American girls. He was laughing, beginning to flirt with them.

"So," he said in the minibus, "we commence the Shaking Minarets. *Two minarets able to shake,*" he read, "*eight kilometres outside the city.* Very famous, ladies-gentlemen, very curious."

The driver started the bus, but the French party shrilly protested, declaring that the man with the moving camera had been left behind. "*Où est-ce qu'il est?*" a woman in red cried.

"I will tell you a Persian joke," Hafiz said to the American girls. "A Persian student commences at a party—"

"*Attention!*" the woman in red cried.

"*Imbécile!*" the professor shouted at Hafiz.

Hafiz smiled at them. He did not understand their trouble, he said, while they continued to shout at him. Slowly he took his spectacles off and wiped a sheen of dust from them. "So a Persian student commences at a party," he began again.

"I think you've left someone behind," Normanton said. "The man with the moving camera."

The driver of the minibus laughed and then Hafiz, realizing his error, laughed also. He sat down on a seat beside the American girls and laughed unrestrainedly, beating his knees with a fist and flashing his very white teeth. The driver reversed the minibus, with his finger on the horn. "Bad man!" Hafiz said to the Frenchman when he climbed into the bus, laughing again. "Heh, heh, heh," he cried, and the driver and the American girls laughed also.

"*Il est fou!*" one of the French party muttered crossly. "*Incroyable!*"

Normanton glanced across the minibus and discovered that Iris Smith, amused by all this foreign emotion, was already glancing at him. He smiled at her and she smiled back.

Hafiz paid two men to climb into the shaking minarets and shake them. The Frenchman took moving pictures of this motion. Hafiz announced that the mausoleum of a hermit was located near by. He pointed at the view from the roof where they stood. He read slowly from one of the leaflets, informing them that the view was fantastic. "At the party," he said to the American girls, "the student watches an aeroplane on the breast of a beautiful girl. 'Why watch you my aeroplane?' the girl commences. 'Is it you like my aeroplane?' 'It is not the aeroplane which I like,' the student commences. 'It is the aeroplane's airport which I like.' That is a Persian joke."

It was excessively hot on the roof with the shaking minarets. Normanton had put on his linen hat. Iris Smith tied a black chiffon scarf around her head.

"We commence to offices," Hafiz said. "This afternoon we visit Vank Church. Also curious Fire Temple." He consulted his leaflets. "An Armenian Museum. *Here you can see a nice collection of old manuscripts and paintings.*"

When the minibus drew up outside the offices of Chaharbagh Tours Hafiz said it was important for everyone to come inside.

He led the way, through the downstairs office and up to the upstairs office. Tea was served. Hafiz handed round a basket of sweets, wrapped pieces of candy locally manufactured, very curious taste, he said. Several men in lightweight suits, the principals of Chaharbagh Tours, drank tea also. When the French professor complained that the tour was not satisfactory, the men smiled, denying that they understood either French or English and in no way betraying that they could recognize any difference when the professor changed from one language to the other. It was likely, Normanton guessed, that they were fluent in both.

"Shall you continue after lunch?" he asked Iris Smith. "The Vank Church, an Armenian museum? There's also the Theological School, which really is the most beautiful of all. No tour is complete without that."

"You've been on the tour before?"

"I've walked about. I've got to know Isfahan."

"Then why—"

"It's something to do. Tours are always rewarding. For a start, there are the other people on them."

"I shall rest this afternoon."

"The Theological School is easy to find. It's not far from the Shah Abbas Hotel."

"Are you staying there?"

"Yes."

She was curious about him. He could see it in her eyes, for she'd taken off her dark glasses. Yet he couldn't believe that he presented as puzzling an exterior as she did herself.

"I've heard it's beautiful," she said. "The hotel."

"Yes, it is."

"I think everything in Isfahan is beautiful."

"Are you staying here for long?"

"Until tomorrow morning, the five o'clock bus back to Teheran. I came last night."

"From London?"

"Yes."

The tea-party came to an end. The men in the lightweight suits bowed. Hafiz told the American girls that he was looking forward to seeing them in the afternoon, at two o'clock. In the evening, if they were doing nothing else, they might meet again. He smiled at everyone else. They would continue to have a happy tour, he promised, at two o'clock. He would be honoured to give them the informations they desired.

Normanton said goodbye to Iris Smith. He wouldn't, he said, be on the afternoon tour either. The people of a morning tour, he did not add, were never amusing in the afternoon: it wouldn't be funny if the Frenchman with the moving camera got left behind again, the professor's testiness and Hafiz's pidgin English might easily become wearisome as the day wore on.

He advised her again not to miss the Theological School. There was a tourist bazaar beside it, with boutiques, where she might find a dress. But prices would be higher there. She shook her head: she liked collecting bargains.

He walked to the Shah Abbas. He forgot about Iris Smith.

□   □

She took a mild sleeping pill and slept on her bed in the Old Atlantic. When she awoke it was a quarter to seven.

The room was almost dark because she'd pulled over the curtains. She'd taken off her pink dress and hung it up. She lay in her petticoat, staring sleepily at a ceiling she couldn't see. For a few moments before she'd slept her eyes had traversed its network of cracks and flaking paint. There'd been enough light then, even though the curtains had been drawn.

She slipped from the bed and crossed to the window. It was twilight outside, a light that seemed more than ordinarily different from the bright sunshine of the afternoon. Last night, at midnight when she'd arrived, it had been sharply different too: as black as pitch, totally silent in Isfahan.

It wasn't silent now. The blue taxis raced their motors as they paused in a traffic-jam outside the Old Atlantic. Tourists chattered in different languages. Bunches of children, returning from afternoon school, called out to one another on the pavements. Policemen blew their traffic whistles.

Neon lights were winking in the twilight, and in the far distance she could see the massive illuminated dome of the Theological School, a fat blue jewel that dominated everything.

She washed herself and dressed, opening a suitcase to find a black and white dress her mother had made her and a black frilled shawl that went with it. She rubbed the dust from her high-heeled sandals with a Kleenex tissue. It would be nicer to wear a different pair of shoes, more suitable for the evening, but that would mean more unpacking and anyway who was there to notice? She took some medicine because for months she'd had a nagging little cough, which usually came on in the evenings. It was always the same: whenever she returned to England she got a cough.

□   □

In his room he read that the Shah was in Moscow, negotiating a deal with the Russians. He closed his eyes, letting the newspaper fall on to the carpet.

At seven o'clock he would go downstairs and sit in the bar and watch the tourist parties. They knew him in the bar now. As soon as he entered one of the barmen would raise a finger and nod. A moment later he would receive his vodka lime, with crushed ice. "You have good day, sir?" the barman would say to him, whichever barman it was.

Since the Chaharbagh tour of the morning he had eaten a chicken sandwich and walked, he estimated, ten miles. Exhausted, he had had a bath, delighting in the flow of warm water over his body, becoming drowsy until the water cooled and began to chill him. He'd stretched himself on his bed and then had slowly dressed, in a different linen suit.

His room in the Shah Abbas Hotel was enormous, with a balcony and blown-up photographs of domes and minarets, and a double bed as big as a nightclub dance-floor. Ever since he'd first seen it he'd kept thinking that his bed was as big as a dance-floor. The room itself was large enough for a quite substantial family to live in.

He went downstairs at seven o'clock, using the staircase because he hated lifts and because, in any case, it was pleasant to walk through the luxurious hotel. In the hall a group of forty or so Swiss had arrived. He stood by a pillar for a moment, watching them. Their leader made arrangements at the desk, porters carried their luggage from the airport bus. Their faces looked happier when the luggage was identified. Swiss archaeologists, Normanton conjectured, a group tour of some Geneva society. And then, instead of going straight to the bar, he walked out of the hotel into the dusk.

□   □

They met in the tourist bazaar. She had bought a brooch, a square of coloured cotton, a canvas carrier bag. When he saw her, he knew at once that he'd gone to the tourist bazaar because she might be there. They walked together, comparing the prices of ivory miniatures, the traditional polo-playing scene, variously interpreted. It was curiosity, nothing else, that made him want to renew their acquaintanceship.

"The Theological School is closed," she said.

"You can get in."

He led her from the bazaar and rang a bell outside the school. He gave the porter a few rials. He said they wouldn't be long.

She marvelled at the peace, the silence of the open courtyards, the blue mosaic walls, the blue water, men silently praying. She called it a grotto of heaven. She heard a sound which she said was a nightingale, and he said it might have been, although Shiraz was where the nightingales were. "Wine and roses and nightingales," he said because he knew it would please her. Shiraz was beautiful, too, but not as beautiful as Isfahan. The grass in the courtyards of the Theological School was not like ordinary grass, she said. Even the paving stones and the water gained a dimension in all the blueness. Blue was the colour of holiness: you could feel the holiness here.

"It's nicer than the Taj Mahal. It's pure enchantment."

"Would you like a drink, Miss Smith? I could show you the enchantments of the Shah Abbas Hotel."

"I'd love a drink."

She wasn't wearing her dark glasses. The nasal twang of her voice continued to grate on him whenever she spoke, but her eyes seemed even more sumptuous than they'd been in the bright light of day. It was a shame he couldn't say to her that her eyes were just as beautiful as the architecture of the Theological School, but such a remark would naturally be misunderstood.

"What would you like?" he asked in the bar of the hotel. All around them the Swiss party spoke in French. A group of Texan oilmen and their wives, who had been in the bar the night before, were there again, occupying the same corner. The sunburnt German couple of the Chaharbagh tour were there, with other Germans they'd made friends with.

"I'd like some whisky," she said. "With soda. It's very kind of you."

When their drinks came he suggested that he should bring her on a conducted tour of the hotel. They could drink their way around it, he said. "I shall be Guide Hafiz."

He enjoyed showing her because all the time she made marvelling noises, catching her breath in marble corridors and fingering the endless mosaic of the walls, sinking her high-heeled sandals into the pile of carpets. Everything made it enchantment, she said: the gleam of gold and mirror-glass among the blues and reds of the mosaic, the beautifully finished furniture, the staircase, the chandeliers.

"This is my room," he said, turning the key in the lock of a polished mahogany door.

"Gosh!"

"Sit down, Miss Smith."

They sat and sipped at their drinks. They talked about the room. She walked out on to the balcony and then came and sat down again. It had become quite cold, she remarked, shivering a little. She coughed.

"You've a cold."

"England always gives me a cold."

They sat in two dark, tweed-covered armchairs with a glass-topped table between them. A maid had been to turn down the bed. His green pyjamas lay ready for him on the pillow.

They talked about the people on the tour, Hafiz and the testy professor, and the Frenchman with the moving camera. She had seen Hafiz and the American girls in the tourist bazaar, in the teashop. The minibus had broken down that afternoon: he'd seen it outside the Armenian Museum, the driver and Hafiz examining its plugs.

"My mother would love that place," she said.

"The Theological School?"

"My mother would feel its spirit. And its holiness."

"Your mother is in England?"

"In Bournemouth."

"And you yourself—"

"I have been on holiday with her. I came for six weeks and stayed a year. My husband is in Bombay."

He glanced at her left hand, thinking he'd made a mistake.

"I haven't been wearing my wedding ring. I shall again, in Bombay."

"Would you like to have dinner?"

She hesitated. She began to shake her head, then changed her mind. "Are you sure?" she said. "Here, in the hotel?"

"The food is the least impressive part."

He'd asked her because, quite suddenly, he didn't like being in this enormous bedroom with her. It was pleasant showing her around, but he didn't want misunderstandings.

"Let's go downstairs," he said.

In the bar they had another drink. The Swiss party had gone, so had the Germans. The Texans were noisier than they had been. "Again, please," he requested the barman, tapping their two glasses.

In Bournemouth she had worked as a shorthand typist for the year. In the past she had been a shorthand typist when she and her mother lived in London, before her marriage. "My married name is Mrs. Azann," she said.

"When I saw you first I thought you had an Indian look."

"Perhaps you get that when you marry an Indian."

"And you're entirely English?"

"I've always felt drawn to the East. It's a spiritual affinity."

129

Her conversation was like the conversation in a novelette. There was that and her voice, and her unsuitable shoes, and her cough, and not wearing enough for the chilly evening air: all of it went together, only her eyes remained different. And the more she talked about herself, the more her eyes appeared to belong to another person.

"I admire my husband very much," she said. "He's very fine. He's most intelligent. He's twenty-two years older than I am."

She told the story then, while they were still in the bar. She had, although she did not say it, married for money. And though she clearly spoke the truth when she said she admired her husband, the marriage was not entirely happy. She could not, for one thing, have children, which neither of them had known at the time of the wedding and which displeased her husband when it was established as a fact. She had been displeased herself to discover that her husband was not as rich as he had appeared to be. He owned a furniture business, he'd said in the Regent Palace Hotel, where they'd met by chance when she was waiting for someone else: this was true, but he had omitted to add that the furniture business was doing badly. She had also been displeased to discover on the first night of her marriage that she disliked being touched by him. And there was yet another problem: in their bungalow in Bombay there lived, as well as her husband and herself, his mother and an aunt, his brother and his business manager. For a girl not used to such communal life, it was difficult in the bungalow in Bombay.

"It sounds more than difficult."

"Sometimes."

"He married you because you have an Indian look, while being the opposite of Indian in other ways. Your pale English skin. Your—your English voice."

"In Bombay I give elocution lessons."

He blinked, and then smiled to cover the rudeness that might have shown in his face.

"To Indian women," she said, "who come to the Club. My husband and I belong to a club. It's the best part of Bombay life, the social side."

"It's strange to think of you in Bombay."

"I thought I mightn't return. I thought I'd maybe stay on with my mother. But there's nothing much in England now."

"I'm fond of England."

"I thought you might be." She coughed again, and took her medicine from her handbag and poured a little into her whisky. She drank a mouthful of the mixture, and then apologized, saying she wasn't being very ladylike. Such behaviour would be frowned upon in the Club.

"You should wear a cardigan with that cough." He gestured at the barman and ordered further drinks.

"I'll be drunk," she said, giggling.

He felt he'd been right to be curious. Her story was strange. He imagined the Indian women of the Club speaking English with her nasal intonation, twisting their lips to form the distorted sounds, dropping "h's" because it was the thing to do. He imagined her in the bungalow, with her elderly husband who wasn't rich, and his relations and his business manager. It was a sour little fairy-story, a tale of Cinderella and a prince who wasn't a prince, and the carriage turned into an ice-cold pumpkin. Uneasiness overtook his curiosity, and he wondered again why she had come to Isfahan.

"Let's have dinner now," he suggested in a slightly hasty voice.

But Mrs. Azann, looking at him with her sumptuous eyes, said she couldn't eat a thing.

□　　□

He would be married, she speculated. There was pain in the lines of his face, even though he smiled a lot and seemed lighthearted. She wondered if he'd once had a serious illness. When he'd brought her into his bedroom she wondered as they sat there if he was going to make a pass at her. But she knew a bit about people making passes, and he didn't seem the type. He was too attractive to have to make a pass. His manners were too elegant; he was too nice.

"I'll watch you having dinner," she said. "I don't mind in the least watching you if you're hungry. I couldn't deprive you of your dinner."

"Well, I am rather hungry."

His mouth curved when he said things like that, because of his smile. She wondered if he could be an architect. From the moment she'd had the idea of coming to Isfahan she'd known that it wasn't just an idea. She believed in destiny and always had.

They went to the restaurant, which was huge and luxurious, like everywhere else in the hotel, dimly lit, with oil lamps on each table. She liked the way he explained to the waiters that she didn't wish to eat anything. For himself, he ordered a chicken kebab and salad.

"You'd like some wine?" he suggested, smiling in the same way. "Persian wine's very pleasant."

"I'd love a glass."

He ordered the wine. She said:

"Do you always travel alone?"

"Yes."

"But you're married?"

"Yes, I am."

"And your wife's a home bird?"

"It's a *modus vivendi*."

She imagined him in a house in a village, near Midhurst possibly, or Sevenoaks. She imagined his wife, a capable woman, good in the garden and on committees. She saw his wife quite clearly, a little on the heavy side but nice, cutting sweet-peas.

"You've told me nothing about yourself," she said.

"There's very little to tell. I'm afraid I haven't a story like yours."

"Why are you in Isfahan?"

"On holiday."

"Is it always on your own?"

"I like being on my own. I like hotels. I like looking at people and walking about."

"You're like me. You like travel."

"Yes, I do."

"I imagine you in a village house, in the Home Counties somewhere."

"That's clever of you."

"I can clearly see your wife." She described the woman she could clearly see, without mentioning about her being on the heavy side. He nodded. She had second sight, he said with his smile.

"People have said I'm a little psychic. I'm glad I met you."

"It's been a pleasure meeting you. Stories like yours are rare enough."

"It's all true. Every word."

"Oh, I know it is."

"Are you an architect?"

"You're quite remarkable," he said.

□   □

He finished his meal and between them they finished the wine. They had coffee and then she asked if he would kindly order more. The Swiss party had left the restaurant, and so had the German couple and their friends. Other diners had been and gone. The Texans were leaving just as Mrs. Azann suggested more coffee. No other table was occupied.

"Of course," he said.

He wished she'd go now. They had killed an evening together. Not for a long time would he forget either her ugly voice or her beautiful eyes. Nor would he easily forget the fairy-story that had gone sour on her. But that was that: the evening was over now.

The waiter brought their coffee, seeming greatly fatigued by the chore.

"D'you think," she said, "we should have another drink? D'you think they have cigarettes here?"

He had brandy and she more whisky. The waiter brought her American cigarettes.

"I don't really want to go back to Bombay," she said.

"I'm sorry about that."

"I'd like to stay in Isfahan for ever."

"You'd be very bored. There's no club. No social life of any kind for an English person, I should think."

"I do like a little social life." She smiled at him, broadening her sensuous mouth. "My father was a counter-hand," she said. "In a co-op. You wouldn't think it, would you?"

"Not at all," he lied.

"It's my little secret. If I told the women in the Club that, or my husband's mother or his aunt, they'd have a fit. I've never even told my husband. Only my mother and I share that secret."

"I see."

"And now you."

"Secrets are safe with strangers."

"Why do you think I told you that secret?"

"Because we are ships that pass in the night."

"Because you are sympathetic."

The waiter hovered close and then approached them boldly. The bar was open for as long as they wished it to be. There were lots of other drinks in the bar. Cleverly, he removed the coffee-pot and their cups.

"He's like a magician," she said. "Everything in Isfahan is magical."

"You're glad you came?"

"It's where I met you."

He rose. He had to stand for a moment because she continued to sit there, her handbag on the table, her black frilled shawl on top of it. She hadn't finished her whisky but he expected that she'd lift the glass to her lips and drink what she wanted of it, or just leave it there. She rose and walked with him from the restaurant, taking her glass with her. Her other hand slipped beneath his arm.

"There's a discotheque downstairs," she said.

"Oh, I'm afraid that's not really me."

"Nor me, neither. Let's go back to our bar."

She handed him her glass, saying she had to pay a visit. She'd love another whisky and soda, she said, even though she hadn't quite finished the one in her glass. Without ice, she said.

The bar was empty except for a single barman. Normanton ordered more brandy for himself and whisky for Mrs. Azann. He much preferred her as Iris Smith, in her tatty pink dress and the dark glasses that hid her eyes: she could have been any little typist except that she'd married Mr. Azann and had a story to tell.

"It's nice in spite of things," she explained as she sat down. "It's nice in spite of him wanting to you-know-what, and the women in the bungalow, and his brother and the business manager. They all disapprove because I'm English, especially his mother and his aunt. He doesn't disapprove because he's mad about me. The business manager doesn't much mind, I suppose. The dogs don't mind. D'you understand? In spite of everything, it's nice to have someone mad about you. And the Club, the social life. Even though we're short of the ready, it's better than England for a woman. There's servants, for a start."

The whisky was affecting the way she put things. An hour ago she wouldn't have said "wanting to you-know-what" or "short of the ready." It was odd that she had an awareness in this direction and yet could not hear the twang in her voice which instantly gave her away.

"But you don't love your husband."

"I respect him. It's only that I hate having to you-know-what with him. I really do hate that. I've never actually loved him."

He regretted saying she didn't love her husband: the remark had slipped out, and it was regrettable because it involved him in the conversation in a way he didn't wish to be.

"Maybe things will work out better when you get back."

"I know what I'm going back to." She paused, searching for his eyes with hers. "I'll never till I die forget Isfahan."

"It's very beautiful."

"I'll never forget the Chaharbagh Tours, or Hafiz. I'll never forget that place you brought me to. Or the Shah Abbas Hotel."

"I think it's time I saw you back to your own hotel."

"I could sit in this bar for ever."

"I'm afraid I'm not at all one for night-life."

"I shall visualize you when I'm back in Bombay. I shall think of you in your village, with your wife, happy in England. I shall

135

think of you working at your architectural plans. I shall often wonder about you travelling alone because your wife doesn't care for it. Your *modus*."

"I hope it's better in Bombay. Sometimes things are, when you least expect them to be."

"It's been like a tonic. You've made me very happy."

"It's kind of you to say that."

"There's much that's unsaid between us. Will you remember me?"

"Oh yes, of course."

Reluctantly, she drank the dregs of her whisky. She took her medicine from her handbag and poured a little into the glass and drank that, too. It helped the tickle in her throat, she said. She always had a tickle when the wretched cough came.

"Shall we walk back?"

They left the bar. She clung to him again, walking very slowly between the mosaiced columns. All the way back to the Old Atlantic Hotel she talked about the evening they had spent and how delightful it had been. Not for the world would she have missed Isfahan, she repeated several times.

When they said goodbye she kissed his cheek. Her beautiful eyes swallowed him up, and for a moment he had a feeling that her eyes were the real thing about her, reflecting her as she should be.

□   □

He woke at half-past two and could not sleep. Dawn was already beginning to break. He lay there, watching the light increase in the gap he'd left between the curtains so that there'd be fresh air in the room. Another day had passed: he went through it piece by piece, from his early-morning walk to the moment when he'd put his green pyjamas on and got into bed. It was a regular night-time exercise with him. He closed his eyes, remembering in detail.

He turned again into the offices of Chaharbagh Tours and was told by Hafiz to go to the upstairs office. He saw her sitting there writing to her mother, and heard her voice asking him if he was going on the tour. He saw again the sunburnt faces of the German couple and the wholesome faces of the American girls and faces in the French party. He went again on his afternoon walk, and after that there was his bath. She came towards him in the bazaar, with her dark glasses and her small purchases. There was her story as she had told it.

For his part, he had told her nothing. He had agreed with her novelette picture of him, living in a Home Counties village, a well-to-do architect married to a wife who gardened. Architects had become as romantic as doctors, there'd been no reason to disillusion her. She would for ever imagine him travelling to exotic places, on his own because he enjoyed it, because his wife was a home bird.

Why could he not have told her? Why could he not have exchanged one story for another? She had made a mess of things and did not seek to hide it. Life had let her down, she'd let herself down. Ridiculously, she gave elocution lessons to Indian women and did not see it as ridiculous. She had told him her secret, and he knew it was true that he shared it only with her mother and herself.

The hours went by. He should be lying with her in this bed, the size of a dance-floor. In the dawn he should be staring into her sumptuous eyes, in love with the mystery there. He should be telling her and asking for her sympathy, as she had asked for his. He should be telling her that he had walked into a room, not in a Home Counties village, but in harsh, ugly Hampstead, to find his second wife, as once he had found his first, in his bed with another man. He should in humility have asked her why it was that he was naturally a cuckold, why two women of different temperaments and characters had been inspired to have lovers at his expense. He should be telling her, with the warmth of her body warming his, that his second wife had confessed to greater sexual pleasure when she remembered that she was deceiving him.

It was a story no better than hers, certainly as unpleasant. Yet he hadn't had the courage to tell it because it cast him in a certain light. He travelled easily, moving over surfaces and revealing only surfaces himself. He was acceptable as a stranger: in two

137

marriages he had not been forgiven for turning out to be different from what he seemed. To be a cuckold once was the luck of
the game, but his double cuckoldry had a whiff of revenge about
it. In all humility he might have asked her about that.

At half-past four he stood by the window, looking out at the
empty street below. She would be on her way to the bus station,
to catch the five o'clock bus to Teheran. He could dress, he could
even shave and still be there in time. He could pay, on her behalf,
the extra air fare that would accrue. He could tell her his story
and they could spend a few days. They could go together to Shi-
raz, city of wine and roses and nightingales.

He stood by the window, watching nothing happening in the
street, knowing that if he stood there for ever he wouldn't find
the courage. She had met a sympathetic man, more marvellous to
her than all the marvels of Isfahan. She would carry that memory
to the bungalow in Bombay, knowing nothing about a pettiness
which brought out cruelty in people. And he would remember a
woman who possessed, deep beneath her unprepossessing surface,
the distinction that her eyes mysteriously claimed for her. In different circumstances, with a less unfortunate story to tell, it
would have emerged. But in the early morning there was another
truth, too. He was the stuff of fantasy. She had quality, he had
none.

JAMES SALTER

American Express

I t's hard now to think of all the places and
nights, Nicola's like a railway car, deep and
gleaming, the crowd at the *Un, Deux, Trois,*
Billy's. Unknown brilliant faces jammed at the
bar. The dark, dramatic eye that blazes for a moment and disappears.

In those days they were living in apartments
with funny furniture and on Sundays sleeping until noon. They were in the last rank of the armies
of law. Clever junior partners were above them,
partners, associates, men in fine suits who had
lunch at the Four Seasons. Frank's father went
there three or four times a week, or else to the
Century Club or the Union where there were men
even older than he. Half of the members can't uri-
nate, he used to say, and the other half can't stop.

Alan, on the other hand, was from Cleveland
where his father was well known, if not detested.
No defendant was too guilty, no case too clear-cut.
Once in another part of the state he was defend-

ing a murderer, a black man. He knew what the jury was thinking, he knew what he looked like to them. He stood up slowly.
It could be they had heard certain things, he began. They may
have heard, for instance, that he was a big-time lawyer from the
city. They may have heard that he wore three-hundred-dollar
suits, that he drove a Cadillac and smoked expensive cigars. He
was walking along as if looking for something on the floor. They
may have heard that he was Jewish.

He stopped and looked up. Well, he was from the city, he
said. He wore three-hundred-dollar suits, he drove a Cadillac,
smoked big cigars, and he was Jewish. "Now that we have that
settled, let's talk about this case."

Lawyers and sons of lawyers. Days of youth. In the morning
in stale darkness the subways shrieked.

"Have you noticed the new girl at the reception desk?"

"What about her?" Frank asked.

They were surrounded by noise like the launch of a rocket.
"She's hot," Alan confided.

"How do you know?"

"I know."

"What do you mean, you know?"

"Intuition."

"Int*ui*tion?" Frank said.

"What's wrong?"

"That doesn't count."

Which was what made them inseparable, the hours of work,
the lyric, the dreams. As it happened, they never knew the girl
at the reception desk with her nearsightedness and wild, full hair.
They knew various others, they knew Julie, they knew Catherine,
they knew Ames. The best, for nearly two years, was Brenda who
had somehow managed to graduate from Marymount and had a
walk-through apartment on West Fourth. In a smooth, thin, silver frame was the photograph of her father with his two daugh-
ters at the Plaza, Brenda, thirteen, with an odd little smile.

"I wish I'd known you then," Frank told her.

Brenda said, "I bet you do."

It was her voice he liked, the city voice, scornful and warm.

They were two of a kind, she liked to say, and in a way it was true. They drank in her favorite places where the owner played the piano and everyone seemed to know her. Still, she counted on him. The city has its incomparable moments—rolling along the wall of the apartment, kissing, bumping like stones. Five in the afternoon, the vanishing light. "No," she was commanding. "No, no, no."

He was kissing her throat. "What are you going to do with that beautiful struma of yours?"

"You won't take me to dinner," she said.

"Sure I will."

"Beautiful what?"

She was like a huge dog, leaping from his arms.

"Come here," he coaxed.

She went into the bathroom and began combing her hair. "Which restaurant are we going to?" she called.

She would give herself but it was mostly unpredictable. She would do anything her mother hadn't done and would live as her mother lived, in the same kind of apartment, in the same soft chairs. Christmas and the envelopes for the doormen, the snow sweeping past the awning, her children coming home from school. She adored her father. She went on a trip to Hawaii with him and sent back postcards, two or three scorching lines in a large, scrawled hand.

It was summer.

"Anybody here?" Frank called.

He rapped on the door which was ajar. He was carrying his jacket, it was hot.

"All right," he said in a loud voice, "come out with your hands over your head. Alan, cover the back."

The party, it seemed, was over. He pushed the door open. There was one lamp on, the room was dark.

"Hey, Bren, are we too late?" he called. She appeared mysteriously in the doorway, barelegged but in heels. "We'd have come earlier but we were working. We couldn't get out of the office. Where is everybody? Where's all the food? Hey, Alan, we're late. There's no food, nothing."

She was leaning against the doorway.

"We tried to get down here," Alan said. "We couldn't get a cab."

Frank had fallen onto the couch. "Bren, don't be mad," he said. "We were working, that's the truth. I should have called. Can you put some music on or something? Is there anything to drink?"

"There's about that much vodka," she finally said.

"Any ice?"

"About two cubes." She pushed off the wall without much enthusiasm. He watched her walk into the kitchen and heard the refrigerator door open.

"So, what do you think, Alan?" he said. "What are you going to do?"

"Me?"

"Where's Louise?" Frank called.

"Asleep," Brenda said.

"Did she really go home?"

"She goes to work in the morning."

"So does Alan."

Brenda came out of the kitchen with the drinks.

"I'm sorry we're late," he said. He was looking in the glass. "Was it a good party?" He stirred the contents with one finger. "This is the ice?"

"Jane Harrah got fired," Brenda said.

"That's too bad. Who is she?"

"She does big campaigns. Ross wants me to take her place."

"Great."

"I'm not sure if I want to," she said lazily.

"Why not?"

"She was sleeping with him."

"And she got fired?"

"Doesn't say much for him, does it?"

"It doesn't say much for her."

"That's just like a man. God."

"What does she look like? Does she look like Louise?"

The smile of the thirteen-year-old came across Brenda's face.

"No one looks like Louise," she said. Her voice squeezed the name whose legs Alan dreamed of. "Jane has these thin lips."

"Is that all?"

"Thin-lipped women are always cold."

"Let me see yours," he said.

"Burn up."

"Yours aren't thin. Alan, these aren't thin, are they? Hey, Brenda, don't cover them up."

"Where were you? You weren't really working."

He'd pulled down her hand. "Come on, let them be natural," he said. "They're not thin, they're nice. I just never noticed them before." He leaned back. "Alan, how're you doing? You getting sleepy?"

"I was thinking. How much the city has changed," Alan said.

"In five years?"

"I've been here almost six years."

"Sure, it's changing. They're coming down, we're going up."

Alan was thinking of the vanished Louise who had left him only a jolting ride home through the endless streets. "I know."

That year they sat in the steam room on limp towels, breathing the eucalyptus and talking about Hardmann Roe. They walked to the showers like champions. Their flesh still had firmness. Their haunches were solid and young.

Hardmann Roe was a small drug company in Connecticut that had strayed slightly outside of its field and found itself suing a large manufacturer for infringement of an obscure patent. The case was highly technical with little chance of success. The opposing lawyers had thrown up a barricade of motions and delays and the case had made its way downwards, to Frik and Frak whose offices were near the copying machines, who had time for such things, and who pondered it amid the hiss of steam. No one else wanted it and this also made it appealing.

So they worked. They were students again, sitting around in polo shirts with their feet on the desk, throwing off hopeless ideas, crumpling wads of paper, staying late in the library and having the words blur in books.

They stayed on through vacations and weekends sometimes

sleeping in the office and making coffee long before anyone came to work. After a late dinner they were still talking about it, its complexities, where elements somehow fit in, the sequence of letters, articles in journals, meetings, the limits of meaning. Brenda met a handsome Dutchman who worked for a bank. Alan met Hopie. Still there was this infinite forest, the trunks and vines blocking out the light, the roots of distant things joined. With every month that passed they were deeper into it, less certain of where they had been or if it could end. They had become like the old partners whose existence had been slowly sealed off, fewer calls, fewer consultations, lives that had become lunch. It was known they were swallowed up by the case with knowledge of little else. The opposite was true—no one else understood its details. Three years had passed. The length of time alone made it important. The reputation of the firm, at least in irony, was riding on them.

Two months before the case was to come to trial they quit Weyland, Braun. Frank sat down at the polished table for Sunday lunch. His father was one of the best men in the city. There is a kind of lawyer you trust and who becomes your friend. "What happened?" he wanted to know.

"We're starting our own firm," Frank said.

"What about the case you've been working on? You can't leave them with a litigation you've spent years preparing."

"We're not. We're taking it with us," Frank said.

There was a moment of dreadful silence.

"Taking it with you? You can't. You went to one of the best schools, Frank. They'll sue you. You'll ruin yourself."

"We thought of that."

"Listen to me," his father said.

Everyone said that, his mother, his Uncle Cook, friends. It was worse than ruin, it was dishonor. His father said that.

Hardmann Roe never went to trial, as it turned out. Six weeks later there was a settlement. It was for thirty-eight million, a third of it their fee.

□　　　□

His father had been wrong, which was something you could not hope for. They weren't sued either. That was settled, too. In place of ruin there were new offices overlooking Bryant Park which from above seemed like a garden behind a dark château, young clients, opera tickets, dinners in apartments with divorced hostesses, surrendered apartments with books and big, tiled kitchens.

The city was divided, as he had said, into those going up and those coming down, those in crowded restaurants and those on the street, those who waited and those who did not, those with three locks on the door and those rising in an elevator from a lobby with silver mirrors and walnut paneling.

And those like Mrs. Christie who was in the intermediate state though looking assured. She wanted to renegotiate the settlement with her ex-husband. Frank had leafed through the papers. "What do you think?" she asked candidly.

"I think it would be easier for you to get married again."

She was in her fur coat, the dark lining displayed. She gave a little puff of disbelief. "It's not that easy," she said.

He didn't know what it was like, she told him. Not long ago she'd been introduced to someone by a couple she knew very well. "We'll go to dinner," they said, "you'll love him, you're perfect for him, he likes to talk about books."

They arrived at the apartment and the two women immediately went into the kitchen and began cooking. What did she think of him? She'd only had a glimpse, she said, but she liked him very much, his beautiful bald head, his dressing gown. She had begun to plan what she would do with the apartment which had too much blue in it. The man—Warren was his name—was silent all evening. He'd lost his job, her friend explained in the kitchen. Money was no problem, but he was depressed. "He's had a shock," she said. "He likes you." And in fact he'd asked if he could see her again.

"Why don't you come for tea, tomorrow?" he said.

"I could do that," she said. "Of course. I'll be in the neighborhood," she added.

The next day she arrived at four with a bag filled with books, at least a hundred dollars worth which she'd bought as a present. He was in pajamas. There was no tea. He hardly seemed to know who she was or why she was there. She said she remembered she had to meet someone and left the books. Going down in the elevator she felt suddenly sick to her stomach.

"Well," said Frank, "there might be a chance of getting the settlement overturned, Mrs. Christie, but it would mean a lot of expense."

"I see." Her voice was smaller. "Couldn't you do it as one of those things where you got a percentage?"

"Not on this kind of case," he said.

It was dusk. He offered her a drink. She worked her lips, in contemplation, one against the other. "Well, then, what can I do?"

Her life had been made up of disappointments, she told him, looking into her glass, most of them the result of foolishly falling in love. Going out with an older man just because he was wearing a white suit in Nashville which was where she was from. Agreeing to marry George Christie while they were sailing off the coast of Maine. "I don't know where to get the money," she said, "or how."

She glanced up. She found him looking at her, without haste. The lights were coming on in buildings surrounding the park, in the streets, on homeward bound cars. They talked as evening fell. They went out to dinner.

At Christmas that year Alan and his wife broke up. "You're kidding," Frank said. He'd moved into a new place with thick towels and fine carpets. In the foyer was a Biedermeier desk, black, tan, and gold. Across the street was a private school.

Alan was staring out the window which was as cold as the side of a ship. "I don't know what to do," he said in despair. "I don't want to get divorced. I don't want to lose my daughter." Her name was Camille. She was two.

"I know how you feel," Frank said.

"If you had a kid, you'd know."

"Have you seen this?" Frank asked. He held up the alumni magazine. It was the fifteenth anniversary of their graduation. "Know any of these guys?"

Five members of the class had been cited for achievement. Alan recognized two or three of them. "Cummings," he said, "he was a zero—elected to Congress. Oh, God, I don't know what to do."

"Just don't let her take the apartment," Frank said.

Of course, it wasn't that easy. It was easy when it was someone else. Nan Christie had decided to get married. She brought it up one evening.

"I just don't think so," he finally said.

"You love me, don't you?"

"This isn't a good time to ask."

They lay silently. She was staring at something across the room. She was making him feel uncomfortable. "It wouldn't work. It's the attraction of opposites," he said.

"We're not opposites."

"I don't mean just you and me. Women fall in love when they get to know you. Men are just the opposite. When they finally know you they're ready to leave."

She got up without saying anything and began gathering her clothes. He watched her dress in silence. There was nothing interesting about it. The funny thing was that he had meant to go on with her.

"I'll get you a cab," he said.

"I used to think that you were intelligent," she said, half to herself. Exhausted, he was searching for a number. "I don't want a cab. I'm going to walk."

"Across the park?"

"Yes." She had an instant glimpse of herself in the next day's paper. She paused at the door for a moment. "Good-bye," she said coolly.

She wrote him a letter which he read several times. *Of all the loves I have known, none has touched me so. Of all the men, no one has given me more.* He showed it to Alan who did not comment.

"Let's go out and have a drink," Frank said.

They walked up Lexington. Frank looked carefree, the scarf around his neck, the open topcoat, the thinning hair. "Well, you know . . ." he managed to say.

147

They went into a place called Jack's. Light was gleaming from the dark wood and the lines of glasses on narrow shelves. The young bartender stood with his hands on the edge of the bar. "How are you this evening?" he said with a smile. "Nice to see you again."

"Do you know me?" Frank asked.

"You look familiar," the bartender smiled.

"Do I? What's the name of this place, anyway? Remind me not to come in here again."

There were several other people at the bar. The nearest of them carefully looked away. After a while the manager came over. He had emerged from the brown-curtained back. "Anything wrong, sir?" he asked politely.

Frank looked at him. "No," he said, "everything's fine."

"We've had a big day," Alan explained. "We're just unwinding."

"We have a dining room upstairs," the manager said. Behind him was an iron staircase winding past framed drawings of dogs—borzois they looked like. "We serve from six to eleven every night."

"I bet you do," Frank said. "Look, your bartender doesn't know me."

"He made a mistake," the manager said.

"He doesn't know me and he never will."

"It's nothing, it's nothing," Alan said, waving his hands.

They sat at a table by the window. "I can't stand these out-of-work actors who think they're everybody's friend," Frank commented.

At dinner they talked about Nan Christie. Alan thought of her silk dresses, her devotion. The trouble, he said after a while, was that he never seemed to meet that kind of woman, the ones who sometimes walked by outside Jack's. The women he met were too human, he complained. Ever since his separation he'd been trying to find the right one.

"You shouldn't have any trouble," Frank said. "They're all looking for someone like you."

"They're looking for you."

148

"They think they are."

Frank paid the check without looking at it. "Once you've been married," Alan was explaining, "you want to be married again."

"I don't trust anyone enough to marry them," Frank said.

"What do you want then?"

"This is all right," Frank said.

Something was missing in him and women had always done anything to find out what it was. They always would. Perhaps it was simpler, Alan thought. Perhaps nothing was missing.

□   □

The car, which was a big Renault, a tourer, slowed down and pulled off the *autostrada* with Brenda asleep in back, her mouth a bit open and the daylight gleaming off her cheekbones. It was near Como, they had just crossed, the border police had glanced in at her.

"Come on, Bren, wake up," they said, "we're stopping for coffee."

She came back from the ladies' room with her hair combed and fresh lipstick on. The boy in the white jacket behind the counter was rinsing spoons.

"Hey, Brenda, I forget. Is it *espresso* or *expresso*?" Frank asked her.

"*Espresso*," she said.

"How do you know?"

"I'm from New York," she said.

"That's right," he remembered. "The Italians don't have an *x*, do they?"

"They don't have a *j* either," Alan said.

"Why is that?"

"They're such careless people," Brenda said. "They just lost them."

It was like old times. She was divorced from Doop or Boos or whoever. Her two little girls were with her mother. She had that quirky smile.

In Paris Frank had taken them to the Crazy Horse. In blackness like velvet the music struck up and six girls in unison kicked their legs in the brilliant light. They wore high heels and a little strapping. The nudity that is immortal. He was leaning on one elbow in the darkness. He glanced at Brenda. "Still studying, eh?" she said.

They were over for three weeks. Frank wasn't sure, maybe they would stay longer, take a house in the south of France or something. Their clients would have to struggle along without them. There comes a time, he said, when you have to get away for a while.

They had breakfast together in hotels with the sound of workmen chipping at the stone of the fountain outside. They listened to the angry woman shouting in the kitchen, drove to little towns, and drank every night. They had separate rooms, like staterooms, like passengers on a fading boat.

At noon the light shifted along the curve of buildings and people were walking far off. A wave of pigeons rose before a trotting dog. The man at the table in front of them had a pair of binoculars and was looking here and there. Two Swedish girls strolled past.

"Now they're turning dark," the man said.

"What is?" said his wife.

"The pigeons."

"Alan," Frank confided.

"What?"

"The pigeons are turning dark."

"That's too bad."

There was silence for a moment.

"Why don't you just take a photograph?" the woman said.

"A photograph?"

"Of those women. You're looking at them so much."

He put down the binoculars.

"You know, the curve is so graceful," she said. "It's what makes this square so perfect."

"Isn't the weather glorious?" Frank said in the same tone of voice.

"And the pigeons," Alan said.

"The pigeons, too."

After a while the couple got up and left. The pigeons leapt up for a running child and hissed overhead. "I see you're still playing games," Brenda said. Frank smiled.

"We ought to get together in New York," she said that evening. They were waiting for Alan to come down. She reached across the table to pick up a magazine. "You've never met my kids, have you?" she said.

"No."

"They're terrific kids." She leafed through the pages not paying attention to them. Her forearms were tanned. She was not wearing a wedding band. The first act was over or rather the first five minutes. Now came the plot. "Do you remember those nights at Goldie's?" she said.

"Things were different then, weren't they?"

"Not so different."

"What do you mean?"

She wiggled her bare third finger and glanced at him. Just then Alan appeared. He sat down and looked from one of them to the other. "What's wrong?" he asked. "Did I interrupt something?"

When the time came for her to leave she wanted them to drive to Rome. They could spend a couple of days and she would catch the plane. They weren't going that way, Frank said.

"It's only a three-hour drive."

"I know, but we're going the other way," he said.

"For God's sake. Why won't you drive me?"

"Let's do it," Alan said.

"Go ahead. I'll stay here."

"You should have gone into politics," Brenda said. "You have a real gift."

After she was gone the mood of things changed. They were by themselves. They drove through the sleepy country to the north. The green water slapped as darkness fell on Venice. The lights in some *palazzos* were on. On the curtained upper floors the legs of countesses uncoiled, slithering on the sheets like a serpent.

In Harry's, Frank held up a dense, icy glass and murmured his father's line, "Good night, nurse." He talked to some people at the next table, a German who was manager of a hotel in Düsseldorf and his girlfriend. She'd been looking at him. "Want a taste?" he asked her. It was his second. She drank looking directly at him. "Looks like you finished it," he said.

"Yes, I like to do that."

He smiled. When he was drinking he was strangely calm. In Lugano in the park that time a bird had sat on his shoe.

In the morning across the canal, wide as a river, the buildings of the Giudecca lay in their soft colors, a great sunken barge with roofs and the crowns of hidden trees. The first winds of autumn were blowing, ruffling the water.

Leaving Venice, Frank drove. He couldn't ride in a car unless he was driving. Alan sat back, looking out the window, sunlight falling on the hillsides of antiquity. European days, the silence, the needle floating at a hundred.

In Padua, Alan woke early. The stands were being set up in the market. It was before daylight and cool. A man was laying out boards on the pavement, eight of them like doors to set bags of grain on. He was wearing the jacket from a suit. Searching in the truck he found some small pieces of wood and used them to shim the boards, testing with his foot.

The sky became violet. Under the colonnade the butchers had hung out chickens and roosters, spurred legs bound together. Two men sat trimming artichokes. The blue car of the *carabiniere* lazed past. The bags of rice and dry beans were set out now, the tops folded back like cuffs. A girl in a tailored coat with a scarf around her head called, *"Signore,"* then arrogantly, *"dica!"*

He saw the world afresh, its pavements and architecture, the names that had lasted for a thousand years. It seemed that his life was being clarified, the sediment was drifting down. Across the street in a jeweler's shop a girl was laying things out in the window. She was wearing white gloves and arranging the pieces with great care. She glanced up as he stood watching. For a moment their eyes met, separated by the lighted glass. She was holding a lapis lazuli bracelet, the blue of the police car. Emboldened, he formed the silent words, *Quanto costa? Trecento settanta mille,* her lips said. It was eight in the morning when he got back to the hotel. A taxi pulled up and rattled the narrow street. A woman dressed for dinner got out and went inside.

The days passed. In Verona the points of the steeples and then its domes rose from the mist. The white-coated waiters appeared from the kitchen. *Primi, secondi, dolce.* They stopped in Arezzo. Frank came back to the table. He had some postcards. Alan was trying to write to his daughter once a week. He never knew what to say: where they were and what they'd seen. Giotto—what would that mean to her?

They sat in the car. Frank was wearing a soft tweed jacket. It was like cashmere—he'd been shopping in Missoni and everywhere, windbreakers, shoes. Schoolgirls in dark skirts were coming through an arch across the street. After a while one came through alone. She stood as if waiting for someone. Alan was studying the map. He felt the engine start. Very slowly they moved forward. The window glided down.

"Scusi, signorina," he heard Frank say.

She turned. She had pure features and her face was without expression, as if a bird had turned to look, a bird which might suddenly fly away.

Which way, Frank asked her, was the *centro,* the center of town? She looked one way and then the other. "There," she said.

"Are you sure?" he said. He turned his head unhurriedly to look more or less in the direction she was pointing.

"Sì," she said.

They were going to Siena, Frank said. There was silence. Did she know which road went to Siena?

She pointed the other way.

"Alan, you want to give her a ride?" he asked.

"What are you talking about?"

Two men in white smocks like doctors were working on the wooden doors of the church. They were up on top of some scaffolding. Frank reached back and opened the rear door.

"Do you want to go for a ride?" he asked. He made a little circular motion with his finger.

They drove through the streets in silence. The radio was playing. Nothing was said. Frank glanced at her in the rearview mirror once or twice. It was at the time of a famous murder in Poland, the killing of a priest. Dusk was falling. The lights were coming on in shop windows and evening papers were in the kiosks. The body of the murdered man lay in a long coffin in the upper right corner of the *Corriere Della Sera*. It was in clean clothes like a worker after a terrible accident.

"Would you like an *aperitivo?*" Frank asked over his shoulder.

"*No,*" she said.

They drove back to the church. He got out for a few minutes with her. His hair was very thin, Alan noticed. Strangely, it made him look younger. They stood talking, then she turned and walked down the street.

"What did you say to her?" Alan asked. He was nervous.

"I asked if she wanted a taxi."

"We're headed for trouble."

"There's not going to be any trouble," Frank said.

His room was on the corner. It was large, with a sitting area near the windows. On the wooden floor there were two worn oriental carpets. On a glass cabinet in the bathroom were his hairbrush, lotions, cologne. The towels were a pale green with the name of the hotel in white. She didn't look at any of that. He had given the *portiere* forty thousand lire. In Italy the laws were very strict. It was nearly the same hour of the afternoon. He kneeled to take off her shoes.

He had drawn the curtains but light came in around them. At one point she seemed to tremble, her body shuddered. "Are you all right?" he said.

She had closed her eyes.

Later, standing, he saw himself in the mirror. He seemed to have thickened around the waist. He turned so that it was less noticeable. He got into bed again but was too hasty. "*Basta,*" she finally said.

They went down later and met Alan in a café. It was hard

for him to look at them. He began to talk in a foolish way. What was she studying at school, he asked. For God's sake, Frank said. Well, what did her father do? She didn't understand.

"What work does he do?"

"Furniture," she said.

"He sells it?"

"Restauro."

"In our country, no *restauro*," Alan explained. He made a gesture. "Throw it away."

"I've got to start running again," Frank decided.

The next day was Saturday. He had the *portiere* call her number and hand him the phone.

"Hello, Eda? It's Frank."

"I know."

"What are you doing?"

He didn't understand her reply.

"We're going to Florence. You want to come to Florence?" he said. There was a silence. "Why don't you come and spend a few days?"

"No," she said.

"Why not?"

In a quieter voice she said, "How do I explain?"

"You can think of something."

At a table across the room children were playing cards while three well-dressed women, their mothers, sat and talked. There were cries of excitement as the cards were thrown down.

"Eda?"

She was still there. *"Sì,"* she said.

In the hills they were burning leaves. The smoke was invisible but they could smell it as they passed through, like the smell from a restaurant or paper mill. It made Frank suddenly remember childhood and country houses, raking the lawn with his father long ago. The green signs began to say Firenze. It started to rain. The wipers swept silently across the glass. Everything was beautiful and dim.

They had dinner in a restaurant of plain rooms, whitewashed, like vaults in a cellar. She looked very young. She looked like a young dog, the white of her eyes was that pure. She said very little and played with a strip of pink paper that had come off the menu.

In the morning they walked aimlessly. The windows displayed things for women who were older, in their thirties at least, silk dresses, bracelets, scarves. In Fendi's was a beautiful coat, the price beneath in small metal numbers.

"Do you like it?" he asked. "Come on, I'll buy it for you."

He wanted to see the coat in the window, he told them inside.

"For the *signorina?*"

"Yes."

She seemed uncomprehending. Her face was lost in the fur. He touched her cheek through it.

"You know how much that is?" Alan said. "Four million five hundred thousand."

"Do you like it?" Frank asked her.

She wore it continually. She watched the football matches on television in it, her legs curled beneath her. The room was in disorder, they hadn't been out all day.

"What do you say to leaving here?" Alan asked unexpectedly. The announcers were shouting in Italian. "I thought I'd like to see Spoleto."

"Sure. Where is it?" Frank said. He had his hand on her knee and was rubbing it with the barest movement, as one might a dozing cat.

The countryside was flat and misty. They were leaving the past behind them, unwashed glasses, towels on the bathroom floor. There was a stain on his lapel, Frank noticed in the dining room. He tried to get it off as the headwaiter grated fresh Parmesan over each plate. He dipped the corner of his napkin in water and rubbed the spot. The table was near the doorway, visible from the desk. Eda was fixing an earring.

"Cover it with your napkin," Alan told him.

"Here, get this off, will you?" he asked Eda.

She scratched at it quickly with her fingernail.

"What am I going to do without her?" Frank said.

"What do you mean, without her?"

"So this is Spoleto," he said. The spot was gone. "Let's have some more wine." He called the waiter. "*Senta.* Tell him," he said to Eda.

They laughed and talked about old times, the days when they were getting eight hundred dollars a week and working ten, twelve hours a day. They remembered Weyland and the veins in his nose. The word he always used was "vivid," testimony a bit too vivid, far too vivid, a rather vivid decor.

They left talking loudly. Eda was close between them in her huge coat. "*Alla rovina,*" the clerk at the front desk muttered as they reached the street, "*alle macerie,*" he said, the girl at the switchboard looked over at him, "*alla polvere.*" It was something about rubbish and dust.

The mornings grew cold. In the garden there were leaves piled against the table legs. Alan sat alone in the bar. A waitress, the one with the mole on her lip, came in and began to work the coffee machine. Frank came down. He had an overcoat across his shoulders. In his shirt without a tie he looked like a rich patient in some hospital. He looked like a man who owned a produce business and had been playing cards all night.

"So, what do you think?" Alan said.

Frank sat down. "Beautiful day," he commented. "Maybe we ought to go somewhere."

In the room, perhaps in the entire hotel, their voices were the only sound, irregular and low, like the soft strokes of someone sweeping. One muted sound, then another.

"Where's Eda?"

"She's taking a bath."

"I thought I'd say good-bye to her."

"Why? What's wrong?"

"I think I'm going home."

"What happened?" Frank said.

Alan could see himself in the mirror behind the bar, his sandy hair. He looked pale somehow, nonexistent. "Nothing happened," he said. She had come into the bar and was sitting at the other end of the room. He felt a tightness in his chest. "Europe depresses me."

Frank was looking at him. "Is it Eda?"

"No. I don't know." It seemed terribly quiet. Alan put his hands in his lap. They were trembling.

"Is that all it is? We can share her," Frank said.

"What do you mean?" He was too nervous to say it right. He stole a glance at Eda. She was looking at something outside in the garden.

"Eda," Frank called, "do you want something to drink? *Cosa vuoi?*" He made a motion of glass raised to the mouth. In college he had been a great favorite. Shuford had been shortened to Shuf and then Shoes. He had run in the Penn Relays. His mother could trace her family back for six generations.

"Orange juice," she said.

They sat there talking quietly. That was often the case, Eda had noticed. They talked about business or things in New York.

When they came back to the hotel that night, Frank explained it. She understood in an instant. No. She shook her head. Alan was sitting alone in the bar. He was drinking some kind of sweet liqueur. It wouldn't happen, he knew. It didn't matter anyway. Still, he felt shamed. The hotel above his head, its corridors and quiet rooms, what else were they for?

Frank and Eda came in. He managed to turn to them. She seemed impassive—he could not tell. What was this he was drinking, he finally asked? She didn't understand the question. He saw Frank nod once slightly, as if in agreement. They were like thieves.

In the morning the first light was blue on the window glass. There was the sound of rain. It was leaves blowing in the garden, shifting across the gravel. Alan slipped from the bed to fasten the loose shutter. Below, half hidden in the hedges, a statue gleamed white. The few parked cars shone faintly. She was asleep, the soft, heavy pillow beneath her head. He was afraid to wake her. "Eda," he whispered, "Eda."

Her eyes opened a bit and closed. She was young and could

stay asleep. He was afraid to touch her. She was unhappy, he knew, her bare neck, her hair, things he could not see. It would be a while before they were used to it. He didn't know what to do. Apart from that, it was perfect. It was the most natural thing in the world. He would buy her something himself, something beautiful.

In the bathroom he lingered at the window. He was thinking of the first day they had come to work at Weyland, Braun—he and Frank. They would become inseparable. Autumn in the gardens of the Veneto. It was barely dawn. He would always remember meeting Frank. He couldn't have done these things himself. A young man in a cap suddenly came out of a doorway below. He crossed the driveway and jumped onto a motorbike. The engine started, a faint blur. The headlight appeared and off he went, delivery basket in back. He was going to get the rolls for breakfast. His life was simple. The air was pure and cool. He was part of that great, unchanging order of those who live by wages, whose world is unlit and who do not realize what is above.

ELIZABETH JOLLEY

The Fellow Passenger

Dr. Abrahams stood watching, for his health, the flying fish. They flew in great numbers like little silver darts, leaping together in curves, away from the ship, as though disturbed by her movement through their mysterious world. Nearby sat his wife with her new friend, a rich widow returning to her rice farms in New South Wales. The two women in comfortable chairs, adjoining, spoke to each other softly and confidingly, helping each other with the burden of family life and the boredom of the voyage.

"Who is that person your daughter is talking to?" said the widow, momentarily looking up from her needlework.

"Oh I've no idea," Mrs. Abrahams said comfortably. And then, a little less comfortably, she said, "Oh I see what you mean. There are some odd people on board." She raised herself slightly and, raising her voice, called, "Rachel! Rachel dear ... mother's over here, we're sitting over here."

161

As the girl reluctantly came towards them, Mrs. Abrahams said in a low voice to her new friend, "I'm so glad you noticed. He does seem to be an unsuitable type, perhaps he's a foreigner of some sort." She lowered her voice even more. "And they do have such ugly heads you know."

Their voices were swallowed up in the wind, which was racing, whipping the spray and pitting the waves as they curled back from the sides of the ship.

Dr. Abrahams walked by himself all over the ship. The sharp fragrance from the barber's shop excited him, and he rested gratefully by the notice boards where there was a smell of boiled potatoes. The repeated Dettol scrubbing of the stairs reminded him of post-natal douchings and the clean enamel bowls in his operating theatre.

Whenever he stood looking at the front of the ship, or at the back, he admired the strength of the structure, the massive construction and the complication of ropes and pulleys being transported, and in themselves necessary for the transporting of the ship across these oceans. It seemed always that the ship was steady in the great ring of blue water and did not rise to answer the sea, and the monsoon had not broken the barrenness. Most of the passengers were huddled out of the wind.

When he returned to his wife he saw the man approaching. For a time he had managed to forget about him and now here he was again, coming round the end of the deck, limping towards them in that remarkably calm manner which Abrahams knew only too well was hiding a desperate persistence.

Knowing the peace of contemplation was about to be broken, Abrahams turned abruptly and tried to leave the deck quickly through the heavy swing doors before the man, with his distasteful and sinister errand, could reach him. There was this dreadful element of surprise and of obligation too. For apart from anything else, the man had an injury with a wound which, having been neglected, must have been appallingly painful. It was something, if seen by a doctor, could not afterwards be ignored.

"All you have to do is to treat me like a fellow passenger," the man had said the first night on board. He entreated rather, with some other quality in his voice and in his bearing which had caused Abrahams to buy him a drink straight away. Perhaps some of the disturbance had come from the unexpected shapeliness of the man's hands.

The Bay of Biscay, unusually calm, had not offered the usual reasons for a day of retreat in the cabin. Abrahams, excusing himself from the company of his wife and daughter, had again invited the man for a drink.

"What about a coupla sangwidges," the fellow said, and he had gobbled rather than eaten them. A little plate of nuts and olives disappeared in the same way.

The two stupid old ladies, they were called Ethel and Ivy and they shared the Abrahams' table, were there in the Tavern Bar. They nodded and smiled and they rustled when they moved, for both were sewn up in brown paper under their clothes.

"To prevent sea sickness," Ethel explained to people whenever she had the chance.

A second little plate of nuts and olives disappeared.

"That'll be good for a growing boy!" Ethel called out. Like Ivy, she was having tomato juice with Worcester sauce. Already they had been nicknamed "The Worcester Sauce Queens" by the Abrahams family.

Abrahams, with the courtesy of long habit, for among his patients were many such elderly ladies, smiled at her. His smile was handsome and kind. The very quality of kindness it contained caused both men and women to confide. It was the nature of this smile, and the years of patient, hard work it had brought upon him, that had necessitated a remedial voyage. For Abrahams was a sick man and was keeping the sickness in his own hands, prescribing for himself at last a long rest. He had been looking forward to the period of suspended peace, which has such tremendous healing power and is the delight of a sea voyage.

At the very beginning the peace was interrupted before it was begun, and Abrahams regretted bitterly the sensitive sympathy his personality seemed to give out. It was all part of his illness. It was as if he were ill because of his sympathetic nature. The burdens he carried sprang from it. That was what he allowed himself to believe but it was not all quite so simple. There were conflicting reasons and feelings which were all perhaps a part of being unwell, perhaps even a part of the cause. He tried to make some sort of acknowledgement, to reach some sort of inner conclusion in the all too infrequent solitary moments.

At the first meeting, Abrahams' feeling was, apart from a sense of obligation on the good manners of not liking to refuse to buy a drink for the stranger, a feeling of gladness, almost happiness, perhaps even a tiny heart bursting gladness which could have made him want to sing. He did not sing, he was not that kind of man. His work did not include singing of any kind. There was not much talking. Mostly he listened. His work kept him quiet and thoughtful. He often bent forward to listen and to examine and to operate. He had good hands. His fingers, accustomed to probing and rearranging, to extracting and replacing, were sensitive and capable. If he frowned it was the frown of attention and concentration. It was his look of kindness and the way in which he approached an examination, almost as if it was some kind of caress, which made his patients like him.

In the bar that first night, he reflected, he had come near singing. A songless song of course because men like Abrahams simply would never burst into song.

Once he did sing and the memory of it had suddenly come back to him clearly even though it had been many years ago. Once his voice, surprisingly powerful, it could have been described as an untrained but ardent tenor, carried a song of love across and down a valley of motionless trees. Throughout his song the landscape had remained undisturbed. He had not realised how, in the stillness, a voice could carry.

"Heard yer singin' this half hour," the woman had said, holding her side, her face old with pain.

"Oh? Was I singing?"

"Yerse, long before you crorsst the bridge, I heard yer comin' thanks to God I sez to meself the doctor's on his way, he's on his way."

It was during a six-month locum in a country town. That day he sang and whistled and sang careering on horseback to a patient in a lonely farm house. He remembered the undisturbed fields and meadows, serene that day because he went through them singing.

The stranger's voice in the bar, and his finely made hands taking the glass from Abrahams, brought back so suddenly the song in the shallow valley.

On the track that day he thought he'd lost his way and he was frightened of his surroundings. The landmarks he'd been told to watch for simply had not appeared. There was no house in sight and no barn and there were no people. He'd been travelling some time. Joyfully he approached some farm machinery but no one was beside it. He almost turned back but thought of his patient and the injection he could give her. In all directions the land sloped gently to the sky, the track seemed to be leading nowhere and he was the only person there.

He came upon the man quite suddenly. He was there as if for no reason except to direct Abrahams, though he had a cart and some tools, but Abrahams in his relief did not really notice. The man's eyes shone as he patted the horse and Abrahams felt as if the intimate caress, because of the way the man looked, was meant for him. He continued his journey feeling this tiny heart-bursting change into gladness, which is really all the greatest change there is, and so he sang.

As he walked or stood on the deck he thought about loneliness. The crowded confined life of the ship was lonely too.

"Give me some money," the man said. "It'll look better if I shout you." So in the temporary duskiness between the double swing doors Abrahams gave him some notes and small change and followed him as he limped into the bar.

"What'll you have?" the man asked the old ladies. They were there as usual, before lunch, their large straw hats were bandaged on with violently coloured scarves. They sat nodding those crazy head-pieces, talking to anyone who would listen to them.

They were pleased to be offered drinks. Abrahams had a drink too, but it was accompanied by disturbing feelings. The thought of his illness crossed his mind. The man's hands had an extraordinary youthful beauty about them, out of keeping with his general appearance. As on the other occasions when glasses had passed between them, their fingers brushed lightly, but it was not so much the caress of fingers as a suggestion of caress in the man's eyes.

Abrahams, with a second drink, found himself wondering had he been on horseback that time in the country or in a car. Had that other man touched the horse or merely put a friendly hand on the door of the car? With his hand he had not touched, only the expression was there in his eyes. This time, all these years later, it was a touching of exceptional hands together with an expression in the eyes.

In the afternoon there was a fancy dress party for the children. Mrs. Abrahams had been making something elaborate with crepe paper. Already the cabin blossomed with paper flowers. Abrahams discovered his daughter sulking.

"Look Rachel darling," Mrs. Abrahams persuaded. "You will be a bouquet, we shall call you 'the language of flowers,'" she said holding up her work. "White roses—they mean 'I cannot,' and this lovely little white and green flower is lily of the valley, it says, 'already I have loved you so long' and here's a little bunch of violets for your hair, Rachel, the violets say 'why so downhearted? Take courage!' and these pretty daisies say ...'"

"Oh no, no!" Rachel interrupted. "I don't want to be flowers, I want to go as a stowaway," and she limped round and round the cabin. "Daddy! Daddy!" she cried with sudden inspiration. "Can I borrow one of your coloured shirts, please. Oh do say I can. Do let me be a stowaway, please!"

Abrahams took refuge among the mothers and photographers at the party. He joined in the clapping for the prize winners, "Little Miss Muffet" and "Alice in Wonderland." "All so prettily dressed!" Mrs. Abrahams whispered sadly. A girl covered in green balloons calling herself "A Bunch of Grapes" won a special prize. The applause was tremendous.

"They must have made a fortune in green umbrellas," the rice farm friend said with delight.

"Spent a fortune on green balloons," Abrahams muttered to himself, almost correcting her aloud. He was unable to forget, for the time being, his sinister companion who was somewhere on the decks waiting with some further demand. Silently he watched his little daughter's mounting disappointment as she limped round unnoticed in one of his shirts, left unbuttoned to look ragged.

He thought he would like to buy her a grown-up-looking drink before dinner, something sparkling with a piece of lemon and a cherry on it, to please her, to comfort her really. If only she could know how much he cherished her. He longed to be free to play with her, she was old enough, he thought, to learn to play chess. But there was the fear that he would be interrupted, and she was old enough too to be indignant and to enquire.

"I am not quite well," he explained to his wife after the first encounter with the man. "It is nothing serious but I am not sleeping well." He did not want her disturbed by something mysterious which he was unable to explain. So he had a cabin to himself and arranged for his wife and daughter to be together. Their new cabin had a window with muslin curtains and a writing table. Mrs. Abrahams took pleasure in comparing it with the cabins of other ladies on board. Dr. Abrahams called for her and Rachel every morning on the way to breakfast.

The children's fancy dress party was depressing. The atmosphere of suburban wealth and competition seemed shallow and useless. The smell of hot children and perfume nauseated him. But it was safer to stay there.

The ship remained steady on her course and the rail of the ship moved slowly above the horizon and slowly below the horizon. There were times when Abrahams felt he was being watched by the stewards and the officers, and even the deck hands seemed to give each other knowing looks. These feelings, he knew, were merely symptoms of his illness which was, after all, nothing serious, only a question of being overtired. All the same, he was worn out with this feeling of being watched. He avoided the sun deck for it was clear from the man's new sunburn that he lay up there, anonymous on a towel, for part of each day.

"You'd better let me have a shirt," the man said. "I'll be noticed by my dirt," he said. He took a set of three, their patterns being too similar for Abrahams to appear in any one of them. He needed socks and underpants and a bag to keep them in. The nondescript one Abrahams had would do very well. It was all settled one evening in the cabin which Abrahams had said he must have to himself. The fellow passenger slept there, coming in late at night and leaving early in the morning. It was there in the cramped space Abrahams dressed the wound on the man's thigh with the limited medical supplies he had with him.

"Easy! Easy!" the fellow passenger said in a low voice.

"It's hot in here," Abrahams complained. He disliked being clumsy. "It's the awkwardness of not having somewhere to put my things."

"It's all right," the fellow passenger said. "You're not really hurting me." He seemed much younger undressed, his long naked body so delicately patched with white between the sunburn, angry only where the wound was, invited Abrahams.

"I'm not wounded all over," he said and laughed, and Abrahams found himself laughing with him.

"Easy! Easy! don't rush!" the younger man said.

That laughter, the tiny heart burst of gladness was a fact, like the fact that the wound was only in one place. They could be careful. It was a question of being careful in every kind of way.

Abrahams knew his treatment to be unsatisfactory but there seemed nothing else to do in the extraordinary circumstances. If only he had not answered the smile in the man's eyes on that first evening; he should have turned away as other people do. Knowing the change and feeling the change, in whatever way it brought gladness, was the beginning and the continuation of more loneliness.

Incredibly the ship made progress, her rail moving gently up and persistently down.

Like many handsome clever men Dr. Abrahams had married a stupid woman. She was quite good at housekeeping and she talked consolingly through kisses. Her body had always been clean and plump, and relaxed, and she was very quiet during those times of love-making, as though she felt that was how a lady, married to a doctor, should behave. Abrahams never sang with her as he sang in the cabin.

"Easy! Easy!" the fellow passenger said, he laughed and Abrahams put the pillow over his head.

"They'll hear you." He buried his own face in the top of the pillow. He could not stop laughing either.

"And they'll hear you too!" Abrahams heard the words piercing through the smothered laughter.

Always unable to discuss things with his wife, Dr. Abrahams did not want to frighten her now and spoil her holiday.

"Your husband is a very quiet man," the rice farm widow said to Mrs. Abrahams. "Still waters run deep, so they say," she said. That was very early in the voyage after a morning in Gibraltar, spent burrowing into little shops choosing antimacassars and table runners of cream coloured lace.

"Did you go to see the apes?" Ethel enquired at lunch.

"Plenty of apes here," Abrahams, burdened and elated by discovery and already bad tempered, would have replied, but instead, he smiled pleasantly and, with a little bow, regretted the family had not had time.

"You see Ethel and I have this plastic pizza," Ivy was explaining to Mrs. Abrahams and Rachel. "At Christmas I wrap it up and go down to Ethel's flat, 'Happy Christmas Ethel,' I say, and she unwraps it and she says, 'Ooh Ivy you are a dear it's just what I wanted,' and then next year she wraps it up and gives it to me, it saves all that trouble of buying presents nobody really wants. Thank you," she said to the steward. "I'll have the curried chicken."

Rachel, accustomed to good meals, ordered a steak. Abrahams could not help reflecting that Ethel and Ivy had both the remedy and the method which simplified their existence. They appeared to be able to live so easily, without emergency, and without burdening other people with their needs. They could, of course, require surgery at any time, though he doubted that this ever occurred to either of them. Perhaps he too, outwardly, gave the same impression.

The fellow passenger's demand was both a pleading and a

promise. At the beginning Abrahams had risen to the entreaty, but, as he understood all too quickly, his response was complicated by an unthought-of need in himself. Walking alone on the ship he was afraid.

The begging for help had, from the first, been a command. Abrahams knew his fellow passenger to be both sinister and evil. In his own intelligent way he tried to reason with himself what, in fact, he was himself. At the start, but on different terms, it was a matching desperation of hunger and thirst and an exhaustion of wits. The fellow passenger had certain outward signs: for one thing, he had a ragged growth of beard which in itself was dangerously revealing. He was dirty too. He needed help, he told Abrahams, to hold out till the first servings of afternoon tea in the lounge, and until such time when the weather would improve and cold buffet lunches would be spread daily in the Tavern Bar and on little tables on the canopied deck by the swimming pool. To be in these delightful places, in order to fill his stomach, he needed to mingle in the company.

"It's dangerous," he said. "Being alone. Being on my own makes me conspicuous and that's what I don't want to be." A companion who was both rich and distinguished was a necessity and it had not taken him long to find the kind of fellow passenger he needed.

"I better have a bit more cash," he said to Abrahams. "I'll shout you and them old Queens. They know a thing or two about life, those two. I'll take care of them." His words sounded like a threat.

They had, without laughter, been sorting out what was to happen next. The cabin had never seemed quite so tall, quite so awkward. He had plans to alter a passport, he knew exactly what had to be done, he needed a passport and it only needed the doctor to produce one.

Like many clever men Dr. Abrahams was easily tired. He had come on the ship, as had the fellow passenger, exhausted, already an easy victim. Now, more tired than ever he hated the man and saw him as someone entirely ruthless. It seemed impossible to consider what might have been the cause. It was clear that there would be no end to the requests. Abrahams realised that soon he would be unable to protect his family and quite unable to protect himself. The voyage no longer had any meaning for him. Together, the two of them went to the bar.

Ethel and Ivy were there as usual.

"It's on me today," Ethel cried and made them sit down. "You must try my tomato juice," she cried. "It's with a difference you know," and she winked so saucily everyone in the bar laughed.

The fellow passenger drank quickly.

"Now it's my turn," Ivy insisted. "It's my turn to shout." She watched with approval as the fellow passenger drank again.

"So good for a growing boy," she declared and she ordered another round.

Dr. Abrahams held his glass too tightly with nervous fingers. After the conversation about the passport he felt more helpless than ever. He could scarcely swallow. He should never have lost his way like this. Quickly he glanced at all the people laughing and talking together and he was frightened of them.

"More tomato juice for my young man," Ethel shrieked. Her straw hat had come loose.

"Ethel dear, watch yourself!" Ivy shrilled. "We're in very mixed company you know dear." Their behaviour drew the attention of the other passengers.

"Steward! Steward!" Ethel called. "Don't forget the you-know-what-oops la Volga! Volga! It makes all the difference. There dear boy, let's toss this off." She raised her fiery little glass to his. "Oops a daisy!" Her hat fell over one eye.

While the fellow passenger drank, Ivy retied Ethel's scarf lovingly. She rocked gently to and fro.

"Yoho heave ho! Volga-Volga," she crooned. "Volga Vodka," she sang, and Ethel joined in.

"Yo ho heave ho! Volga-Worcester-saucy-vodka-tommy-ommy-artah—All together now—Yo ho heave ho-Volga-Vodka," they sang together and some of the other passengers joined in. Above the noise of the singing and the laughing Abrahams heard a familiar voice, but it was much louder than usual.

"Go on dear boy! Go on! Go on! Don't stop now!" Ethel and

Ivy cried together, their absurd hats bobbing. "Tell us more," they screamed.

It seemed to Abrahams that the fellow passenger was telling stories to Ethel and Ivy and to anyone else who cared to listen. Hearing the voice he thought how ugly it was. The ugliness filled him with an unbearable sadness.

"So you're wanted in five countries!" Ethel said. "Why that's wonderful!" she encouraged. She bent forward to listen. Ivy examined the young man's shirt. She patted his shoulder.

"This is such good quality," she breathed. "Look at this lovely material Ethel dear." But Ethel would not have the subject changed.

"Rape!" she shrieked with delight. "And murder too, how splendid! What else dear boy. Being a thief is so exciting, do tell us about the watches and the jewels and the diamonds. You must be very clever. Ivy and I have never managed anything more expensive than a pizza and then it turned out to be quite uneatable."

The fellow passenger did not join in the laughter. He began to despise his audience.

"Look at you!" he sneered. "You two old bags and you lot— you've all paid through the nose to be on this ship. But not me, I'm getting across the world on my wits. That's how I do things. I've got brains up here," he tapped his head with a surprisingly delicate finger. "It isn't money as has got me here," he said and he tapped his head again.

For the first time Abrahams noticed the ugliness of the head. He thought he ought to find the Purser and speak to him.

"It's all my fault about the head," he would confide, and explain to the officer about the arching of soft white thighs and the exertion. "It's like this," he would say. "When you see the baby's head appear on the perineum it's like a first glimpse of all the wonder and all the magic, a preview if you like to call it that, of all the possibilities." The Purser would understand about the shy hope and the tenderness when it was explained to him. Abrahams thought the Purser might be in his cabin changing for lunch. He could find the cabin.

"What has happened?" he wanted to ask the Purser. "What has happened?" he wanted to shout. "What is it that happens to the tiny eager head to bring about this change from the original perfection?"

He walked unsteadily towards the open end of the bar. Really he should speak and protect his fellow passenger. He felt ashamed as well as afraid, knowing that he needed to protect himself. Of course he could not speak to anyone, his own reputation mattered too much.

He was appalled at the sound of the boasting voice and, at the same time, had a curious sense that he was being rescued. The fellow passenger was giving himself to these people.

Abrahams did not turn round to watch the man being led away by two stewards in dark uniforms.

"Mind my leg!" He heard the pathetic squeal as the three of them squeezed through a narrow door at the back of the bar. It was a relief that the wound, which he was convinced needed surgery, would receive proper attention straight away.

There were still a few minutes left before lunch. For the first time he went up on the sun deck. Far below, the sea, shining like metal, scarcely moving, invited him. For a moment he contemplated that peace.

"Yoo hoo doctor! Wear my colours!" Ethel shrieked. Turning from the rail he saw the Worcester Sauce Queens playing a rather hurried game of deck tennis. Ethel unpinned a ragged cluster of paper violets from her scarf and flung them at his feet. Politely he bent forward to pick them up.

"You must watch Rachel beat us after lunch," Ivy shrilled.

The pulse of the ship, like a soft drum throbbing, was more noticeable at the top of the ship. To Abrahams it was like an awakening not just in his body but in his whole being. He stood relaxed letting life return as he watched the grotesque game and, with some reservations belonging to his own experience, he found the sight of the Worcester Sauce Queens charming.

STEVEN MILLHAUSER

The Sepia Postcard

I was tense, irritable, overworked; the city stifling, my nerves stretched taut; life was a foul
farce with predictable punchlines; things were
not going well between Claudia and me; one
morning in early September I threw a suitcase in
the back of the car, and toward dusk I came to the
village of Broome. A single street wound down to
the darkening cove. The brochure had shown
sunny red-and-white buoys lying against piles of
slatted lobster pots, with brilliant blue water beyond, but tomorrow would be time enough for
that. I expected no miracles; I wasn't young
enough for dreams; I knew in my bones that I
couldn't escape my troubles by changing the view
from my window. But I hoped for a little respite,
do you know, a little forgetfulness, and perhaps a
freshness of spirit, too. Was it asking so much? At
the bottom of the street I rolled down my window
and breathed the sharp chill air, drew it deep into
my lungs. The brochure had shown a girl in a

white bathing suit lying on a golden beach, but if the season was over, what was that to me? I needed the cleansing air, the purifying otherness, of Broome. The inn was a rambling many-gabled Victorian with a broad front porch and paired brackets under the eaves. It stood near the top of the hill, on a lane off the winding street of shops. And if the lamplit sign on the sloping lawn said OCEAN GABLES, what was that to me? Claudia would have found the perfect words for the sign, with its black iron lighthouse screwed into the wood. Claudia would have had something to say about the rockers on the porch, the old brass chandelier over the mahogany dining table, the square stairpost with its dark globe, the carpeted creaking stairs, the framed engraving on the landing (a little girl in a bonnet embracing a Saint Bernard), the ruffled pink bedspread, but Claudia hadn't smiled at me in a month. I was here alone.

I slept well enough, not well, but well enough, and woke almost refreshed to a gray morning. Downstairs a brisk woman in a half apron was clearing the table in a small room off the main dining room. Her apron had a design of purple plums, red apples, and yellow pears, all with stems and little leaves. A white-haired couple sat at one table, sipping heavy-looking cups of coffee. "Am I late for breakfast?" I asked in surprise; it was 8:45. The brisk woman hesitated and glanced sharply at a blue wooden clock shaped like a teapot. "I can fix you up something," she said, banging a knife onto a saucer. I sat down at a table covered with a clean white tablecloth with crisp fold-lines. Despite the slightly unpleasant note, the breakfast when it came proved generous—a tall, fluted glass of orange juice, two eggs with bacon, two slices of toast with blackberry jam, a yellow porcelain pot of superb coffee—and I rose in a buoyant mood, determined to make the best of the gray day.

Outside it was drizzling lightly, barely more than a mist. I turned up the collar of my trench coat and walked along the lane to the steep street that curved down to the water. Most of the shops had the look of houses, with curtained windows above the converted main floors. Between the shops on the shore side of the street I caught glimpses of grass, cove, and stormy sky. Once, through a large window containing giraffes and trains, I saw an open doorway, and through the doorway another window, with a view of rushing clouds. It was as if the shop were flying through the sky, like Dorothy's house in the tornado. On the other side of the street I passed winding roads of white clapboard houses with bracketed porch posts, bay windows, and gingerbread along the gables. It was a village meant for brilliant sun and hard-edged shadow, for sharp rectangles of blue between the shingled shops. But what was it to me that the sun didn't shine, that a cold drizzle matted my lashes and trickled down my neck? I wasn't out for sun. I was here because it was not there, I was here because it was anywhere else, because Broome was—well, Broome; and I was set on taking it as it was, in dazzle or drizzle.

I stopped at every shop window, every one. I studied the realtor's corkboard display of slightly blurred black-and-white photographs of houses in sun-dappled woods, I browsed in the window of the garden shop with its baked-earth flowerpots and shiny green hoses and country-humor lawn ornaments, including a pink wooden piglet and a fat woman bending over and showing her polka-dot underpants, I paused under the awning of the stationer's to examine the table that offered half-price notepads stamped with treble clefs and called Musical Notes, gigantic pencils as thick as towel bars, pencil sharpeners shaped like typewriters, mice, and black shoes. I admired the striped pole turning in a misted tube of glass and the melancholy barber with heavy-lidded eyes who stared out the window at the rain and me. I studied the ice cream parlor, the grocery store, the drugstore with its display of rubber-tipped crutches, aluminum walkers, and back-to-school specials. I passed two gift shops and entered a third. I like gift shops; I like the variety of invention within a convention of rigorous triteness. I looked at the flashlight pens that said BROOME; the little straw brooms with wooden handles that said BROOME; erasers shaped like chipmunks, rabbits, and skunks; little slatted lobster pots containing miniature red plastic lobsters; tiny white-and-gray seagulls perched on wooden piles the size of cigarettes; porcelain thimbles painted with lighthouses; little wind-up kangaroos that flipped over once and landed on their feet; foot-high porcelain fishermen with pipes and yellow slickers; red wax apples with wicks for stems; a rack of comic postcards, one of which bore the legend LOBSTER DINNER FOR TWO and showed two lobsters in bibs seated at a table before plates of shrimp; black mailboxes with brass lobsters on them; sets of plastic teeth that clacked noisily when you wound them up; a bin of porcelain coin banks shaped like lobster pots, Victorian houses with turrets, and mustard-covered hot dogs in buns; and a basket of red, blue, and green brachiosauruses. When I stepped out of the gift shop I saw that the sky had darkened. I was more than halfway down the main street of Broome and it was not yet eleven in the morning. I didn't know what to do. I passed a window filled with watches, two of which formed the eyes of a cardboard mouse. I passed a window with a white crib in which slept a red cotton lobster and a polar bear. The rain began to fall harder. The steep sidewalk turned sharply, and at the end of the street I saw wet grass, a stretch of slick dirt with pools of trembling rainwater, a gray pier leading into gray water.

The shops were more thickly clustered here, as if backing away from the muddy bottom of the street. They seemed darker and shabbier than the shops above, and the steepness of the descent gave everything a tilted and precarious look. I passed a red-lit window crowded with the glimmering lower halves of sawed-off women in panty hose; some appeared to be dancing wildly, some were lounging about, and some were upside down, their legs straining desperately upward, as if at any moment they would be pulled underground. There was a window with a handwritten sign that said BOOTS BAIT TACKLE. There was an empty dark window with a telephone number written across it in white soap, and another dark window that said PLUMSHAW'S RARE BOOKS. A dim light burned inside. Here the sidewalk was so steep that the left-hand edge of the window began at my knees, the right-hand edge at my stomach. I felt oddly unbalanced, but something about the place drew me, and I lingered uncertainly under the narrow green awning.

It was a crowded, scattered sort of display, with here an open children's book showing a boy trundling a hoop, there a set of twelve cracked leather volumes called *Barnsworth's Geographic Cy-clopaedia.* In one corner a doll dressed like Little Boy Blue was leaning with his eyes closed against a globe on a dusty stand, not far from a large atlas open to a faded map of the Roman Empire in 200 A.D. It was difficult to know what to make of this shop, where a Victorian toy theater with a red paper curtain sat next to a book of fairy tales open to a color print of a princess drawing a bucket out of a well, where a stereoscope mounted on a wooden bar lay aslant on its wooden handle in front of a glass-covered engraving of the Place de la Concorde, and thirteen volumes of a sixteen-volume set of Hawthorne rose like a crooked red chimney behind an old top hat and a pair of opera glasses. Plumshaw's taste was odd and eccentric, but I seemed to detect in the display a secret harmony. The rain had begun to fall in earnest. I stepped inside.

A bell tinkled faintly over the door. The room was small and gloomy, lit by a single bare bulb at the bottom of a green-stained brass ceiling fixture shaped like flower petals. A dark passage led to a room beyond. On the counter stood an old black cash register and a small wire rack hung with cellophane bags of butterscotch squares, jelly beans, and gumdrops. Behind the counter was a tall woman with high hair who looked at me without smiling. Plumshaw, I decided. Her voluminous gray hair was pulled tightly upward and piled on top of her head in masses of sharp-looking little curls. She wore a high-necked black dress with long sleeves ending in stiff bursts of faded lace. A pearl circle pin was fastened at her throat, and on one wrist she wore a yellowed ivory bracelet composed of a ring of little elephants each holding in its trunk the tail of the elephant in front. Plumshaw, without a doubt. Oh, maybe some other Plumshaw had started the shop, maybe she was the unmarried daughter of Plumshaw the First, but she had taken it over and had stood motionless and unsmiling behind that cash register for forty years. The dark walls were lined with books, but here and there stood knickknacks of brass or ivory and boxes of stereoscopic views, and in one corner stood an umbrella stand containing three walking sticks with ivory handles, one of which was shaped like a hand curved over a ball.

Evidently PLUMSHAW'S RARE BOOKS had fallen on hard days and was forced to drum up extra trade in antiques. Or perhaps—the thought struck me—perhaps these odds and ends were Plumshaw's own possessions, brought down one by one from the backs of closets and the depths of attic trunks to be offered for sale. The books themselves, arranged carefully by category, were the mediocre used books of any second-rate bookshop (sets of Emerson, sets of Poe), and among them were library discards, with the Dewey Decimal number printed in white ink on the spine and the melancholy DISCARDED stamped across the card pocket in back. I lingered politely under Plumshaw's severe gaze for as long as I could stand it and then escaped through the dark passage into the next room.

I saw at once that there were other rooms; PLUMSHAW'S RARE BOOKS was a warren of small rooms connected by short dark passages lined with books. The invasion of alien objects was more noticeable as I moved deeper into the back, where entire shelves had been cleared to make way for stacks of maroon record albums containing heavy, brittle 78's as thick as roof slates, boxes of old postcards, empty cardboard cylinders the size of soup cans each bearing the words EDISON GOLD MOULDED RECORD and an oval photograph of Thomas A. Edison, daguerreotypes, tintypes, stacks of pen-and-ink illustrations torn from old books, a moldering gray Remington typewriter with dark green keys, a faded wooden horse with red wheels, little porcelain cats, a riding crop, old photographs (Green Point, 1926) with upcurled corners showing traces of rubber cement, a cribbage board with ivory pegs, a pair of high cracked black lace-up shoes. Here and there I saw brass standing lamps with cloth shades and yellowed ivory finials, and armchairs with faded doilies; I wondered whether they were for sale. All the rooms were gloomily lit by dim yellow bulbs with tarnished brass chains.

I had slipped into one room to examine a little music box with a red-jacketed monkey on top, who turned slowly round and round and raised and lowered his cup as the melody played, when I happened to look up to see a figure standing in the doorway. At first she said nothing, but only looked at me from the shadows. I placed the music box back on the shelf—the tinkling music was playing, the monkey was turning and raising its cup. "May I be of help?" Plumshaw said at last, decisively. "I was just browsing—a nice little fellow!" I answered, wanting to strangle the little monster. I turned to push it deeper into the shelf, as if to conceal a crime; when I looked up, Plumshaw was gone. I cursed her suspicions—did she think I'd pocket him?—but felt obscurely obliged to purchase some trifle, as if my visit to the shop were an intrusion that required apology. With this in mind I began looking at engravings, stereoscopic views, a box of black-and-white photographic portraits on glass. It seemed there was nothing here for me, nothing in all of Broome for me, or in all the gray universe, and with a dull sort of curiosity I came to a table on which stood a black wire rack filled with old postcards.

They were black-and-white and sepia and tinted postcards, showing topiary gardens, and Scottish castles, and boats on the Rhine, and public buildings in Philadelphia. Some bore stamps and postmarks and messages in ink: *Dear Robert, I cannot tell you how lovely our rooms are*—but then, I've never been interested in other people's mail. The pictures had a faded and melancholy air that pleased me; there is a poetry of old postcards, which belong in the same realm as hurdy-gurdy tunes, merry-go-round horses, circus sideshows, silent black-and-white cartoons, tissue-paper-covered illustrations, old movie theaters, kaleidoscopes, and storm-faded figureheads of women with their wooden hair blown back. I examined the postcards one by one, turning now and then to look at the doorway, which remained ominously empty, and after a while I found myself lingering over a sepia postcard. The back was clean; it had never been sent. The melancholy brown photograph showed a rocky point extending into a lake or river; on the other side of the water was a brown forest of pines, and above the trees were long thin brown clouds and a setting brown sun. In the upper left-hand corner of the sky, in small brown capital letters, was the single word INNISCARA. On the farthest rock two small figures were seated, a man and a woman, looking out at the water. Beside the man I could make out a straw hat and a walking stick. The woman was bareheaded, her hair full and tumbling. The details were difficult to distinguish in the dim light, but the very uncertainty seemed part of the romantic melancholy of the brown scene. I decided to purchase it. Perhaps I would send it to Claudia, with a terse, ambiguous message.

There was no price on the rack of cards, no price penciled on the backs. It occurred to me that I hadn't seen a price anywhere in PLUMSHAW'S RARE BOOKS. I wandered back through the jumble of ill-lit rooms and when I reached the cash register I presented my postcard with a flourish to Plumshaw. Majestically, with her torso flung back, she took it from me. She looked at the picture, turned the card over and studied the blank side, and gave me a sharp glance, as if estimating my bank account. She held the card up and appeared to examine one corner. At last she lowered the postcard to the counter, where she rested it on its edge and supported it lightly with both hands. She drew her shoulders back and looked directly at me.

"That will be three dollars," she said.

"Three dollars! For a postcard!" I couldn't stop myself.

She hesitated; looked at the card again; reached her decision. "Some postcards are two dollars, some are three, and some are five. It depends on the condition. This is in very good condition, as you can see—no postmark, no stains, no creases. Only here, at the corner"—she held the card toward me—"it is bent a little. It hardly touches the picture itself, but the card is not in mint condition. I can let you have it for two dollars and fifty cents, but I cannot possibly—"

"Please," I said, holding up my hand. "I'll take it for three. I was just curious."

"My customers never complain. If you think three is too high—"

"I think three is perfect—perfect." Quickly, one after the other, I placed three dollar bills on the counter. She slipped them one by one into her hand and rang open the cash register.

"If you would care to see other cards, I have a number of unopened boxes—"

I assured her that I wanted only the one card. She picked it up, glanced at it once more, and slipped it into a small flat paper bag. She folded the top over and flattened the fold with a single slow stroke of her long thumb. She held it out to me and said, "A very nice postcard."

"Thank you," I replied; it seemed the only thing to say. She banged the drawer of the cash register shut. No smile from Plumshaw—no flicker of friendliness—only, for a moment, she turned to look at the streaming window, as if imagining my misfortune.

Through cold, gusting rain I trudged uphill, keeping under the occasional awnings. Rain coursed down my face and neck and trickled onto my collarbone; the bottoms of my pants darkened. I walked with bent head, my hands thrust deep in my trench coat pockets. Between the shops the gray of the water met the darker gray of the sky. Somewhere on the water a bell clanged, and I heard ropes creaking and a faint tinkling sound. It struck me that Columbus had been wrong. The earth was flat, and ended right here, at Broome—you could fall over the edge into grayness, and be lost forever.

In my room I rubbed my hair with a towel and changed into dry clothes and slippers. Despite the chill the radiator was cold, and I put on my summer bathrobe, wishing I had brought my winter one. I had placed the paper bag on the night table and I now drew out the postcard and propped it up against the white porcelain base of the lamp. I had chosen well. The sepia sun, the sepia lovers on their rock, the gloomy reflections in the lake, all these pleased me. In the light of the lamp I saw details I had failed to notice in Plumshaw's cavern: the tips of grasses rising through the shallow water in front of the pines, a pine root twisting through the bank and hanging over the water, a ribbon in her hair; and it was now plain that the figures were not looking out over the water, but were turned slightly toward each other. I could make out part of his face, and she was turned almost in profile. Her miniature features were sharply caught by the camera: I could see her eyelashes, her slightly open lips, a brown shadow of cheekbone. She was beautiful, but it was difficult to read her expression; I seemed to detect something questioning or uncertain in her face.

Lunch was served in the chilly room of small tables. There were seven other guests at OCEAN GABLES, all of them elderly except for a thin, fragile-looking, thirtyish woman with eyeglasses and sharp elbows, who sat hugging herself as she leaned over a book held open by a saucer at one edge and the top of a sugar bowl at the other and who looked up now and then with large, startled eyes. Even among the three couples there was no conversation, as if the presence of others compelled secrecy. After a hefty lunch I sought out the manager, John Kearns. I found him sitting in the living room reading a newspaper: a boyish gray-haired man with round, clear-rimmed eyeglasses and shiny cheeks, wearing a corduroy jacket with leather elbow patches over a buttoned sweater that revealed at the throat a red-and-black lumberjack shirt. He continued to hold open the paper while looking up with a big, hearty smile. "A cold snack," he said, and shook his paper sharply once. I realized that I must have heard incorrectly: a cold snap. "We never turn the heat on before the first of October. By law I can wait till the fifteenth." He paused and lowered his voice. "There's a man coming to look at the furnace next week. Unusual weather for this time of year. Bracing. You'll see: in two, three days people will be complaining about the heat and humidity. Never fails, does it." The last sentence seemed not quite to fit, but I was certain there would be no heat at OCEAN GABLES.

I sat for a while in a small room off the living room, in a plump, flowered armchair beside a bay window dripping with rain. The room contained a small bookcase filled with faded forty-year-old best-sellers and back issues of an architectural journal. I felt myself falling into a black mood and I suddenly sprang up and went upstairs for my coat and umbrella. Outside the rain ran in black rivulets along the sides of the lane. When I reached the main street I walked down the other side, stopping in a warm store to look at bamboo napkin holders, lacquered wicker picnic baskets lined with red-and-white-checked cloth, and white wicker wine carriers each with an empty green wine bottle, and then stopping in an even warmer store to examine a perforated wall hung with big shiny brass numerals, brass knockers, barrel bolts, cabinet catches, and double-pronged door hooks. Toward the bottom of the hill I looked across the street for PLUMSHAW'S RARE BOOKS, but it had disappeared. I imagined Plumshaw folding it all up like a cardboard box and walking away with it under a black umbrella. A moment later I caught sight of a white telephone number in a dark window; beside it Plumshaw's dripping black window reflected a white storefront, through which a dim book was visible. At the bottom of the street I walked through the muddy field past a gray rowboat half-filled with water. On the slippery pier I stood looking at a lobster boat with its piles of wet buoys, its slick tarpaulin spread over something with sharp edges, and its dark crate with a slightly open lid from which emerged a single brown-green pincer.

Back in my chilly room I wrapped myself in my bathrobe and walked back and forth rubbing my arms. The windows rattled. I began turning the sash locks, and discovered that one was missing—there were four little holes for screws. Still in my bathrobe I got into bed and lay reading one page in turn of the three impossible books I had brought with me: a history of the United States beginning with the Bronze Age, a complete Shakespeare in double columns, and a novel set in ancient Rome. I tossed the books aside and tried to sleep, but I was too bored for sleep. Rain lashed the windows—hammer-blows of rain. At any moment the panes were going to crack like eggshells. Then the rain would fall on the cold radiator, on the bedspread, on the open suitcase sitting on the wooden chair. Slowly the room would fill with water, slowly my bed would rise—and turning and turning, I would float out through the window into the angry sky. In the lamplit dusk of midafternoon I reached for my postcard. Despite a first, general impression of brown softness, I was struck again by the sharpness of the image as I drew the card close. I could distinguish the woman's brown iris from her darker brown pupil, and I could see her individual eyelashes. With surprise I now saw that the man faced her directly: his forehead, the straight line of his nose, even his lips, were distinctly visible. I detected a harshness about his expression; she for her part appeared sorrowful, the set of her lips mournful. On the rock beside him I could see the interwoven pattern of straw on his boater and the tiny ivory monkey, his hands pressed over his eyes, on top of the walking stick.

I replaced the card against the lamp and tried to nap, but the rain splattering against the windows, and the rattling sashes with the missing lock, and the rattling gray universe, all banished sleep, and I lay with my arm over my eyes waiting for dinner in my darkening room.

Dinner at OCEAN GABLES was served from six to eight. At one minute past six I stepped into the room of small tables covered with fresh white tablecloths and lit by fat candles in colorless glass globes. A small electric heater with a black rubber cord rattled in the center of the room. I wondered what occasion called forth the use of the main dining room and chose a corner table beside a curtained window. As I sat down the woman with sharp elbows appeared in the doorway, wearing a heavy baggy sweater that came down to her thighs and clutching her book against her stomach. She cast an alarmed look in my direction and chose a table in a far corner, where she sat down with awkward suddenness and bent her head over her book. Slowly the other couples came in and took their silent places. "Still raining," one man said, perhaps to his wife, perhaps to no one in particular, and "Yes," a woman from another table answered, "it certainly is coming down," before we subsided into silence. Dinner dazzled us: duck à l'orange with wild rice, hot homemade bread, hot apple crisp for dessert. I lingered over a superb cup of coffee and wondered how on earth I would pass the time till bed. The expression struck me: how on earth. Was it possible I needed some other place? Slowly the room emptied, leaving only me and my destined companion. She had the look of a librarian or a third-grade teacher. We would be married in a white church on a green hill and open a gift shop in Broome. I stared at the bowed top of her head and began counting slowly, but at two hundred thirty she had not looked up. I finished a second cup of coffee and rose, but my fading bride remained rigidly bent over her book. In the living room a number of guests and John Kearns sat on flowered armchairs and couches and watched television. The screen showed rolls of smiling antacid tablets, dancing. Kearns wore a heavy, ribbed sweater and thick shoes with spongy soles; he looked like a happy bear. At the reception desk in the front hall I found a boy of ten reading a toy catalogue open to a page of robots. When I asked about movie theaters he said there was one over in Rock Ridge, at which moment a door opened and Mrs. Kearns came out, holding a tissue to her reddish nostrils and suddenly turning her face away to give a delicate, suppressed sneeze. Rock Ridge was twenty-five miles away through heavy rain. There was a drive-in theater ten miles away but sometimes the bridge was washed out and you had to go through Ashville. I recommended tea with lemon juice and three thousand milligrams of Vitamin C and returned upstairs, where I took a hot bath in a claw-foot tub. In my room I sat in pajamas, shirt, and bathrobe on a hard wooden chair at a small writing table and held my ballpoint poised above the back of a postcard I had found in the drawer, showing on the front a pen-and-ink sketch of OCEAN GABLES. I wrote the C of *Claudia,* brooded for ten minutes, and went to bed.

Before turning off the lamp I took my sepia postcard from the table and lay holding it upright on my chest. With surprise I realized that I had been looking forward impatiently to this moment, as if in the brown rectangle of the postcard I could forget for a while the rain and the room and the town and my restless, oddly askew life. In the light of the close-pulled lamp the sharpness of the image was almost startling. I could see the needles in the pine trees and the wingtip of a bird on a branch; in a tiny opening in the pines the spotted back of a fawn was visible. I could see the knot in the ribbon in the woman's hair and the minuscule lines streaming outward from the knot. The hardness of the man's expression was unmistakable, the tension in lip and nostril sharp and clear. For the first time I noticed that his face was tilted toward hers, which was pulled back slightly, as if from a fire. A long brown cloud was reflected with a single ripple beneath the reflected pines. Uncomfortably I returned the postcard to the base of the lamp and turned out the light.

Perhaps it was the unnatural earliness, perhaps it was the second cup of coffee, perhaps it was only my life, my life, but I could not fall asleep. I listened to the rain, the dark rain of Broome, to the heavy creak and crack of footsteps on the stairs, to the always opening and closing bathroom door—and long after the floor had grown quiet, and I was drifting off to sleep, again I heard the creaking of the stairs as someone climbed slowly, very slowly, pausing as if abashed at each loud crack of wood, until I wanted to shout into the night: and still the steps ascended, timidly, crashingly, and suddenly stopped forever. I fell into a restless sort of half-waking sleep and dreamed that I was wandering ankle-deep in water in a dark tangle of decaying rooms. I came to a massive door with a handle so high I could not reach it. The wood of the door was slippery and covered with greenish slime, and when the door sprang open I saw Plumshaw before me, but she was grinning wildly and her hair was blowing in the wind. I turned over and Plumshaw vanished but the rooms remained, filled now with small tables heaped with bowls of soup. Claudia was complaining about the soup, knocking one bowl after another from the tables, and when I crouched down to pick up a bowl I saw a woman seated on the floor with her head bowed, who looked up with startled eyes as I woke in the dark. My windows were rattling. I turned on the lamp. It was 11:46. Grimly I threw off the covers and marched to the writing table, where I folded the OCEAN GABLES postcard in half and in half again before thrusting it between the clattering pair of unlocked sashes. Back in my bed I lay in lamplight listening to the rain. As I turned on my side and reached up to turn off the lamp I glanced at the postcard.

There was no possibility of misreading their expressions: she was in anguish, his face was twisted in anger. The dark sun seemed to have slipped lower, it was barely visible above the pines. His body leaned harshly toward her and she was straining away. The dark brown sun half-sunk behind the trees, the unpeaceful lovers, the sharp rocks, the brown clouds, all were burdened with sorrow, and with a sense of oppression I thrust the picture back against the lamp.

I must have fallen into a light, uneasy sleep, for I was wakened by what sounded like a faint gasp or cry. I lay listening, but heard only the harsh rain. In that black room my chest felt heavy, my lungs labored, I could barely breathe. With a feeling of anxiety I sat up and switched on the lamp, which instantly sprang up in a black window. I snatched the postcard and looked in anguish at her face stricken with terror, his face taut with fury. A tendon stood out sharply on his neck and I saw that his slightly raised right hand grasped a small sharp rock. I could see the tense knuckles and the tiny, carefully manicured nails.

I tore my eyes away and saw on the lamp table the small, flat paper bag. Quickly I thrust the postcard into the bag.

I turned off the lamp and could not sleep. The oppressive postcard, the clattering rain, the labyrinth of tangled bedclothes, my racing mind, all lashed me into heavy wakefulness. Sometime in that hellish night I heard a dim cry, a thud, a splash, but I was sick to death of Broome, I was sick to death of it all, and lay with clenched fists in the streaming dark, imagining the bloody stone, the circle of spreading ripples, the floating hair. Toward dawn I slept, and was wakened not long after by the banging of the bathroom door.

I was the first one down for breakfast, and I rose wiping my lips as two silent couples were studying the menu. Through the cold morning rain I made my way down the steep street, leaning forward in the wind and holding my umbrella with two hands, one on the curving handle and one under the spokes. Though it was ten of eight, Plumshaw was there. I had known she would be. The look she gave me, when I entered under the tinkling bell, seemed to say: no returns accepted. I balanced my dripping umbrella carefully against the counter and strode toward the passage as the handle began to slide in a dream-slow arc. In the warren of rooms and passages I lost my way and came to a room filled with old furniture: a flattish rolled-up carpet lay bent across an armchair, and a dressmaker's dummy, wearing nothing but a wide-brimmed black hat, rose up from behind an upside-down bicycle. After that I found myself in a room with a boarded-up window, and then I stepped through a narrow passage into the room with the rack of postcards. At the table I kept looking at the entrance, but Plumshaw didn't appear. Furtively I pulled the

189

paper bag from my pocket and slipped out the postcard, pausing for an instant before thrusting it into the middle of a cluster of cards. In that pause I glanced at it, but in the poor light I saw only a vague brown scene, with something dim, perhaps a figure, at the end of the rocky point. Wildly I spun the teetering rack and turned away. At that moment I was seized by a violent curiosity, like a hand gripping my throat, and stepping back to the rack I began searching desperately through postcards of baroque fountains and Alpine huts and old railroad trains. It was Plumshaw who saved me: she walked into the room and I whirled around. She was carrying a shoebox under one arm.

"I thought you might like to see these," she said, taking off the lid and holding out a box tightly stuffed with postcards. "There are some very nice views."

"Not today, no, not right now. Here, allow me." I took the box from her, tucked it under my arm, and followed her to the front of the shop. My umbrella hung by its handle from the side of the counter. I set down the box next to the cash register and pulled from the candy rack a cellophane bag of gumdrops. "One of these instead." There was no price on any of the candy; I looked forward to being amazed. Plumshaw disappointed me by ringing up seventy-five cents. "More rain," I said, gesturing vaguely toward the window.

"It rains often, here in Broome." She paused a moment, drew herself up, and added, "The jellybeans are also very good."

In my room I ate two gumdrops and packed my bag, which seemed to contain nothing but damp clothes. As I swung across the landing I nearly knocked into the woman with the book, who looked at me in alarm and stepped back against a wall. "Wonderful weather!" I said. She blinked at me through her glasses and said quietly, as if reproachfully, "I love it when it rains." She looked disapprovingly at my suitcase. I reached into my pocket and held out the open bag of gumdrops. She shook her head quickly. I imagined staying at Broome, taking her out to dinner, marrying her. "I don't like gumdrops," she said. "Goodbye," I said, and bounded down the stairs. At the desk in the front hall Mrs. Kearns looked at my suitcase with red, rheum-glittering eyes. I had paid for three nights; she said nothing at all as I nodded at her and stepped onto the front porch.

Rain splashed on the flagstone path and ran from the roof gutters. I turned up the collar of my trench coat and made my way through cuff-high wet grass to the gravel parking lot pooled with rain. My windshield was covered with large wet leaves. I threw my dripping suitcase in the car and backed out onto the muddy lane, remembering suddenly the black-and-silver ballpoint I had left on the writing table, and making a mental gift of it to John Kearns. It would look good in the pocket of his corduroy jacket. As I turned onto the steep street, in the uphill direction, I saw the shops plunging downhill in the rearview mirror, and I was seized by the certain feeling that the moment the street vanished from view, suddenly the clouds above the shop would part, a big yellow sun would burst forth, the sky would turn bright, dazzling blue.

PAUL THEROUX

Portrait of a Lady

A hundred times, Harper had said to himself: *I am in Paris*. At first he had whispered it with excitement, but as the days passed he began mouthing it in a discouraged way, almost in disbelief, in the humiliated tones of a woman who realizes that her lover is not ever going to turn up. His doubt of the city made him doubt himself.

He was in Paris waiting for a sum of money in cash to be handed to him. He was expected to carry this bundle back to the States. That was the whole of his job: he was a courier. The age of technology demanded this simple human service, a return to romance: he tucked his business under his arm—the money, the message—as men had a century ago. It was a delicate matter; also, it was illegal.

Harper had been hired for his loyalty and resourcefulness. His employer demanded honesty, but implied that cunning would be required of him. He had impressed his employer because he wasn't hungry and wasn't looking for work. And, a recent graduate of Harvard Business School, Harper was passionate about real estate investment. Afterward he discovered that real estate investment was carrying a flat briefcase with eighty-five thousand dollars in used hundreds from an Iranian in Paris to an office in Boston, to invest in an Arizona supermarket or a chain of hamburger joints. They probably didn't even eat hamburgers, the Iranians—probably against their religion; so much was. Money (he, from Harvard Business School, had to be told this) shows up in a luggage x-ray at an airport security check as innocently as laundry, like so many folded hankies.

I am in Paris. But his first sight of the place gave him the only impression that stayed with him: there were parts of Paris that resembled Harvard Square.

He had told his wife that he would be back by the following weekend, and had flown to Paris on Sunday believing that he could pick up the cash on Monday. A day to loaf, then home on Wednesday, and his surprised wife seeing him grinning in the doorway would say, "So soon?"

He had not known that Monday was a holiday; this he spent furiously walking, wishing the day away. On Tuesday, he found Undershaw's office closed—Undershaw was the Iranian's agent, British: everyone got a slice. Harper's briefcase felt ridiculously light. That afternoon he tried the telephone. The line was busy; that made him hopeful. He took a taxi to the office but found it as he had that morning, locked, with no message on the dusty glass. On Wednesday he canceled his flight and tried again. This time there was a secretary in the outer office. She did not know Undershaw's name; she was temporary, she explained. Harper left a message, marked it *Urgent* and returned to his hotel near Les Invalides and waited for the phone to ring. Then he regretted that he had left his number, because it obliged him to stay in his room for the call. There was no call. He tried to ring his wife, but failed; he wondered if the phone was broken. Thursday he wasted on three trips to the office. Each time, the secretary smiled at him and he thought he saw pity in her eyes. He became awkward under her gaze, aware that a certain frenzy showed in his rumpled clothes.

"I will take your briefcase," she said. She was French, a bit buck-toothed and angular, not what he had expected.

Harper handed it over. Not realizing its lightness until it was too late, she juggled it and almost dropped it. Harper wondered whether he had betrayed his errand by disclosing the secret of its emptiness. A man with an empty briefcase must have a shady scheme.

The street door opened and a man entered. Harper guessed this might be Undershaw; but no, the fellow was young and a moment later Harper knew he was American—something about the tortoise-shell frames, the new raincoat, the wide-open face, the way he sat with his feet apart, his shoes and the way he tapped them. Brisk apology and innocent arrogance inhabited the same body. Still sitting, he spoke to the secretary in French. She replied in English. He gave her his name—it sounded to Harper like "Bumgarner." He turned to Harper and said, "Great city."

Harper guessed that he himself had been appraised. He said, "Very nice."

Bumgarner looked at his watch, did a calculation on his fingers, and said, "I was hoping to get to the Louvre this afternoon."

He is going to say, You can spend a week there and still not see everything.

But Bumgarner said, "What part of the States are you from?"

Harper told him: Boston. It required less explanation than Melrose.

"I'm from Denver," Bumgarner said, and before Harper could praise it, Bumgarner went on, "I'm over here on a poetry grant. National Endowment for the Arts."

"You write poems?" But Harper thought of his taxes, paying for this boy's poems, the glasses, the new raincoat.

Bumgarner smiled. "I've published quite a number. I'll have enough for a collection soon."

The secretary stared at them, seeing them rattling away in their own language. Bumgarner seemed to be addressing her as well as Harper.

"I've been working on a long poem ever since I got here. It was going to be simple, but it's become the history of Europe, and in a way kind of autobiographical."

"How long have you been in Paris?"

"Two semesters."

Harper thought: *Doesn't that just sum it up.*

"Are you interested in poetry?" Bumgarner asked.

"I read the usual things at college. Yeats, Pound, Eliot. 'April is the cruellest month.'" Bumgarner appeared to be waiting for him to say something more. Harper said, "There's a lot of naive economic theory in Pound."

"I mean modern poetry."

"Isn't that modern? Pound? Eliot?"

Bumgarner said, "Eliot's kind of a back number."

And Harper was offended. He had liked Eliot and found it a relief from marketing and accountancy courses; even a solace.

"What do you think of Europe?" Bumgarner asked.

"That's a tough one, like, 'Is science good?'" But seeing that Bumgarner looked mocked and wary, Harper added, "I haven't seen much more than my hotel and this office. I can't say."

"Old Europe," said Bumgarner. "James thought it corrupted you—Daisy Miller, Lambert Strether. I've been trying to figure it out. But it does do something to you. The freedom. All the history. The outlook."

Harper said, "I can't imagine any place that has more freedom than the States."

"Ever been to Colorado?"

"No," said Harper. "But I'll bet Europeans go. And for the same reason that characters in Henry James used to come here. To escape, find freedom, live a different life. Listen, this is a pretty stuffy place."

"Depends," Bumgarner said. "I met a French girl. We're living together. That's why I'm here. I mean, I have to see this lawyer. My wife and I have decided to go our separate ways."

"Sorry to hear it." *He will go home,* thought Harper, *and he will regret his folly here.*

"It's not like that. We're going to make a clean break. We'll still be friends. We'll sell the house in Boulder. We don't have any kids."

Harper said, "Is this a lawyer's office?"

"Sure. Are you in the wrong place?"

"Anywhere away from home is the wrong place," said Harper. "I'm in brokerage. I haven't fallen in love yet. As a matter of fact, I'm dying to leave. Is Undershaw your lawyer?"

"I don't know Undershaw. Mine's Haebler—Swiss. Friend of a friend." Then Bumgarner said, "Give Paris a chance."

"Paris is an idea, but not a new one," said Harper. "I tried to call my wife. The phones don't work. Where do these people park? The restaurants cost an arm and a leg. Call this a city?"

Bumgarner laughed in a patronizing way; he didn't argue. It interested Harper to discover that there were still Americans— poets—finding Paris magical. But this poet was getting a free ride: who was paying? Only businessmen and subsidized students could afford the place. Harper had had a meal at a small restaurant the previous day. The portions were tiny, the waiter was rude, the tables were jammed together, his knees ached from the forced confinement. The meal had cost him forty-seven dollars, with wine. No wonder poets had credit cards. It was a world he understood, but not one that he had expected.

Soon after, a tall man entered: Bumgarner's lawyer. Recognizing him, Bumgarner galloped after him. Harper was annoyed that the poet had shown so little interest in him, and *Eliot's kind of a back number* had stung him. The divorce: he would make it into a poem, deal with it like a specimen in a box and ask to be excused. But the other things—the dead phones, the restaurants, the bathtubs that couldn't take your big end, the pillow bolster that was hard as a log, the expense account, the credit card—they couldn't be poems. Too messy; they didn't rhyme. *Go home!* Harper wanted to scream at Bumgarner. *Europe's more boring than Canada!*

The secretary made a sorrowful click of her tongue when Harper rose to go. She had to remind him that he had left his briefcase; empty, it hardly seemed to matter. He was thinking about his wife.

On Friday, Undershaw rang him at ten-thirty, moments before Harper, who had started sleeping late—it was boredom—was preparing to leave his hotel room. Undershaw said he had been out of town, but this was not an apology.

"I've come for the merchandise," said Harper. He wanted to say, *I've wasted a week hanging around for you to appear.* He said, "I'd like to pick up the bundle today."

"Out of the question."

Harper tried to press him, but gently: the matter was illegal.

Undershaw said, "These things take time. I won't be able to do much before next week."

"Monday?"

"I can't be that definite," said Undershaw. "I'll leave a message at your hotel."

No, thought Harper. But he could not protest. He was a courier, no more than that. Undershaw did not owe him any explanation.

Harper had come to the city with one task to perform, and as he had yet to perform it his imagination wouldn't work. He had concentrated his mind on one thing; thwarted, he could think of nothing else. He was on the hook. His boss had sent him here to hang. Paris seemed very small.

Waiting in Paris reminded Harper of his childhood, which was a jumpy feeling of interminable helplessness. And childhood was another country, too, one governed like this by secretive people who would not explain their schemes to him. He had suspected as a child that there were rules he did not know. In adulthood he learned that there were no particular rules, only arbitrary courtesies. Children were not important, because they had no power and no menace: it took a man twenty-eight years old to realize that. You wait; but perhaps it is better, less humiliating, if people don't know you're waiting. Children were ignorant. The strength of adulthood lay in being dignified enough not to expose this impatience. It was worse for women. Now Harper could say to his wife: *I know how you feel.*

Portrait of a Lady

The weekend was dreary. Sunday in a Catholic country punished atheists by pushing them into the empty streets. Harper felt unwelcome. He did not know a soul except Bumgarner, who was smug and lucky and probably in bed with his "mistress"—the poet from Colorado would have used that silly word. Harper lay on his bed alone, studying the repetitions in the patterned wallpaper, and it struck him that it is the loneliest traveler who remembers his hotel wallpaper. He was exhausted by inaction; he wanted to go home.

He had been willing to offer the city everything. There were no takers. He thought: All travelers are like aging women, now homely beauties; the strange land flirts, then jilts and makes a fool of the stranger. There is less risk, at home, in making a jackass of yourself: you know the rules there. The answer is to be ladylike about it and maintain your dignity. But he knew as he thought this that he was denying himself the calculated risks that might bring him romance and a memory to carry away. There was no hell like a stranger's Sunday.

□ □

I'll leave a message at your hotel, Undershaw had said. That was a command. So Harper loitered in the hotel on Monday and when he was assailed by the sense that he was lurking he went out and bought a *Herald Tribune;* then he felt truant. At five there was no message. He decided to go for a walk, and soon he discovered himself to be walking fast toward Undershaw's office.

"He is not here," the secretary said. She knew before he opened his mouth what Harper wanted.

To cover his embarrassment, Harper said, "I knew he wasn't here. I just came to say hello."

The girl smiled. She began to cram papers and envelopes and keys into her handbag.

"I thought you might want a drink," said Harper, surprising himself at his invitation.

The girl tilted her head and shrugged: it was neither yes nor no. She picked up her coat and switched off the lights as she walked to the door. Still, Harper was not sure what all this meant, until with resignation she said, "We go."

At the bar—she chose it; he would never have found it in that alley—she told him her name was Claire.

Harper began describing the emptiness he had felt on Sunday, how the only thing it was possible to do was go to church.

Claire said, "I do not go to church."

"At least we've got that in common."

A man in the bar was reading a newspaper; the headline spoke of an election. Harper mentioned this.

Claire thrust forward her lower lip and said, "I am an anarchist." She pronounced the word *anarsheest*.

"Does that mean you don't take sugar?" Harper playfully moved the sugar bowl to one side as she stirred her coffee.

She said, "You have a ring." She tapped it with a pretty finger. "Are you married?"

Harper nodded and made a private vow that he would not deceive his wife.

She said, "How is it possible to be married?"

"I know," Harper said. "You don't know anyone who's happily married. Right? But how many single people are happy?"

"Americans think happiness is so important."

"What do the French think is important?"

"Money. Clothes. Sex. That is why we are always so sad."

"Always?"

"We have no humor," she said, proving it in her solemn tone of voice. "We are—how do you say—*mélancolique*?"

And Harper, who knew almost no French, translated the word. Then he complimented her on her English. Claire said that she had lived for two years in London, with an English family.

He wanted her to drink. She said she only drank wine, and that with meals. He took her to a restaurant—again she chose: a narrow noisy room. Why did they all look like ticket offices? Harper stared at the young men and women in the restaurant. The men had close-cropped hair and earrings, the women were white-faced and smoked cigarettes over their food. Harper said, "There's something about this place."

Claire smiled briefly.

"That guy in the corner," Harper said. "He's gay." Claire squinted at Harper. "A pederast."

Claire glanced at the man and made a noise of agreement. Harper smiled. "A sodomite."

"No," she said. "I am a sodomite. But he is a pederast. *Un pédé.*"

"I knew there was something about this place." Harper's scalp prickled.

"You seem a bit shocked."

"Me?" Harper tried to laugh.

"Didn't you do it at school? Playing with the other boys?"

"They would have killed me. I mean, the teachers. Anyway, I didn't want to. What about you?"

She thrust out her lower lip and said, "Of course."

"And now?"

"Of course."

The food came. They ate in silence. Harper could think of nothing to say. She was an anarchist who had just disclosed that she was also a lesbian. And he? A courier with an empty briefcase, killing time. He thought of the poet Bumgarner: Paris belonged to him. Harper could not imagine the feeling, but Bumgarner would know what to say now.

"It is easier for a woman," said Claire. He guessed that she had perceived his confusion. "I don't care whether I make love to a man or a woman. Though I have a fiancé—he is a nice boy. It is the personality that matters. I like clever men and stupid women."

"That guy who was in the office the other day," Harper said. "He's a poet. He writes poems."

Claire said, "I hate poems."

It was the most passionate thing she had said so far, but it killed his ardor.

In the twilight, under a pale watery-blue sky, they walked

past biscuity buildings to the river. Although this was his eighth day in Paris, Harper's yearning for home had deserted him, and he could ignore his errand, which seemed trivial to him now. He no longer felt humiliated by suspense; and another thing released him: the girl Claire, who was neither pretty nor ugly, seemed indifferent to him. It did not matter whether he slept with her or not—he felt no desire, so there could be no such thing as failure. He enjoyed this perverse freedom, walking along the left bank of the Seine, on a mild spring evening, feeling no thrill, only a complacent lack of urgency. But that was how it was, in spite of Paris; and urgency had been no help the previous week. He did not speak French. The churches and stonecrusts were familiar; he recognized them from free calendars and jigsaw puzzles and the lids of fancy cookie tins. He had never been overseas before. It was the stage set he had imagined, but he felt unrehearsed.

"I'm tired," he said, to give Claire an excuse to go home.

She shrugged as she had before, but now the gesture irritated him because she did it so well, using her shoulders and hands and sticking out her lower lip.

"I'm staying at a hotel near Les Invalides," he said. "Would you like a drink there?"

She shrugged again. This one meant yes—it was pliable and positive.

By the time they found a taxi rank it was ten-thirty. There was traffic—worse than Boston—and they did not arrive at the hotel until after eleven. The concierge stepped from behind a palm to tell Claire the bar was closed.

Harper said, "We can drink in my room," although he had nothing there to drink.

In the room, Harper filled a tumbler with water from the sink. This he brought to Claire and presented it with a waiter's flourish. She drank it without a word.

He said, "Do you like it?"

"Yes. Very much. It is a pleasant drink."

"Would you like some more?"

"Not now," she said.

He sat beside her on the bed, and kissed her with a clownish sweetness, holding her elbows, and she responded innocently, putting her cool nose against his neck. Then she said, "Wait."

She untied the drawstring at her waist and shook herself out of her dress. She did this quickly, like someone impatient to swim. When she was naked they kissed again, and he was almost alarmed by the way her tongue insisted in his mouth and her foraging hands pulled clumsily at his clothes. Soon after, they made love, and in the darkness, when it had ended, Harper thought he heard her whimper with dissatisfaction.

He woke. She was across the room, speaking French.

"What is it?"

"I am calling a taxi, to go home."

"Don't go," he said. "Besides, I don't think the phone works."

"I have to take my pill."

The phone worked. *I am in Paris:* he said it in a groggy foolish voice.

Claire, who was dressing, said, "Pardon?"

The next day was a repetition of the previous day. He waited at the hotel for Undershaw to ring. At four, he went to the office. This time there were no preliminaries; only romance required them, and this was no romance. Harper was glad of that, and glad too that he was not particularly attracted to Claire. Since his marriage—and he was happy with his wife—he had not been attracted to any other woman. It did not make him calm; indeed, it worried him, because he knew that if he did fall for another woman it would matter and he would have to leave home. They skipped the bar, ate quickly, then hurried to the hotel and went to bed, hardly speaking.

In the pitch dark of early morning, he waited for her to make her telephone call. But she was asleep. He woke her. She was startled, then seemed to remember where she was. He said, "Don't you have to go?"

She muttered rapidly in French, then came fully awake and said, "I brought my pill."

Harper slept badly; Claire emitted gentle satisfied snores. In the morning she opened her eyes wide and said, "I had a *cauchemar.*"

"Really?" The word, which he knew, bewitched him.

She said, "You have a beautiful word in English for *cauchemar.*"

"*Cauchemar* is a beautiful word," he said, and quoted,

How much it means that I say this to you—
Without these friendships—life, what *cauchemar!*

"I don't understand," she said.

"A poem," said Harper.

She pretended to shudder. She said, "What is *cauchemar* in English?"

"Nightmare."

"So beautiful," she said.

"What was your *cauchemar* about?"

"My—nightmare"—she smiled, savoring the word—"it was about us. You and me. We were in a house together, with a cat. It was quite an ordinary cat, but it was very hungry. I wanted to make love with you. That is my trouble, you see. I am too direct. The cat was in our bedroom."

"Where was this bedroom—Europe?"

"Paris," she said. "The cat was so hungry it was sitting on the floor and crying. We couldn't make love until we had fed it. We gave it some food. But when the cat ate the food it caught fire and burned—oh, it was horrible! Each time it swallowed it burned some more. It did not burn like a cat, but like a human, like Jan Palach. You know Jan Palach?"

Harper did not know the name. He said, "A saint?"— because her tone seemed to describe a martyr.

"No, no, no," said Claire. She was troubled.

Harper said, "It's about being a lesbian—your dream. Killing the cat, us making love."

"Of course," she said. "I have thought of that."

Her troubled look had left her; now she was abstracted, her features stilled by thought.

A fear rose in Harper that he was not in Europe at all, but trapped in a strange place with a sad crazy woman. He had made a great mistake in becoming involved with her. It was worse when they were dressing, for the telephone rang and Harper panicked and screamed, "Don't touch it!" He imagined that it was his wife, and he felt guilty and ashamed to be in this room with this incomprehensible woman. He had never loved his wife more. He seized the phone: Undershaw.

"It's ready. You can come over."

"Thank you," said Harper, tongue-tied with gratitude. He turned to Claire. "I've got to go to the office."

But she was buckling her small watch to her wrist. "Look at the time," she cried. "I'm late!"

They arrived separately—it was his idea—so that no one would suspect what they had done. Harper, who had spent days wishing to punch Undershaw in the face, introduced himself to the gray, rather tall Englishman feeling no malice at all. He took the parcel of money and locked himself in a small room to count it. He repeated the procedure, and when he was satisfied the amount was correct he packed the money in neat bundles in the briefcase. And, as if he knew how long it took to count eighty-five thousand dollars, Undershaw knocked at the door just as Harper finished.

"If everything's in order I'll be off then," said Undershaw.

"Take care," said Harper, and watched him go.

In the outer office, Claire was filling her handbag. Harper paused, because he believed it was expected of him to ask her out to dinner—he would not be able to leave until the next day.

Claire said, "I can't see you tonight. I am meeting a woman. I may have an adventure. You can stay—shut the door and it will lock."

"I hope she's nice," said Harper. "Your woman."

"Yes," said Claire, ladylike in concentration. She went to the door and stuck out her lower lip. "She is my fiancé's girl friend."

When she had left, Harper wanted to sit down. But the chairs disgusted him. There were four of them in this dreadful yellow room, this rallying place for the crooked—they were not evil, but idle. The room had held Bumgarner, and Claire, and Undershaw; and now they had gone on their tired errands. But their snailtracks were still here. There are rooms—his hotel room was one—in which the weak leave their sour hope behind; from which they set out to succeed at small deceptions and fail in the hugest way. Harper wanted to be home. He felt insulted and had never hated himself more. The briefcase, weighted with money, reminded him that he was still in Paris, and that he would have to complete his own shameful errand before he could look for a new job in the United States of America.

PAUL BOWLES

You Have Left
Your Lotus Pods
on the Bus

I soon learned not to go near the windows or to
draw aside the double curtains in order to
look at the river below. The view was wide
and lively, with factories and warehouses on the
far side of the Chao Phraya, and strings of barges
being towed up and down through the dirty water. The new wing of the hotel had been built in
the shape of an upright slab, so that the room was
high and had no trees to shade it from the poisonous onslaught of the afternoon sun. The end of
the day, rather than bringing respite, intensified
the heat, for then the entire river was made of
sunlight. With the redness of dusk everything out
there became melodramatic and forbidding, and
still the oven heat from outside leaked through
the windows.

Brooks, teaching at Chulalongkorn University,
was required as a Fulbright Fellow to attend regular classes in Thai; as an adjunct to this he arranged to spend much of his leisure time with

Thais. One day he brought along with him three young men wearing the bright orange-yellow robes of Buddhist monks. They filed into the hotel room in silence and stood in a row as they were presented to me, each one responding by joining his palms together, thumbs touching his chest.

As we talked, Yamyong, the eldest, in his late twenties, explained that he was an ordained monk, while the other two were novices. Brooks then asked Prasert and Vichai if they would be ordained soon, but the monk answered for them.

"I do not think they are expecting to be ordained," he said quietly, looking at the floor, as if it were a sore subject all too often discussed among them. He glanced up at me and went on talking. "Your room is beautiful. We are not accustomed to such luxury." His voice was flat; he was trying to conceal his disapproval. The three conferred briefly in undertones. "My friends say they have never seen such a luxurious room," he reported, watching me closely through his steel-rimmed spectacles to see my reaction. I failed to hear.

They put down their brown paper parasols and their reticules that bulged with books and fruit. Then they got themselves into position in a row along the couch among the cushions. For a while they were busy adjusting the folds of their robes around their shoulders and legs.

"They make their own clothes," volunteered Brooks. "All the monks do."

I spoke of Ceylon; there the monks bought the robes all cut and ready to sew together. Yamyong smiled appreciatively and said: "We use the same system here."

The air-conditioning roared at one end of the room and the noise of boat motors on the river seeped through the windows at the other. I looked at the three sitting in front of me. They were very calm and self-possessed, but they seemed lacking in physical health. I was aware of the facial bones beneath their skin. Was the impression of sallowness partly due to the shaved eyebrows and hair?

Yamyong was speaking. "We appreciate the opportunity to use English. For this reason we are liking to have foreign friends.

English, American; it doesn't matter. We can understand." Prasert and Vichai nodded.

Time went on, and we sat there, extending but not altering the subject of conversation. Occasionally I looked around the room. Before they had come in, it had been only a hotel room whose curtains must be kept drawn. Their presence and their comments on it had managed to invest it with a vaguely disturbing quality; I felt that they considered it a great mistake on my part to have chosen such a place in which to stay.

"Look at his tattoo," said Brooks. "Show him."

Yamyong pulled back his robe a bit from the shoulder, and I saw the two indigo lines of finely written Thai characters. "That is for good health," he said, glancing up at me. His smile seemed odd, but then, his facial expression did not complement his words at any point.

"Don't the Buddhists disapprove of tattooing?" I said.

"Some people say it is backwardness." Again he smiled. "Words for good health are said to be superstition. This was done by my abbot when I was a boy studying in the *wat*. Perhaps he did not know it was a superstition."

We were about to go with them to visit the *wat* where they lived. I pulled a tie from the closet and stood before the mirror arranging it.

"Sir," Yamyong began. "Will you please explain something? What is the significance of the necktie?"

"The significance of the necktie?" I turned to face him. "You mean, why do men wear neckties?"

"No. I know that. The purpose is to look like a gentleman."

I laughed. Yamyong was not put off. "I have noticed that some men wear the two ends equal, and some wear the wide end longer than the narrow, or the narrow longer than the wide. And the neckties themselves, they are not all the same length, are they? Some even with both ends equal reach below the waist. What are the different meanings?"

"There is no meaning," I said. "Absolutely none."

He looked to Brooks for confirmation, but Brooks was trying out his Thai on Prasert and Vichai, and so he was silent and thoughtful for a moment. "I believe you, of course," he said graciously. "But we all thought each way had a different significance attached."

As we went out of the hotel, the doorman bowed respectfully. Until now he had never given a sign that he was aware of my existence. The wearers of the yellow robe carry weight in Thailand.

A few Sundays later I agreed to go with Brooks and our friends to Ayudhaya. The idea of a Sunday outing is so repellent to me that deciding to take part in this one was to a certain extent a compulsive act. Ayudhaya lies less than fifty miles up the Chao Phraya from Bangkok. For historians and art collectors it is more than just a provincial town; it is a period and a style—having been the Thai capital for more than four centuries. Very likely it still would be, had the Burmese not laid it waste in the eighteenth century.

Brooks came early to fetch me. Downstairs in the street stood the three bhikkus with their book bags and parasols. They hailed a cab, and without any previous price arrangements (the ordinary citizen tries to fix a sum beforehand) we got in and drove for twenty minutes or a half-hour, until we got to a bus terminal on the northern outskirts of the city.

It was a nice, old-fashioned, open bus. Every part of it rattled, and the air from the rice fields blew across us as we pieced together our bits of synthetic conversation. Brooks, in high spirits, kept calling across to me: "Look! Water buffaloes!" As we went further away from Bangkok there were more of the beasts, and his cries became more frequent. Yamyong, sitting next to me, whispered: "Professor Brooks is fond of buffaloes?" I laughed and said I didn't think so.

"Then?"

I said that in America there were no buffaloes in the fields, and that was why Brooks was interested in seeing them. There were no temples in the landscape, either, I told him, and added, perhaps unwisely: "He looks at buffaloes. I look at temples." This struck Yamyong as hilarious, and he made allusions to it now and then all during the day.

The road stretched ahead, straight as a line in geometry,

across the verdant, level land. Paralleling it on its eastern side was a fairly wide canal, here and there choked with patches of enormous pink lotuses. In places the flowers were gone and only the pods remained, thick green disks with the circular seeds embedded in their flesh. At the first stop the bhikkus got out. They came aboard again with mangosteens and lotus pods and insisted on giving us large numbers of each. The huge seeds popped out of the fibrous lotus cakes as though from a punchboard; they tasted almost like green almonds. "Something new for you today, I think," Yamyong said with a satisfied air.

Ayudhaya was hot, dusty, spread-out, its surrounding terrain strewn with ruins that scarcely showed through the vegetation. At some distance from the town there began a wide boulevard sparingly lined with important-looking buildings. It continued for a way and then came to an end as abrupt as its beginning. Growing up out of the scrub, and built of small russet-colored bricks, the ruined temples looked still unfinished rather than damaged by time. Repairs, done in smeared cement, veined their façades.

The bus's last stop was still two or three miles from the center of Ayudhaya. We got down into the dust, and Brooks declared: "The first thing we must do is find food. They can't eat anything solid, you know, after midday."

"Not noon exactly," Yamyong said. "Maybe one o'clock or a little later."

"Even so, that doesn't leave much time," I told him. "It's quarter to twelve now."

But the bhikkus were not hungry. None of them had visited Ayudhaya before, and so they had compiled a list of things they most wanted to see. They spoke with a man who had a station wagon parked nearby, and we set off for a ruined *stupa* that lay some miles to the southwest. It had been built atop a high mound, which we climbed with some difficulty, so that Brooks could take pictures of us standing within a fissure in the decayed outer wall. The air stank of the bats that lived inside.

When we got back to the bus stop, the subject of food arose once again, but the excursion had put the bhikkus into such a state of excitement that they could not bear to allot time for anything but looking. We went to the museum. It was quiet; there were Khmer heads and documents inscribed in Pali. The day had begun to be painful. I told myself I had known beforehand that it would.

Then we went to a temple. I was impressed, not so much by the gigantic Buddha which all but filled the interior, as by the fact that not far from the entrance a man sat on the floor playing a *ranad* (pronounced *lanat*). Although I was familiar with the sound of it from listening to recordings of Siamese music, I had never before seen the instrument. There was a graduated series of wooden blocks strung together, the whole slung like a hammock over a boat-shaped resonating stand. The tones hurried after one another like drops of water falling very fast. After the painful heat outside, everything in the temple suddenly seemed a symbol of the concept of coolness—the stone floor under my bare feet, the breeze that moved through the shadowy interior, the bamboo fortune sticks being rattled in their long box by those praying at the altar, and the succession of insubstantial, glassy sounds that came from the *ranad*. I thought: If only I could get something to eat, I wouldn't mind the heat so much.

We got into the center of Ayudhaya a little after three o'clock. It was hot and noisy; the bhikkus had no idea of where to look for a restaurant, and the prospect of asking did not appeal to them. The five of us walked aimlessly. I had come to the conclusion that neither Prasert nor Vichai understood spoken English, and I addressed myself earnestly to Yamyong. *"We've got to eat."* He stared at me with severity. "We are searching," he told me.

Eventually we found a Chinese restaurant on a corner of the principal street. There was a table full of boisterous Thais drinking *mekong* (categorized as whiskey, but with the taste of cheap rum) and another table occupied by an entire Chinese family. These people were doing some serious eating, their faces buried in their rice bowls. It cheered me to see them: I was faint, and had half expected to be told that there was no hot food available.

The large menu in English which was brought us must have been typed several decades ago and wiped with a damp rag once a week ever since. Under the heading SPECIALITIES were some dishes that caught my eye, and as I went through the list I began to laugh. Then I read it aloud to Brooks.

> *"Fried Sharks Fins and Bean Sprout*
> *Chicken Chins Stuffed with Shrimp*
> *Fried Rice Birds*
> *Shrimps Balls and Green Marrow*
> *Pigs Lights with Pickles*
> *Braked Rice Bird in Port Wine*
> *Fish Head and Bean Curd"*

Although it was natural for our friends not to join in the laughter, I felt that their silence was not merely failure to respond; it was heavy, positive.

A moment later three Pepsi-Cola bottles were brought and placed on the table. "What are you going to have?" Brooks asked Yamyong.

"Nothing, thank you," he said lightly. "This will be enough for us today."

"But this is terrible! You mean no one is going to eat *anything?*"

"You and your friend will eat your food," said Yamyong. (He might as well have said "fodder.") Then he, Prasert, and Vichai stood up, and carrying their Pepsi-Cola bottles with them, went to sit at a table on the other side of the room. Now and then Yamyong smiled sternly across at us.

"I wish they'd stop watching us," Brooks said under his breath.

"They were the ones who kept putting it off," I reminded him. But I felt guilty, and I was annoyed at finding myself placed in the position of the self-indulgent unbeliever. It was almost as bad as eating in front of Moslems during Ramadan.

We finished our meal and set out immediately, following Yamyong's decision to visit a certain temple he wanted to see. The taxi drive led us through a region of thorny scrub. Here and there, in the shade of spreading flat-topped trees, were great round pits, full of dark water and crowded with buffaloes; only their wet snouts and horns were visible. Brooks was already crying: "Buffaloes! Hundreds of them!" He asked the taxi driver to stop so that he could photograph the animals.

"You will have buffaloes at the temple," said Yamyong. He was right; there was a muddy pit filled with them only a few hundred feet from the building. Brooks went and took his pictures while the bhikkus paid their routine visit to the shrine. I wandered into a courtyard where there was a long row of stone Buddhas. It is the custom of temple-goers to plaster little squares of gold leaf onto the religious statues in the *wats*. When thousands of them have been stuck onto the same surface, tiny scraps of gold come unstuck. Then they tremble in the breeze, and the figure shimmers with a small, vibrant life of its own. I stood in the courtyard watching this quivering along the arms and torsos of the Buddhas, and I was reminded of the motion of the bô-tree's leaves. When I mentioned it to Yamyong in the taxi, I think he failed to understand, for he replied: "The bô-tree is a very great tree for Buddhists."

Brooks sat beside me on the bus going back to Bangkok. We spoke only now and then. After so many hours of resisting the heat, it was relaxing to sit and feel the relatively cool air that blew in from the rice fields. The driver of the bus was not a believer in cause and effect. He passed trucks with oncoming traffic in full view. I felt better with my eyes shut, and I might even have dozed off, had there not been in the back of the bus a man, obviously not in control, who was intent on making as much noise as possible. He began to shout, scream, and howl almost as soon as we had left Ayudhaya, and he did this consistently throughout the journey. Brooks and I laughed about it, conjecturing whether he was crazy or only drunk. The aisle was too crowded for me to be able to see him from where I sat. Occasionally I glanced at the other passengers. It was as though they were entirely unaware of the commotion behind them. As we drew closer to the city, the screams became louder and almost constant.

"God, why don't they throw him off?" Brooks was beginning to be annoyed.

"They don't even hear him," I said bitterly. People who can tolerate noise inspire me with envy and rage. Finally I leaned over and said to Yamyong: "That poor man back there! It's incredible!"

"Yes," he said over his shoulder. "He's very busy." This set me thinking what a civilized and tolerant people they were, and I marvelled at the sophistication of the word "busy" to describe what was going on in the back of the bus.

Finally we were in a taxi driving across Bangkok. I would be dropped at my hotel and Brooks would take the three bhikkus on to their *wat*. In my head I was still hearing the heartrending cries. What had the repeated word patterns meant?

I had not been able to give an acceptable answer to Yamyong in his bewilderment about the significance of the necktie, but perhaps he could satisfy my curiosity here.

"That man in the back of the bus, you know?"

Yamyong nodded. "He was working very hard, poor fellow. Sunday is a bad day."

I disregarded the nonsense. "What was he saying?"

"Oh, he was saying: 'Go into second gear,' or 'We are coming to a bridge,' or 'Be careful, people in the road.' Whatever he saw."

Since neither Brooks nor I appeared to have understood, he went on. "All the buses must have a driver's assistant. He watches the road and tells the driver how to drive. It is hard work because he must shout loud enough for the driver to hear him."

"But why doesn't he sit up in front with the driver?"

"No, no. There must be one in the front and one in the back. That way two men are responsible for the bus."

It was an unconvincing explanation for the grueling sounds we had heard, but to show him that I believed him I said: "Aha! I see."

The taxi drew up in front of the hotel and I got out. When I said good-by to Yamyong, he replied, I think with a shade of aggrievement: "Good-by. You have left your lotus pods on the bus."

MARIA THOMAS

Summer

Opportunity

Mr. and Mrs. Warren P. Stegler request the pleasure of the company of *Ms. Gwendolyn Johnson* at a reception on *Tuesday July 2* from 7:00–9:00 P.M.

182 Embassy Crescent

RSVP (regrets only)   Tel. 01627

and written below:

"To welcome Ms. Gwendolyn Johnson
to Lagos, Summer IDI program."

Gwendolyn leans back, fingers the invite like a playing card, and takes a drag on her Benson & Hedges (airplane stash: duty free). She tries it on, "Beens'n 'n Hey-ges! Whoooooo? I say, Ben-Son and Hedge-Es." She tries IDI, "Ah-dee-ah," laughs around a little, and says, "I-D-I spells In-ter-na-tion-al Deee-vel-op-

ment In-tern. Me." Summer program means minority program.
Minority summer opportunity. An opportunity for a minority for
a summer.

"Gwind'lin!" her mother had shouted when she heard about
the trip six months ago. "You ain't goin' to *no Africa.*"

Gwendolyn's mother never got used to minority opportunity.
Way back in the fourth grade in Mississippi, sometime in the
middle sixties, Gwendolyn had been selected to integrate the
white school.

"Oh, yeah, well they's 'on haf ta come git you!" her mother
hollered; and when the white social worker showed up to drag
the girl off to school, Ida Johnson (five foot ten and two hundred
pounds) picked up the skinny, pale lady and heaved her out of
the front yard—never opened the gate.

But they finally got Gwendolyn for the ninth grade and kept
her right through high school. She had no friends save that skin-
and-bones Ralphy Wilkins, the other minority with an opportunity. Those two looked like Jack Sprat and his wife. Gwendolyn
was already beginning to look like her mother. But she did very
well in school and graduated in the top fifteen percent of her
class. She was selected for an IBM minority training program. It
meant she would have to go to New York. The night before she
was to leave, Mrs. Johnson set fire to her suitcase while the girl
wailed in her room and her brothers and sisters roared with
laughter.

She had to stay home. Miserable. Fat Gwendolyn. In her
room, she ate potato chips, drank Cokes, cried herself silly, and
read novels. Her mother wanted her to forget IBM and get a job
in town waiting tables or running the cash register at the local
grocery store. "You work for black folks or you be sorry," she
said. Gwendolyn refused. She was too ashamed to be seen around
town. She tried to explain to her mother that she had been given
opportunities. Now she was a failure. And no fault of her own.

"I coulda gone places," she told her brother Melchior. "Don't
you let Mamma tromp you down." Melchior also went to the
white high school and was already at the top of his class.
Melchior told Gwendolyn not to worry; he had an idea that

Summer Opportunity

would take her places. From the library at school, he got college
catalogues for his sister. Black colleges. Exclusively for black kids.
Melchior's idea was that Mamma would agree to that. And so it
was. Gwendolyn: on a big scholarship to Howard.

"Satan's own Washington!" her mother moaned.

"Chocolate city, they calls it," Uncle Charlie said. And they
pressed the frightened Ida Johnson into agreeing.

Gwendolyn threw herself right into things at Howard. Before
she had been there a month, this Melchior sent her a little button
said, BLACK IS BEAUTIFUL. And it was. Howard girls with their
afros and tinted shades, their slender butts and their bouncy
braless tits. Howard cats, tall, flat-bellied, shiny big afros, dashi-
kis, sandals, and pants tight on their slick sides.

Gwendolyn did not date. She was too fat. But the kids liked
Gwen. She always had the joke. At Howard she got herself a
style. She wore tent dresses in bright African prints, cut her hair
into a huge, high afro, and covered herself with lots of cheap
bangles and necklaces. She bought lots of big fringed shawls.

Now, one day, over on 11th Street, this Gwendolyn is walking, humming and swaying her lots of flesh side to side. She just
made honor grades again and she's on the way to something special. She's just a leeetle high—a postprandial pipe with Walter
Jackson and Sally B. A Washington spring, and black folks are
out and turning on. In the window of this little hole-in-the-wall,
factory-to-you-prices, no-name shoe store, Gwendolyn sees the
sandals of every woman's dreams. No white cat of a shoe man
ever made those steppers.

"These shoes," the man inside tells her, "are custom designed.
One fine lady over Alexandria had them made special. But like
it go," he says, "she hit bad luck. Never come git 'em. Now,
young lady, you ain' never gonna see a-nuvver pair of shoes like
these!"

Gwen smiles, puts them on, and struts her stuff, just a little
top heavy on these four-inch platforms.

"On'y the fines' leather," the man tells her—thin leather
straps in twelve dark, wild colors woven into dazzling baskets
out of which peeks the shocking pink of Gwendolyn's toenails.

219

"Ever' place you goes," the man says, "people gon' look at you an' say, *Lookit 'em shoes!*"

And they did. In Mississippi, when Gwen went home for spring vacation, people went pale and speechless in the wake of those shoes. And her mother, accusing Gwendolyn of having become a whore, threatened to destroy the sandals.

"You a fine howdy-do!" her mother told her, tossing the shoes at her.

□   □

Gwendolyn told Uncle Charlie first. An intercessor. "The government has picked me to go on a program to Africa. 'Count I got good grades and things. They gonna pay me all kind a money jes' to write a paper. I get a trip, my credits at school, and a chance for a job when I get out. Tell Mamma I'll buy her a new stove and icebox the day I get home. It's only for three month," she said. "You tell Mamma."

"AFRICA!" she heard her mother roar in the other room, and then the phrases coming in an excited garble: "... wil' animals ... heyd huntahs ... mumbo jumbo ... too many niggers ..." Gwendolyn smiled at Melchior, the two of them down on the floor with an atlas, looking for Nigeria.

Gwendolyn packed up to get out of there in a hurry in case Mrs. Johnson had a change of mind. As it was, her mother vacillated, threatening to drown herself or take the gas pipe or do both to Gwendolyn. She was frightened, she allowed in one of her quieter moments, that Gwendolyn might not come home. Not because her daughter might get hurt—what could be worse than Satan's own Washington?—but because her daughter might just like it there.

"When you walk down the street," she mused, "an' someone there in a car or standing behin' a tree, or comin' out 'roun' a corner ... when a man got his back to you and that man turn 'roun', his face gonna be a black face."

"Yeah, an' all the cops be black," said Uncle Charlie.

"All the doctors, the nurses, the judges, the pilots," said Melchior.

"All the teachers," said Sukie.

"An' telephone operators," said Phyllis.

"Car sellers and car buyers," said Roger.

"Car fixers and car builders," said Benjamin.

Gwendolyn and her brothers and sisters danced around the table. They made a party with Cokes and chocolate cakes and a banner saying, BON VOYAGE, GWEN BABY.

□ □

When Gwendolyn arrived in Lagos, Nigeria, a Mrs. Stegler was at the airport to welcome her and drive her to a small flat. She was a slender blond woman and she smiled and chatted about what life was like in this hectic town. Perhaps Gwendolyn was tired, she suggested, perhaps Gwendolyn would like a day or two to rest. "Jet lag," she called it, a phrase that made Gwendolyn feel like she had just *arrived,* honey, not *lagged.* Gwendolyn Johnson in the jet set. Gwendolyn thanked the lady, plopped down on a couch, and expected to sleep, but she was wound up, like the highest high, she was tuning in on all channels, running on all cylinders.

She opened up her big, new, red suitcase, pulled out her big blue jeans, her bright green, sleeveless turtleneck jersey and her multicolored four-inch platform sandals. Ready for battle on the town. She grabbed a bus in what she reckoned was the right direction, hit what looked like the downtown, and wound up in a place called Dixie Fried Chicken, with a menu right out of Colonel Sanders and a picture of some black dude in a Colonel Sanders outfit smiling out of a kinky beard and saying, "Real U.S. fried chicken. Try our crinkle-fry chips and fish burgers." Right there she met her first man, a skinny kid about half her size. He made the proposition and she didn't hesitate. She grabbed the opportunity and took him back to the flat and stayed there with him until the next day.

And then, two nights later, there was the Hausa trader, a tall wiry man, very black but with the features of a white man. He wore a long shirtlike thing and an embroidered skull cap. He chewed on kola nut and betel and his fine mouth was tinted deep red. He smelled of leather and came to her door selling statues and hassocks. She had just had a bath and had tied herself in a robe, pulling the sash tight around her waist. His eyes froze on her breasts when she leaned forward to look at his wares. She made the Hausa shower first and then, still wet, he twisted his long ebony body around her like a snake, his breath perfumed with betel nut. She bought a carving from him, a ripe woman holding out huge breasts over a big belly and carefully etched below, the fine details of her sex. "Like this dude had statues that looked like *me,*" she wrote in an X-rated letter to Sally B. at Howard.

□   □

When Ellie Stegler called Gwendolyn to say, "We would like to have a welcoming get-together for you, Gwen," Gwendolyn wanted to say, "Missus, I already *been* welcomed!"

Instead, she said, "Oh, thank you, Mrs. Stegler, I'd really like that." Summer opportunity. The invitation went in her scrapbook along with the plane ticket vouchers and the chit from the Dixie Fried Chicken. "Shittin' in the tall corn, as we say in Mississippi," she muttered, thinking, An' I'm gonna razzle dazzle them with my coon shoes, four big inches up, soaring over the host and hostess sky high.

The reception, your typical honky do with the chamber music muted in the background and scrawny white ladies on diets dwarfed in big African caftans, was a good time after all. Practically all the Nigerian guys, guys who worked in the office, guys who worked in the ministries alongside American technicians, guys who were teachers at American-sponsored colleges, guys who studied in the States, all these guys clustered around Gwendolyn. She was American, rich (so they thought), in transit, so clearly loose, and she was *magnificent.* Before the night was over, she had four dates for the next night. She somehow intended to keep them all.

She ended up going out with the first guy that showed. His name was Adedeji. He took her to dinner. He told her about the couple of years he spent in the States at Yale University, freezing his ass off and pumping gas to get pocket money. He told her about his village in Western State, about his family, his father who had seven wives.

"But I'll only have one wife," he told her. He took her to his small flat. He took her to his bed. He told her she was beautiful and sweet. He said it in Yoruba. *O dun. O wu mi.* A language that rose and fell like a song.

She laughed, "Hey, you know, back home, I'm just fat Gwendolyn. I tell jokes."

"Here you are a goddess," only he wasn't joking. He caressed her rich flesh, the mound of her belly. He tasted the thick folds of her neck.

Gwendolyn breaks all her other dates forever. When the Hausa comes, she tells him she doesn't want any teehee. When the skinny kid from the Dixie Fried shows up, she doesn't invite him in. She spends all her time with Adedeji. She should be writing her paper, doing her research. Grabbing the opportunity. But she doesn't even go into the office.

Mrs. Stegler checks in: "Is everything okay, Gwen? Is there any kind of problem? I don't want to pry, but if I can help ..." She starts saying things that sound like they're supposed to make Gwendolyn feel responsible, possibly grateful, as though she were standing there for her whole race and her whole sex. She's using tired old phrases like "... times of change ... black women in demand in the job market of the future ... a real chance ... a golden opportunity."

Gwendolyn interrupts, "You don't mind me asking this do you, but, like, what are you, personally, doing about all these movements—all this stuff you're laying on me?"

Ellie Stegler looks kind of embarrassed. "I don't know what I'm doing. I'm sorry. I wish I was your age. I wish I had your chance."

"Okay, okay, I'll get the work done," Gwen tells her, with absolutely no intention of doing a thing.

□   □

Adedeji invites her to come to his village for a few days. She agrees, excited. She goes with him dressed in Yoruba duds, a wrapper and a *gele,* the wild turban of Western Nigeria, big as a dream flower opening on the wide African morning. On her platform sandals she is nearly as tall as he is. He gives her a golden bangle that she knows he can't afford. He takes her picture with his instant camera, twice, giving one print to her and keeping the other for himself. And there she is, beaming in Kodacolor, rainbow Gwen, looking for all the world like an authentic, indigenous, Yoruba native.

On the bus, she loosens the wrapper. Air rushes into the folds of the cloth over her hot, moist skin. Adedeji looks cool, used to the heat. People talk in Yoruba to her and she laughs, telling them that she is American. Maybe she is Yoruba, she tells Adedeji. They buy boxes of yogurt and spicy cakes made of mashed beans, eggs, sardines, and hot pepper, steamed in green leaves.

"Just like my Mamma said," she tells Adedeji. "I see a little kid behind a bush, a woman bent over a child, a guy resting on his belly in the shade: I see that person there ahead of me standing in the dark shadow of a porch and I don't have to worry or even go close up to see his face. I know he's black. You understand what that means?" Did she really believe it though? Did her mother really believe it? That there was safety in color? That no one here would hurt her? She drank the light as it washed over Adedeji's perfect face, modeled on soft curves, his almond eyes set high on his cheekbones, strangely Oriental eyes, and his skin, not brown like hers but dark, jet black. She wondered if her mother had been right, if she might not just stay here with this man. Why was he taking her to his home? Was it a proposal?

His father's compound—enclosed in high terra-cotta walls, clouded in red dust, a path to it over dried mud and rocks. She carries the precious sandals like a wedding bouquet. Inside the old man's wives have their houses, single-room houses, huts, neat, grass covered, clothes drying, hung on bushes and sticks. Kids. So many kids. Adedeji's mother greets her with a closed, sardonic grin. She gestures for her to sit down on an awkward chair, something that angles back in a way that Gwendolyn can't possibly fit her body into. Someone brings a stool and Gwendolyn settles onto it. Adedeji tells her that she looks like a queen. People peer from doorless houses, from behind trees. They gather behind her, giggling, adolescent girls, cloths held tight over high hard breasts and boys rushing around while Adedeji heaps presents on them all.

The mother smiles open-mouthed this time. A tooth is gone. Gwendolyn smiles back.

Someone brings tea.

The hut they bring her to that night is dark. The bed is iron—a spring on legs and a thin mattress made of some dried grass. An earthen jug of water and a plastic cup so old that dirt is imbedded in it are there on an unsteady table. One of the young girls comes in with a lantern, a bowl of rice, and a spoon. The rice has some oily leaves and a few pieces of yellow meat on top of it. The girl stares at Gwendolyn with distrust, moving around her at the same distance. She pours some water and backs out of the hut. Gwendolyn cannot eat the stuff. She takes some papers out and tries to work. She gets out her novel, a mystery by Alistair MacLean. The lantern is too weak. She tries to drink some of the water but it's slimy and tastes of clay. The sheet on her bed is rough, washed in strong chemicals. The room smells of acid and insect spray. Gwendolyn had expected Adedeji would be there. She stretches out on the bed and waits.

In the morning Adedeji comes and tells her that he had to spend the night with his father and some friends in a nearby compound. "Gentlemen affairs," he says. "I will come to you tonight," he says, "but today I have more things to do. I own a few farms around here. Everyone will look after you."

He leaves her. His mothers and sisters (or whoever the hell they are) try to involve her in their work but she understands nothing of what is going on. One girl—a sister?—hovers around her more than the others with an intense curiosity that Gwendolyn knows is jealousy. The girl is tall and lean from hard work. She has deep brown skin and her hair is plaited in cornrows to the nape of her long neck, where it makes a delicate fringe. Her eyes, like Adedeji's, are ovals slanted back over high cheekbones. Her shoulders and back are narrow, angled down to a slender waist where her body curves out to a woman's hips and long dancer's legs.

After a long pantomime, it becomes clear that she wants to see Gwendolyn carry something on her head in the manner of a Yoruba woman. Gwendolyn removes her sandals to give it a try. She becomes the center of interest, her great, clumsy body swaying, her neck too weak, her hair a high pillow on which nothing will sit. The girl gestures, offering to plait Gwendolyn's hair.

The American's hair is soft and the African girl makes a high, surprised sound when she touches it, calling the others over to feel it. They all come shyly with tentative fingers, giggling when they contact it and then running away with excited cries. The girl braids Gwendolyn's hair, standing back to admire her handiwork and then admiring Gwendolyn with awe. Finally she dares to poke the flesh around Gwendolyn's neck and presses a palm on the woman's large breast, smiling and nodding in approval and envy.

Gwendolyn tries the basket on her head again. They teach her the words: *Wa gbe ru mi.* "Come put it on my head." Funny nasal syllables. She laughs now, tipping nearly over and looking, she thinks, like a token in some Walt Disney film. The girl meanwhile has taken Gwendolyn's mighty shoes and is walking around on them, or trying to, as unsteadily as Gwendolyn with the basket of pineapples on her head. Everyone is laughing. A small boy rushes in and pushes the girl over. She falls on Gwendolyn and the two of them crumple in a heap of dust giggling like little kids.

The girl shows Gwendolyn some onions. Teaches her how to say it, *alubosa.* Makes it clear that Gwendolyn is supposed to cut these onions into slices and put them in this pot. She has a fire going and is boiling some yams and goat meat. Gwendolyn is frying the onions in red palm oil while her friend is tossing in hot peppers and demonstrating what they are going to do to Gwendolyn's mouth when she tastes them.

Then suddenly the girl grabs Gwendolyn's arm. "Adedeji!"

she announces, smiling and nodding. The man steps through the gate and comes across the red compound. Huge. His shoulders are wide and the cloth of his great robe has golden threads woven into it, embroidered at the neck with spiraling gold symbols. He seems to float, shimmering in the red sun, glistening in the dusk.

□   □

"Is she your wife?" Gwendolyn asks him that night. He sits in her dark hut fingering the lantern.

"Yes," he says.

"What did you bring me here for then, huh?" she asks.

"I wanted you to see my home, my family—"

"Your *wife?*"

"Not necessarily that, but you're American, black. I thought the village ... the ..."

"You were with her last night? Tonight me?"

"Look," he said, "it isn't that way here. You're using some ideas you bring from America. It's different in Africa."

"You think she doesn't know?"

"She knows. Of course she knows."

"You think she doesn't care?"

"That's anther matter. It hasn't any relevance though. Besides, she's lucky. She knows I only plan to have one wife. She won't have to face—all this. My mother hated being the third wife. The first wife hates her. My wife won't have that."

"Oh, Jee-sus, and when do you, like, *plan* to get her out of all this? When do you take her to Lagos so you can't mess around? What's the difference between you and your old man is what I want to know? Except you're cheap. And I ain't about to be your second wife, you bastard," she says. "So get your black ass out of here."

She dusts her multicolored sandals, ties the heel straps together with a little bow she digs out of her purse, and takes them to Adedeji's wife. The young woman is hunkered alone by her fire stirring the soup she and Gwendolyn had made so happily that afternoon. Her feet are cracked and caked with ashes; ashes streak her face. (Have there been tears?)

227

Gwendolyn hands her the shoes. She doesn't understand at first but gets the picture and brightens. She dusts off her sorry-looking feet and puts the glorious sandals on, towering and strutting and smiling at Gwendolyn.

"Lookit 'em shoes!" Gwendolyn sings.

□　　□

After that it wasn't so hard for Gwendolyn to get her work done. She swore off men. Mrs. Stegler got excited and helped the kid with some of the fine grammatical points of her paper and Gwendolyn, the scholar-nun, turned the thing into something she knew she was going to fly with. Title: "Cottage Industries in Polygamous Yoruba Households." Thesis: That Yoruba women produced all the goods and ran all the businesses in the rural areas of Western Nigeria and that any development efforts in the area should be focused on them and not their menfolk. She gave the paper in Washington at a World Bank seminar on Women in Development and was awarded a scholarship to attend courses at the Hague.

When she got home to Mississippi, her mother was in despair. Melchior was going to Boston, to that citadel of honkydom, Harvard University ("I cain't even pronounc't it," she said), on a very big scholarship. She was sure they would turn him into a cracker or one of them fancy niggers who marries white gals. When Gwendolyn muttered something about Holland, it seemed to be the end of everything. Mrs. Johnson shrieked, "Ain't *no* black folks in Holland. NONE!" She was standing there ironing Melchior's shirts to absolute perfection and she had sunk every penny she had into a new wardrobe for that boy.

"I bought you a new stove, Mamma, and an icebox," Gwendolyn said. But the woman was not talking.

Everyone stood around then and Gwendolyn started digging out presents. Bright cloths, afro combs, beads, a couple of batiks to hang on the walls, carvings of people who looked just like them, and a little black hand-sewn doll for her baby sister Louise who was already talking up a storm. In the rubble of the unpacked things, this little Louise finds a picture of her sister in Yoruba duds, and she stands there looking and holding the thing for a while.

"Dat you, Gwind'lin!!!" she finally says. The little girl gives a funny laugh like someone who is already used to trick photography, and then off the track says, "Hey, Gwind'lin, you gonna give me them bes' shoes I grows up? You gonna give me them hi' hi' shoes?"

"I don't have them shoes no more," Gwendolyn tells her. "I already give them to someone over in Africa. Someone who didn't have no shoes atall."

"It far 'way, ain't it?" says the little kid. "Someplace far 'way like Mamma say?"

"Jest 'bout as far 'way as you can git."

JOHN UPDIKE

Cruise

Islands kept appearing outside their windows. Crete, Cythera, Capri, Ponza. Calypso, who had become Neuman's cruisemate, his wife at sea, liked to make love sitting astride him while gazing out the porthole, feeling between her legs the surging and the bucking of the boat. Her eyes, the color of a blue hydrangea, tipped toward the violet end of the spectrum in these moments. Her skin was as smooth as a new statue's. He called her Calypso because the entire cruise, consisting of sixty-five passengers and forty crewpersons, was marketed as a duplicate of the tortuous homeward voyage of Ulysses, though everyone, including their lecturers, kept forgetting which port of call represented what in the Odyssey. Were the cliffs of Bonifacio, a chic and slanty tourist trap on the southern tip of Corsica, *really* the cliffs from which the giant, indiscriminately carnivorous Laestrygones had pelted the fleet with rocks, sinking all but the wily captain's dark-prowed hull? Was

Djerba, a sleepy hot island off of the Tunisian coast, distinguished by a functioning synagogue and a disused thirteenth-century Aragonese fort, *really* the land of the Lotus Eaters?

"Well, what is 'really'?" their male lecturer asked them in turn, returning a question for a question in Socratic style. "Τί ἐστι η αλήθεια?" Or, as the French might put it, *"Le soi-disant 'Ding an sich,' c'existe ou non?"*

Their onboard lecturers were two: a small man and a large woman. The man preached a wry verbal deconstructionism and the woman a ringing cosmic feminism. Clytemnestra was her idea of a Greek hero. Medea and Hecuba she admired also. She wore gold sickles around her neck and her hair was done up in snakes of braid. Our lovers—cruel and flippant vis-à-vis the rest of humanity in their ecstasy of love newly entered upon—called her Killer. The male lecturer they called Homer. Homer sat up late in the ship's lounge each night, smoking cigarettes and planning what he was going to say the next day. He looked exhausted by all his knowledge, all his languages, and sallow from too much indoors. Even while trudging up and down the slippery, scree-ridden slopes of archeological digs, he wore a button-down shirt and laced black shoes. The lovers felt superior to him, in the exalted state brought on by repeated orgasms in the little cabin's swaying, clicking, cunningly outfitted space. *"Aiiiieeee!"* they cried. *"Aiae, aiae!* We are as gods!"

There were rough seas between Malta and Djerba. Neuman threw up, to his own surprise and disgust. He had thought, on the basis of several Atlantic crossings in the era before jet planes, that he was seaworthy. Calypso, who in her terrestrial life had been raised on a Nebraska wheat farm and had not seen the ocean until she was twenty-one and unhappily married, had no *mal-de-mer* problem; when he bolted from their table in the see-sawing dining room she stayed put, finished her poached sea trout, helped herself to his squid stew, ate all of the delicious little Maltese biscuits in the breadbasket, and ordered caramelized *pomme Charlotte* for dessert, with Turkish coffee. In the tranquillity of her stomach she was indeed as a goddess—Calypso, the daughter of Tethys by Oceanus. Fleeing the dining room, Neuman held acid vomit back against his teeth for the length of his run down the second-deck corridor; when he got into his own bathroom, he erupted like a fountain, disgustingly, epically. What is man but a bit of slime in the cistern of the void?

"You poor baby," she said, descending to him at last. Her kiss smelled of caramel and brought on a minor attack of gagging. "I think I'll spend the night back in my own cabin," she told him. "After a spot of anisette."

"Don't go up to the lounge," Neuman begged, feeble and green-faced yet nevertheless sexually jealous. "There's a hard-drinking crowd up there every night. Hardened cruisers. Good-time Charlies. Tonight they're having a sing-along, followed by a showing of 'Casablanca.' Whenever they show 'Casablanca' on one of these boats, all hell breaks loose."

"I'll be fine," she told him, her complicated blue eyes drifting evasively to the porthole, which was black but for the dim glow of the starboard lights and a diagonal slap of spray at the nadir of an especially sickening flop into watery nothingness. "Just because we have good sex," she told him firmly, "you don't own me, Buster. I paid for this cruise with my own money and I intend to have a good time."

She was one of the new women and he, despite his name, one of the old men. Female equality struck him as a brutish idea. Just the idea of her having a good time—of trying to milk some selfish happiness out of this inchoate hyperactive muddle of a universe—doubled and redoubled his nausea. "Go, go, you bitch," he said. His stomach, like a filmy jellyfish floating within him, was organizing itself for a new convulsion, and he was planning his dash to the toilet once she had removed the obstacle of her trim, compact body, in its chiton of starched blue linen, belted with a rope of gold. Good sturdy legs, like a cheerleader's without the white socks. Hips squared off like small bales of cotton. Narrow feet in gilded sandals. "Easy come," he told her queasily, with false jauntiness, "easy go."

□   □

They had sized each other up at the start, in the ruins of Troy. She was standing in khaki safari slacks and a lime-green tennis visor on Level VIIa, thought to be Priam's Troy if anything on this site "really" was, and he was down in Level II, not far from where Schliemann and his racy Greek wife, Sophia, had discovered and surreptitiously hidden a hoard of golden treasures from the middle of the third millennium before Christ. Now it was all a muddle of mounds and pebbles and blowing grasses and bobbing poppies and liquid-eyed guides and elderly Americans and tightly made limestone walls probably too small to have been the walls of fabled Troy. "Can this be all there was?" Homer was murmuring to their group. "*Est-ce que c'est tout?* A little rubbly village by the marshes? Schliemann decided, '*Es ist genug*. This was Troy.'" The poppies bobbed amid the nodding grasses. The rubble underfoot had been trod by Cassandra and Aeneas, venerable Priam and ravishing Helen.

The destined lovers' glances met, and remet; they measured each other for size and age and signs of socioeconomic compatibility, and he carefully climbed through the levels to edge into her group. Their group's guide, a local Turk, was telling about the Judgment of Paris as if it had happened just yesterday, in the next village: "So poor Zeus, what to do? One woman his wife, another his daughter, straight from head—*boom!*" He hit his fist against his broad brown brow. "Each lady say she the absolute best, *she* deserve golden apple. So Zeus, he looking around in bad way and see far off in Mount Ida, over there, you can almost see"—he gestured, and the tourists looked, but all they saw was the plains of Troy, vast if not as windy as in the epic—"he see this poor shepherd boy, son of King Priam, minding own business, tending the sheeps. His name, Paris. Zeus tell him, 'You choose.' 'Who, me?' 'Yes, you.'" The American tourists, broiling in the sun, obligingly laughed; the guide smiled, showing a gold fang. "'Oh, boy,' Paris think to self. 'Problem.' One offered him much riches, Hera. Another say, 'No, have some much glory in battle and wars, thanks to me.' That was Athena, daughter straight out of Zeus' head. Third say, Aphrodite say, 'No, forget all that. I give you most beautiful woman in world to be your wife.' And Paris say, 'O.K., you win. Good deal.'"

By now Neuman had drawn level with his tennis-visored prey. He murmured in her ear, "The 'O.K.' that launched a thousand ships." A gravelly American witticism, here in this remote, archaic place. He liked her ear very much, the marble whiteness and the squarish folds of it. It was feminine yet no-nonsense, like her level gaze.

She had sensed his proximity. The soul has hairs, which prickle. In profile Calypso barely smiled at the pleasantry, then turned to appraise him, calculating his suitability and the length of the cruise ahead of them. Návplion, Valletta, Bonifacio, Sperlonga. O.K. As if by destiny, without planning it, they arrived at the lounge for predinner drinks at the same moment. With utmost diffidence they chose the same banquette and, their increasingly excited recountings of their separate pasts far from finished, asked to be seated at the same dining table, as the sleek white cruise ship slipped off the tight-fitting Dardanelles and slipped on the sequinned blue gown of the Aegean.

□   □

Malta, a fairy-tale island. Everything was sand-colored—a series of giant sand castles unfolded as the ship wormed into the harbor. Groggy from one of their seaborne nights of love, Neuman and Calypso, strolling slightly apart from the sixty-three other cruisers, moved hand in hand through the bustling streets of Valletta, where every swivel-hipped pedestrian wore a scowl. The prehistoric Maltese blood had been suffused with centuries of Italian immigration. The palace of the grand masters of the famous persecuted Knights was gloomy with tapestries, and the ruins of the temples of Tarxien were so ancient and their purpose was so conjectural that one went dizzy, right there in the roofless maze of it all, under the blazing overhead sun.

In the harbor of Marsaxlokk, the little fishing boats had painted eyes on the prows. Neuman wondered, though, if they were sincerely magical or just painted on to keep the tourists happy. So many things were like that now—the hex signs on Pennsylvania barns, the Beefeater costumes at the Tower of London. The world had become a rather tatty theme park, its attractions trumped-up and suspect. A little rusty playground existed here in Marsaxlokk, and Calypso got on one of the swings. Neuman gave her a push, both of them fighting the sadness welling from underneath—a black sludge leaking up through the grid of the "x"s in Maltese place-names, a dark liquid sliding beneath the progress of the tightly scheduled days, the certainty that the cruise would one day be over. They were both between divorces, which was worse than being between marriages. Their spouses had point-blank declined to come on this educational cruise, and their refusals hung in the air like the humming in the eardrums after a twenty-one-gun salute. In the heat of Malta, on the hike from the bus up to the standing stones of Hagar Qim, her hand in his felt as sticky as a child's.

Marvels began to beset them. Mrs. Druthers, a grossly overweight widow from Paterson, New Jersey, who maneuvered herself about on metal arm-crutches—very gallantly, everybody agreed, especially when she, several days before, had made it all the way to the top of the hilltop fortress of Mycenae, through the stupendous Lion Gate, and along the lip of the great shaft tomb—wearily sat down on one of the stones of Hagar Qim in her sand-colored raincoat and simply vanished. Vanished! A concerted search led by the ship's captain and the Maltese secret service failed to uncover her whereabouts, though a rubber crutch-tip turned up in a crevice and a local archeologist said there seemed to be one more stone than usual, somehow.

Then, at sea, the captain's Bolivian fiancée, with her striped poncho and bowler hat, began to dress diaphanously and to drape herself at the U-shaped bar with the ship's purser for hours at a time, while the stern-visaged captain steadfastly steered the ship. The purser was a grave, mustached young man given to exceedingly slow calculations as he turned dollars into drachmas and dinars; lachrymosely reading a French translation of John Grisham by the ship's bathtub-size pool while his surprisingly muscular body acquired a glowering, narcissistic tan, he had been thought by the passengers to be a still-closeted gay. Now he was revealed as a Lothario, a Prometheus flying in the face of authority, and all the female passengers began to need to have their money changed and their accounts audited; they found on the office door a sign saying "HOURS/HEURES/HORAS/STUNDEN" but not giving any hours, the blank space left blank. One night, long after midnight, the passengers turned and moaned in their dreams as the ship made an unscheduled stop in mid-Mediterranean; the captain put his rival ashore on a barren rock, crinkled like papier-mâché, east of Ustica. Then in a rage he reduced his fiancée to the form of a bright-green parrot and wore her on his epauletted shoulder when he descended, fiery-eyed, from the bridge. He was an erect, middle-aged Macedonian, very proud, his uniform very clean. The parrot kept twisting its glistening small head and affirming, with a croak and a lisp, "*Sí. Sí.*"

But most marvellous was what happened to old Mr. Breadloaf. He was the oldest passenger, well into his eighties. His mouth lacked some of its teeth, but he smiled nevertheless, at a benign slant; his white countenance was rendered eerie by the redness of the sagging lids below his eyes, like two bright breves on an otherwise unaccented page. From Djerba, a group including the elderly gentleman passed over to the Tunisian mainland on a ferry noisome with Mercedes-Benz diesel trucks. A bus met the cruise passengers and carried them through miles of olive groves to the ruin of a Roman city in Gigthis. Here, close to the sea, pale stones—pavements, steps, shattered columns, inverted Corinthian capitals—still conveyed the sense of a grid; milling about in their running shoes and blue cruise badges, the Americans could feel the presence of an ancient hope, an order projected from afar. "*AVRELIO VERO CAESARI GIGTHENSIS PVBLICE,*" an upstanding reddish stone stated. Killer stood on a truncated pillar and, with a jaunty diction designed to capture the attention of her inner-city students, translated it for them: "I, Emperor Aurelian, am sending you this nice little Roman town, with its forum and wine shops and public baths and spiffy grid street plan, as a sample of what the power of Rome can do for *you.* Yo, guys, get with the program!"

Dinnertime was nearing; the bus drivers, slim men with two-day beards, smoking over in the dunes, were letting their Arabic conversation become louder, as a sign of growing impatience. The blue sky above them was turning dull; the shadows were lengthening in the orderly ruins. But as the tourists began to gather and to straggle toward the bus through the collapsed arcades of limestone, Mr. Breadloaf, standing alone in a paved space like a slightly tilting column, was transfigured. He grew taller. His cane dangled down like a candy cane, and his knobby old hand released it with a clatter. His irradiated white face spread out along a smiling diagonal bias. His wife of fifty-six years, hard of sight and hearing both, stared upward in habitual admiration. Her husband's radiance was by now quite diffuse, and his disturbing eyelids were smeared into two thin red cloudlets near the horizon, above the storied wine-dark sea. Mr. Breadloaf had become a sunset—the haunting end to a day satisfyingly full of sights.

□   □

Ah, as the ancients knew, nothing lasts. The lovers' bliss was disturbed on the eleventh night by Calypso's repeated sniffing. "There's a funny smell in this cabin," she said. "Worse than funny. It's terrible."

Neuman felt insulted. "Do you think it's me?"

She bent down and sniffed his chest, his armpits. "No. You're normal masculine. Nice." She dismounted him gingerly and walked, nude, around his cabin, opening doors, bending down, sniffing. Glimmers from the starboard lights, bounced back by the waves, spotlit now her squarish buttocks, now the crescent of her shoulders and the swaying fall of her hair, unbound from its pins of spiralled gold wire. Her voice pounced: "It's in here, down low." She was at his closet, in the narrow corridor to his bathroom. "Oh, it's foul."

They turned on the light. There was nothing there but his shoes, including a pair of sandals he had bought in a row of shops near Houmt Souk. "One dollar, one dollar," the Tunisian outside had been chanting, but when Neuman went inside, and was trapped in a back room between walls of worked leather and horsehair fly whisks and souvenir mugs with a picture of the Aragonese fort on them, men kept tapping him and thrusting sandals in his face and saying, "Thirty-five dollars, only thirty-five." He had panicked, but as he crouched to barrel his way through the scrum and back into the open a voice had said, "Ten," and he—as keen as Odysseus to avoid unnecessary violence—had said, "It's a deal." The sandals were beige and cut rather flatteringly, he thought, across his instep. He had worn them once or twice to the ship's pool, which had been deserted since the purser had been marooned for hubris.

Calypso held the sandals up close to her pretty Doric nose, with its sunburned nostril wings. "Ugh," she said. "Fish. Rotten fish. They used fish glue to hold the soles on. Throw them *out,* honey."

Her tone reminded Neuman unpleasantly of his land wife, his legal wife, thousands of air miles away. "Listen," he told her. "I paid good money for those sandals. I risked my life for them. Suppose one of those guys in the back room had pulled a knife."

"They were poor Tunisians," she sniffed, "trying to make a sale to a disgusting rich Westerner. You like to dramatize every little encounter. But you're wrong if you think I'm going to keep making love to a man whose cabin smells of dead fish."

"I didn't even notice the smell," he argued.

"You're not immensely sensitive, I can only conclude."

"If you were really as carried away by me as you pretend, you wouldn't have noticed."

"I *am* carried away, but I'm not rendered absolutely insensible. Drop those sandals overboard, Neuman, or do the rest of this cruise by yourself."

"Let's compromise. I'll wrap them in a plastic shirt bag and tuck them under my dirty laundry."

She accepted his compromise, but the relationship had taken a wound. The islands seen through the porthole kept coming faster and faster: Stromboli, Panarea, Lipari, Sicily. In the Strait of Messina, they held their breaths, between the Scylla of having loved and lost and the Charybdis of never having loved at all.

On Corfu, supposedly the land of the obliging Phaeacians, who turned Ulysses from a scruffy castaway into a well-fed, well-clad guest worthy of being returned to the island where he was king, Calypso took a dislike to the Achilleion palace, built in 1890 to humor the Empress Elizabeth of Austria's extraordinary fondness for Achilles. "It's so *pseudo*," she said. "It's so *German*."

Her dislike of his sandals' fishy smell still rankled with Neuman. "To me," he said, "this grand villa in the neoclassical style has a lovely late-Victorian charm. Statues without broken noses and arms, for once, and infused with a literalist sensibility. Who says the nineteenth century couldn't sculpt? See how with what charming anatomical accuracy the boy and the dolphin, here in the fountain, are intertwined! And look, darling, in Ernst Herter's 'Dying Achilles,' how the flesh of the tendon puckers around the arrow, almost erotically! Scrap the 'almost.' It *is* erotic. It's us."

But she was harder to beguile, to amuse, each day. In anticipation of the injury that her susceptible and divine nature would soon suffer, she was trying to make their inevitable parting her own deed. No longer riding the boat's rise and fall, she huddled deep under the blankets beside him as the wistful scattered lights of coastal Greece and benighted Albania slid away to port. Just the sun-kissed pink tip of her Doric nose showed, and when he touched it, it, too, withdrew into the carapace of blankets.

In the little fan-shaped lecture hall, with its feeble slide projector and slippery green blackboard that resisted the imprint of chalk, Homer tried to prepare them for Ithaca. His sallow triangular face was especially melancholy, lit from beneath by the dim lectern bulb. The end of the journey meant for him the return to his university—its rosy-cheeked students invincible in their ignorance, its demonic faculty politics, its clamorous demands for ever higher degrees of political correctness and cultural diversity. "ΚΡΙΝΩ," he wrote on the blackboard, pronouncing, "*krino*—to discern, to be able to distinguish the real from the unreal. To do this, we need *noös,* mind, consciousness." He wrote, then, "ΝΟΟΣ." His face illumined from underneath was as eerie as that of a jack-in-the-box or a prompter hissing lines to stymied thespians.

"We need *no-os*," he pronounced, scrabbling with his invisible chalk in a fury of insertion, "to achieve our *nos-tos*, our homecoming." He stood aside to reveal the completed word: "ΝΟΣΤΟΣ." In afterthought he rapidly rubbed out two of the letters, created "ΠΟΝΤΟΣ," and added with a small sly smile, "After our crossing together of the sea, the *pontos*."

□   □

And the marvellous thing about Ithaca was that it *did* feel like a homecoming, to the quintessence of islands, green and brimming with memories and precipitous: *ithaki*, precipitous. The bus taking them up the hairpin road to the monastery at Kathara and to Ulysses' soi-disant citadel repeatedly had to back around, with much labored chuffing of the engine and shrieking of the brakes. Had the driver's foot slipped, Calypso and Neuman, sitting in the back holding hands, would have been among the first tourists killed, the bus tumbling down, down in Peckinpahish slow motion, over the creamy white crags of Korax to the wooded plateau of Marathia, where loyal Eumaeus had watered his pigs and plotted with the returned monarch his slaughter of the suitors—the suitors whose only fault, really, had been to pick up on the languishing queen's mixed signals. The lovers' hands gripped, as tightly as their loins had gripped, at the thought of the long fall with death—*aiae!*—at the end.

But the driver, a tough local kid called Telemachus, drove this route all the time. In the monastery, bougainvillea was in bloom and a demented old blind monk waggled his hand for money and occasionally shrieked, sitting there on a stone bench intricately shaded by grapevines. "At home, he'd be homeless," Neuman shyly said.

"Somehow," she said, unsmiling, "it offends me, the suggestion that one must be insane to be religious." A dirty white dog slept before a blue door, a blue of such an ineffable rightness that Calypso photographed it with bracketed exposure times. Below them, the cruise ship was as white as a sliver of soap in the blue harbor. At the Nekromanteion of Ephyra, once thought to be the mouth of Hades, they were led, in stark sunlight, through the

241

maze that credulous pilgrims had long ago traced in the dark, in
an ordeal that took days and many offerings. The modern pilgrims were shown the subterranean room where the priests
shouted prophecies up through the stone floor of the final chamber. The stones smelled of all those past lives, stumbling from
birth to death by the flickering light of illusion.

The bus went down a different way, and stopped at the
sunny, terraced village of Stavros. Here in a small park a bust of
Odysseus awaited them. Neuman posed for Calypso's camera beside it; though he had no bronze beard, there was a resemblance,
that of all men to one another. Wanderers, deserters, returners.
Now in a mood of terminal holiday, the Harvard graduates posed
for the Yale graduates, and vice versa, while those marginal
cruise passengers from Columbia and the University of Chicago
looked on scornfully.

Calypso and Neuman drifted away from the square with its
monuments and taverna, and found a small store down a side
street, where they bought souvenir scarves and aprons, baskets
and vases for their spouses and children. He said, thinking of the
grip of her loins, so feminine yet no-nonsense, "I can't bear it."

"Life is a voyage," Calypso said. "We take our pleasure at a
price. The price is loss."

"Don't lecture me," he begged.

She shrugged, suggesting, "Stay with me, then, and I'll make
you divine."

Neuman would never forget the electric, static quality she
projected, there with her arms full of cloth and her hands full of
drachmas, staring at him in the wake of this celestial challenge
with irises as multiform as hydrangea blooms. Did her lower lip
tremble? This was as vulnerable as the daughter of Oceanus
could allow herself to appear; he defended himself as best he
could, distinguishing the real from the unreal: "I am a mere
man," he said. "Only gods and animals can withstand the monot-
ony of eternity, however paradisaical."

She snapped her profile at him, with a wisecrack: "So now
who's lecturing?"

By mutual agreement they slept, on this last night at sea, in separate cabins. But at four in the morning, Aurora Mergenthaler, their melodious chief stewardess, announced to every cabin over the loudspeaking system that the ship was about to pass through the Corinth Canal. The project, cherished by Periander and Caligula, and actually begun by Nero, had been taken up by a French company in 1881 and completed by the Greeks in 1893. The canal is four miles long, twenty-four yards wide, and two hundred sixty feet at the highest point. Dug entirely by hand, it transformed the Peloponnese from a peninsula into an island.

In the dark of the hour, the walls of earth slid by ominously, growing higher and higher. There seemed to be many horizons, marked by receding bluish lights. The ship, formerly so free, plodded forward in the channel like a blinkered ox. The damp upper deck was surprisingly well populated by conscientious cruisers, some wearing ghostly pajamas, others fanciful jogging outfits, and still others fully dressed for disembarkation on the mainland at Piraeus. Personalities that had grown distinct over the days now melted back into dim shapes, shades. Calypso was not among them. Or if she was—and Neuman searched, going from face to face with a thrashing heart—she had been transformed beyond recognition.

ALICE MUNRO

Hold Me Fast, Don't Let Me Pass

Ruins of "Kirk of the Forest." Old graveyard, William Wallace declared Guardian of Scotland here, 1298.

Courthouse where Sir Walter Scott dispensed judgment, 1799–1832.

Philiphaugh? 1945.

Gray town. Some old gray stone like Edinburgh. Also grayish-brown stucco, not so old. Library once the jail (gaol).

Country around very hilly, almost low mountains. Colors tan, lilac, gray. Some dark patches, look like pine. Reforestation? Woods at edge of town, oak, beech, birch, holly. Leaves turned, golden-brown. Sun out, but raw wind and damp feels like coming out of the ground. Nice clean little river.

One gravestone sunk deep, crooked, name, date, etc., all gone, just skull and crossbones. Girls with pink hair going by, smoking.

Hazel struck out the word "judgment" and wrote in "justice." Then she struck out "lilac," which seemed too flimsy a word to describe the gloomy, beautiful hills. She didn't know what to write in its place.

She had pressed the button beside the fireplace, hoping to order a drink, but nobody had come.

Hazel was cold in this room. When she checked into the Royal Hotel, earlier in the afternoon, a woman with a puff of gilt hair and a smooth, tapered face had given her the once-over, told her what time they served dinner, and pointed out the upstairs lounge as the place where she was to sit—ruling out, in this way, the warm and noisy pub downstairs. Hazel wondered if women guests were considered too respectable to sit in the pub. Or was she not respectable enough? She was wearing corduroy pants and tennis shoes and a windbreaker. The gilt-haired woman wore a trim pale-blue suit with glittery buttons, white lacy nylons, and high-heeled shoes that would have killed Hazel in half an hour. When she came in after a couple of hours' walk, she thought about putting on her one dress but decided not to be intimidated. She did change into a pair of black velvet pants and a silk shirt, to show she was making some effort, and she brushed and repinned her hair, which was gray as much as fair now, and fine enough to have got into an electric tangle in the wind.

Hazel was a widow. She was in her fifties, and she taught biology in the high school in Walley, Ontario. This year she was on a leave of absence. She was a person you would not be surprised to find sitting by herself in a corner of the world where she didn't belong, writing things in a notebook to prevent the rise of panic. She had found that she was usually optimistic in the morning but that panic was a problem at dusk. This sort of panic had nothing to do with money or tickets or arrangements or whatever dangers she might encounter in a strange place. It had to do with a falling-off of purpose, and the question why am I here? One could as reasonably ask that question at home, and some people do, but generally enough is going on there to block it out.

Now she noticed the date that she'd written beside "Philiphaugh": 1945. Instead of 1645. She thought that she must have

246

been influenced by the style of this room. Glass-brick windows, dark-red carpet with a swirly pattern, cretonne curtains with red flowers and green leaves on a beige background. Blocky, dusty, dark upholstered furniture. Floor lamps. All of this could have been here when Hazel's husband, Jack, used to come to this hotel, during the war. Something must have been in the fireplace then—a gas fire, or else a real grate, for coal. Nothing was there now. And the piano had probably been kept open, in tune, for dancing. Or else they'd had a gramophone, with 78s. The room would have been full of servicemen and girls. She could see the girls' dark lipstick and rolled-up hair and good crêpe dresses with their sweetheart necklines or detachable white-lace collars. The men's uniforms would be stiff and scratchy against the girls' arms and cheeks, and they would have a sour, smoky, exciting smell. Hazel was fifteen when the war ended, so she did not get to many parties of that sort. And even when she did get to one, she was too young to be taken seriously, and had to dance with other girls or maybe a friend's older brother. The smell and feel of a uniform must have been just something she imagined.

Walley is a lake port. Hazel grew up there and so did Jack, but she never knew him, or saw him to remember, until he turned up at a high-school dance escorting the English teacher, who was one of the chaperones. By that time Hazel was seventeen. When Jack danced with her, she was so nervous and excited that she shook. He asked her what the matter was, and she had to say that she thought she was getting the flu. Jack negotiated with the English teacher and took Hazel home.

They were married when Hazel was eighteen. In the first four years of marriage they had three children. No more after that. (Jack told people that Hazel had found out what was causing it.) Jack had gone to work for an appliance-sales-and-repair business as soon as he got out of the Air Force. The business belonged to a friend of his who had not gone overseas. Until the day of his death Jack worked in that place, more or less at the same job. Of course, he had to learn about new things, like microwave ovens.

After she had been married for about fifteen years, Hazel

started to take extension courses. Then she commuted to a college fifty miles away, as a full-time student. She got her degree and became a teacher, which was what she had meant to do before she got married.

Jack must have been in this room. He could easily have looked at these curtains, sat in this chair.

A man came in, at last, to ask what she would like to drink. Scotch, she said. That made him smile.

"*Whisky*'ll do it."

Of course. You don't ask for Scotch whisky in Scotland.

Jack was stationed near Wolverhampton, but he used to come up here on his leaves. He came to look up, and then to stay with, the only relative in Britain that he knew of—a cousin of his mother's, a woman named Margaret Dobie. She was not married, she lived alone; she was middle-aged then, so she would be quite old now, if indeed she was still alive. Jack didn't keep up with her after he went back to Canada—he was not a letter writer. He talked about her, though, and Hazel found her name and address when she was going through his things. She wrote Margaret Dobie a letter, just to say that Jack had died and that he had often mentioned his visits to Scotland. The letter was never answered.

Jack and this cousin seemed to have hit it off. He stayed with her in a large, cold, neglected house on a hilly farm, where she lived with her dogs and sheep. He borrowed her motorbike and rode around the countryside. He rode into town, to this very hotel, to drink and make friends or get into scraps with other servicemen or go after girls. Here he met the hotelkeeper's daughter Antoinette.

Antoinette was sixteen, too young to be allowed to go to parties or to be permitted in the bar. She had to sneak out to meet Jack behind the hotel or on the path along the river. A most delectable, heedless, soft, and giddy sort of girl. *Little Antoinette.* Jack talked about her in front of Hazel and to Hazel as easily as if he had known her not just in another country but in another world. Your Blond Bundle, Hazel used to call her. She imagined Antoinette wearing some sort of woolly pastel sleeper outfit, and she thought that she would have had silky, babyish hair, a soft, bruised mouth.

Hazel herself was a blonde when Jack first met her, though not a giddy one. She was shy and prudish and intelligent. Jack triumphed easily over the shyness and the prudery, and he was not as irritated as most men were, then, by the intelligence. He took it as a kind of joke.

Now the man was back, with a tray. On the tray were two whiskies and a jug of water.

He served Hazel her drink and took the other drink himself. He settled into the chair opposite her.

So he wasn't the barman. He was a stranger who had bought her a drink. She began to protest.

"I rang the bell," she said. "I thought you had come because I rang the bell."

"That bell is useless," he said with satisfaction. "No. Antoinette told me she had put you in here, so I thought I'd come and inquire if you were thirsty."

Antoinette.

"Antoinette," Hazel said. "Is that the lady I was speaking to this afternoon?" She felt a drop inside: her heart or her stomach or her courage—whatever it is that drops.

"Antoinette," he said. "That's the lady."

"And is she the manager of the hotel?"

"She is the owner of the hotel."

The problem was just the opposite of what she had expected. It was not that people had moved away and the buildings were gone and had left no trace. Just the opposite. The very first person that she had spoken to that afternoon had been Antoinette.

She should have known, though—she should have known that such a tidy woman, Antoinette, wouldn't employ this fellow as a barman. Look at his baggy brown pants and the burn hole in the front of his V-neck sweater. Underneath the sweater was a dingy shirt and tie. But he didn't look ill cared for or downhearted. Instead, he looked like a man who thought so well of himself that he could afford to be a bit slovenly. He had a stocky, strong body, a square, flushed face, fluffy white hair springing up in a vigorous frill around his forehead. He was pleased that she had mistaken him for the barman, as if that might be a kind of trick he'd played on her. In the classroom she would have picked him for a possible troublemaker, not the rowdy, or the silly, or the positively sneering and disgusted kind, but the kind who sits at the back of the class, smart and indolent, making remarks you can't quite be sure of. Mild, shrewd, determined subversion—one of the hardest things to root out of a classroom. What you have to do—Hazel had said this to younger teachers, or those who tended to get discouraged more easily than she did—what you have to do is find some way of firing up their intelligence. Make it a tool, not a toy. The intelligence of such a person is underemployed.

What did she care about this man anyway? All the world is not a classroom. I've got your number, she said to herself; but I don't have to do anything about it.

She was thinking about him to keep her mind off Antoinette.

He told her that his name was Dudley Brown and that he was a solicitor. He said that he lived here (she took that to mean he had a room in the hotel) and that his office was just down the street. A permanent guest—a widower, then, or a bachelor. She thought a bachelor. That twinkly, edgy air of satisfaction didn't usually survive married life.

Too young, in spite of the white hair, a few years too young, to have been in the war.

"So have you come over here looking for your roots?" he said. He gave the word its most exaggerated American pronunciation.

"I'm Canadian," Hazel said quite pleasantly. "We don't say 'roots' that way."

"Ah, I beg your pardon," he said. "I'm afraid we do that. We do tend to lump you all together, you and the Americans."

Then she started to tell him her business—why not? She told him that her husband had been here during the war and that they had always planned to make this trip together, but they hadn't, and her husband had died, and now she had come by herself. This was only half true. She had often suggested such a trip to Jack, but he had always said no. She thought this was because of her—he didn't want to do it with her. She took things more personally than she ought to have done, for a long time. He probably meant just what he said. He said, "No, it wouldn't be the same."

He was wrong if he meant that people wouldn't be in place, right where they used to be. Even now, when Dudley Brown asked the name of the cousin in the country and Hazel said Margaret Dobie, Miss Dobie, but in all probability she's dead, the man just laughed. He laughed and shook his head and said, Oh, no, by no means, indeed not.

"Maggie Dobie is far from dead. She's a very old lady, certainly, but I don't believe she's got any thought of dying. She lives out on the same land she's always lived on, though it's a different house. She's pretty sound."

"She didn't answer my letter."

"Ah. She wouldn't."

"Then I guess she wouldn't want a visitor, either?"

She almost wanted him to say no. *Miss Dobie is very much the recluse, I'm afraid. No, no visitors.* Why, when she'd come so far?

"Well, if you drove up on your own, I don't know, that would be one thing," Dudley Brown said. "I don't know how she would take it. But if I was to ring up and explain about you, and then we took a run out, then I think you'd be made most welcome. Would you care to? It's a lovely drive out, too. Pick a day when it isn't raining."

"That would be very kind."

"Ah, it isn't far."

□   □

In the dining room, Dudley Brown ate at one little table, and Hazel at another. This was a pretty room, with blue walls and deep-set windows looking out over the town square. Hazel sensed none of the gloom and neglect that prevailed in the lounge. Antoinette served them. She offered the vegetables in silver serving dishes with rather difficult implements. She was very correct, even disdainful. When not serving, she stood by the side-board, alert, upright, hair stiff in its net of spray, suit spotless, feet slim and unswollen in the high-heeled shoes.

Dudley said that he would not eat the fish. Hazel, too, had refused it.

"You see, even the Americans," Dudley said. "Even the Americans won't eat that frozen stuff. And you'd think they'd be used to it; they have everything frozen."

"I'm Canadian," Hazel said. She thought he'd apologize, re-membering he'd been told this once already. But neither he nor Antoinette paid any attention to her. They had embarked on an argument whose tone of practiced acrimony made them sound al-most married.

"Well, I wouldn't eat anything else," Antoinette said. "I wouldn't eat any fish that hadn't been frozen. And I wouldn't serve it. Maybe it was all right in the old days, when we didn't have all the chemicals we have now in the water, and all the pol-lution. The fish now are so full of pollution that we need the freezing to kill it. That's right, isn't it?" she said, turning to in-clude Hazel. "They know all about that in America."

"I just preferred the roast," Hazel said.

"So your only safe fish is a frozen one," Antoinette said, ig-noring her. "And another thing: they take all of the best fish for freezing. The rejects is all that is left to sell fresh."

"Give me your rejects, then," Dudley said. "Let me chance it with the chemicals."

"More fool you. I wouldn't put a bite of fresh fish in my mouth."

"You wouldn't get a chance to. Not around here."

While the law was being laid down in this way about the fish, Dudley Brown once or twice caught Hazel's eye. He kept a very straight face, which indicated, more than a smirk would have done, a settled mixture of affection and contempt. Hazel kept looking at Antoinette's suit. Antoinette's suit made her think of Joan Crawford. Not the style of the suit but its perfect condition. She had read an interview with Joan Crawford, years ago, that described many little tricks Joan Crawford had for keeping hair, clothes, footwear, fingernails in a most perfect condition. She remembered something about the way to iron seams. Never iron seams open. Antoinette looked like a woman who would have all that down pat.

She hadn't, after all, expected to find Antoinette still babyish and boisterous and charming. Far from it. Hazel had imagined— and not without satisfaction—a dumpy woman wearing false teeth. (Jack used to recall Antoinette's habit of popping caramels into her mouth between kisses, and making him wait until she'd sucked the sweetness out of the last shred.) A good-natured soul, chatty, humdrum, a waddly little grandmother—that was what she had thought would be left of Antoinette. And here was this pared-down, vigilant, stupid-shrewd woman, sprayed and painted and preserved to within an inch of her life. Tall, too. It wasn't likely she'd been any kind of cozy bundle, even at sixteen.

But how much would you find in Hazel of the girl Jack had taken home from the dance? How much of Hazel Joudry, a pale, squeaky-voiced girl who held her fair hair back with two bows of pink celluloid, in Hazel Curtis? Hazel was thin, too—wiry, not brittle like Antoinette. She had muscles that came from gardening and hiking and cross-country skiing. These activities had also dried and wrinkled and roughened her skin, and at some point she'd stopped bothering about it. She threw out all the colored pastes and pencils and magic unguents she had bought in moments of bravado or despair. She let her hair grow out whatever color it liked and pinned it up at the back of her head. She broke open the shell of her increasingly doubtful and expensive prettiness; she got out. Years before Jack died, even, she did that. It had something to do with how she took hold of her life. She has said and thought that there came a time when she had to take hold of her life, and she has urged the same course on others. She urges action, exercise, direction. She doesn't mind letting people know that when she was in her thirties she had what used to be called a nervous breakdown. For nearly two months she was unable to leave the house. She stayed in bed much of the time. She crayoned the pictures in children's coloring books. That was all she could do to control her fear and unfocussed grief.

Then she took hold. She sent for college catalogues. What got her going again? She doesn't know. She has to say she doesn't know. Maybe she just got bored, she has to say. Maybe she just got bored, having her breakdown.

She knew that when she had got out of bed (this is what she doesn't say), she was leaving some part of herself behind. She suspected that this was a part that had to do with Jack. But she didn't think then that any abandonment had to be permanent. Anyway, it couldn't be helped.

When he had finished his roast and vegetables, Dudley got up abruptly. He nodded to Hazel and said to Antoinette, "I'm off now, my lamb." Did he really say that—"lamb"? Whatever it was, it had the satirical inflection that an endearment would need between him and Antoinette. Perhaps he said "lass." People did say "lass" here. The driver on the bus from Edinburgh had said it to Hazel, that afternoon.

Antoinette served Hazel a piece of apricot flan and started immediately to fill her in on Dudley. People were supposed to be so reserved in Britain—that was what Hazel had been led to believe, by her reading, if not by Jack—but it didn't always seem to be the case.

"Off to see his mother before she's tucked up for the night," Antoinette said. "Always off home early on a Sunday night."

"He doesn't live here?" Hazel said. "I mean, in the hotel?"

"He didn't say that, did he?" said Antoinette. "I'm sure he didn't say that. He has his own home. He has a lovely home. He shares it with his mother. She's in bed all the time now—she's one of those ones who have to have everything done for them. He's got a day nurse for her and a night nurse, too. But he always looks in and has a chat Sunday nights, even if she doesn't know him from Adam. He must have meant that he gets his meals here. He couldn't expect the nurse to get his meals. She wouldn't do it, anyway. They won't do anything extra at all for you now. They want to know just what they're supposed to do, and they won't do a tick more. It's just the same with what I get here. If I say to them, 'Sweep the floor,' and I don't say, 'Put up the broom when you're finished,' they'll just leave the broom lying."

Now is the time, Hazel thought. She wouldn't be able to say it if she put it off longer.

"My husband used to come here," she said. "He used to come here during the war."

"Well, that's a long time ago, isn't it? Would you like your coffee now?"

"Please," Hazel said. "He came here first on account of having a relative here. A Miss Dobie. Mr. Brown seemed to know who she would be."

"She's quite an elderly person," Antoinette said—disapprovingly, Hazel thought. "She lives away up in the valley."

"My husband's name was Jack." Hazel waited, but she didn't get any response. The coffee was bad, which was a surprise, since the rest of the meal had been so good.

"Jack Curtis," she said. "His mother was a Dobie. He used to come here on his leaves and stay with this cousin and he would come into town in the evenings. He used to come here, to the Royal Hotel."

"It was a busy place during the war," Antoinette said. "Or so they tell me."

"He would talk about the Royal Hotel and he mentioned you, too," Hazel said. "I was surprised when I heard your name. I didn't think you'd still be here."

"I haven't been here the whole time," Antoinette said—as if to suppose that she had been would be to insult her. "I lived in England while I was married. That's why I don't talk the way they do around here."

"My husband is dead," Hazel said. "He mentioned you. He said your father owned the hotel. He said you were a blonde."

"I still am," Antoinette said. "My hair is just the same color it always was; I never have had to do anything to it. I can't remember the war years very well. I was such a wee little girl at the time. I don't think I was born when the war started. When did the war start? I was born in 1940."

Two lies in one speech, hardly any doubt about it. Blatant, smooth-faced, deliberate, self-serving lies. But how could Hazel tell if Antoinette was lying about not knowing Jack? Antoinette would have no choice but to say that, given the lie she must have told all the time about her age.

◻ ◻

For the next three days it rained, off and on. When it wasn't raining, Hazel walked around the town, looking at the exploded cabbages in kitchen gardens, the unlined flowered window curtains, and even at such things as a bowl of waxed fruit on the table in a cramped, polished dining room. She must have thought that she was invisible, the way she slowed down and peered. She got used to the houses' being all strung together. At the turn of the street she might get a sudden, misty view of the enthralling hills. She walked along the river and got into a wood that was all beech trees, with bark like elephant skin and bumps like swollen eyes. They gave a kind of gray light to the air.

When the rains came, she stayed in the library, reading history. She read about the old monasteries that were here in Selkirk County once, and the Kings with their Royal Forest, and all the fighting with the English. Flodden Field. She knew some things already from the reading she had done in the Encyclopedia Britannica before she ever left home. She knew who William Wallace was, and that Macbeth killed Duncan in battle instead of murdering him in bed.

Dudley and Hazel had a whisky in the lounge now, every night before dinner. An electric radiator had appeared, and was set up in front of the fireplace. After dinner Antoinette sat with them. They all had their coffee together. Later in the evening Dudley and Hazel would have another whisky. Antoinette watched television.

"What a long history," said Hazel politely. She told Dudley something of what she'd read and looked at. "When I first saw the name Philiphaugh on that building across the street I didn't know what it meant."

"At Philiphaugh the fray began," Dudley said, obviously quoting. "Do you know now?"

"The Covenanters," Hazel said.

"Do you know what happened after the battle of Philip-haugh? The Covenanters hanged all their prisoners. Right out there in the town square, under the dining-room windows. Then they butchered all the women and children on the field. A lot of families travelled with Montrose's army, because so many of them were Irish mercenaries. Catholics, of course. No—they didn't butcher all of them. Some they marched up toward Edinburgh. But on the way they decided to march them off a bridge."

He told her this in a most genial voice, with a smile. Hazel had met this smile before and she had never been sure what it meant. Was a man who smiled in this way daring you not to be-lieve, not to acknowledge, not to agree, that this was how things must be, forever?

□   □

Jack was a hard person to argue with. He put up with all kinds of nonsense—from customers, from the children, probably from Hazel as well. But he would get angry every year on Remem-brance Day, because the local paper would run some lugubrious story about the war.

"NOBODY WINS IN A WAR" was the headline of one such story. Jack threw the paper on the floor.

"Holy Christ! Do they think it'd be all the same if *Hitler* had won?"

He was angry, too, when he saw the Peace Marchers on tele-vision, though he usually didn't say anything, just hissed at the screen in a controlled, fed-up way. As far as Hazel could see, what he thought was that a lot of people—women, of course, but, as time went on, more and more men, too—were determined to spoil the image of the best part of his life. They were spoiling it with pious regrets and reproofs and a certain amount of out-and-out lying. None of them would admit that any of the war was fun. Even at the Legion you were supposed to put on a long face about it; you weren't supposed to say anymore than you wouldn't have missed it for the world.

When they were first married, Jack and Hazel used to go to

dances, or to the Legion, or just to other couples' houses, and sooner or later the men would begin telling their stories about the war. Jack did not tell the most stories, or the longest, and his were never thick with heroics and death staring you in the face. Usually he talked about things that were funny. But he was on top then, because he had been a bomber pilot, which was one of the most admired things for a man to have been. He had flown two full tours of operations ("ops"—even the women referred to "ops"). That is, he had flown on fifty bombing raids.

Hazel used to sit with the other young wives and listen, meek and proud and—in her case, at least—distracted by desire. These husbands came to them taut with proved courage. Hazel pities women who had given themselves to lesser men.

Ten or fifteen years later the same women sat with strained faces or caught one another's eyes or even absented themselves (Hazel did, sometimes) when the stories were being told. The band of men who told these stories had shrunk, and it shrank further. But Jack was still at the center of it. He grew more descriptive, thoughtful, some might say long-winded. He recalled now the noise of the planes at the American airfield close by, the mighty sound of them warming up in the early dawn and then taking off, three by three, flying out over the North Sea in their great formations. The Flying Fortresses. The Americans bombed by day, and their planes never flew alone. Why not?

"They didn't know how to navigate," Jack said. "Well, they did, but not the way we navigated." He was proud of an extra skill, or foolhardiness, that he would not bother to explain. He told how the R.A.F. planes lost sight of one another almost at once and flew for six or seven hours alone. Sometimes the voice that directed them, over the radio, was a German voice with a perfect English accent, providing deadly false information. He told about planes appearing out of nowhere, gliding above or beneath you, and of the death of planes in dreamlike flashes of light. It was nothing like the movies, nothing so concentrated or organized—nothing made sense. Sometimes he had thought he could hear a lot of voices, or instrumental music, weird but familiar, just beyond or inside the noises of the plane.

Then he seemed to come back to earth—in more ways than one—and he told his stories about leaves and drunks, fights in the blackout outside pubs, practical jokes in the barracks.

□   □

On the third night Hazel thought that she had better speak to Dudley about the trip to see Miss Dobie. The week was passing, and the idea of the visit didn't alarm her so much, now that she'd got a little used to being here.

"I'll ring up in the morning," Dudley said. He seemed glad to have been reminded. "I'll see if it would suit her. There's a chance of the weather's clearing, too. Tomorrow or the next day we'll go."

Antoinette was watching a television show in which couples selected each other, by a complicated ritual, for a blind date, and then came back the next week to tell how everything went. She laughed outright at disastrous confessions.

Antoinette used to run out to meet Jack with nothing but her nightie on under her coat. Her daddy would have tanned her, Jack used to say. Tanned us both.

□   □

"I'll drive you out, then, to see Miss Dobie," Antoinette said to Hazel at breakfast. "Dudley's got too much on."

Hazel said, "No, no, it's all right, if Dudley is too busy."

"It's all set up now," Antoinette said. "But we'll go a bit earlier than Dudley planned. I thought later this morning, before lunch. I just have a couple of things to see about first."

So they set out in Antoinette's car, around half past eleven. The rain had stopped, the clouds had whitened, the oak and beech trees were dripping last night's rainwater with the stirring of their gold and rusty leaves. The road went between low stone walls. It crossed the clear, hard-flowing little river.

"Miss Dobie has a nice house," Antoinette said. "It's a nice little bungalow. It's on a corner of the old farm. When she sold off the farm, she kept one corner of it and built herself a little bungalow. Her other old house was all gone to rookery."

Hazel had a clear picture in her mind of that other, old house. She could see the big kitchen, roughly plastered, with its uncurtained windows. The meat safe, the stove, the slick horsehair couch. A great quantity of pails and implements and guns, fishing rods, oilcans, lanterns, baskets. A battery radio. On a backless chair a big husky woman, in trousers, would be sitting, oiling a gun or cutting up seed potatoes or gutting a fish. There was not a thing she couldn't do herself, Jack had said, providing Hazel with this picture. He put himself in it as well. He had sat on the steps outside the kitchen door, on days of hazy radiance like today's—except that the grass and the trees had been green—and he passed the time fooling with the dogs or trying to get the muck off the shoes he had borrowed from his hostess.

"Jack borrowed Miss Dobie's shoes once," she said to Antoinette. "She had big feet, apparently. She always wore men's shoes. I don't know what had happened to his. Maybe he just had boots. Anyway, he wore her shoes to a dance and he went down to the river, I don't know what for"———it was to meet a girl, of course, probably to meet Antoinette—"and he got the shoes soaked, covered with muck. He was so drunk he didn't take anything off when he went to bed, just passed out on top of the quilt. Miss Dobie did not say a word about it. Next night he came home late again and he crawled into bed in the dark, and a pailful of cold water hit him in the face! She'd rigged up this arrangement of weights and ropes, so that when the springs of the bed sagged under him, the pail would be tipped over and the water would hit him like that, to serve him right."

"She mustn't have minded going to a lot of trouble," Antoinette said. Then she said they would stop for lunch. Hazel had thought that the whole point of leaving when they did had been to get the visit over with early, because Antoinette was short of time. But now, apparently, they were taking care not to arrive too soon.

They stopped at a pub that had a famous name. Hazel had read about a duel fought there; it was mentioned in an old ballad. But the pub now seemed ordinary, and was run by an Englishman who was in the middle of redecorating. He heated their sandwiches in a microwave oven.

"I wouldn't give one of those houseroom," Antoinette said. "They irrigate your food."

She began to talk about Miss Dobie and the girl Miss Dobie had to look after her.

"Well, she's hardly a girl anymore. Her name is Judy Armstrong. She was one of those what-do-you-call-thems—orphans. She went to work for Dudley's mother. She worked there for a while, and then she got herself in trouble. The result was she had a baby. The way they often do. She couldn't stay in town so easily after that, so it was fortunate Miss Dobie was just getting in the way of needing somebody. Judy and her child went out there, and it turned out to be the best arrangement all round."

They delayed at the pub until Antoinette judged that Judy and Miss Dobie would be ready for them.

The valley narrowed in. Miss Dobie's house was close to the road, with hills rising steeply behind it. In front was a shining laurel hedge and some wet bushes, all red-leaved or dripping with berries. The house was stuccoed, with stones set here and there in a whimsical suburban style.

A young woman stood in the doorway. Her hair was glorious—a ripply fan of red hair, shining over her shoulders. She was wearing a rather odd dress for the time of day—a sort of party dress of thin, silky brown material, shot through with gold metallic thread. She must have been chilly in it—she had her arms crossed, squeezing her breasts.

"Here we are, then, Judy," Antoinette said, speaking heartily as if to a slightly deaf or mutinous person. "Dudley couldn't come. He was too busy. This is the lady he told you about on the phone."

Judy blushed as she shook hands. Her eyebrows were very fair, almost invisible, giving her dark-brown eyes an undefended look. She seemed dismayed by something—was it the fact of visitors, or just the flamboyance of her own spread-out hair? But she was the one who must have brushed it to this gloss and arranged it on show.

Antoinette asked her if Miss Dobie was well.

A clot of phlegm thickened Judy's voice as she tried to answer. She cleared her throat and said, "Miss Dobie's kept well all this year."

Now there was some awkwardness about getting their coats off—Judy not knowing quite when to reach for them, or how to direct Antoinette and Hazel where to go. But Antoinette took charge and led the way down the hall to the sitting room, which was full of patterned upholstery, brass and china ornaments, pampas grass, peacock feathers, dried flowers, clocks and pictures and cushions. In the midst of this an old woman sat in a high-backed chair, against the light of the windows, waiting for them. Though she was old, she was not at all shrivelled. She had thick arms and legs and a bushy halo of white hair. Her skin was brown, like the skin of a russet apple, and she had large purplish pouches under her eyes. But the eyes themselves were bright and shifty, as if some intelligence there looked out just when it wanted to— something as quick and reckless as a squirrel darting back and forth behind this heavy, warty, dark old face.

"So you are the lady from Canada," she said to Antoinette. She had a strong voice. Spots on her lips were like blue-black grapes.

"No, that's not me," Antoinette said. "I'm from the Royal Hotel, and you've met me before. I'm the friend of Dudley Brown's." She took a bottle of wine—it was Madeira—out of her bag and presented it, as a credential. "This is the kind you like, isn't it?"

"All the way from Canada," Miss Dobie said, taking possession of the bottle. She still wore men's shoes—she was wearing them now, unlaced.

Antoinette repeated what she had said before, in a louder voice, and introduced Hazel.

"Judy! Judy, you know where the glasses are!" Miss Dobie said. Judy was just coming in with a tray. On it was a stack of cups and saucers, a teapot, a plate of sliced fruitcake, milk, and sugar. The demand for the glasses seemed to throw her off course, and she looked around distractedly. Antoinette relieved her of the tray.

"I think she'd like a taste of the wine first, Judy," Antoinette said. "Isn't this nice! Did you make the cake yourself? May I take a piece back to Dudley when we go? He's so fond of fruitcake. He'll believe it was made for him. That can't be true, since he only called this morning and fruitcake takes a lot longer than that, doesn't it? But he'll never know the difference."

"I know who you are now," Miss Dobie said. "You're the woman from the Royal Hotel. Did you and Dudley Brown ever get married?"

"I am already married," Antoinette said irritably. "I would get a divorce, but I don't know where my husband is." Her voice quickly smoothed out, so that she ended up seeming to reassure Miss Dobie. "Perhaps in time."

"So that's why you went to Canada," Miss Dobie said.

Judy came in with some wineglasses. Anybody could see that her hands were too unsteady to pour the wine. Antoinette got the bottle out of Miss Dobie's clasp and held a wineglass up to the light.

"If you could just fetch me a napkin, Judy," Antoinette said. "Or a clean tea towel. Mind it's a clean one!"

"My husband, Jack," Hazel broke in resolutely, speaking to Miss Dobie—"my husband, Jack Curtis, was in the Air Force, and he used to visit you during the war."

Miss Dobie picked this up all right.

"Why would your husband want to visit me?"

"He wasn't my husband then. He was quite young then. He was a cousin of yours. From Canada. Jack Curtis, Curtis. But you may have had a lot of different relatives visiting you, over the years."

"We never had visitors. We were too far off the beaten track," Miss Dobie said firmly. "I lived at home with Mother and Father and then I lived with Mother and then I lived alone. I gave up on the sheep and went to work in town. I worked at the post office."

"That's right, she did," Antoinette said thoughtfully, handing round the wine.

"But I never lived in town," Miss Dobie said, with an obscure, vengeful-sounding pride. "No. I rode in every day, all that way on the motorbike."

"Jack mentioned your motorbike," Hazel said, to encourage her.

"I lived in the old house then. Terrible people live there now."

She held out her glass for more wine.

"Jack used to borrow your motorbike," Hazel said. "And he went fishing with you, and when you cleaned the fish, the dogs ate the fish heads."

"Ugh," Antoinette said.

"I'm thankful I can't see it from here," Miss Dobie said.

"The house," Antoinette explained, in a regretful undertone. "The couple that live in it are not married. They have fixed it up but they are not married. And, as if naturally reminded, she said to Judy, "How is Tania?"

"She's fine," said Judy, who was not having any wine. She lifted the plate of fruitcake and set it down. "She goes to kindergarten now."

"She goes on the bus," Miss Dobie said. "The bus comes and picks her up right at the door."

"Isn't that nice," Antoinette said.

"And it brings her back," Miss Dobie continued impressively. "It brings her back right to the door."

"Jack said you had a dog that ate porridge," Hazel said. "And that one time he borrowed your shoes. I mean Jack did. My husband."

Miss Dobie seemed to brood over this for a little while. Then she said, "Tania has the red hair."

"She has her mother's hair," Antoinette said. "And her mother's brown eyes. She is Judy all over again."

"She is illegitimate," Miss Dobie said, with the air of somebody sweeping aside a good deal of nonsense. "But Judy brings her up well. Judy is a good worker. I am glad to see that they have a home. It is the innocent ones, anyway, that get caught."

Hazel thought that this would finish Judy off completely, send her running to the kitchen. Instead, she seemed to come to a decision. She got up and handed around the cake. The flush had never left her face or her neck or the part of her chest left bare by the party dress. Her skin was burning as if she had been slapped, and her expression, as she bent to each of them with the plate, was that of a child who was furiously, bitterly, contemptuously holding back a howl. Miss Dobie spoke to Hazel. She said, "Can you say any recitations?"

Hazel had to think for a moment to remember what a recitation was. Then she said that she could not.

"I will say one, if you like," Miss Dobie said.

She put down her empty glass and straightened her shoulders and placed her feet together.

"Excuse my not rising," she said.

She began to speak in a voice that seemed strained and faltering at first but that soon became dogged and preoccupied. Her Scottish pronunciation thickened. She paid less attention to the content of the poem than to the marathon effort of getting it out in the right order—word after word, line after line, verse after verse. Her face darkened further with the effort. But the recitation was not wholly without expression; it was not like those numbing presentations of "memory work" that Hazel remembered having to learn at school. It was more like the best scholar's offering at the school concert, a kind of willing public martyrdom, with every inflection, every gesture, rehearsed and ordained.

Hazel started picking up bits and pieces. A rigmarole about fairies, some boy captured by the fairies, then a girl called Fair Jennet falling in love with him. Fair Jennet was giving back talk to her father and wrapping herself in her mantle green and going to meet her lover. Then it seemed to be Halloween and the dead of night, and a great charge of fairies came on horseback. Not dainty fairies, by any means, but a fierce lot who rode through the night making a horrid uproar.

"Fair Jennet stood, with mind unmoved,
The dreary heath upon;
And louder, louder wax'd the sound,
As they came riding on!"

265

Judy sat with the cake plate in her lap and ate a large slice of fruitcake. Then she ate another—still with a fiery, unforgiving face. When she had bent to offer the cake, Hazel had smelled her body—not a bad smell, but nevertheless a smell that washing and deodorizing had made uncommon. It poured out hotly from between the girl's flushed breasts.

Antoinette, not bothering to be very quiet, possessed herself of a tiny brass ashtray, got her cigarettes out of her bag, and began to smoke. (She said she allowed herself three cigarettes a day.)

"And first gaed by the black black steed,
And then gaed by the brown;
But fast she gript the milk-white steed,
And pu'd the rider down!"

Hazel thought that there was no use asking anymore about Jack. Somebody around here probably remembered him—somebody who had seen him go down the road on the motorbike or talked to him one night in the pub. But how was she to find that person? It was probably true that Antoinette had forgotten him. Antoinette had enough on her mind, with what was going on now. As for what was on Miss Dobie's mind, that seemed to be picked out of the air, all willfulness and caprice. An elf-man in her yammering poem took precedence now.

"They shaped him in Fair Jennet's arms,
An esk, but and an adder;
She held him fast in every shape,
To be her bairn's father!"

A note of gloomy satisfaction in Miss Dobie's voice indicated that the end might be in sight. What was an eskbut? Never mind, Jennet was wrapping her lover up in her mantle green, a "mother-naked man," and the Queen of the Fairies was lamenting his loss, and just about at the point where the audience might be afraid that some new development was under way—for Miss

Dobie's voice had gone resigned again, and speeded up a bit as if for a long march—the recitation was over.

"Good Lord," Antoinette said when she was sure. "How ever do you keep all that in your head? Dudley does it, too. You and Dudley, you are a pair!"

Judy began a clattering, distributing cups and saucers. She started to pour out the tea. Antoinette let her get that far before stopping her.

"That's going to be a bit strong by now, isn't it, dear?" Antoinette said. "I'm afraid too strong for me. We have to be getting back anyway, really. Miss Dobie'll be wanting her rest, after all that."

Judy picked up the tray without protest and headed for the kitchen. Hazel went after her, carrying the cake plate.

"I think Mr. Brown meant to come," she said to Judy quietly. "I don't think he knew that we were leaving as early as we did."

"Oh, aye," said that bitter, rosy girl, as she splashed the poured tea down the sink.

□   □

"If you wouldn't mind opening my bag," Antoinette said, "and getting me out another cigarette? I have to have another cigarette. If I look down to do it myself, I'll feel sick. I've got a headache coming, from that moaning and droning."

The sky had darkened again, and they were driving through a light rain.

"It must be a lonely life for her," Hazel said. "For Judy."

"She's got Tania."

The last thing that Antoinette had done, as they were leaving, was to press some coins into Judy's hand.

"For Tania," she'd said.

"She might like to get married," Hazel said. "But would she meet anybody out there to marry?"

"I don't know how easy it'd be for her to meet anybody anywhere," Antoinette said. "Being in the position she is in."

"It doesn't matter so much nowadays," Hazel said. "Girls

267

have children first and get married later. Movie stars, ordinary girls, too. All the time. It doesn't matter."

"I would say it matters around here," Antoinette said. "We aren't movie stars around here. A man would have to think twice. He'd have to think about his family. It'd be an insult to his mother. It would be even if she was past knowing anything about it. And if you make your living dealing with the public, you have to think about that, too."

She was pulling the car off the road. She said, "Excuse me," and got out and walked over to the stone wall. She bent forward. Was she weeping? No. She was vomiting. Her shoulders were hunched and quivering. She vomited nearly over the wall into the fallen leaves of the oak forest. Hazel opened the car door and started toward her, but Antoinette waved her back with one hand.

The helpless and intimate sound of vomiting, in the stillness of the country, the misty rain.

Antoinette leaned down and held on to the wall for a moment. Then she straightened up and came back to the car and wiped herself off with tissues, shakily but thoroughly.

"I get that," she said, "with the kind of headaches I get."

Hazel said, "Do you want me to drive?"

"You aren't used to this side of the road."

"I'll go carefully."

They changed places—Hazel was rather surprised that Antoinette had agreed—and Hazel drove slowly, while Antoinette sat with her eyes closed most of the time and her hands against her mouth. Her skin showed gray through the pink makeup. But near the edge of town she opened her eyes and dropped her hands and said something like "This is Cathaw."

They were going past a low field by the river. "Where in that poem," Antoinette said—speaking hastily, as one might if one was afraid of being overtaken by further vomiting—"the girl goes out and loses her maidenhead, and so on."

The field was brown and soggy and surrounded by what looked like council housing.

Hazel was surprised to recall a whole verse now. She could hear Miss Dobie's voice chanting it hard at them.

"Now, gowd rings ye may buy, maidens,
Green mantles ye may spin;
But, gin ye lose your maidenheid,
Ye'll ne'er get that agen!"

A ton of words Miss Dobie had, to bury anything.

□   □

"Antoinette isn't well," Hazel said to Dudley Brown when she came into the lounge that evening. "She has a sick headache. We drove out today to see Miss Dobie."

"She left me a note to that effect," Dudley said, setting out the whisky and water.

Antoinette was in bed. Hazel had helped her get there, because she was too dizzy to manage by herself. Antoinette got into bed in her slip and asked for a facecloth, so that she could remove what was left of her makeup and not spoil the pillowcase. Then she asked for a towel, in case she should be sick again. She told Hazel how to hang up her suit—still the same one, and still miraculously unspotted—on its padded hanger. Her bedroom was mean and narrow. It looked out on the stucco wall of the bank next door. She slept on a metal-frame cot. On the dresser was displayed all the paraphernalia that she used to color her hair. Would she be upset when she realized that Hazel must have seen it? Probably not. She might have forgotten that lie already. Or she might be prepared to go on lying—like a queen, who makes whatever she says the truth.

"She had the woman from the kitchen go up to see about dinner," Hazel said. "It'll be on the sideboard, and we're to help ourselves."

"Help ourselves to this first," Dudley said. He had brought the whisky bottle.

"Miss Dobie was not able to remember my husband."

"Was she not?"

"A girl was there. A young woman, rather. Who looks after Miss Dobie."

"Judy Armstrong," Dudley said.

She waited to see if he could keep himself from asking more, if he could force himself to change the subject. He couldn't. "Has she still got her wonderful red hair?"

"Yes," Hazel said. "Did you think she would have shaved it off?"

"Girls do terrible things to their hair. I see sights every day. But Judy is not that sort."

"She served a very nice dark fruitcake," Hazel said. "Antoinette mentioned bringing a piece home to you. But I think she forgot. I think she was already feeling ill when we left."

"Perhaps the cake was poisoned," Dudley said. "The way it often is, in the stories."

"Judy ate two slices herself, and I ate some and Miss Dobie ate some, so I don't think so."

"Perhaps only Antoinette's."

"Antoinette didn't have any. Just some wine, and a cigarette."

After a silent moment Dudley said, "How did Miss Dobie entertain you?"

"She recited a long poem."

"Aye, she'll do that. Ballads, they're rightly called, not poems. Do you recall which one it was?"

The lines that came into Hazel's mind were those concerning the maidenhead. But she rejected them as being too crudely malicious and tried to find others.

"First dip me in a stand of milk?" she said tentatively. "Then in a stand of water?"

"But hold me fast, don't let me pass," Dudley cried, very pleased. "I'll be your bairn's father!"

Quite as tactless as the first lines she had thought of, but he did not seem to mind. Indeed, he threw himself back in his chair, looking released, and lifted his head and started reciting—the same poem that Miss Dobie had recited, but spoken with calm relish now, and with style, in a warm, sad, splendid male voice.

His accent broadened, but, having absorbed a good deal of the poem once already, almost against her will, Hazel was able to make out every word. The boy captured by fairies, living a life of adventures and advantages—not able to feel pain, for one thing—but growing wary as he gets older, scared of "paying the teint to hell," and longing for a human climate, so seducing a bold girl and instructing her how she can get him free. She has to do it by holding on to him, holding on no matter what horror the fairies can change him into, holding on until all their tricks are exhausted, and they let him go. Of course Dudley's style was old-fashioned, of course he mocked himself, a little. But that was only on the surface. This reciting was like singing. You could parade your longing without fear of making a fool of yourself.

> "They shaped him in her arms at last,
> A mother-naked man;
> She wrapt him in her green mantle,
> And so her true love wan!"

You and Miss Dobie, you are a pair.

□　　□

"We saw the place where she went to meet him," Hazel said. "On the way back, Antoinette showed it to me. Down by the river." She thought that it was a wonder to be here, in the middle of these people's lives, seeing what she'd seen of their scheming, their wounds. Jack was not here, Jack was not here after all, but she was.

"Carterhaugh?" Dudley said, sounding scornful and excited. "That's not down by the river! Antoinette doesn't know what she's talking about! That's the high field, it overlooks the river. That's where the fairy rings were. Fungi. If the moon were out, we could drive out tonight and look at it."

Hazel could feel something, as if a cat had jumped into her lap. Sex. She felt her eyes widen, her skin tighten, her limbs settle, attentively. But the moon was not going to be out—that was the other thing his tone made clear. He poured out more whisky, and it wasn't in aid of a seduction. All the faith and energy, the adeptness, the forgetfulness that is necessary to manage even a tiny affair—Hazel knew, for she'd had two tiny affairs, one at college and one at a teachers' conference—all that was beyond them at present. They would let the attraction wash over them and ebb away. Antoinette would have been willing, Hazel was sure of that. Antoinette would have tolerated someone who was going away, who didn't really matter, who was only a sort of American. That was another thing to make them draw back— Antoinette's acceptance. That was enough to make them thought-ful, fastidious.

"The little girl," Dudley said, in a quieter voice. "Was she there?"

"No. She goes to kindergarten." Hazel thought how little was required, really—a recitation—to turn her mind from needling to comforting.

"Does she? What a name that child has got. Tania."

"That's not so odd a name," Hazel said. "Not nowadays."

"I know. They all have outlandish international names, like Tania and Natasha and Erin and Solange and Carmen. No one has family names. Those girls with the rooster hair I see on the streets. They pick the names. They're the mothers."

"I have a granddaughter named Brittany," Hazel said. "And I have heard of a little girl called Cappuccino."

"Cappuccino! Is that true? Why don't they call one Cassou-let? Fettucini? Alsace-Lorraine?"

"They probably do."

"Schleswig-Holstein! There's a good name for you!"

"But when did you see her last?" Hazel said. "Tania?"

"I don't see her," Dudley said. "I don't go out there. We have financial matters, but I don't go out."

Well, you ought to go, she was about to say to him. You must go, and not make stupid arrangements that Antoinette can step in and spoil, as she did today. He was the one, however, who spoke first. He leaned across and spoke to her with slightly drunken sincerity.

"What am I to do? I can't make two women happy."

A statement that might have been thought fatuous, conceited, evasive.

Yet it was true. Hazel was stopped. It was true. At first the claim seemed to be all Judy's, because of her child and her loneliness and her lovely hair. But why did Antoinette have to lose out, just because she had been in the running for a long time, could calculate, and withstand defections, and knew how to labor at her looks? Antoinette must have been useful and loyal and perhaps privately tender. And she didn't even ask for a man's whole heart. She might shut her eyes to a secret visit once in a while. (She'd be sick, though; she'd have to turn her head away and vomit.) Judy wouldn't put up with that at all. She'd be bursting with ballad fervor, all vows and imprecations. He couldn't bear such suffering, such railing. So had Antoinette foiled him today for his own good? That was the way she must see it—the way he might see it, too, after a little while. Even now, perhaps—now that the ballad had stirred and eased his heart.

Jack had said something like that once. Not about two women, but about making a woman—well, it was Hazel—happy. She thought back to what he had said. *I could make you very happy.* He meant that he could give her an orgasm. It was something men said then, when they were trying to persuade you, and that was what they meant. Perhaps they still said it. Probably they were not so indirect nowadays. And he had been quite right about what he promised. But nobody had said that to Hazel before, and she was amazed, taking the promise at face value. It seemed rash and sweeping to her, dazzling but presumptuous. She had to try to see herself, then, as somebody who could be *made happy*. The whole worrying, striving, complicated bundle of Hazel—was that something that could just be picked up and *made happy*?

One day, about twenty years later, she was driving down the main street of Walley and she saw Jack. He was looking out the front window of the appliance store. He wasn't looking in her direction, he didn't see the car. This was while she was going to college. She had errands to do, classes to get to, papers, labs, housework. She could notice things only if she was halted for a minute or two, as she was now, waiting for the light. She noticed Jack—how slim and youthful he looked, in his slacks and pullover—how gray and insubstantial. She didn't have anything like a clear intimation that he was going to die there, in the store. (He did die there; he slumped over while talking to a customer— but that was years later.) She didn't take account, all at once, of what his life had become—two or three nights a week at the Legion, the other nights spent lying on the sofa from supper to bedtime, watching television, drinking. Three drinks, four. Never mean, never noisy, he never passed out. He rinsed his glass at the kitchen sink before he went to bed. A life of chores, routines, seasons, pleasantries. All she saw was the stillness about him, a look you could have called ghostly. She saw that his handsomeness—a particular Second World War handsomeness, she felt, with a wisecracking edge to it and a proud passivity—was still intact but drained of power. A ghostly sweetness was what he showed her, through the glass.

She could be striving toward him, now as much as then. Full of damaging hopes, and ardor, and accusations. She didn't let herself then—she thought about an exam, or groceries. And if she let herself now, it would be like testing the pain in a lost limb. A quick test, a twinge that brings the whole shape into the air. That would be enough.

□   □

She was a little drunk herself by this time, and she thought of saying to Dudley Brown that perhaps he *was* making those two women happy. What could she mean by that? Maybe that he was giving them something to concentrate on. A hard limit that you might someday get past in a man, a knot in his mind you might undo, a stillness in him you might jolt, or an absence you might make him regret—that sort of thing will make you pay attention, even when you think you've taught yourself not to. Could it be said to make you happy?

Meanwhile, what makes a man happy?

It must be something quite different.

LORRIE MOORE

Which Is More
Than I Can Say
About Some People

Tt was a fear greater than death, according to
the magazines. Death was No. 4. After muti-
lation, three, and divorce, two. No. 1, the real
fear, the one death could not even approach, was
public speaking. Abby Mallon knew this too well.
Which is why she had liked her job at American
Scholastic Tests: she got to work with words in a
private way. The speech she made was done in the
back, alone, like little shoes cobbled by an elf: Spider is to web as weaver is to *blank*. That one was
hers. She was proud of that.

Also, *blank* is to heartache as forest is to bench.

But then, one day, the supervisor and A.S.T.
district coördinator called her upstairs. She was
good, they said, but perhaps she had become *too*
good, too *creative*, they suggested, and gave her a
promotion out of the composing room and into
the high-school auditoriums of America. She
would have to travel and give speeches, tell high-
school faculty how to prepare students for the en-

trance exams, meet separately with the juniors and seniors and answer their questions unswervingly, with authority and grace. "You may have a vacation first," they said, and handed her a check.

"Thank you," she said doubtfully. In her life she had been given the gift of solitude, a knack for it, but now it would be of no professional use. She would have to become a people person.

"A *peeper* person?" queried her mother, on the phone from Pittsburgh.

"*People,*" said Abby.

"Oh, those," said her mother, and she sighed the sigh of death, though she was strong as a brick.

□   □

Of all Abby's fanciful ideas for self-improvement (the inspirational video, the breathing exercises, the hypnosis class) the Blarney Stone, with its whoring barter of eloquence for love—"O gift of gab" read the T-shirts—was perhaps the most extreme. Perhaps. There had been, after all, her marriage to Bob, her boyfriend of many years, after her dog, Randolph, had died of kidney failure and marriage to Bob seemed the only way to overcome her grief. Of course, she had always admired the idea of marriage, the citizenship and public speech of it, the innocence rebestowed, and Bob was big and comforting. But he didn't have a lot to say. He was not a verbal man. Rage gave him syntax—but it just wasn't enough! Soon Abby had begun to keep him as a kind of pet, while she quietly looked for distractions of depth and consequence. She looked for words. She looked for ways with words. She worked hard to befriend a lyricist from New York—a tepid, fair-haired, violet-eyed bachelor. She and most of the doctors' wives and arts administrators in town. He was newly arrived, owned no car, and wore the same tan blazer every day. "Water, water everywhere but not a drop to drink," said the bachelor lyricist once, listening wanly to the female chirp of his phone messages. In his apartment there were no novels or bookcases. There was one chair, a large television set, the phone machine, a rhyming dictionary continually renewed from the library, and a coffee table. Women brought him meals, professional introductions, jingle commissions, and cash grants. In return, he brought them small, piebald stones from the beach, or pretty weeds from the park. He would stand behind the coffee table and recite his own songs, then step back and wait fearfully to be seduced. To be lunged at and devoured by the female form was, he believed, something akin to applause. Sometimes he would produce a rented lute and say, "Here, I've just composed a melody to go with my 'Creation' verse. Sing along with me."

And Abby would stare at him and say, "But I don't know the tune. I haven't heard it yet. You just made it up, you said."

Oh, the vexations endured by a Man of Poesy! He stood paralyzed behind the coffee table, and when Abby did at last step forward, just to touch him, to take his pulse, perhaps, *to capture one of his arms in an invisible blood-pressure cuff!* he crumpled and shrank. "Please don't think I'm some kind of emotional Epstein-Barr," he said, quoting from other arguments he'd had with women. "I'm not indifferent or dispassionate. I'm calm. I'm romantic, but I'm calm. I have appetites, but I'm very calm about them."

When Abby went back to her husband ("Honey, you're home!" Bob exclaimed), she lasted only a week. Shouldn't it have lasted longer—the mix of loneliness and lust and habit she always felt with Bob, the mix that was surely love, for it so often felt like love, how could it not be love, surely nature intended it to be, surely nature with its hurricanes and hail was counting on this to suffice? Bob smiled at her and said nothing. And the next day she booked a flight to Ireland.

□   □

How her mother became part of the trip, Abby still couldn't exactly recall. It had something to do with a stick shift: how Abby had never learned to drive one. "In my day and age," said her mother, "everyone learned. We all learned. Women had skills. They knew how to cook and sew. Now women have no skills."

The stick shifts were half the rental price of the automatics.

"If you're looking for a driver," hinted her mother, "I can still see the road."

"That's good," said Abby.

"And your sister Theda's spending the summer at your aunt's camp again." Theda had Down's syndrome, and the family adored her. Every time Abby visited, Theda would shout, "Look at you!" and throw her arms around her in a terrific hug. "Theda's, of course, sweet as ever," said her mother, "which is more than I can say about some people."

"That's probably true."

"I'd like to see Ireland while I can. Your father, when he was alive, never wanted to. I'm Irish, you know."

"I know. One-sixteenth."

"That's right. Of course, your father was Scottish, which is a totally different thing."

Abby sighed. "It seems to me that *Japanese* would be a totally different thing."

"*Japanese?*" hooted her mother. "Japanese is close."

□ □

And so in the middle of June they landed at the Dublin airport together. "We're going to go all around this island, every last peninsula," said Mrs. Mallon, in the airport parking lot, revving the engine of their rented Ford Fiesta, "because that's just the kind of crazy yuppies we are."

Abby felt sick from the flight, and sitting on what should have been the driver's side but which didn't have a steering wheel suddenly seemed emblematic of something.

Her mother lurched out of the parking lot and headed for the nearest roundabout, crossing into the other lane only twice. "I'll get the hang of this," she said. She pushed her glasses farther up on her nose, and Abby could see for the first time that her mother's eyes were milky with age. Her steering was jerky, and her foot jumped around on the floor, trying to find the clutch. Perhaps this had been a mistake.

"Go straight, Mom," said Abby, looking at her map.

Which Is More Than I Can Say About Some People

They zigged and zagged to the north, up and away from Dublin, planning to return there at the end, but now heading toward Drogheda, and the N1, Abby snatching up the guidebook and then the map again and then the guidebook, and Mrs. Mallon shouting, "What?" or "Left?" or "This can't be right, let me see that thing." The Irish countryside opened up before them, its pastoral patchwork and stone walls and chimney aroma of turf fires like something from another century, its small stands of trees, and fields populated with wildflowers and sheep dung and cut sod and cows with ear tags, beautiful as women. Perhaps fairy folk lived in the trees! Abby saw immediately that to live amidst the magic feel of this place would be necessarily to believe in magic. To live here would make you superstitious, warmhearted with secrets, unrealistic. If you were literal, or practical, you would have to move—or you would have to drink.

They drove uncertainly past signs to places unmarked on the map. They felt lost—but not in an uncharming way. The old, narrow roads with their white markers reminded Abby of the vacations her family had taken when she was little, the cow-country car trips through New England or Virginia—in those days before there were interstates or plastic cups or a populace depressed by asphalt and French fries. Ireland was a trip into the past of America. It was years behind, unmarred, like a story or a dream or a clear creek. I'm a child again, Abby thought. I'm back. And just as when she was a child, she suddenly had to go to the bathroom.

"I have to go to the bathroom," she said. To their left was a sign that said "Road Works Ahead" and underneath someone had scrawled, "No, it doesn't."

Mrs. Mallon veered the car over to the left and slammed on the brakes. There were some black-faced sheep, haunch-marked with bright blue, munching grass near the road.

"Here?" asked Abby.

"I don't want to waste time stopping somewhere else and having to buy something. You can go behind that wall."

"Thanks," said Abby, groping in her pocketbook for Kleenex. Already she missed her own house. She missed her neighbor-

279

hood. She missed the plentiful U-Pump-'Ems, where she often said, at least they spelled the word "pump" right! She got out and hiked back down the road a little way. On one of the family road trips thirty years ago, when she and Theda had had to go to the bathroom, their father had stopped the car and told them to "go to the bathroom in the woods." They had got out and wandered through the woods for twenty minutes, looking for the bathroom, before they came back out to tell him they hadn't been able to find it. Their father had looked perplexed, then amused, and then angry—his usual pattern.

Now Abby struggled over a short stone wall and hid, squatting, eying the sheep warily. She was spacey with jet lag, and when she got back to the car she realized she'd left the guidebook on a stone and had to turn around and retrieve it.

"There," she said, getting back in the car.

Mrs. Mallon shifted into gear. "I always feel that if people would just be like animals and excrete here and there rather than in a single agreed-upon spot, we wouldn't have any pollution."

Abby nodded. "That's brilliant, Mom."

"Is it?"

They stopped briefly at an English manor house, to see the natural world cut up into moldings and rugs, wool and wood captive and squared, the earth stolen and embalmed and shellacked. Abby wanted to leave. "Let's leave," she whispered.

"What is it with you?" complained her mother. From there they visited a Neolithic passage grave, its design like a birth in reverse, its narrow stone corridor spilling into a high, round room. They took off their sunglasses and studied the Celtic curlicues. "Older than the pyramids," announced the guide, though he failed to address its most important feature, Abby felt: its deadly maternal metaphor.

"Are you still too nervous to cross the border to Northern Ireland?" asked Mrs. Mallon.

"Uh-huh." Abby bit at her thumbnail, tearing the end of it off like a tiny twig.

"Oh, come on," said her mother. "Get a grip."

And so they crossed the border into the north, past the flak-jacketed soldiers patrolling the neighborhoods and barbed wire of Newry: young men holding automatic weapons and walking backward, block after block; their partners across the street, walking forward, on the watch. Helicopters flapped above. "This is a little scary," said Abby.

"It's all show," said Mrs. Mallon breezily.

"It's a scary show."

"If you get scared easily."

Which was quickly becoming the theme of their trip—Abby could see that already. That Abby had no courage and her mother did. And that it had been that way forever.

"You scare too easily," said her mother. "You always did. When you were a child, you wouldn't go into a house unless you were reassured that there were no balloons in it."

"I didn't like balloons."

"And you were scared on the plane coming over," said her mother.

Abby grew defensive. "Only when the flight attendant said there was no coffee because the percolator was broken. Didn't you find that alarming? And then, after all that slamming, they still couldn't get one of the overhead bins shut." Abby remembered this as if it were a distant, bitter memory, though it had only been yesterday. The plane had taken off with a terrible shudder, and when it proceeded with the rattle of an old subway car, particularly over Greenland, the flight attendant had gotten on the address system to announce that there was nothing to worry about, "especially when you think about how heavy air really is."

Now her mother thought she was Tarzan. "I want to go on that rope bridge I saw in the guidebook," she said.

On page 98 in the guidebook was a photograph of a rope-and-board bridge slung high between two cliffs. It was supposed to be for fishermen, but tourists were allowed, though they were cautioned about strong winds.

"Why do you want to go on the rope bridge?" asked Abby.

"*Why?*" replied her mother, who then seemed stuck and fell silent.

□   □

For the next two days, they drove east and to the north, skirting Belfast, along the coastline, past old windmills and sheep farms, and up onto vertiginous cliffs that looked out toward Scotland, a pale sliver on the sea. They stayed at a tiny stucco bed-and-breakfast, one with a thatched roof like Cleopatra bangs. They slept lumpily, and in the morning, in the breakfast room with its large front window, they ate their cereal and rashers and black-and-white pudding in an exhausted way, going through the motions of good guesthood. "Yes, the troubles," they agreed, for who could say for certain to whom you were talking? It wasn't like a race-riven America, where you always knew. Abby nodded. Out the window there was a breeze, but she couldn't hear the faintest rustle of it. She could only see it silently moving the dangling branches of the sun-sequinned spruce, just slightly; it was like looking at objects hanging from a rearview mirror in someone else's car.

She charged the bill to her Visa, tried to lift both bags, and then lifted just her own.

"Goodbye! Thank you!" she and her mother called to their host. Back in the car, briefly, Mrs. Mallon began to sing "Toora-loora-looral." "Over in Killarney, many years ago," she warbled. Her voice was husky, vibrating, slightly flat, coming in just under each note like a saucer under a cup.

And so they drove on. The night before, the whole day ahead could have shape and design. But when it was upon you, it could vanish tragically into air.

They came to the sign for the rope bridge.

"I want to do this," said Mrs. Mallon, and swung the car sharply right. They crunched into a gravel parking lot and parked; the bridge was a quarter-mile walk from there. In the distance dark clouds roiled like a hemorrhage, and the wind was picking up. Rain mizzled the windshield.

"I'm going to stay here," said Abby.

"You are?"

"Yeah."

"Whatever," said her mother in a disgusted way, and she got

out scowling and trudged down the path to the bridge, disappearing beyond a curve.

Abby waited, now feeling the true loneliness of this trip. She realized she missed Bob and his warm, quiet confusion; how he sat on the rug in front of the fireplace, where her dog Randolph used to sit; sat there beneath the five Christmas cards they'd received, and placed on the mantel—five including the one from the paperboy—sat there picking at his feet or naming all the fruits in his fruit salad, remarking life's great variety or asking what was wrong (in his own silent way) while poking endlessly at a smoldering log. She thought, too, about poor Randolph, at the vet with his patchy fur and begging, dying eyes. And she thought about the pale bachelor lyricist, how he had once come to see her, and how he hadn't even placed enough pressure on the doorbell to make it ring, and so had stood there waiting on the porch, holding a purple coneflower, until she just happened to walk by the front-room window and see him standing there. *O poetry!* When she invited him in, and he gave her the flower and sat down to decry the coded bloom and doom of all things, decry as well his own unearned deathlessness, how everything hurtles toward oblivion except words, which assemble themselves in time like molecules in space, for God was an act—an act!—of language, it hadn't seemed silly to her, not really, at least not *that* silly.

The wind was gusting. She looked at her watch, worried now about her mother. She turned on the radio to find a weather report, though the stations all seemed to be playing strange, redone versions of American pop songs from 1970. Every so often there was a two-minute quiz show—Who is the president of France? Is a tomato a vegetable or a fruit?—questions that the callers rarely if ever answered correctly, which made the show quite embarrassing to listen to. Why did they do it? Puzzles, quizzes, game shows. Abby knew from A.S.T. that a surprising percentage of those taking the college-entrance exams never actually applied to college. People just loved a test. Wasn't that true? People loved to put themselves to one.

Her mother was now knocking on the glass. She was muddy

and wet. Abby unlocked the door and pushed it open. "Was it worth it?" Abby asked.

Her mother got in, big and dank and puffing. She started the car without looking at her daughter. "What a bridge!" she said finally.

□　□

The next day they made their way along the Antrim coast, through towns bannered with Union Jacks and lines from Scottish hymns, down to Derry with its barbed wire, and I.R.A. scrawlings on the city walls—"John Major is a Zionist Jew." ("Hello," said a British officer, when they stopped to stare.) Then they escaped across bandit country, and once more down across the border into the south, down the Donegal coast, its fishing villages like some old, never-was Cape Cod. Staring out through the windshield, off into the horizon, Abby began to think that all the beauty and ugliness and turbulence you found scattered through nature you could also find in people themselves, all collected in them, all together in one place. No matter what terror or loveliness the earth could produce—winds, seas—a person could produce the same, lived with the same, lived with all that mixed-up nature swirling inside, every bit. There was nothing as complex in the world—no flower or stone—as a single "hello" from a human being.

□　□

Once in a while Abby and her mother broke their silences with talk of Mrs. Mallon's job as office manager at a small flashlight company—"I had to totally rearrange our insurance policies. The dental and major-medical were eating our lunch!"—or with questions about the route signs, or the black dots signifying auto deaths. But mostly her mother wanted to talk about Abby's shaky marriage and what she was going to do. "Look, another ruined abbey," she took to saying, every time they passed a heap of medieval stones.

"When are you going back to Bob?"

"I went back," said Abby. "But then I left again. Whoops."

284

Her mother sighed. "Women of your generation are always hoping for some other kind of romance than the one they have," said Mrs. Mallon. "Aren't they?"

"Who knows?" said Abby. She was starting to feel a little tight-lipped with her mother, crammed into this space together like astronauts. She was starting to have a highly inflamed sense of event: a single word rang and vibrated. The slightest movement could annoy, a breath, an odor. Unlike her sister Theda, who had always remained sunny and cheerfully intimate with everyone, Abby had always been darker and left to her own devices; she and her mother had never been very close. When Abby was a child, her mother had always repelled her a bit—the oily smell of her hair, her belly button like a worm curled in a pit, the sanitary napkins in the bathroom wastebasket, horrid as a war, then later strewn along the curb by raccoons who would tear them from the trash cans at night. Once, at a restaurant, when she was little, Abby had burst into an unlatched ladies' room stall, only to find her mother sitting there, in a dazed and unseemly way, peering out at her from the toilet seat, like a cuckoo in a clock.

There were some things one should never know about another person.

Later, Abby decided that perhaps it hadn't been her mother at all.

Yet now, here she and her mother were, sharing the tiniest of cars, reunited in a wheeled and metal womb, sharing small double cots in bed-and-breakfasts, waking up with mouths stale and close upon each other or backs turned and rocking in angry-seeming humps. *The land of ire!* Talk of Abby's marriage and its possible demise trotted before them on the road like a herd of sheep, insomnia's sheep, and it made Abby want to have a gun.

"I never bothered with conventional romantic fluff," said Mrs. Mallon. "I wasn't the type. I always worked, and I was practical, put myself forward, and got things done and over with. If I liked a man, I asked him out myself. That's how I met your father. I asked him out. I even proposed the marriage."

"I know."

"And then I stayed with him until the day he died. Actually, three days after. He was a good man." She paused. "Which is more than I can say about some people."

Abby didn't say anything.

"Bob's a good man," added Mrs. Mallon.

"I didn't say he wasn't."

There was silence again between them now as the countryside once more unfolded its quilt of greens, the old roads triggering memories as if this were a land she had travelled long ago, its mix of luck and unluck like her own past; it seemed stuck in time like a daydream or a book. Up close the mountains were craggy, scabby with rock and green, like a buck's antlers losing their fuzz. But distance filled the gaps with moss. Wasn't that the truth? Abby sat quietly glugging Ballygowan water from a plastic bottle and popping Extra Strong Mints. Perhaps she should turn on the radio, listen to one of the call-in quizzes or to the news. But then her mother would take over, fiddle and re-tune. Her mother was always searching for country music, songs with the words "devil woman." She loved those.

"Promise me one thing," said Mrs. Mallon.

"What?" said Abby.

"That you'll try with Bob."

At what price? Abby wanted to yell, but she and her mother were too old for that now.

Mrs. Mallon continued, thoughtfully, with the sort of pseudo-wisdom she donned now that she was sixty. "Once you're with a man you have to sit still with him. As scary as it seems. You have to be brave and learn to reap the benefits of inertia," and here she gunned the motor to pass a tractor on a curve. "Loose chippings," said the sign. "Hidden dip." But Abby's mother drove as if these were cocktail-party chatter. A sign ahead showed six black dots.

"Yeah," said Abby, clutching the dashboard. "Dad was inert. Dad was inert except that once every three years he jumped up and socked somebody in the mouth."

"That's not true."

"It's basically true."

Which Is More Than I Can Say About Some People

In Killybegs, they followed the signs for Donegal City. "You women today," Mrs. Mallon said. "You expect too much."

□   □

"If it's Tuesday, this must be Sligo," said Abby. She had taken to making up stupid jokes. "What do you call a bus with a soccer team on it?"

"What?" They passed a family of gypsies, camped next to a mountain of car batteries they hoped to sell.

"A football coach." Sometimes Abby laughed raucously and sometimes not at all. Sometimes she just shrugged. She was waiting for the Blarney Stone. That was all she'd come here for, so everything else she could endure.

They stopped at a bookshop to get a better map and inquire, perhaps, about a bathroom. Inside there were four customers: two priests reading golf books, and a mother with her tiny son who traipsed after her along the shelves begging: "Please, Mummy, just a wee book, Mummy. Please just a wee book." There was no better map. There was no bathroom. "Sorry," the clerk said, and one of the priests glanced up quickly. Abby and her mother went next door to look at the Kinsale smocks and wool sweaters—tiny cardigans that young Irish children, on sweltering summer days of seventy-one degrees, wore on the beach, over their bathing suits. "So cute," said Abby, and the two them wandered through the store, touching things. In the back, by the wool caps, Abby's mother found a marionette hanging from a ceiling hook and began to play with it a little, waving its arms to the store music, which was a Beethoven concerto. Abby went to pay for a smock, ask about a bathroom or a good pub, and when she came back her mother was still there, transfixed, conducting the concerto with the puppet. Her face was arranged in girlish joy, luminous, as Abby rarely saw it. When the concerto was over, Abby handed her a bag. "Here," she said. "I bought you a smock."

Mrs. Mallon let go of the marionette, and her face darkened. "I never had a real childhood," she said, taking the bag and looking off into the distance. "Being the oldest, I was always my

287

mother's confidante. I always had to act grown-up and responsible. Which wasn't my natural nature." Abby steered her toward the door. "And then when I really was grown-up, there was Theda, who needed all my time, and your father, of course, with his demands. But then there was you. You I liked. You I could leave alone."

"I bought you a smock," Abby said again.

They used the bathroom at O'Hara's pub, bought a single mineral water and split it, then went on to the Drumcliff cemetery to see the dead Yeatses. Then they sped on toward Sligo City to find a room, and the next day were up and out to Knock, to watch lame women, sick women, women who wanted to get pregnant ("Knocked up," said Abby) rub their rosaries on the original stones of the shrine. They drove down to Clifden, around Connemara, to Galway and Limerick—"There once were two gals from America, one named Abby and her mother, named Erica. . . ." They sang, minstrel speed demons around the Ring of Kerry, its palm trees and blue and pink hydrangea like a set from an operetta. "Playgirls of the Western World!" exclaimed her mother. They came to rest, at dark, near Ballylicky, in a bed-and-breakfast, a former hunting lodge, in a glen just off the ring. They had a late supper of toddies and a soda bread their hostess called Curranty Dick.

"Don't I know it," said Mrs. Mallon. Which depressed Abby, like a tacky fixture in a room, and so she excused herself and went upstairs, to bed.

□　　□

It was the next day, through Ballylicky, Bantry, Skibbereen, and Cork, that they entered Blarney. At the castle the line to kiss the stone was long, hot, and frightening. It jammed the tiny winding stairs of the castle's suffocating left tower, and people pressed themselves against the dark wall to make room for others who had lost their nerve and were coming back down.

"This is ridiculous," said Abby. But by the time they'd reached the top, her annoyance had turned to anxiety. To kiss the stone, she saw, people had to lie on their backs out over a parapet, stretching their necks out to place their lips on the underside of a supporting wall where the stone was laid. A strange-looking, leprechaunish man was squatting at the side of the stone, supposedly to help people arch back, but he seemed to be holding them too loosely, a careless and sadistic glint in his eyes, and some people were changing their minds and going back downstairs, fearful and inarticulate as ever.

"I don't think I can do this," said Abby hesitantly, tying her dark raincoat more tightly around her.

"Of course you can," said her mother. "You've come all this way. This is why you came." Now that they were at the top of the castle, the line seemed to be moving quickly. Abby looked back, and around, and the view was green and rich, and breathtaking, like a photo soaked in dyes.

"Next!" She heard the leprechaun shouting.

Ahead of them a German woman was struggling to get back up from where the leprechaun had left her. She wiped her mouth and made a face. "That vuz awfhul," she grumbled.

Panic seized Abby. "You know what? I don't want to do this," she said to her mother. There were only two people ahead of them in line. One of them was now getting down on his back, clutching the iron supports and inching his hands down, arching at the neck and waist to reach the stone, exposing his white throat. His wife stood above him, taking his picture.

"But you came all this way! Don't be a ninny!" Her mother was bullying her again. It never gave her courage; in fact, it deprived her of courage. But it gave her bitterness and impulsiveness, which could look like the same thing.

"Next," said the leprechaun nastily. He hated these people, one could see that. One could see he half hoped they would go crashing down off the ledge in a heap of raincoats, limbs, and traveller's checks.

"Go on," said Mrs. Mallon.

"I can't," Abby whined. Her mother was nudging and the leprechaun was frowning. "I can't. You go."

"No. Come on. Think of it as a test." Her mother, too, gave her a frown, then a lunatic scowl. "You work with tests. And in school you always did well on them."

"For tests you have to study."

"You studied!"

"I didn't study the right thing."

"Oh, Abby."

"I can't," Abby whispered. "I just don't think I can." She breathed deeply and moved quickly. "Oh—O.K." She threw her hat down and fell to the stone floor fast, to get it over with.

"Move back, move back," droned the leprechaun, like a train conductor.

She could now feel no more space behind her back; from her waist up she was out over air and hanging on only by her hands clenched around the iron rails. She bent her head as far back as she could, but it wasn't far enough.

"Lower," said the leprechaun.

She slid her hands down farther, as if she were doing a trick on a jungle gym. Still, she couldn't see the Stone itself, only the castle wall.

"Lower," said the leprechaun.

She slid her hands even lower, bent her head back, her chin skyward, could feel her windpipe pressing out against the skin, and this time she could see the Stone. It was about the size of a microwave oven and was covered with moisture and dirt and lipstick marks, in the shape of lips—lavender, apricot, red. It seemed very unhygienic for a public attraction, filthy and wet, and so now, instead of giving it a big smack, she blew a peck at it, then shouted, "O.K. help me up, please," and the leprechaun helped her back up.

Abby stood and brushed herself off. Her raincoat was covered with whitish mud. "Eeyuhh," she said. But she had done it! At least sort of. She put her hat back on. She tipped the leprechaun a pound. She didn't know how she felt. She felt nothing. Finally, these dares one made with oneself didn't change a thing. They were all a construction of wish and string and distance.

"Now my turn," said her mother with a kind of reluctant determination, handing Abby her sunglasses. As her mother got down stiffly, inching her way toward the stone, Abby suddenly saw something she'd never seen before: her mother was terrified. For all her bullying and bravado, she was proceeding, and proceeding badly, through a great storm of terror in her brain. As her mother tried to inch herself back toward the Stone, Abby, now privy to her bare face, saw that this fierce bonfire of a woman had gone twitchy and melancholic—it was a ruse, all her formidable display. She was only trying to prove something, trying pointlessly to defy and overcome her fears—instead of just learning to live with them, since, hell, you were living with them anyway.

"Mom, you O.K.?" Mrs. Mallon's face was in a grimace, her mouth open and bared. The former auburn of her hair had descended, Abby saw, to her teeth, which she'd let rust with years of coffee and tea.

Now the leprechaun was having to hold her more tightly than he had the other people. "Lower, now lower."

"Oh, God, not any lower," cried Mrs. Mallon.

"You're almost there."

"I don't see it."

"There, you got it?" He loosened his grip and let her slip further.

"Yes," she said. She let out a puckering, spitting sound. But then, when she struggled to come back up, she seemed to be stuck. Her legs thrashed out before her, her shoes loosened from her feet; her skirt rode up revealing the brown tops of her pantyhose. She was bent too strangely—from the hips, it seemed—and she was plump and didn't have the stomach muscles to lift herself back up. The leprechaun seemed to be having difficulty.

"Can someone here help me?"

"Oh, my God," said Abby, and she and a man in line immediately squatted next to Mrs. Mallon to help her. She was heavy, stiff with fright, and when they had finally lifted her and got her sitting, then standing again, she looked stricken and pale.

A guard near the staircase volunteered to escort her down.

"Would you like that, Mom?" Abby asked. Mrs. Mallon simply nodded.

"You get in front of us," the guard said to Abby in the singsong accent of County Cork, "just in case she falls." And Abby got in front, her coat taking the updraft and spreading to either side as she circled slowly down into the dungeon dark of the stairwell, into the black, like a bat new to its wings.

□   □

In a square in the center of town an evangelist was waving a Bible and shouting about "the brevity of life," how it was a thing grabbed by one hand and then gone, escaped through the fingers. "God's word is quick!" he called out.

"Let's go over there," said Abby, and she took her mother to a pub called Brady's Public House for a restorative Guinness. "Are you O.K.?" Abby kept asking. They still had no place to stay that night, and though it remained light quite late and the inns stayed open until ten, she imagined the two of them temporarily homeless, sleeping under the stars, snacking on slugs. Stars the size of Chicago! Dew like a pixie bath beneath them! They would lick it from their arms.

"I'm fine," Mrs. Mallon said, waving her daughter's questions away. "What a stone!"

"Mom," said Abby, frowning; she was now wondering about a few things. "When you went across that rope bridge, did you do that O.K.?"

Mrs. Mallon sighed. "Well, I got the idea of it," she said huffily. "But there were some gusts of wind that caused it to buck a little, and though some people thought that was fun, I had to get down and crawl back. You'll recall there was a little rain."

"You crawled back on your hands and knees."

"Well, yes," she admitted. "There was a nice Belgian man who helped me." She felt unmasked before her daughter and now gulped at her Guinness.

Abby tried to take a cheerful tone, switching the subject a little, and that reminded her of Theda, Theda somehow living in Abby's voice, her larynx suddenly a summer camp for the cheer-

ful and slow. "Well, look at you!" said Abby. "Do you feel eloquent and confident, now that you've kissed the stone?"

"Not really." Mrs. Mallon shrugged.

Now that they had kissed it, or sort of, would they become
self-conscious? What would they end up talking about? Movies,
probably. Just as they always had at home. Movies with scenery,
movies with songs.

"How about you?" asked Mrs. Mallon.

"Well," said Abby, "mostly I feel like we've probably caught
strep throat. And yet, and yet—" here she sat up and leaned forward. No tests, or radio quizzes, or ungodly speeches, or brain-
dead songs, or kookie prayers, or shouts, or prolix conversations
that with drink and too much time always revealed how stupid
and mean even the best people were, just simply this: "A toast. I
feel a toast coming on."

"You do?"

"Yes, I do." No one had toasted Abby and Bob at their little
wedding, and that's what had been wrong, she believed now. No
toast. There had been only thirty guests, and they had simply
eaten the ham canapés and gone home. How could such a marriage go right? It wasn't that such ceremonies were important in
and of themselves. They were nothing. They were zeros. But they
were zeros as placeholders; they held numbers and equations intact. And once you underwent them you could move on, know
the empty power of their blessing, and not spend time missing
them.

From here on in, she would believe in toasts. One was collecting itself now, in her head. She gazed over at her mother and
took a deep breath. Perhaps her mother had never shown Abby
affection, not really, but she had given her a knack for solitude,
with its terrible lurches outward and its smooth glide back to
peace. Abby would toast her for that. It was really the world that
was your brutal mother, the one that nursed and neglected you,
and your own mother was only your sibling in that world. Abby
lifted her glass. "May the worst always be behind you, may the
sun daily warm your arms. . . ." She looked down at her cocktail
napkin for assistance, but there was only a cartoon of a big-

chested colleen, two shamrocks over her breasts. Abby looked back up. *God's word is quick!* "May your car always start. . . ." But perhaps God might also begin with tall, slow words: the belly bloat of a fib, the distended tale. "And may you always have a clean shirt," she continued, her voice growing gallant, public, and loud, "and a holding roof, healthy children, and good cabbages— and may you be with me in my heart, Mother, as you are now, in this place, always and forever, like a flaming light."

There was noise in the pub.

Blank is to childhood as journey is to lips.

"Right," said Mrs. Mallon, looking into her stout in a concentrated, bright-eyed way. She had never been courted before, not once in her entire life, and now she blushed, ears on fire, lifted her pint, and drank.

KATE BRAVERMAN

Virgin of Tenderness

M aggie Decker has always wanted to fall off the world as it is ordinarily known and it seems she has finally done it. She is looking at icons in the crypt beneath the Church of Alexander Nevsky on Ruskie Boulevard in Sofia. She pauses in front of the Virgin of Tenderness, noting how abstract and isolated she seems. She is insulated by a background painted with a pigment derived from lapis lazuli. Half a millennium later the color is undamaged. It glares like a permanent blue truth. The Virgin of Tenderness has a garish silver hand. She has been kissed by so many that parts of her body have been covered with a protective metal.

"Did you see the Virgin of Tenderness?" Maggie asks.

"No. I'm blind," Heather answers. And, after a moment, "Of course I saw it. You always ask the worst questions."

Maggie is quiet as they climb marble stairs.

She pauses in the chapel to light a candle for her daughter. Bless her in her cynicism, she thinks, and her aggressive ignorance.

Then they are sitting in the car again and the chauffeur is taking them out of the city. There are yellow trollies on boulevards bordered by dead birch and oak. She can see snow on the Balkan Mountains beyond the Palace of Culture. The gold dome of the Church of Alexander Nevsky is behind them. They are passing empty parks with dismissed chestnuts and bronze soldiers on horseback. There is the soft red fluttering of communist flags above cobblestones. It is late winter. The sun seems distant and flat.

She studies her daughter's face. Heather has black hair and creamy pale skin. Her cheeks are the color of apricots. When the sun strikes her hair, it becomes shades of brown and red like the tones of certain polished woods. She thinks of violins and cellos and the music lessons Heather took when she was seven. Even then she had a temper.

"You're staring again," Heather accuses.

"It gives me pleasure to look at you," Maggie says.

"It's always about you," Heather replies. She's been waiting for this. "But *you* are making *me* uncomfortable."

Maggie wills her head to turn and it does. The suburbs of Sofia are behind them. Everything is behind them, the Ottoman Empire, the German occupation, the way the Greeks and Romans came. Even the Turks who stayed for five hundred years, smoking hash and playing with themselves, are finally gone.

They are passing mining villages with brick town houses on ruts of dirt streets. The land seems unadorned. Donkeys pull carts. Sheep walk the shoulder of the road like a form of punctuation, something in the margin one could forget to mention. They are on the road to the Rila Monastery. There are occasional patches of snow. A sudden herd of bulls passes. Below are hillsides where apples and walnuts will later grow.

They are parked near the entrance to the compound. The air is sharp with implications, angels and gray devils with the cool sheen of reptiles are painted on ceilings and arches and the edges of balconies. These are the creatures of fever and dream and a severity of winter. This is why they have wound up mountains through a density of birch and chestnut. She opens the door for her daughter.

"My feet hurt," Heather tells her. "You go."

"But you'll never have another chance to see Rila," Maggie says.

"Is that a promise?" Heather is staring at her with contempt. She lights a cigarette with slow deliberation. "I hope I'm never within two thousand miles of this ugly backward country for the rest of my life."

"Heather, please," Maggie Decker begins. She is always beginning.

"You go. I know what's there. They're selling pieces of the saints. They've got their bones in carved filigree boxes. Jesus, this is worse than Mexico."

Maggie Decker walks alone through Rila, past the old women selling bones of the saints in small wooden boxes. She studies an altar cross said to contain six hundred separate carved figures in scenes from the New Testament. It took the monk twelve years to carve. Maggie makes the mistake of asking the tour guide what happened to the monk.

"He went blind on the day it was finished," the guide replies.

"Of course," Maggie says, in English. "What else?"

Then they are passing illuminated manuscripts in Cyrillic, royal decree scrolls with gold seals, and six-foot wooden candles donated by Turkish sultans. There are carved chalices and Russian shrouds with raised figures woven with gold and silver fibers, with gems and pearls for emphasis. It is a tiered world and the skies and underground are also filled.

When she returns to the car, Heather is smoking. She tosses the cigarette out the window, onto the snow. "This place is even worse than I thought," Heather tells her. "This has got to be the country from hell." Then Heather closes her eyes and pretends to fall asleep.

Maggie Decker does not look at her daughter. She does not

reach out and touch her arm. She does not speak. The road feels south, even with your eyes closed, she decides. You can feel the drift.

□　　□

After a time she notices the skeletons of grapevines planted between apartments along a river. There is a snowstorm. Then there are factories and towns without names beside train tracks.

A cold drizzle begins. It is late afternoon in Melnick near the Greek border. Peasant women bend over tobacco. They have passed through the Bulgarian wine country in rolling valleys below mountains with snow. Goats push up hillsides. She is drawn to the sudden yellow of leaves in a gully by a fast-moving stream. It is a stasis of winter. Only russet and orange, red and brown and gray are permitted.

They walk through the town. Heather always walks ahead of her. The town is mostly stone houses with broken porches on which white gourds hang. There is radio disco in subterranean cafés that look dark and gouged as caves.

They sit on a wall Romans built. It is all a matter of suggestion, she thinks. The ruins of a thousand-year-old mineral bath are below them. It is all stone upon stone, one at a time, relentless as cells, she is realizing. And stone is the DNA of the exterior world. And doesn't man build dimensional metaphors of his interior, obsessively constructing what he only subliminally recognizes? And it occurs to Maggie Decker that you can know yourself absolutely in any ancient ruin.

Maggie remembers her daughter at seven. How she would sit on her lap in the morning before school. How she would brush her hair. Or the way they would look into one another's eyes when they spoke. Now she tries to explain the historical significance of the site to Heather.

"Oh, be quiet," her daughter says, annoyed. "History is just the way you try to contaminate me. History is your private excuse. This is not about the Romans."

"What is it about?" Maggie wants to know.

"It's about your petty failures and fear of death." Heather turns away.

Maggie Decker considers her daughter's concept of history. They are driving through trees. These are the woods you don't picnic in but survive, she decides. And it seems she is watching the world through branches, through hillsides of stark crucifixions. And there is only stone and oak and the way bark is between late snows, bark like charred wood when its skin is carved away, when it rises into the cold air waiting to be born.

□   □

She wakes up in the middle of the night in Plovdiv, the city she has added to their itinerary because her grandmother was born there. It is raining. She has dreamed about the hospital again, specifically the radiation treatment. She has dreamed she is strapped to the metal table, the invisible rays are entering her body. She can feel them. They are blue and cold like the distilled essence of some profound evil.

Later she watches the day assemble itself from her hotel window. She notes the first random truck, the first taxi and then another. She has spent her life watching cities she is merely passing through wake up. It never meant anything and she wonders, vaguely, why she has adhered to this empty ritual. Outside it is a cold gray falling into the river, the buildings and air.

In the elevator a man says, "There are still forbidden zones in Russia."

"Don't be absurd," the woman with him answers in French. "That is obvious propaganda."

Then they are driving through Plovdiv and the city seems old and bloody, ancient and infected. They are passing streets of low apartment houses beyond the gray river in the sharp gray air.

"Grandmother walked from this city," she tells Heather. "She walked carrying an infant to Antwerp."

Heather doesn't hear her. Heather has a cassette player with earphones on her head. She listens exclusively to punk rock. She writes one postcard after another. It does not seem possible she can know that many people. She avoids even a stray glance out the window.

Maggie Decker had planned to find her grandmother's neighborhood and somehow pay her respects. She has maps and documents with lists of names and reference numbers. But now she decides it is not possible to navigate this density of gray. There are no gestures from her time and region that can apply here.

They have crossed the river. There are flatlands between mountains. She starts to say it could be Northern California, Salinas, perhaps, in winter, but Heather has the earphones on. They are passing a town where clothing has been left to dry on apartment balconies. Snow falls across the sheets. The side streets are the color of leaves. The houses are brick behind a veil of what could be fog or chimney smoke. Everything is the tone of winter and rock and a God who would be hard, severe with his delineations.

In her hotel room, she notices that she is bleeding. There is a moment when she almost faints but she doesn't. She washes her underwear. She dreams of the radiation treatment again. They are staying in a hotel in the Balkan Mountains. She dreams of the hotel. In this dream, she has become the Virgin of Tenderness. She is draped in blue and her hand is a kind of metal hook. She waves her hook at the doctor and says, "It's still winter in the mountains. In the towns, it's still the Middle Ages."

At breakfast, Heather orders wine with her eggs. She drinks in slow motion, letting their eyes meet. "I went to a disco last night," Heather reveals. "And no one would dance with me."

Have your cruelties become apparent, even to strangers? Maggie wonders. Can they sense your callous indifference? She is interested. At last, she asks her daughter why.

"Because I'm from Los Angeles. They know we've got the plague. They were afraid of catching something." Heather pauses. She looks at the ceiling. "This country sucks," she says finally.

Later they are winding into the mountains, into a blizzard, and the car is skidding. They slide onto the shoulder, crashing into branches. This catches Heather's attention. She removes her earphones. Oak trees along the road look solemn and crocheted. They seem frozen in midstep, in some autistic repetition. In this protracted moment they calibrate the movement of stars and who can say what they know or why they chose to point that way at the road? Maggie tells the driver to wait. She can see a small church.

"Why are you going in there?" Heather shouts.

"I want to light candles," Maggie tells her. She is walking.

"You've been lighting candles since Sofia," Heather says. "Is it a new addiction?"

"I wouldn't worry about that," Maggie says. "You need all the illumination you can get."

She is walking and the snow is deeper than she imagined. She steps in past her knees. She can sense Heather behind her now. She can hear her daughter, the car door shutting and some rustling of fur in snow.

The chapel is carved wood and gilt, gilt thrones and icons with metal hands and metal halos. There are Oriental carpets on the stone floor which bear the scars from past fires. Plastic roses in vases rest on the altar beneath icons. Maggie buys ten candles from an old woman with a black birthmark on her cheek.

She stands near the carved wood on the side of the church. Everything is carved in this country, as if men sat in a trance through perpetual winters, playing with knives. Two peasants pass near her and retreat into shadow. They look like movie extras. They have faces lifted from nightmares. They carry the props of bit players, berets and canes and candles and pipes. They dress entirely in black. They have brilliant eyes. Perhaps this is where the grandmothers go to die, she thinks, in Balkan mountain villages where they whisper over brandy while it snows. They stand near the entrances of compounds with thick ankles in black socks and they make sweeping motions at the illusionary ground. It is even possible that her grandmother is already here, waiting for her.

"Are you okay?" Heather asks. They walk in silence across the snow, back to the car. Now Heather looks worried.

"I was dizzy for a moment," Maggie says, suddenly frightened. She is about to tell Heather about the blood. She bites her lip and doesn't.

"It's always something with you," Heather says. Her tone is bitter.

"Why are you so angry?" Maggie studies her face. "Is it about your father?"

"Dad?" Heather's eyes are fixed. "They buried the Dead Hippie in 1969. Then you carried the corpse around for twenty years."

"What else?"

"Your style," Heather tells her. "It offends me. How you stand center stage and suck up all the air. All that drama with the drugs and the paramedics and rehabs. Then the high ritual you turned AA into. Every meeting was opening night. Now this." Heather looks out the window.

The car is moving into the snow. It seems as if the snow is throwing itself against the windshield. It looks purposeful, capable of intention and malice. And they are leaving the mountains behind them. Sheets are drying on apartment balconies as snow falls. There is more brick and stripped trees, streams and wooden fences and the carcasses of grapes.

She dreams she is cold and something blue is forcing its way into her body. She could stop this, but her hands are encased in metal and she has no thumbs. It is an invasion of subtle disguised particles. She wakes up with a start and they are parked in front of the hotel in Turnovo.

It is late afternoon. Maggie wants to see the ruins of the city now. She has spent her life waiting and there can be no more deferments. She knows this. She is walking up a hill, picking her way through rocks and weeds and walking through one of the walled entrances with its remnant of a drawbridge. The river is below. The country is the color of ruins, mustard yellow, brick red, and gray. Somehow the land, the rock and air have coalesced into these lost monuments.

The afternoon is darkening and the bus loads of Russian tourists have left the walled ruins. The plump women with dyed blond hair and bad skin and poorly fitting dull clothing are gone. Below are hillsides of houses, one upon another, a uniform white. The orange roofs seem part of the earth. There is a truth in all this that she can't quite grasp. In the narrow stone and mud streets of Turnovo, men and women wear brown coats and carry loaves of round bread.

Maggie Decker is alone in the ruins of Turnovo. Heather is far below, at the drawbridge, sharing her cassette player with the chauffeur. Nothing moves in the hills or on the river. Maggie reads a description of the annihilation of this city by the Turks in the fourteenth century.

Perhaps because it is winter and almost night and she is alone in these ruins, the idea of what it is to live in a walled city suddenly becomes clear to her. To dwell here would be to live in the only enclosure of civilization in hundreds of savage miles. How unlikely it would be that one would ever reach another city, a Constantinople or Athens. It seems almost impossible to take such a journey, even now.

Maggie Decker considers what it is to be invaded and to have your city burned. It is to erase you and your ancestors from the earth absolutely. There is nothing on microfilm. You and your history, your gods and poetry and children are utterly gone and gone forever. The fall of your city is the fall of the world.

□   □

"But you don't know you have a recurrence," Heather points out at dinner. She finishes a second bottle of wine. She glares at her mother.

"No, I don't know absolutely," Maggie agrees. It is important for Heather to believe that she doesn't know. So Maggie does not tell her intoxicated daughter about her intuition or dreams, or how she can feel it growing and spreading. She can feel it moving through her body the way you can feel a shadow across your skin. She doesn't tell Heather about the blood. She turns her eyes away from the wine bottle.

Later she lies in the darkness of her hotel room. Four men are playing cards in the hallway, arguing in Russian. She can hear the church bells, the many bells of Turnovo breaking the night with surgical precision, slicing the hours in half with the inevitability of centuries of slow winters, icons and stone churches, nights they invented vodka for.

Finally there is dawn with its terrible chill, with its icy rivers and bridges and stones. The old world moves in tortuous small circles and goes nowhere. It's been in a coma for a thousand years. You can barely recognize the forms beneath the rain and stupor, beneath the socialist art, gigantic and brain dead. And there are always the church bells with their ugly repetitions, their interminable chorus of gray.

□　　□

Between Turnovo and the Black Sea, Maggie Decker cannot help but consider her life and the wrong turns that deposited her in this car with the daughter who despises her and the driver who is no longer even bothering to offer suggestive gestures with his lips or fingers. On the streets, whole segments of the population look tainted. There is a ghastly sense of irrevocable winter and a squalor that seems almost intrinsic. They are driving through a city. All the women's coats are either black or brown or navy blue. Spring will never come to this region.

"This is a country where the female orgasm is unheard of," Heather observes. She says this and puts the earphones back on.

The mountains are behind them now. Of course the road is a borderline between time. This country has a tradition of blind singers in marginal areas. Nothing is accidental. It is a country of apple trees and symbols like all others. Now there is a hillside with blue beehives in the snow. A deer the color of blanched leaves regards them by a riverbank.

We come to bring flowers to apartments where our grandmothers once lived. We drive through streets they walked on, but they are dead and their memories are gone and the streets belong to someone else. We journey to abstract ruins. The stones are serene in their insignificance. We are the more wounded.

Heather sleeps and allows herself to slide against her mother, this woman who sits at the center of all drama, taking up the air.

Heather sleeps with her head on her mother's shoulder and it occurs to Maggie that it will be easier for her daughter to breathe soon. Now, because she is asleep, Maggie dares to brush her lips against the cheek which is the pink of the sides of apricots in July. She closes her eyes and breathes in the smell of Heather's hair, how forested it seems, how of damp moonlight and some essence of mahogany.

The driver has stopped. The cessation of movement wakes Heather, who bolts upright. They have stopped because the Black Sea is below them. It is a pale blue. Maggie experiences a sharp disappointment.

"What were you expecting?" Heather is regarding her with contempt. "Some real dark drama? I can read you like a book."

Indeed, Maggie Decker thinks. The dénouement is coming and ten to one you don't even know it.

Then they are driving down to the Black Sea port of Varna. She can see the ocean liners with their Russian flags, the cruise ships with the tourists from Moscow. The sun smells fresh.

They walk through the Roman ruins in Varna. When the baths were built, in the second century, the city was called Odessos. She starts to tell this to Heather and then remembers that Heather does not care. She does not believe that the fall of your city is the end of the world, that you are scratching with stone into dirt again. You are naked. You are an animal again and fear the night and the stars and the rain and predators. There are wild cats and sea gulls and the afternoon seems simultaneously ancient and possible. The sounds of haunted seabirds ricochet against the walls. After the fall of the world there are still seabirds.

"Is this it?" Heather asks.

Yes, this is it, Maggie thinks, but says nothing. You sit on a wall where the stones are the color of air in a light sun. From certain angles they seem invisible. You could almost walk through them. Then Maggie remembers there is one more town, Nessebyr. She tells the driver to take them there.

The Black Sea is a gauze below them, a pale restrained blue to the right. It could be the Santa Monica Bay of her youth. She went there with her brother. They would fish for halibut from the pier. If they found enough glass soda bottles to return, they could buy food. The bottles were two cents apiece. Most of the time, there was only enough for one hot dog or doughnut. Her brother would split the food with her, even though he was bigger. Sometimes they found enough bottles to take the bus back home. Other afternoons they would walk.

Now there are peach trees in a ravine off the road, yellow blossoms on a bush, and a carpet of sheep beneath trees near train tracks. It seems that the sun should set, it's seemed that way for hours, but it doesn't.

There are peach trees in flower. The forests are stripped. The sides of the road are thick with sheep the color of ruins and leaves and air. There is a sense of bells and Nessebyr.

Maggie knows it is the last stop on this awful journey. This is the last walled city Romans built that they will see. She is suddenly hungry and buys cakes from a street vendor. She eats as she walks. She stops to buy shell necklaces from a little boy. She puts them around her neck, one string then two more. She winds a string around her wrists and ankles. She intuits this is necessary. It is still afternoon.

It seems that Nessebyr is on an island. They have crossed a kind of bridge. She is walking on cobblestones. The cottages along the sea are wood and stone and like any beach resort, deserted in winter. She notices small sailboats below her. There are round piles of tiny clam shells in the ancient winter sand.

She has been sitting on the wall of a tenth-century church. There is the constant dialogue of seabirds in the ruins near her. Below and behind her, she can see the bridge they crossed. On the other side of that thin channel is a blue haze and what might be the twentieth century.

She wants to put her hands in the Black Sea. She walks across the sand, bends down, and knows instantaneously what this blue is. This is the blue of prophecy and she can correctly decipher it at last. This is the blue she has dreamed of, what she must anoint her face with.

The rocks are behind her. It is good to think of the world this way, as rock and wood and sand and flat sky and blue water. They raze your city and you are a baboon again. Small quiet-seeming boats with sails are in the water. Tree branches reach out from the shore. There is nothing more.

Maggie Decker is beginning to understand why the Virgin of Tenderness is depicted with lapis lazuli. It is the particular blue of this gulf. She could open her mouth and breathe faith in. There is so much air. It is incredible, but the higher the water touches her, the more clarity and knowledge she is given. She could swim past the stray fishing boats to the breakwater, or even beyond. Her feet can no longer touch the bottom. She can still see Heather standing on the far side of the bridge. It is a construction into a different millennium. Of course time is fluid. If Heather were to cross the bridge, two thousand years would pass. But Heather could never cross it fast enough.

ALLEN BARNETT

Succor

It was said that the reason Italian pilots flew so close to the ground was to follow the roads, but Kerch Slattery thought they might just be taking in the view. His plane circled Rome awaiting a ground crew's impromptu strike—*un sciopero*—which could last days or just the length of a coffee break. Fortunately, he had a window seat. The flight around Rome reminded him of Manhattan's Circle Line cruise; once around the island, you've seen the town, and you can go back to Joliet without another thought, the victor, the survivor, triumphant, alive. If Kerch had been handed a microphone, he could have identified sights out the window for the other passengers. It was fifteen years since he last had been in Rome, but he knew all the domes: St. Peter's was easy, and S. Andrea della Valle, but there was S. Ivo's, S. Eustachio, and the handsome and humble square dome on the synagogue. He knew the streets and piazzas as well: the Via Arenula, Via del Corso, the Campidoglio, Piazza Navona; that way was the S. Luigi dei Francesi with its three Caravaggios; around the corner was S. Agostino's, which only had one, the Madonna of the Pilgrims (to look at her one imagines the model was a streetwalker), but that served as an interesting contrast to the classical Junoesque sculpture of the Madonna by Sansovino, covered with jewel votive offerings, as ancient statues of goddesses often were. "To see her surrounded by blazing candles and to watch her devotees touch the foot that has been worn smooth by the millions [necessitating, Kerch recalled, a silver prosthesis] who have gone before is to realize that the cult of the mother strikes some deep atavistic chord in the Roman mind" is how his guidebook mildly put it. Did the real idea of mother fall somewhere between the two images, Kerch asked himself, or was there really that much of a difference between a goddess you paid for favors or the voluptuous one who held you in her arms as if you, not she, were the object of worship? But that thought was replaced quickly by another one: I've been here before.

"Go back," Father Casey had said to him, and left a small amount of money after his death for Kerch to do so. "The city won't have changed, but you'll have." Casey implied that as he himself was dying of AIDS, Kerch, by virtue of being seropositive for the virus, would become ill, also. It was just a matter of time.

The thought came back, or actually, the thought progressed, as he stood beneath the Bernini angel (there was actually some doubt about that, as he recalled) on the Ponte S. Angelo. The angel was covered with scaffolding and straw matting; a sign claimed that a major corporation was paying for the restoration; he couldn't see which instrument of the Passion this angel held. The restorer, wearing white overalls like an American house painter, opened a door into the scaffolding, then closed it behind himself. Kerch opened it again, and the restorer said, *"Buon giorno."* He looked up.

It was the angel with the nail. The head of the nail was rounded and sloped, rather like a mushroom, but more like something else, Kerch observed. The smile on the angel was not without its own knowledge of the private joke. That is when Kerch thought, Perhaps I should have gone someplace else.

Henry James had said that Rome can increase tenfold one's liability toward misery, and his first time here, as a melancholic nineteen-year-old, Kerch had indeed been miserable. Either James was right or the city was just obliging; misery loves company, or least a good mirror. The city's moods and one's own tended to be concomitant, or maybe there was just a lag time on the city's part, like someone who will go for a walk with you if given enough time to comb her hair.

"To love and have my love returned was my heart's desire, and it would be all the sweeter if I could also enjoy the body of the one who loved me." St. Augustine's *Confessions*. Well, that was the crux of it, right there, the real reason Kerch had been miserable in Rome, young and gay, and in a strange town where every man was more handsome than the last.

Dr. Palermo, the psychiatrist he had gone to only once, surmised as much himself, believing as he did that time spent celibate was a sad waste of time, and arranged for a meeting between his own son, Niccolo, who had a passion for American poetry, and Kerch, a literature major at an American school that had a campus in Rome. "How do you say this word?" Niccolo asked, pointing to his Whitman.

"Athwart," Kerch said.

"A—thwart," Niccolo attempted, the English *th* as difficult for him as the Italian rolled *r* or the *gli* sound was for Kerch. "Read the line to me," Niccolo demanded.

Kerch read as Niccolo nervously pounded his fingers on the tabletop, and his heart raced to catch up with their quickening beat. " 'You settled your head athwart my hips and gently turned over upon me, and parted the shirt from my bosom-bone, and plunged your tongue to my barestript heart, and reached till you felt my beard, and reached till you held my feet.' "

Where he now stood on the Ponte Sant'Angelo, Kerch could see the shuttered window that overlooked the Tiber where he and his psychiatrist's son had made love in the cloudy light of a February afternoon. Dr. Palermo sent him a bill for his single consultation.

They had never become lovers, though they continued to have sex three or four times a week. Sex was possible, a relationship prohibited. It had been a matter of class, almost illegal in an ancient Roman sense, Niccolo a patrician, Kerch a plebe. But they had become companions. On the back of Niccolo's Vespa, Niccolo maneuvering the streets of Rome, Kerch would sing, "Whenever blues becomes my only song, I concentrate on you."

□　　□

Promiscuous (adj.), consisting of diverse things or members: miscellaneous, indiscriminate, mixed, motley, multifarious. Lacking a definite plan, purpose, or pattern: random, desultory, haphazard, irregular, spot.

"You've brought dying people into your home," the magazine writer said to him, "people who had no place else to go. Why do you do it?"

"I have a spare room," Kerch said.

The spare room overlooked a sliver of a park at the top of West End Avenue. A motley assortment of men—he had been indiscriminate in whom he let in—had died in the room, looking down at the statue in the park built in memory of Ida and Isidor Straus, who had gone down in the *Titanic*. When he had moved into the rent-stabilized apartment as a graduate student, he thought the Strauses were sisters; to himself, he called the statue *Remembrance*. She lay across the top of a granite wall, reclining on one arm, the fingers of one hand loose across her lips. From a distance, she looked as if she might be smiling. Up close, one saw her sad hooded eyes contemplating an empty basin and dried pool, as if she were reading Eliot, "Dry the pool, dry concrete, brown edged ... human kind/Cannot bear very much reality."

The apartment was filled with medical apparatus; sometimes it looked like an infirmary; I.V. poles, sturdy plastic containers for medical waste, a kitchen cabinet devoted to medications—some effective, most useless. The police came each time someone died in his apartment, as was the law. They always knew that AIDS was the cause of death. Kerch once overheard one of the cops say, "This place is like a Roach Motel. They check in and they don't check out." The comment didn't bother him; he had had the same thought himself, as did the men who came there and died.

He used to be a buddy, but that was when people volunteered out of a sense of identification with the sick. That time seemed to have passed. The volunteers who helped the sick were still called buddies, but the people who were sick were called clients.

"My client doesn't think he needs me, but he will, he will," Kerch heard a man say as he wandered through the last party for volunteers.

"You really have to tell them what your limits are," another said. "Otherwise, they expect you to drop everything and come running over just because they're lonely."

"I understand that Terry has been in the hospital for six months, but all he does is gossip about the doctors and the nurses, and it's boring. Maybe I should speak to him about that."

"My client hemorrhaged last week."

"Mine died; I'm waiting to be assigned another," said a woman.

"You're really wonderful to be doing this," someone told her. She smiled, then looked sad and then neutral, a Juno among the volunteers.

Kerch wondered whether the buddies would speak with more humility if they were called succors instead.

□　　□

Father Casey's remains had been the last to be carried from the spare room. Kerch had tried to talk Casey out of leaving the hospital when it was obvious that doctors could do nothing more for him. "If you start coughing and you can't stop, I won't know what to do for you," Kerch said. "If you're in pain, I'll be helpless."

"I'm not afraid of that, if you aren't," Casey said.

Casey had been living in a Catholic community in upstate New York when he was diagnosed, and came to Manhattan for better medical care. The Jesuits had tossed him out for his homosexuality, but the Vatican wouldn't defrock him.

Kerch assumed that Casey was too close to death to suffer the rejection of his order, that he wasn't angry, because the dying so often let go of such things. But that wasn't the case. "No, I'm grateful to the Jesuits. They educated me, satisfied answers to old questions, and gave me moments of mystery and serenity. They helped me find an inner ground, the place of my being. I think that's where I'll go when I die," Casey told him. "You, on the other hand, secular humanist that you are, God only knows where you'll end up."

"Hell, then."

"No, the devil hates a liberal."

Kerch said, "So Hell is filled with Republicans."

"Yes." The priest smiled. "And they just love the place."

Kerch had been with him when Casey died, knew the moment. Whatever pain Casey had been in, he was not telling Kerch. Kerch had learned over and over again how little can be done for someone who was ill, even as hard as it was to know the contents of another's heart. With the sick, he was not outside looking in as their interior worlds were changed by drugs and viruses and bacteria; he was outside looking *at* them, as if through a shop window, or at someone hallucinating. When Casey died, however, something happened that had nothing to do with the body in the bed. It was as if the inner garden he had spoken of simply overflowed into the room. Casey was there, and was there for three days after the remains—the remains to be seen—had been carried out. And Kerch sat in the room, smoking cigarettes, drinking coffee and wine, as if he was in a garden, or a park, or even the Piazza S. Maria in Trastevere, watching the foot traffic pass, the light change across the face of the church.

□   □

He feared that Casey's death, and the deaths before him, had settled like sediment to the bottom of his heart, layer over layer, like the level of civilizations here in the Eternal City.

On the Ponte S. Angelo, he remembered a teacher, Fink, an

Austrian, a handsome man, who always wore one of two turtle-neck sweaters, black or gray cashmere. Maybe as much as Niccolo, Fink had determined Kerch's impression of the city. It was rumored—and probably not true—that he had four doctorates. He taught everything, from Baroque architecture to the plays of Bertolt Brecht. Little he ever said in class could be corroborated in texts or art history books. Kerch could remember a class huddled in a fine fog, Fink, his gray hair shiny with jewel-like mist, pointing to the elongated figures of the angels, saying that they were designed to give the impression of fluidity and movement to passengers in carriages going over the bridge. "Your own speed and motion gives them flight," Fink said. Since then, Fink and his young son had been killed in a car crash on the coast of Spain. His wife, back in Austria, sent money for the bodies to be buried there.

There was a current trend for the dying young to request that there be no funeral, no wake, just a memorial service a month or two after their deaths. The fashion did not consider the needs of the living; it did not help their bereavement process. It was being forced to feel loss long after mourning had become memory. Even two months after a death, time had tempered grief to some extent; death had been accepted, the dead gone for good. If one was not exactly over it, you were past the public display of sadness. For a while, friends and associates joked that they only saw one another at memorial services. Eventually, Kerch observed that people merely nodded to him, and he to them, from across the room, and then rushed for the door afterward, like opera-goers who rush out during ovations to get to parked cars, dinner reservations, the baby-sitter back home.

One who died in his apartment requested that there be no funeral for him, so Kerch looked at the death notices in the newspaper and found a funeral in the neighborhood with the casual interest of one looking for a movie. Then he put on a dark jacket, a white shirt. He signed the registration book and was handed a program. He was ready to sit with strangers and have a good cry. As he looked around the church, however, he found that he recognized a good many mourners.

315

Kerch opened the program. A snapshot had been inserted of the deceased, a fortyish man with a sexy bald head and sexier overlapped front teeth. "What luck," Kerch said to himself, "I knew this one."

A woman was moving up the aisle of the church from one pew to another. People were looking at her, horrified. She sat down next to Kerch and said, "I didn't know the dead, but I offer my condolences. Were the two of you close?"

Kerch considered her a moment, then said, "We met at a j.o. party."

After a pause the woman said, "What a coincidence. I love Jo Stafford. I always have. And the two of you so young."

During the service, friends of the deceased read a poem by Edna St. Vincent Millay, "Dirge Without Music," sentimental but appropriately touching, and someone else read from "Little Gidding." Kerch was in his element, although he saved his enthusiasm for the hymns, "Jerusalem, My Happy Home" and "Amazing Grace," for he had been frustrated out of familiar expressions of grief at a succession of Jewish funerals. (He knew the Jews at this service—they were the ones trying to look up the hymns in *The Book of Common Prayer.*)

When he got back home, the victim's family was attempting to move everything that belonged to Kerch out of his own apartment. The police were called and stopped them.

"Money," the family said. "Wasn't there any money? We sent him five hundred dollars."

"He was here six months," Kerch said. "What do you think that went for?"

Kerch saw the mother look around the room, for a picture or a shirt, anything so as not to leave empty-handed. He pulled off the watch he had gotten as a confirmation present when he was eleven; he pulled off a ring he had bought in Rome. "He gave these to me," Kerch said. "But he had a fever; he was probably delirious. I'm sure he meant for you to have them."

She tried the ring on, and began to weep. She held the watch up to her cheek, and turned it over in her hand. On the back of the watch, she read Kerch's name, including the one he had chosen for himself, the date April 11, 1966, the words *God's love.* She handed them back to him.

"Sebastian must be your confirmation name. I bet the nuns helped you pick it out," she said. "He was the patron saint of plagues."

"I thought he was the patron saint of cowboys."

Her face collapsed. "My son would have said something like that, too," she said. "He left me nothing, then. No keepsakes. Nothing to take home with me."

"We'll find something," Kerch said, and took her into the spare room.

"A scrapbook," she said when he pulled out the album that was stuck between the bed and the wall.

Kerch had never seen it before, either. "No, it's a commonplace book," he said. It was filled with passages from books and magazine articles, and illustrated with postcards the man had found in museum gift shops. It was definitely the commonplace book of a sick man, the passages that filled it colored by months spent ill in this room. Kerch recognized almost all the excerpts, like the one from Whitman's *Specimen Days.* "The dead, the dead, the dead—*our* dead—ours all (all, all, all, finally dear to me) ... our young men once so handsome and so joyous, taken from us, the son from the mother, the husband from the wife, the dear friend from the dear friend." Then Kerch recognized his own handwriting along the margin of a poem torn out of *The Collected Poems of Emily Dickinson.* The source of the commonplace book were the books from his own shelves.

" 'There is a pain—so utter—It swallows substance up,' " the man's mother read, pausing at the dashes. She read formally and well, as if she was reading from the Bible to a Sunday school class. "This must have given him so much comfort in his final days," she said.

"Well, it certainly kept him busy," Kerch said.

"Thank you for finding this," she said. "To know what he was thinking all these months, I'll feel as if I had been with him."

□   □

On top of the Castel Sant'Angelo was the archangel Michael brandishing his sword. Kerch opened *The Companion Guide to Rome,* which had been the guidebook of choice for something like twenty years, and read, "In 590 ... the first year of Gregory the Great's reign, Rome was decimated by plague and the pope ordered forty processions to make their way through the city to intercede for God's help. People fell out of the ranks, dying by the wayside, as men and women, priests and children, marched through the empty streets. Just as Gregory was about to enter St. Peter's, he saw a vision of the Archangel Michael, on the summit of what was left of Hadrian's tomb, sheathing his sword. The pestilence ceased. . . ."

"Yeah, sure," Kerch said. Once, his Catholic-taught mind would not have questioned the miracle. Even after he stopped believing, he went on to believe that there must have been an historical fact to explain the miracle, a coincidence. Across town was a portrait of the Madonna, supposedly hand-delivered by two angels to Pope John in the year 523. In two other epidemics, 590 and 1656, the image was carried through the streets in a penitential procession, and wherever the Madonna passed, the pestilence or plague was said to cease. It would not have occurred to him before, nor to the Church, which had its own explanation for illness, that whatever the cause of the pestilence, virus or bacteria, it had simply killed who it could kill.

He had a casual acquaintance with a man in his own neighborhood, someone he did not even know was ill until they met by chance one morning in a coffeehouse across from Straus Park. On any other occasion, Kerch probably would have said hello and sat at another table, but the sight of the man's face, the loss of weight, the color of his complexion, but especially the lesion that had turned the white of one eye deep red, had the effect of sudden confession, sudden intimacy, as if in truth they shared an accomplished past, a war, an addiction, a struggle, in common.

"The weather has been marvelous, hasn't it?" Dennis said, almost as if he had something to do with it.

And Kerch said it had, as if to give him credit for it. It had indeed been a beautiful Indian summer, a reprieve after October's tongue lashings and premature snow. The leaves on the ginkgo trees in Straus Park, always the last to fall, were lemon; the air bright as seltzer. An old Chinese couple were picking up the fecund ginkgo berries off the ground.

"You recall the weather two weeks ago, the snow?" Dennis asked.

"Wednesday."

"I really thought I was dying that night," Dennis said. "I went to sleep not expecting to wake up."

"Well, you look pretty good."

"I healed myself," he said to Kerch.

"Why, that's terrific," Kerch said, wishing that he had sat at another table. "I'm very happy for you."

"Oh, I can see you looking at my lesions," Dennis said, "but they are disappearing; I know they are."

"No, I'm glad for you," Kerch said, and squeezed the man's hand. Who was he to doubt, to question?

"I called my father, whom I haven't spoken to in six years. We're going to spend Thanksgiving together," Dennis said. He looked out the window and said after a moment, "Really, I have no idea why anyone would call AIDS into his life."

'Yes, well, you know."

This had been a man, Kerch knew, who used to read newspaper articles all the way to the end, hungry for the world. He had stopped reading papers, however, because the bad news interfered with his state of grace, his positive attitude. Kerch thought that this must explain why men in other times went into monasteries, to close out a world beyond their control, protected by the monastery walls, and from their own thoughts by a theology that rationalized chaos. It did not occur to him that this was much the same reason he brought homeless people with AIDS into his own home.

"Do you have anyone staying with you now?" Dennis asked. It was well known that Kerch brought people into his home.

"Yes, he's not doing so well."

319

"If your friend is sick, it is because he wants to be sick," Dennis said.

"But, darling," Kerch said. "Don't we both know people who died even though they wanted to live?"

"They accepted a different reality," Dennis said.

Shortly after Thanksgiving, though, they ran into one another again. The weather had turned bad; the fleshy ginkgo berries were squashed against the gray cobblestone in Straus Park. By this time, the KS had overwhelmed Dennis's face. He had lost another twenty pounds; his clothes hung off of him as if they were borrowed from a larger man. Dennis looked away from Kerch, and wouldn't speak to him, as if embarrassed, as if defeated. A few months later, he died.

□　　□

Kerch stepped off the Ponte Sant'Angelo and walked down the Via dei Coronari, the street of the rosary makers, who once sold their wares to poor pilgrims on their way to St. Peter's. No rosaries now, but antique shops whose wares were beyond the reach of any but the very rich. A shopkeeper once told Kerch he could always come back to look at something he couldn't afford to buy. "It's enough to know that beautiful things exist," she said.

Kerch turned down the Via della Pace and into the piazza of the same name. The day, the piazza, and the church were the color of tarnished silver. Fink used to give a three-hour morning lecture beneath the ceiling fresco at the Il Gesù for his seminar in Art and Ideas, and then they would come here and look at the facade of the S. Maria della Pace. Of course, the ideas were generally his own; if a student said something he disagreed with, Fink would shout, *"Ma che stronzo."* His lecture beneath the ceiling fresco was on persuasive splendor ("the very opposite of Brecht's alienation effect"), the premise behind the opulent and exuberant theatrics of the Baroque church, that the riches of heaven could be previewed here on earth, or that the mystery of Christ's love did not need priestly mediators, as could be seen in the face of Bernini's St. Teresa, that, yes, someday all this would be yours, was yours now, did indeed exist.

Succor

What did we need to be persuaded of now? Kerch wondered. The world had gotten away from us. Did we now have a raw and chafing need for others to tell us that everything would be all right, perhaps, that the universe provides, and what it won't we needn't worry over? Did we just need someone to undress us and undress for us, touch our bodies gently, and put us to bed?

Fink's lecture had ended in front of the S. Maria della Pace. "The convex atrium, the concave wings give the illusion of taking up greater space than they actually do. The church itself is really quite small, but the multiplicity of details, including even the grain of the travertine, a stone common to the region and to Baroque masonry, focus the eye and extend our attention."

Kerch thought, What am I seeing, what am I seeing really?

There was his memory of the church, and there was the church itself right in front of him, and in that the whole of the church and the piazza seemed more articulated to him. It seemed that he was seeing them both at the same time, as if through an antique stereograph at twin photographs that were taken at slightly different angles (in his case, the angle of fifteen years, though time meant nothing in Rome) to give the impression of depth.

He stepped back to get another view of the church within the piazza designed for the traffic jam of horse-drawn carriages, when the church had become fashionable for its afternoon Mass. As he did so, several boys entered the piazza on their way home from school, kicking a ball among them. The ball hit the leg of an old woman who had come behind them, her hands full from shopping.

"*Prego, signora, mi scusa,*" a little boy with dark, sad eyes said to her. He looked up at Kerch, his eyes now moist with faked mortification. "*Mi scusa, signore.*" The woman turned to Kerch, impressed herself by the boy's little act, and spoke as if she were a Renaissance courtesan: "They kick with their feet, not with their eyes."

□　　□

He came into a piazza where Cellini boasted he had killed a rival jeweler. There had been a plague in Cellini's time as well, and it

321

had been blamed on the conjunction of Jupiter and Mars. A man of the Church, at the time, Cardinal Gastaldi, said that anything the doctors wrote about the pestilence produced "Much smoke and little light." He said that medical remedies against the plague were no use and at times dangerous. The only remedy for it were pills made of three ingredients: *cito, longe,* and *tarde*—"run swiftly, go far, and return late." Doctors had to be compelled to tend the sick who were kept in lazarettos, or pesthouses.

In his confessions, Cellini wrote, "The epidemic disease continuing to rage for many months, I took to a freer course of life, because many of my acquaintances had died of it, while I remained in perfect health." He was twenty-three at the time, and eventually stricken himself, though he survived.

Kerch traversed the short length of the Via Giulia, then stopped to look back at it. So much had the city become a part of him when first he came here, he believed that a surgeon opening him up would not see viscera but this particular view. The street had once been envisioned as a major thoroughfare to the Vatican, the enclosed bridge just above his head was designed by Michelangelo and was to have gone clear across the river and to have connected two palaces. Now one of the few straight roads of the inner city, it seemed hardly more than a passionate alley. It did not seem to suffer, didn't demand attention, didn't even need a human being on its cobblestone to give it scale or purpose. It set out for a certain greatness and fell so far short of it, lasted and survived, that it could be smug in its established existence.

To his left was the Mascherone fountain, one of three huge, puzzling masks in the city that dated back to the ancient city. In a former life, it might have been a sewer cap; who knew? It, too, had been intended for greater things when it was placed in the wall; it was meant to have been fed by a major aqueduct that never made it quite this far. Water merely dribbled over its huge bottom lip now and made the face seem all the more human because of it, unblinking and insentient, someone who can only sigh and babble, drool and spit, because he knows more than he can make sense of. Or as Festus said to Saul, later Paul, "Much learning does make thee mad."

The S. Maria dell'Orazione e Morte just beyond the arch of Michelangelo's abbreviated bridge, according to his guidebook, belonged to an order whose purpose was to collect the bodies of the unknown dead and give them a Christian burial. A winged skeleton on the facade pointed to a scroll that read, "ME TODAY, YOU TOMORROW."

Kerch's doctor had called him about a month before he left for Rome with the results of his last blood tests, including a new test that allegedly measured viral activity. It was eleven o'clock on a Sunday night; Kerch was already asleep when the phone rang. Casey answered it and woke him up. Kerch and his doctor stayed on the phone for nearly an hour and a half.

"There doesn't seem to be active virus. Your T-4 cells are very low, but low T-4 cells is not incompatible with normal life," the doctor said. "You're more vulnerable now, but it doesn't mean that you will get an infection."

"If my viral activity is negligible," Kerch asked, "how do you explain this depletion of T-cells?"

"Attrition of the players."

"You can't tell by these dwindling numbers whether or not I'll go on to develop full-blown AIDS?"

"No, and if more people start taking AZT as an antiviral, or aerosol pentamidine as a penumonia prophylaxis, we won't know; we'll never know. It all remains to be seen."

Kerch asked when he should start AZT. Everyone knew it was highly toxic, there was bone-marrow depletion, some muscle atrophy. It was feared to be a carcinogen that would invade every cell in the body. But the real reason that he was afraid to take the drug was that it would change the way he saw himself; it meant that there was something wrong with him; that if he didn't take it, he would probably become ill.

"There is no magic number," his doctor said. "If you decide to start taking it, I will support your decision. I am seeing other patients with higher counts than yours; they have lymphadenopathy, impetigo, anal herpes, fatigue, erosion of platelets ... still normal, moving to abnormal."

"I could have been at that point years ago," Kerch said.

"We're all different ... individual science."

Casey stood by listening to the whole conversation. When Kerch hung up the phone, Casey placed a bottle of AZT in front of him. "What are you waiting for?" Casey asked. "Do you think that your T-cells are going to turn around and start going up on their own?"

"They don't mean anything," Kerch said. "I know someone who has had less than two hundred for five years, and no opportunistic infections."

"Don't forget, I was where you are now just eight months ago," Casey said. "You are afraid of identifying with me, and if you don't, you will end up like me, treading time in the darkness waiting for a cure."

"I don't know," Kerch said. "What if I can't handle it?"

"Soon there might be something else. You just have to be prepared to take it," Casey said. "It's too late for me, obviously, but it looks like the disease will become a manageable chronic condition."

"When? And what does that mean ... manageable chronic condition? Manageable for whom? What's being managed?"

"There's hope."

"When?"

Casey backed off. He knew of Kerch's kitchen cabinet totally filled with useless chemicals and drugs that had neither prolonged a life, nor decreased the duration of an illness, nor saved anyone any pain. Each drug had been the harbinger of the end of the epidemic. They both had read an editorial in the newspaper that had waxed rhapsodic about a new drug, alleged evidence at how far science had progressed in combating the disease. Everyone was talking about it. Casey had tried to get into the trial and was told that he was too ill. Kerch was told that he was too healthy. And then the trial was canceled. The drug was totally forgotten and hope transferred to the next drug that showed promise in the test tube.

Casey asked, "Do you have any idea what you want to do with the rest of your life?"

"No, I don't even know how to plan for it. Do I live for the moment? And what is the moment? Is the moment basing my hopes in a future that may not even exist? Do I tie my puny savings up in long-term or short-term investments? Do I go back to Rome, where I was happy once? Or someplace I've never been before? The only thing I know anything about anymore is AIDS. I know more about this epidemic than I can recall of my college major. I've thought about going back to school to get a degree in public health, but what if I get sick after two years at Yale or Columbia, and I wasted all that time? Or just as bad, what if they find a cure? Then what do I do?"

"If you could have anything . . ."

Kerch said, "Sex with abandon."

□   □

He walked back out to the Tiber to the Ponte Sisto, which crossed the Tiber like a spine of sun-bleached bone. On one parapet, he saw something that took a moment for him to translate. It was the Star of David surrounded by question marks. The Jewish question. That was painted in red. Beneath that was painted in black, HITLER WAS RIGHT. On the opposite parapet was the inscription carved there when the bridge was built: YOU WHO PASS BY HERE OFFER A PRAYER TO GOD SO THAT SIXTUS IV, EXCELLENT PONTIFEX MAXIMUS, MAY BE HEALTHY AND FOR LONG SO PRESERVED. ANY OF YOU, WHOEVER YOU ARE, TO WHOM THIS REQUEST IS MADE, BE HEALTHY, TOO.

The people who used the word *hope* were usually uninfected and/or heterosexual, whose only source of information about the epidemic was the mainstream media. And, of course, none of these people were tending the sick. They confused hope with certainty, the fait accompli. They grasped at the simplest mechanical description of how some new drug would theoretically work, and discussed it as if it had already eradicated the disease, as if they had been released from worrying about it anymore. Their hope absolved them even of the necessity to be sympathetic. Fear of the new drug, let alone skepticism, was not allowed into discussion.

It was not their hope that Kerch minded; like any particular faith, it was a private matter. He only wanted his friends to say outright that his fears were justified, and that they hoped he did not get sick, and that if he did get sick, they hoped that some new drug or drugs would work for him and have no toxic side effects, and that they would pay for that drug if he couldn't himself. And that they would be there for him if the drug did not work.

The chestnut trees were bare. The river swelled with mud. It was the warmest winter Rome had had in—twenty, thirty-five, fifty years, the century? Everyone told him a different story. He was now hurrying to meet Niccolo at the Sora Lella, a restaurant on the Tiberina, the little island in the middle of the river. There was a hospital on the island where Niccolo worked as a pathologist. A hospice had existed on that site since the Middle Ages, and a religious order had founded this hospital on that site during the settecento.

At the Ponte Fabricio, Kerch stopped to look at the four-headed Janus, the Roman god who guarded over all beginnings. He opened *The Companion Guide to Rome,* which said, "The island has long been associated with the art of healing; a Temple of Aesculapius was built there after the great plague in 291 B.C. The temple was very large and constructed with porticoes where sick people could sleep the night in the hope that the god would visit them in their dreams and prescribe a cure."

Over the temple, a Christian church was built at the end of the tenth century, and people used to come with ex-votos, models of human arms and legs, in the hopes of, or with thanks for, cures. They brought tiny replicas of their arms and legs made in silver. He wondered what they had brought for other maladies—jewel-encrusted hearts, or tiny heads carved in ivory, flesh-colored silks for cancers, wooden dolls if it was a child sick? What, he wondered, could represent and heal his own immune system? A bottle of wine, a bucket of blood, his confirmation watch, the numbers and hands of which had long stopped glowing in the dark?

□　　□

Casey was in the hospital for six weeks before the doctors and the pathologists and the neurologists and the oncologists decided that there was nothing they could do for him because they could not find what was wrong with him. He had left Kerch the money to come to Rome, dying just the month before. Casey was out of his room getting more tests when Kerch came to visit, but there was a man in his mid-to-late twenties in the other bed reading a biography of Natalie Wood.

"My name is Max. It is very lonely here, and I don't get many visitors. GMHC sent a buddy, but this was very hard for him. I was his first client. They should have started him out on someone healthier," he said. He held up a stuffed dog that must have been as old as its owner. "This is Curly."

He held the stuffed dog to his own face and looked it in a beaded eye. "I love Curly," he said, and then walked the dog over the hill of his knees.

It was an effort to look up and smile. Max was hardly more than a rag and a bone and a hank of hair. His skin was the color of fog. He could not eat because of abscesses in his mouth, he said, and had lost fifty pounds. His lover had died six weeks ago, both of his parents to cancer in the last year. A catheter implanted in his chest had exploded the first time it was used to give him a medication that might have halted at least one of his infections. Immediate open-heart surgery was needed to get the plastic pieces out of his body's most active muscle.

"So you see, Kerch," he said, "my life has been rather sad lately."

Casey, it seemed, was dying, and Kerch saw Max as a candidate to take his place. The greater the horror, the greater the suffering, the more remote the possibility that this would happen to him, Kerch often thought, as if these poor people were totems against the activity of the virus within him. But when Casey was brought back into the room, it was hard to tell which person would last longer.

"Are you a positive person, Kerch?" Max asked.

"I'm sero-positive. Is that what you mean?"

"No, I mean, are you positive about being positive?" Max

asked with the earnest smile of a born-again Christian, as if the next question would be, Have you accepted Jesus into your heart as a personal savior?

"I have a good attitude about it," Kerch said. "Yes, I have a positive outlook."

"You have to structure it," Max said. "The mornings are best for meditation." He held up a little blue book that he kept on his nightstand. "These are meditations for people with AIDS. There is one written for every day of the year," he said. "And one of these days, I might just get over this hump."

Max laid his head back on his pillow as if on a layer of truth he had plumped up for himself. "Are you taking AZT yet, Kerch?"

"Not yet, though I'm thinking about it."

"You should, Kerch. You really should. It helped me a lot, but I can't take it anymore. My body just can't handle it," Max said. "You can see I'm something of a chatterbox. Well, at least I haven't lost my voice."

Kerch smiled for him.

"I don't hate my disease. I am loving it. That way, I help it to leave my body. There are only two emotions, Kerch, love and fear. I wish I could have told that to my parents. It's a good thing to know." And then he said, "I am at peace with myself, Kerch."

Kerch went up to him and kissed Max's forehead. "I can see that, Max. It was nice meeting you. Here's my number if there's anything that I can do for you."

□   □

"Ecco me," Kerch said.

Niccolo stood to embrace Kerch as he entered the Sora Lella. They kissed one another on the cheeks the way Italian men do, right there in public, which had a comforting effect. "I saw you cross the Ponte Fabricio. What took you so long to come into the restaurant?"

"I was sight-seeing," Kerch said.

A waiter came to their table and called them both Dottore,

though Niccolo was the only one wearing a white lab coat. Kerch noticed that Niccolo, like so many Italian men of his class, was thin and elegant, although he had a slouch and was getting a stomach. "Will we practice your Italian or my English?" Niccolo asked.

"If I'm going to speak Italian, it will have to be in very, very simple sentence structures."

Niccolo smiled and said, "Good then, Dottore, my English. You are looking well. I always forget how handsome you are. How long has it been?"

"Seven years, eight. When you were in New York, just before the epidemic," Kerch said. "And your father, how is he? Have you persuaded him to give up his practice yet?"

"Not exactly. He'll take on clients who are as old as he is," Niccolo said. "He's in Ferrara trying to get a chair established to study and preserve a Jewish culture that seems to be disappearing in towns like Parma and Modena. What the Nazis didn't destroy, it seems that time has neutralized. We won't expire at the gates of our libraries like the Alexandrians did, but stumbling out the doors asphyxiated by the dust and library paste."

"I was shocked—when was it? two years ago?—when the synagogue was bombed."

"No, longer ago than that. I was sitting right here, as a matter of fact," Niccolo said. "I ran out to see what I could do, and a man came stumbling down the steps of the synagogue clutching the body of a child. He stood there and cried out, '*Siamo anche italiani.* We have been here since Caesar.' Well, you might imagine the scene yourself. Have you eaten here before? Any of the house specialties are good. Why are you smiling like that? You look like you're going to cry."

The waiter had set down a basket of bread, and Kerch had cracked open a rosetta, a crusty bun that tears apart in mouth-proportioned pieces, each part as fleshy as the plump of one's hand. "I haven't had one of these in years."

Kerch described the graffiti on the Ponte Sisto. "The red was painted by the Communists," Niccolo said, "the footnote in black was done by the fascisti."

"Doesn't it disturb you?"

"If offends me, yes, but you know, the hate is so ancient, so irrational, it seems to exist only in the past, like the atrocities that happened in the Colosseum, or the sacking of Jerusalem by Titus. Well, maybe not that ancient, but the Italians who are anti-Semitic haven't even met a Jew, or wouldn't know one when they did. Even Mussolini's heart wasn't in the deportation, and he regretted what part he had in it."

"Oh, I suppose that would make him a humanist in the Italian tradition."

"Suppose we change the subject," Niccolo said. "I'd much rather talk about you. What else did you see today?"

Kerch's pleasure at seeing Niccolo tapered off. Being with him had always been like sitting in a dark room with a mirror; it takes and gives nothing back, but you know it's there because you saw it before the lights went out. Even in bed with him, Kerch thought he might as well be alone, might as well be making love to himself, and so he'd lay claim to Niccolo's body—this is what I would do to myself if I could—and licked and smelled, and was wordlessly affectionate, because finally, it was someone else's body, someone else's smell.

"I went to see the restoration of the Sistine Chapel," Kerch said, "I got there early, just like when I was a student, and tipped the guard so that he would let me lie on the floor to look at the ceiling."

"How far along are they?"

"About halfway through the Creation."

"It must have been like seeing it for the first time," Niccolo said. "You'll have to come back for the Last Judgment."

"All of the city seems more articulated to me. I must have been half-asleep when I was here the first time, or I walked around with one eye closed."

"You were often wrapped up in yourself. I often felt as if we had to plan our days around your moods."

"Well, I don't seem to be capable of those depths of unhappiness anymore," Kerch said.

"You were young,"Niccolo said. "The Italians would say that you needed a mule's swift kick to the back of the head."

"I rather liked your father's prescription better, though I could have used a stronger dose."

Niccolo missed a quarter beat, hardly enough for a singer to breathe before a note. "Are you here alone?" he asked.

"Yes, what of it?"

"Just that the city closes up at seven-thirty. People go home to their families. There really isn't anything to do here by way of meeting people when you are by yourself, you know, no bars, no clubs. I'd hate to see you get lonely."

"I don't suppose that is something you would see," Kerch said, and was silent. If the food hadn't been brought, if it hadn't been so delicious, he might even have wept. He felt as if he had been reprimanded, judged and found wanting.

"Did I tell you that I am getting married?" Niccolo asked.

"Married? You? Surely that isn't expected of you, not your parents."

"My mother passed away," he said. Kerch said he was sorry. Niccolo shrugged. "And my father is not going to live forever. Once he's gone, I'll have no family. I don't want to grow old alone."

"And your fiancée?"

"She's a wonderful girl," Niccolo said.

"Girl? She's only twelve?"

"We have much in common. She loves poetry," he said, "and she's ready to have children."

Kerch raised his wineglass in salute. "You will be a fine parent, I'm sure. Will you keep a boyfriend on the sly, or does one just assume that sort of thing?"

"I haven't thought that far ahead," Niccolo replied.

An older man at another table slapped the table, and his hand rose quickly in a precise and emphatic gesture up to his head. The three younger men at the table laughed, as did the waiter who was standing there. They looked like family. The movements of the old man's hands fascinated Kerch. The man picked

up an orange with one hand and a sharp knife in the other. Even
Niccolo turned to watch.

"He is saying that in his day we did not need amniocentesis
to determine a child's sex," Niccolo translates. "The midwife
would just take an orange and carve a little baby out of the rind
over the woman's stomach." Kerch could see the old man carving
the baby's head, his arms and legs, then he began to tear the
limbs and body away from the pulp of the fruit.

"This is an old joke. I've seen it before," Kerch said. When
the bambino was pulled away from the fruit of the orange, the
core in the center stuck out like a long, thin penis. The other
men at the table, and even the waiter, rolled their eyes and
looked away.

"I do think about you,'" Niccolo said over the second course,
"especially now."

Kerch didn't know what he meant. "Now that you're getting
married, you mean."

"No, I mean the epidemic. I've wondered about your health."

"Oh, that." Kerch told him everything. "My doctor hasn't said
it in so many words, but I think he'd be relieved if I started taking AZT."

"I think I would agree with him."

"Yes, but you're in the medical mode."

"As opposed to?"

"The spiritual mode," Kerch said. "There's a movement
abroad, part of the new age, which says that fear causes illness, or
lack of love, or fear of love. Even sick people have told me that
worrying about AIDS would ensure my getting it, as if illness
were punishment for impure thoughts. And I've been told by the
healthy not to spend so much time helping the sick, because everyone is responsible for their own lives."

"You Americans, with all your freedom," Niccolo said, "are
afraid to admit that you aren't in control of everything."

"I am not often afraid," Kerch said. "I've known for years
that I was sero-positive, but I do have moments of paralysis,
when I feel as if I have awakened to the sound of thieves ran-
sacking my apartment, that they are about to come into my room

and shine a flashlight in my face to see if I'm asleep. If nothing else, I would like to feel safe again, know how to think about the future."

"You live for the day," Niccolo said, "and plan for the long haul."

"I saw the Monte Testaccio yesterday for the first time," Kerch said, referring to an ancient mound of shards of amphorae, which were shattered to discharge their contents of oil, wine, and grain at the nearby river port.

"It's beautiful, isn't it?"

"I read where they used to drive oxen and swine off of it during festivals for swordsmen to kill."

"Really?"

"Then I visited the Protestant Cemetery," Kerch said.

"You always liked it there."

"Yes, I once wanted to be buried there under an obelisk."

Niccolo said, "That would have been an appropriate memorial, as I recall."

Kerch said, "I was wondering if they still sold plots."

"I suspect that you would have to have a significant connection to Rome to be buried there."

"Yes, that's what I was thinking, too," Kerch said. "Do you think that you could find out for me?"

"And if they don't, I mean, I'm sure that they haven't buried anyone there in years," Niccolo said. "And, if they did, the bureaucracy it would entail!"

"Maybe you could spread my ashes there. Could there be anything wrong with that, if they don't catch you?"

Niccolo said, "Why don't I just toss your urn against the Monte Testaccio with the rest of the broken amphorae."

Kerch said, "Because it would probably just bounce off."

"What if I just toss fistfuls of your ashes around your favorite sites, how about that, in the Forum, on the Campidoglio, in Trastevere and the Borgo."

"I wouldn't want to be any trouble," Kerch said.

"You wouldn't even know you were in Rome."

"It's not a trip I look forward to."

"Really, Kerch, you still have this morbid streak. Even Shelley said that that cemetery could make you half in love with death. You're just excited about being back in Rome. When you are back in New York, you will change your mind."

Kerch said, "That's why I bring it up now, Niccolo. If you told me now that you would ... You're right, it won't matter then." He suspected that he had committed a social faux pas by asking Niccolo to see to his remains; people are more loyal to a dead man's requests if they are not facing him over lunch. "I'm sorry I upset you. That was asking a lot."

The waiter set a glass of Sambuca down in front of both of them. Niccolo raised his and said, "To your health, then."

□   □

Kerch walked up the steps of the cordonata to the Campidoglio, as opposed to the parallel steps of the Aracoeli, where he was actually heading. The steps to the church were too many and too steep. There were 122 of them and they had been built in 1348 as thanks for sparing Rome the brunt of the Black Death, which had killed over half the population of Florence and ravaged most of Western Europe. The number of steps and their steep incline symbolized life as a dreary ascent to heaven; pilgrims still climbed it on their knees, he'd been told.

Marcus Aurelius was gone. That was the first thing Kerch saw when he stepped onto the Campidoglio. Michelangelo had designed the piazza as a pedestal for Aurelius and his horse. Once the nostrils of the horse had poured wine and water during a festival, and supposedly the horse's forelock would sing to announce the end of the world, but from where, no one now knew. The statue was said to be beyond repair. Acid rain had rotted it, inside and out, and there were no funds to replicate it. But the Romans didn't seem to mind so very much. The piazza was still beautiful without it, and they felt the statue had been spared once already from the crucible that melted all pagan statues to cannonballs; Marcus Aurelius had been mistaken for Constantine, the first Christian emperor, instead of the pagan that he was; that is how the statue had survived. And maybe he got even more than he deserved. Originally, a bronze barbarian stood beneath the horse's hoof, and in more recent times, the fascists had declared the statue an enormous influence on modern art, though on whose art and what had been forgotten. Marcus Aurelius had had his extra centuries in the sun; his day was gone, but this made Kerch sad, as if it said that Rome was not eternal after all, or that eternity fed on the fodder of memory and memorials; the empty spot seemed even more a memento mori than the winged skeleton at the church on the Via Giulia.

A priest was coughing on the altar of the Aracoeli. He crossed it in a long black bathrobe, his chest bare to the damp cold. In a back chapel was the Santo Bambino, supposedly carved from the wood of an olive tree from the Garden of Gethsemane. There were a handful of letters stuck in front of its glass case, sent by the sick, mail-order prayers. Once, the infant had had its own carriage, which carried him to sickbeds and hospitals. Even fascist soldiers believed in its powers, and had let it pass through a crowd that had gathered to hear Mussolini speak. But to Kerch, the baby Jesus, swaddled in gold lamé and covered with cheap-looking jewelry, was a tacky little drag queen dressed for bingo in Cherry Grove. He covered his mouth when he started to laugh, and a nun entered the chapel with holy cards. She must have seen tears in his eyes, for she whispered, "Such devotion in one so young."

□   □

Kerch continued on down the Via del Corso, weaving in and out of the streets, window-shopping. He had not packed much; he had planned to buy. He was not going to deny himself anything to which he took a liking, as he'd done when he was young and had to tell the shopkeeps that a sweater was *"troppo caro per me, sono un povero studente."*

And yet he didn't see anything that he wanted, as if his ability to want things had atrophied, or that this season's fashions, the bright aqua, for example, or the blowsy denim shirts, could neither contribute to nor augment the image he had finally come to of himself; and in that, he was somehow out of time, out of step.

That was how he felt back home, out of step with the fashionable vocabulary, where a person with AIDS was not sick but surviving, as if severe damage to the immune system was an auto accident from which they had walked away—done, over, complete in and of itself, the danger passed—instead of an ongoing condition with all its variables and vagaries. He and Casey were watching television one night when a person with AIDS said that he was not a victim, and Casey, who would be dead in a week, said, "I don't know about him, but I feel like a victim. I didn't choose this." It was as if the only way to rationalize the confusion of the world was to control the language used to describe it.

"Oh, but it's empowering," Kerch was told at a party where he had had too much to drink and become contentious.

"Empowering," he said. "If I was really empowered, I would make this all go away."

Then a woman in her mid-twenties pounded her chest with an open palm, squared out her chin at him, and with her eyes bulging screamed, "I feel empowered inside."

He had raised his hand and said in a staccato shout, "Duce, Duce, Duce." Empowering, he thought, if people were empowered by merely changing the way something was called, how weak were they really, how illusory was language?

And then there was the Quilt touring the country like a movable wake, panel upon panel of fabrics stitched together like a foldable, dry-cleanable cemetery. Seeing a beautiful man reduced to a name sewn on a bedspread had made him call a woman friend, an artist, to say, "Karen, you're the only one I'd trust with my panel." She said to him, "Why don't I make one up now and you can sleep with it."

□　　□

At Casey's instigation, he went to a group called Body Positives to hear how others were dealing with being infected. "I've had a hundred and twenty-five friends die of AIDS," the team leader said. "They all led very stressful lives, so it's no wonder they got sick. I take a lighthearted attitude to the whole thing, but that's the reality I created for myself."

The team leader put on a tape made by a woman who had written a book that told people they could heal themselves. "I believe that we are one hundred percent responsible for our lives," the woman said. "Our health is a mirror of what we believe about ourselves. The very fact that you have found this tape and have discovered me means that you are ready to make a new positive change in your life. Acknowledge yourself for this." There was a silence of several seconds, and then, "The past has no power over us. The past has no power over us," she said with a lift in her voice. "Isn't it wonderful to realize that this is a new moment, a fresh beginning."

The team leader was smiling like a child with his head on his mother's lap, when she has returned home from a day in the factory. But another man stood and started to leave the room. "Excuse me," he said, "but this isn't what I came here for."

"If you don't intellectualize her," the team leader said, "she can be very helpful."

"I'm glad that it works for you," the fellow said as he headed toward the door. Kerch was going for his coat, as well.

The team leader said, "All she is saying is that you have to love yourself."

"No," the man said at the door, "I read her book. She says that AIDS is caused by self-hatred."

"Some gay men do hate themselves," the team leader said.

"You'd pretty much have to to believe this stuff."

The leader turned to the rest of the room and said, "She just doesn't want to see anyone get sick."

Kerch met up with the man on the steps. "Are you all right?" He said, "I hate that metaphysical snake oil."

"It gives them a sense of control."

"Spiritual fascism."

"You can't take away their hope," Kerch said, arguing their viewpoint, though he didn't know why. "You can't deny the power of a positive outlook."

"Yeah, and an addict loves his drugs."

"They'd call you negative. They'd say you're a cynic."

"A cynic is a romantic gone sour," the man said. "I never did that."

"If you have all the answers already, why did you come to-night?" Kerch asked.

"I don't have all the answers. I wanted to know how others were handling this. I wanted to talk about issues, like do you tell someone you just met in a bar that you're sero-positive before you go home and have sex? Or do you wait on the chance that he wants to see you again, and then how do you tell him? I'm of a generation of gay men who never even needed to know another man's name to have sex with him."

Leaning against the opposite walls of the building's foyer, they stopped and faced each other. Kerch himself sometimes felt that the world was being divided into the HIV's and HIV-not's. Tell a man in a bar that you were sero-positive and he would look you in the eye, squeeze your arm, thank you for your hon-esty, wish you luck, and excuse himself to a distant corner.

"Well," Kerch said, "I don't know your name, but I do know you're sero-positive."

In the long pause, the man looked Kerch over with a slow-dawning, lopsided smile. "You live around here?"

"Yes, but I've got a sick roommate." Kerch said.

"Now I recognize you. You're the guy with the dying room," the man said.

"That's what the press called it."

The man put one arm out, leaned forward, and caught him-self on the wall above Kerch's shoulder. He looked down into Kerch's face. "There's one other thing I'll ask you. Do you think oral sex is an acceptable risk?"

"It's one I'm willing to take," Kerch said. "If you let me."

□   □

Finally, in the church of Santa Maria del Popolo, Kerch found himself back in front of the Caravaggio, *The Conversion of St. Paul.* He opened his *Companion Guide* and read, "So much has

338

been written about it, and it has been so frequently reproduced, that any comment seems superfluous."

He almost said, Don't fail me now. He had an impulse to shake the guidebook for more information, as if more history would come fluttering out of the bindings, like notes, or roses, or a dollar bill stuck between the pages. There was no one else in the chapel. Kerch put the *Companion Guide* back into his bag. He pulled out a small flashlight he had brought from America, because it was impossible ever to carry enough change in Italy for the light meters that illuminated everything one could want to look at.

There was Saul lying on the foreground where he had just fallen. He had been on his way to Damascus to find Jews who had been persuaded by the teachings of Jesus. He would root out these early Christians, the blasphemers, and they would be stoned until they collapsed and died. Kerch's teacher, Fink, had told them that the executioners would strip so as not to be encumbered by their clothes, and Saul stood guard over the clothes.

The moment in the painting varied whenever it appeared in the Bible. Saul is blinded by the light and hears the voice; his companions hear only the voice, or they see only the light. Here a servant's brow is lined with concern over the horse, not Saul. The perspective of the painting made the horse seem little more than a pony next to the servant, but compared to Saul lying on the ground, he is enormous. The saddle has fallen off the other side, the horse looks down at Saul, and Kerch laughed to paraphrase Frost's line: "My little horse must think it queer to stop without Damascus near."

Saul's arms were raised in a wide gesture, almost like one whose arms are being spread for a crucifixion. Yet his shoulders were beginning to relax, his knees were up and parted, his hips raised slightly, his mouth just open, like a man who is ready for his lover. He was an ugly man in Caravaggio's vision, ugly as a corpse; his eyes seemed rolled into his head like an epileptic having a seizure. His nipples were extraordinary and manly though, the body nice, his chest bare and his breeches pulled down as far as they could go without exposing him entirely. "If this is divine love, then I know it," someone had said of Bernini's *Ecstasy of St. Teresa,* her mystical union with Christ. The same could be said of this painting, Kerch thought. Not only know it, but to have been responsible for it as well, that moment of penetration when your lover looks at you, helpless with the knowledge that you have brought him to the edge of something, counting on you to maintain the moment, his security, his safety.

"For the sake of argument," Fink had said, "let's say that Jesus had come to Saul and told him everything he needed to know in that moment of light on the way to Damascus. Wouldn't Saul's own self-assigned role as executioner shape that revelation? Isn't it possible that love, all love, even the love of Jesus, can be misconstrued? Paul brought the arrogance and self-righteousness of an executioner to the new religion, tearing Christianity away from Judaism membrane by membrane," Fink had said, "certain he had a right to determine what the laws, the new codes would be. And Paul would be among the first to blame the Jews for killing Christ."

Kerch looked at the light on Saul's arms and across the horse's bulk. Surface into depth, the Italian trick, but the genius of the painting was not in the light, what use was a light that made the world fall back in shadow? Or was that the point?

Kerch considered the woman who wrote the book that said we were responsible for our own lives, that we could heal ourselves, that the past had no power over us. Hers was not the promise of life everlasting, but life now, if one would just believe her, if one would just believe in himself, if one would just love himself enough. Well, of course, he thought, who wouldn't take the guarantee of life now over the promise of life later? What in an unknown heaven could compare to what you had already developed a taste for—coffee in the morning, whiskey at night? So Kerch turned to leave the church, finished with Rome. There were cities he had never been to—Carthage, Alexandria, Babylon. The empty arms convinced him: Nothing remained but what remained to be seen.

HAROLD BRODKEY

Verona: A Young Woman Speaks

I know a lot! I know about happiness! I don't mean the love of God, either: I mean I know the human happiness with the crimes in it.

Even the happiness of childhood.

I think of it now as a cruel, middle-class happiness.

Let me describe one time—one day, one night.

I was quite young, and my parents and I— there were just the three of us—were traveling from Rome to Salzburg, journeying across a quarter of Europe to be in Salzburg for Christmas, for the music and the snow. We went by train because planes were erratic, and my father wanted us to stop in half a dozen Italian towns and see paintings and buy things. It was absurd, but we were all three drunk with this; it was very strange; we woke every morning in a strange hotel, in a strange city. I would be the first one to wake; and I would go to the window and see some tower or palace; and then I would wake my mother and be

341

justified in my sense of wildness and belief and adventure by the way she acted, her sense of romance at being in a city as strange as I had thought it was when I had looked out the window and seen the palace or the tower.

We had to change trains in Verona, a darkish, smallish city at the edge of the Alps. By the time we got there, we'd bought and bought our way up the Italian peninsula: I was dizzy with shopping and new possessions: I hardly knew who I was, I owned so many new things: my reflection in any mirror or shopwindow was resplendently fresh and new, disguised even, glittering, I thought. I was seven or eight years old. It seemed to me we were almost in a movie or in the pages of a book: only the simplest and most light-filled words and images can suggest what I thought we were then. We went around shiningly: we shone everywhere. *Those clothes.* It's easy to buy a child. I had a new dress, knitted, blue and red, expensive as hell, I think; leggings, also red; a red loden-cloth coat with a hood and a knitted cap for under the hood; marvelous lined gloves; fur-lined boots and a fur purse or carryall, and a tartan skirt—and shirts and a scarf, and there was even more: a watch, a bracelet: more and more.

On the trains we had private rooms, and Momma carried games in her purse and things to eat, and Daddy sang carols off-key to me; and sometimes I became so intent on my happiness I would suddenly be in real danger of wetting myself; and Momma, who understood such emergencies, would catch the urgency in my voice and see my twisted face; and she—a large, good-looking woman—would whisk me to a toilet with amazing competence and unstoppability, murmuring to me, "Just hold on for a while," and she would hold my hand while I did it.

So we came to Verona, where it was snowing, and the people had stern, sad faces, beautiful, unlaughing faces. But if they looked at me, those serious faces would lighten, they would smile at me in my splendor. Strangers offered me candy, sometimes with the most excruciating sadness, kneeling or stopping to look directly into my face, into my eyes; and Momma or Papa would judge them, the people, and say in Italian we were late, we had to hurry, or pause and let the stranger touch me, talk to me, look into my face for a while. I would see myself in the eyes of some strange man or woman; sometimes they stared so gently I would want to touch their eyelashes, stroke those strange, large, glistening eyes. I knew I decorated life. I took my duties with great seriousness. An Italian count in Siena said I had the manners of an English princess—at times—and then he laughed because it was true I would be quite lurid: I ran shouting in his *galleria,* a long room, hung with pictures, and with a frescoed ceiling: and I sat on his lap and wriggled: I was a wicked child, and I liked myself very much; and almost everywhere, almost every day, there was someone new to love me, briefly, while we traveled.

I understood I was special. I understood it *then*.

I knew that what we were doing, everything we did, involved money. I did not know if it involved mind or not, or style. But I knew about money somehow, checks and traveler's checks and the clink of coins. Daddy was a fountain of money: he said it was a spree; he meant for us to be amazed; he had saved money—we weren't really rich but we were to be for this trip. I remember a conservatory in a large house outside Florence and orange trees in tubs; and I ran there, too. A servant, a man dressed in black, a very old man, mean-faced—he did not like being a servant anymore after the days of servants were over—and he scowled—but he smiled at me, and at my mother, and even once at my father: we were clearly so separate from the griefs and weariness and cruelties of the world. We were at play, we were at our joys, and Momma was glad, with a terrible and naive inner gladness, and she relied on Daddy to make it work: oh, she worked, too, but she didn't know the secret of such—unreality: is that what I want to say? Of such a game, of such an extraordinary game.

□　　□

There was a picture in Verona Daddy wanted to see: a painting; I remember the painter because the name Pisanello reminded me I had to go to the bathroom when we were in the museum, which was an old castle, Guelph or Ghibelline, I don't remember which; and I also remember the painting because it showed the hind end of the horse, and I thought that was not nice and rather funny, but Daddy was admiring; and so I said nothing.

He held my hand and told me a story so I wouldn't be bored as we walked from room to room in the museum/castle, and then we went outside into the snow, into the soft light when it snows, light coming through snow; and I was dressed in red and had on boots, and my parents were young and pretty and had on boots, too; and we could stay out in the snow if we wanted; and we did. We went to a square, a piazza—the Scaligera, I think; I don't remember—and just as we got there, the snowing began to bellow and then subside, to fall heavily and then sparsely, and then it stopped: and it was very cold, and there were pigeons everywhere in the piazza, on every cornice and roof, and all over the snow on the ground, leaving little tracks as they walked, while the air trembled in its just-after-snow and just-before-snow weight and thickness and gray seriousness of purpose. I had never seen so many pigeons or such a private and haunted place as that piazza, me in my new coat at the far rim of the world, the far rim of who knew what story, the rim of foreign beauty and Daddy's games, the edge, the white border of a season.

I was half mad with pleasure anyway, and now Daddy brought five or six cones made of newspaper, wrapped, twisted; and they held grains of something like corn, yellow and white kernels of something; and he poured some on my hand and told me to hold my hand out; and then he backed away.

At first, there was nothing, but I trusted him and I waited; and then the pigeons came. On heavy wings. Clumsy pigeony bodies. And red, unreal birds' feet. They flew at me, slowing at the last minute; they lit on my arm and fed from my hand. I wanted to flinch, but I didn't. I closed my eyes and held my arm stiffly; and felt them peck and eat—from my hand, these free creatures, these flying things. I liked that moment. I liked my happiness. If I was mistaken about life and pigeons and my own nature, it didn't matter *then*.

The piazza was very silent, with snow; and Daddy poured grains on both my hands and then on the sleeves of my coat and on the shoulders of the coat, and I was entranced with yet more stillness, with this idea of his. The pigeons fluttered heavily in the heavy air, more and more of them, and sat on my arms and on my shoulders; and I looked at Momma and then at my father and then at the birds on me.

Oh, I'm sick of everything as I talk. There is happiness. It always makes me slightly ill. I lose my balance because of it.

The heavy birds, and the strange buildings, and Momma near, and Daddy, too: Momma is pleased that I am happy and she is a little jealous; she is jealous of everything Daddy does; she is a woman of enormous spirit; life is hardly big enough for her; she is drenched in wastefulness and prettiness. She knows things. She gets inflexible, though, and foolish at times, and temperamental; but she is a somebody, and she gets away with a lot, and if she is near, you can feel her, you can't escape her, she's that important, that echoing, her spirit is that powerful in the space around her.

If she weren't restrained by Daddy, if she weren't in love with him, there is no knowing what she might do: she does not know. But she manages almost to be gentle because of him; he is incredibly watchful and changeable and he gets tired; he talks and charms people; sometimes, then, Momma and I stand nearby, like moons; we brighten and wane; and after a while, he comes to us, to the moons, the big one and the little one, and we welcome him, and he is always, to my surprise, he is always surprised, as if he didn't deserve to be loved, as if it were time he was found out.

Daddy is very tall, and Momma is watching us, and Daddy anoints me again and again with the grain. I cannot bear it much longer. I feel joy or amusement or I don't know what; it is all through me, like a nausea—I am ready to scream and laugh, that laughter that comes out like magical, drunken, awful, and yet pure spit or vomit or God knows what, makes me a child mad with laughter. I become brilliant, gleaming, soft: an angel, a great bird-child of laughter.

I am ready to be like that, but I hold myself back.

There are more and more birds near me. They march around

my feet and peck at falling and fallen grains. One is on my head. Of those on my arms, some move their wings, fluff those frail, feather-loaded wings, stretch them. I cannot bear it, they are so frail, and I am, at the moment, the kindness of the world that feeds them in the snow.

All at once, I let out a splurt of laughter: I can't stop myself and the birds fly away but not far; they circle around me, above me; some wheel high in the air and drop as they return; they all returned, some in clouds and clusters driftingly, some alone and angry, pecking at others; some with a blind, animal-strutting abruptness. They gripped my coat and fed themselves. It started to snow again.

I was there in my kindness, in that piazza, within reach of my mother and father.

Oh, how will the world continue? Daddy suddenly understood I'd had enough, I was at the end of my strength—Christ, he was alert—and he picked me up, and I went limp, my arm around his neck, and the snow fell. Momma came near and pulled the hood lower and said there were snowflakes in my eyelashes. She knew he had understood, and she wasn't sure she had; she wasn't sure he ever watched her so carefully. She became slightly unhappy, and so she walked like a clumsy boy beside us, but she was so pretty: she had powers anyway.

We went to a restaurant, and I behaved very well, but I couldn't eat, and then we went to the train and people looked at us, but I couldn't smile; I was too dignified, too sated; some leftover—pleasure, let's call it—made my dignity very deep; I could not stop remembering the pigeons, or that Daddy loved me in a way he did not love Momma; and Daddy was alert, watching the luggage, watching strangers for assassination attempts or whatever; he was on duty; and Momma was pretty and alone and *happy,* defiant in that way.

And then, you see, what she did was wake me in the middle of the night when the train was chugging up a very steep mountainside; and outside the window, visible because our compartment was dark and the sky was clear and there was a full moon, were mountains, a landscape of mountains everywhere, big mountains, huge ones, impossible, all slanted and pointed and white with snow, and absurd, sticking up into an ink-blue sky and down into blue, blue shadows, miraculously deep. I don't know how to say what it was like: they were not like anything I knew: they were high things: and we were up high in the train and we were climbing higher, and it was not at all true, but it was, you see. I put my hands on the window and stared at the wild, slanting, unlikely marvels, whiteness and dizziness and moonlight and shadows cast by moonlight, not real, not familiar, not pigeons, but a clean world.

We sat a long time, Momma and I, and stared, and then Daddy woke up and came and looked, too. "It's pretty," he said, but he didn't really understand. Only Momma and I did. She said to him, "When I was a child, I was bored all the time, my love—I thought nothing would ever happen to me—and now these things are happening—and you have happened." I think he was flabbergasted by her love in the middle of the night; he smiled at her, oh, so swiftly that I was jealous, but I stayed quiet, and after a while, in his silence and amazement at her, at us, he began to seem different from us, from Momma and me; and then he fell asleep again; Momma and I didn't; we sat at the window and watched all night, watched the mountains and the moon, the clean world. We watched together.

Momma was the winner.

We were silent, and in silence we spoke of how we loved men and how dangerous men were and how they stole everything from you no matter how much you gave—but we didn't say it aloud.

We looked at mountains until dawn, and then when dawn came, it was too pretty for me—there was pink and blue and gold in the sky, and on icy places, brilliant pink and gold flashes, and the snow was colored, too, and I said, "Oh," and sighed; and each moment was more beautiful than the one before; and I said, "I love you, Momma." Then I fell asleep in her arms.

That was happiness then.

BIOGRAPHICAL NOTES

WILLIAM MAXWELL was born in 1908 in Lincoln, Illinois. He has published an autobiographical memoir, a children's book, and several works of fiction, including the novel *So Long, See You Tomorrow* and the short-story collections *Over the River and Other Stories* and *Billy Dyer and Other Stories*. For more than forty years he was an editor at *The New Yorker*.

DIANE JOHNSON was born in Moline, Illinois, and lives in San Francisco. She is a novelist, critic, biographer, and screenwriter. Among her recent works is *Natural Opium*, a collection of travel stories.

WARD JUST is the author of nine novels, including *Jack Gance* and *Ambition and Love*, and three short-story collections, including *Twenty-one Stories*. Originally from Indiana, he lives in Vineyard Haven, Massachusetts.

SUE MILLER lives in Boston. She is the author of the novels *The Good Mother*, *Family Pictures*, and *For Love*, and *Inventing the Abbots and Other Stories*.

Biographical Notes

JAMES LASDUN was born in England in 1958. His first short-story collection was published there in 1985 as *The Silver Age* and in the United States and Canada as *Delirium Eclipse & Other Stories*.

FAY WELDON was raised in New Zealand and lives in London and Somerset, England. Among her twenty novels and short-story collections are: *Trouble, Life Force, The Cloning of Joanna May*, and *The Life and Loves of a She-Devil*.

WILLIAM TREVOR was born in Cork, Ireland, in 1928. He is the author of twelve novels, eight volumes of short stories, a book of personal memoirs, and a play. His *Collected Stories* was published in 1992.

JAMES SALTER is the author of the novels *Light Years, A Sport and a Pastime*, and *Solo Faces*, and the collection *Dusk and Other Stories*, which won the 1989 PEN/Faulkner Award.

ELIZABETH JOLLEY is a former nurse who wrote for twenty years before publishing her first novel, after which she became one of Australia's most prominent writers. Among her novels is *My Father's Moon Cabin Fever*. Her collection, *Stories*, was published in the United States in 1988.

STEVEN MILLHAUSER is the author of *Edwin Mullhouse, Portrait of a Romantic, In the Penny Arcade, From the Realm of Morpheus*, and *Little Kingdoms*. He lives in Saratoga Springs, New York.

PAUL THEROUX was born in Medford, Massachusetts, in 1941. His books of fiction include *The Mosquito Coast, O Zone, Chicago Loop*, and *World's End and Other Stories*. Among his nonfiction travel books are *The Great Railway Bazaar, The Old Patagonian Express*, and *The Happy Isles of Oceania*.

PAUL BOWLES has lived for many years as an expatriate in Tangier, Morocco. Among his novels are *The Sheltering Sky, Let It Come Down*, and *Up Above the World*. Among his short-story collections is *Collected Stories 1939–1976*.

MARIA THOMAS, which is a pseudonym, was the author of the novel *Antonia Saw the Oryx First* and the short-story collections *Come to Africa and Save Your Marriage* and *African Visa*, published posthumously. She died in the summer of 1989 while accompanying U.S. Representative Mickey Leland on a relief mission to refugee camps on the border of Ethiopia and Somalia.

JOHN UPDIKE was born in Shillington, Pennsylvania, in 1932. He graduated from Harvard College in 1954 and spent a year in England on the Knox Fellowship, at the Ruskin School of Drawing and Fine Art in Oxford. Since 1957 he has lived in Massachusetts. He is the father of four children and the author of sixteen novels—among them *Rabbit at Rest* and *Brazil*—numerous short-story collections—most recently, *The Afterlife and Other Stories*—several volumes of poetry, a memoir, and collected essays and criticism. His fiction has won the Pulitzer Prize, the National Book Award, the American Book Award, and the National Book Critics Circle Award.

ALICE MUNRO is the author of a novel and several collections of short stories, among them *The Beggar Maid* and *Friend of My Youth*. A native Canadian, she lives in Clinton, Ontario.

LORRIE MOORE is the author of a children's book and several works of fiction, including *Self-Help*, *Anagrams*, *Like Life*, and *Who Will Run the Frog Hospital?* She teaches at the University of Wisconsin in Madison. Her stories frequently appear in *The New Yorker*.

KATE BRAVERMAN lives in Los Angeles. She is the author of several books of poetry, the novels *Lithium for Medea* and *Palm Latitudes*, and the short-story collection *Squandering the Blue*.

ALLEN BARNETT's short-story collection, *The Body and Its Dangers*, published in 1990, was awarded a special citation from the Ernest Hemingway Foundation in 1991. He died shortly thereafter of AIDS.

HAROLD BRODKEY was born in 1930 in Staunton, Illinois, and grew up in Missouri. He is the author of two collections of short stories, *First Love and Other Sorrows* and *Stories in an Almost Classical Mode*, and the novels *The Runaway Soul* and *Profane Friendship*.